"Sharon K. Souza has taken the coming of age story and upped the ante. In *Unraveled*, we find a young woman who discovers that everything she thought was solid and real is shifting sand beneath her feet. This expertly crafted novel, at turns affecting, funny and aching, is a story that will engross and reveal. A beautiful book."

~ BONNIE GROVE, award winning author of *Talking to the Dead.*

"Sharon has crafted a lovely story of youthful enthusiasm and idealism, shattered by doubt and unexpected crisis. With a heroine who runs away from what she thought was a clear-cut mission, the young woman is soon forced to face the truth about her own lack of faith. In the process, grace finds a way to invade her heart and plant seeds of hope that will bring a mighty harvest, even in the darkest of circumstances."

~ KATHI MACIAS, named 2011 Author of the Year by BooksandAuthors.net, has authored more than 35 books, including *Deliver Me From Evil* and *Red Ink*.

"Once again, as in her previous novels *Lying on Sunday* and *Every Good & Perfect Gift*, Sharon Souza reminds us that we are sometimes only one decision away from circumstances that could forever change our lives, but do not forever have to define us. In *Unraveled*, a young woman learns that sometimes it's only when all we know about ourselves is taken away, that we learn most about who we really are. Sharon creates a story that is beautifully woven with threads of humor and hope and heart."

~ CHRISTA ALLAN, author of *Walking on Broken Glass* and *The Edge of Grace.*

UNRAVELED

A NOVEL

Sharon K. Souza

ISBN-13: 978-1-47506-962-4
ISBN-10: 1-47506-962-6

Printed in the United States of America.

Most Scripture quotations in this publication are taken from the HOLY BIBLE: NEW INTERNATIONAL VERSION. Copyright © 1973, 1978, 1984 by International Bible Society.

This is a work of fiction. Names, characters, places and incidents are either the product of the author's imagination or are used fictitiously.

Cover Design by Kathleen Popa, www.cottonbond.com
Sunflower Photos by Michelle Dennis
Author Photo by Mindy Grant

For Janice,
a lover of sunflowers

One

I lost my faith at twenty-four. Well, that isn't true. I didn't lose it. I left it. In a small village in Moldova, right there amongst the sunflowers. Just took it off like a vesture discarded. Not outgrown. Discarded. It left me feeling exposed, I'll admit, but I figure if God isn't capable of protecting the weakest among us, I'd rather work for someone else. Oh sure, he makes it plain that pure and undefiled religion is caring for the widows and orphans, as if it's my job and not his. And that was the thing, he let us down in the worst way. So I tipped my hat and shook the dust off my feet.

Which left me instantly unemployed half a world away from home. No one ever said I was farsighted. They did, on occasion, say I was rash.

After high school I earned my AA at Modesto JC, because the commute from where I lived in Linden, California, was easier than driving to Sacramento in rush hour. And if you ask me, one JC's as good as another. Sure, Delta College in Stockton was closer than Modesto, but that was too close to home. I wanted to feel to some degree I was going off to college, even if I came back home every afternoon.

I chose a community college instead of a four-year institution because, quite frankly, I had no earthly idea what I wanted to be when I grew up. I knew one thing for sure. I did not want to spend the whole of my adult working life in the family business, on the family compound, though that's exactly where I ended up after tucking my Associate in Arts certificate in between the pages of the family Bible. That's where we keep our important papers. Most everything pertaining to me can be found in the pages of the Gospel of John. Which is exactly where you'd expect to find my sister Johnnie, but no, I'm the firstborn, so I got first choice, and I chose John.

To understand this little quirk among our oh-so-many family quirks, we have to go back to my grandparents on my mother's side, krystal and blue karma, the original flower children of the San Joaquin Valley. As you might have guessed, those were not their given names. Mam was actually born Georgeanne Cattano, and Opa was christened Gary Ray Shunk.

They met at a commune in Santa Cruz the summer of '65. My mother was born the following spring on the floor of their flower power VW bus. They named their baby girl celestial bliss. No way do I want to know the source of their inspiration. They call her Celie and so do I, because I love the sound of it.

Mam and Opa took their new names the day they united themselves in togetherness, as a symbol of the new life they were creating. They exchanged love beads, rechristened themselves krystal blue karma, meant to always be said together, for as long as they were together, which was never intended to be forever.

But then the Jesus Movement came along. Mam and Opa went braless and barefoot, respectively, to the first church they found, sat on the floor in front of the first row, and grew up in God. They traded in their love beads for a marriage license, and went back to Shunk to make the whole thing legal, but they kept krystal and blue as their first names, and that's how they've been known ever since.

Celie married Michael Winters, my dad, at eighteen, had me, Aria

Sage Winters, at nineteen, and my sister, Johanna Anise, at twenty-one. Celie loves classical music and Dad loves to cook. I bet you'd never have guessed.

The Shunk-Winters compound is one hundred twenty acres of prime farmland in Linden, California—and we're talking the filet mignon of farmland—only because Opa had the foresight of Superman or the inspiration of God, depending in whom you believe, to buy it in exponential increments, starting with ten acres in 1972, on which he planted orchards and more orchards of almonds, walnuts and pistachios. Mam, the one vegetarian holdout in our family, hates when I refer to our land as filet mignon, but the Shunk-Winters orchards are the best and most beautiful in the whole valley, maybe all of California. Anyone who knows anything about living off the land will tell you.

In the center of that one hundred twenty acres are four five-acre parcels, all connected like squares on a granny quilt. Mam and Opa's home is built on one square, the home Johnnie and I grew up in, where Celie and Dad still live, is another. The third belongs to Johnnie. She and Matt already have their plans drawn for a two-story Colonial. They'll break ground next spring, six months before their wedding.

I adore Matt, who was my first honest-to-goodness boyfriend, and I'd have been the one marrying him if it weren't for his name. Not that there's anything intrinsically wrong with the name Matthew Farmer. It's nice and balanced. And so is he. But one day during World History class my sophomore year of high school, instead of taking notes on Mr. Gates' lecture, I filled an entire sheet of purple college-ruled binder paper writing Aria Farmer. I wrote it with a back slant, a forward slant, no slant, printed, in cursive, in my finest calligraphy. *Aria Farmer*, ARIA FARMER. ARIA FARMER. And then, at the bottom of the page I found I had written, "Well, are he?" And there went the magic. I knew I couldn't go through life with that question on everyone's lips. Johnnie Farmer is no better, to be sure, especially since Johnnie's a political science major and plans to run for office one day. They'd do well to take her name instead of his if you ask me. But no one has.

The fourth square of the compound, of course, is mine, and I'd like nothing better than to drop the stitch that connects us and let the whole thing unravel. Don't get me wrong. I love my family, but I need my space. My forebears were at Woodstock, you know? It doesn't get any freer than that.

One year into my stint as the family business office manager, following my graduation from Modesto JC, inspiration hit like a tsunami. I wanted to be a missionary. In a far, faraway place. So off I went to Bethany College in Santa Cruz. Accidentally, the Shunk family had come full circle.

Ten days after graduating with a major in English and a minor in Missions, I was on a plane for Moldova.

_____

"Window seat. Yes!"

I slide my carry-on into the overhead compartment, and myself into the third seat in my row, which is—dang!—right over the wing. What is it they say about the wing? Is it the best or the worst place to sit? I have a fifty-fifty chance of getting the answer right, and a ninety-five percent chance of getting it wrong. That's how the odds work with me. Regardless, it certainly interferes with the view. But, hey, what can you do? I fasten my seatbelt, turn the air on full speed, and pull out my iPod.

Saying goodbye at the security checkpoint was hard for Dad, harder still for Celie. Not so much for me. I'm the adventurer of the family, the one who'd have sailed with Columbus toward that questionable edge on the way to the New World. Anything that would take me away from the compound. Celie fingered the chopped ends of my hair, then hugged and kissed me one more time. Her own blond hair, which, in my life, had always been short and funky, was now loads longer than mine. I smiled, she smiled, but I saw in her eyes that the changes taking place in her little girl's life were more than about a haircut, and couldn't we please just turn back the clock?

But it was hardest of all for Johnnie. Oddly enough, my sister and I are the closest of friends. We're seventeen months apart, which hasn't mattered since Johnnie started junior high. The longest we'd ever been apart, before college, was seven days when I went to summer camp while she stayed home with tonsillitis. Now here I was flying halfway around the world on a one-year missions assignment. She was brave, for Johnnie, when she bid me farewell, but her eyes did glisten. They're normally blue-gray like Celie's, but whenever she cries they turn to sapphire. No one would believe she isn't wearing tinted contact lenses, when she cries.

I admit, when I hugged her goodbye I had to swallow a lump the size of the bagel I passed up at the airport Starbucks, and didn't get to say what I wanted to say. So instead I said, "See ya," like I always do, though the pitch of my voice was a good octave higher than normal. Then I handed over my passport to the lady in uniform, hoping I didn't look like a terrorist. Because I certainly didn't look like me. The image thrown back from every reflective surface I'd passed the past day and a half still caused me to catch my breath and stop for a second look. My hair, the one feature that had defined me most of my life, was all but gone. Until a day and a half ago I had Pantene-commercial hair. Long, lustrous, perfect. It's the one thing I don't mind being vain about because here's the thing: acquiring it was completely out of my control. I thank Celie, Dad and God, not necessarily in that order.

When I walked into Snippits, the salon I've been going to forever, sat down at Tana's station, saying, "Off with her hair!" Tana looked at me as if I were the Queen of Hearts, and brought a hand to her neck in defense.

"Off with it?" she said.

"Like this." I handed her a photo I'd Googled of a closely-sheared Winona Ryder taken at the Oscars a few years ago.

Tana dropped into the empty chair beside me and gaped at the photo. She'd been keeping the split ends at bay since I was old enough to care, and took as much pride in my hair as I did. "Like this?"

"I won't have time for deep conditioning in Moldova."

"Oh, but there's this new—"

"Off with it."

She stood and paced behind her station. "What if we—"

"No." I sounded bold as the Queen of Hearts even though my insides were quaking.

"Well, then we could—"

"No. Just do it. It'll grow back."

She shook her head. "You'll never grow it back, not like this. I can give you the stats. At your age once it's gone, it's gone."

At my age? I snatched the photo of Winona out of her hand and studied it. "I can live with this," I said at last. "Assuming I don't beat the odds." Which it was most unlikely I would.

"For a wedding?" Tana said.

"I'm not getting married, I'm going to the mission field."

"You're not getting married today, or anytime soon perhaps. But you will get married eventually, Ree, and you won't want to look like the head of a Greek philosopher on your wedding day. Trust me, I know about these things."

"There are extensions."

"And to what would we attach them?"

"I'm going short, not hairless."

Tana stopped pacing and stood behind my chair, her violet eyes catching mine in the mirror, imploring me. "I don't know if I can do it."

I huffed out a breath. "Tana. I'm not asking for assisted suicide. Now come on."

"I just don't think I can."

"Then have Will make the first cut. You know how long he's wanted to get his hands on my hair."

Will's head appeared around the column that separated his station from Tana's. "Did I hear my name?"

"And everything else, I'm sure."

He smiled, winked. "I'm your man, Aria."

"Oh yeah? What would Tad say to that?"

Will raised his left hand and wiggled his fingers. "It's not like he's given me a ring or anything."

"That wasn't legal here before it was legal before it wasn't legal again. But it's never been legal in God's universe."

"Now, doll, don't get preachy on me. Again."

"Okay, well here's the deal." I held up a tantalizing strand of hair. "I'll let you make the first cut, but the next time Opa comes in for a trim you have to give him your undivided attention for fifteen minutes." No one could share the love of Christ like Opa, without an ounce of condemnation. Because once upon a time that's exactly how blue karma needed it.

"Make it ten minutes and we have a deal. I think I can hold out that long."

"Fifteen or I cut it myself." I reached for Tana's scissors to make good on my threat.

"Okay! Fifteen, but not one second more."

"Deal." I stuck out my hand and we shook, as I made a mental note to have Opa come in for a trim tomorrow. Strike while the curling iron is sizzling hot, I always say.

Will moved behind my chair and tied a plastic zebra-print drape around my neck. He lifted the scissors in one hand and a strand of my hair in the other. The smile on his face was ghoulish.

"Wait!" I cried. "Wait. Turn me around, away from the mirror. And make it count, Will. The point of no return."

Tana closed her eyes like shutters on the world, as Will swiveled my chair one hundred eighty degrees. "You got it," he said. I heard the scissors slice through the strand, then Tana gasped as Will held up a two-foot long hank of hair thick as a willow branch. "There you are, doll. Your point of no return."

I watched as the hair fell in a heap on the floor. "Fifteen minutes," I whimpered.

"Not a second more."

Thirty minutes later, with a mangled mane of hair at my feet, Tana turned me back to the mirror. I swallowed, or tried to.

"Is it right?" There was a quaver in her voice.

It was exactly right. I blinked and blinked, and somehow managed to keep the tears from filling my eyes.

"It'll grow back," Tana said, though neither of us was convinced of it.

"I want a streak the color of Johnnie's hair right here." I indicated a spot just to the right of my barely-there bangs.

"What a sweet idea. So you can take your baby sister with you."

I pointed to the back of the shop. "Go. Mix." As soon as she was out of sight I pulled a laundered towel out of her drawer and blotted my eyes. By the time she came back with the color mixed and ready to streak on my hair I was hanging onto my self control, but only by a hair.

The controlled rumble of the Boeing 777 fills the cabin as a full load of passengers waits for take-off. I tighten my seatbelt, dump a packet of Airborne into my Avian and give it a good shake.

"Where ya headed?"

I turn toward the questioner in the seat beside me, the bottle just inches from my mouth. "Bucharest," I say, because no one seems to have heard of Moldova. At least they're in the same neighborhood. The woman could be a cousin, if not a sister, to Mam. She has the same spiky hair—sort of like mine now—the same wide mouth, the same sagging earlobes from the weight of her shoulder-length earrings. I can actually hear them tinkle when she moves her head, over the noise of the engine, no less. Mam would love them.

"Bucharest. Well." She seems impressed. "I'm only going to Queens."

I sit up straighter, thinking she might be an assignment the Lord has placed in my path. Someone who needs to hear the gospel message I'm traveling over seven thousand miles to share. Why not start now? Or, she might be a guardian angel. I mean, who better to bring along than Mam? I think about the lectures I heard in Bible class about the soul winning that takes place on airplanes, clear my throat, and am about to say, "Yes, I'm going to teach English to eastern European children, using the Bible as a text." That should open the door. But while I'm donning my best missionary face, the woman slips on a Lone Ranger mask, tucks a travel pillow around her neck, and doesn't so much as twitch a finger all the way to New York.

The businessman in the aisle seat keeps his eyes on his laptop and does his best to look busy—though I really think he's playing Spider Solitaire—but it's tough to talk around a passenger asleep in the middle seat anyway. Especially one who whiffle-snores. So, I work the crossword puzzle in the flight magazine the first hour, thinking what good fortune it was to have an early morning flight, if for no other reason than finding the puzzle unworked. I stick a four-dollar postage-stamp of a pillow between my head and the window and try to nap for the next hour, giving me a terrible crick in the neck. Then, till we land in New York, I browse through *Destination Bucharest*, the book Opa gave me just as I left the compound, because he couldn't find a *Destination Moldova*.

Okay, so it's not really a compound. It's a picture postcard of a setting, especially during the summer when all you can see forever are the treetops melding into a huge expanse of powder blue sky, uninterrupted with anything except Mt. Diablo off to the west, rising up like a perky breast on the surface of the world. I know, the analogy would be better suited for a mountain named Mt. Diabla, but you get the idea. And all around the granny squares are a mélange of non-nut-bearing trees, two, three, even four times older than I am, shading our little nucleus from the hot sun that's so good for the nuts. And I don't mean the human variety. And, oh, the sunsets, so resplendent with color they're as much pain to the eye as they are pleasure.

A hard-slanting rain is falling when we land in New York. Not that it matters. With only a three-and-a-half-hour layover, I'm not going anywhere. Not that I wouldn't like to. It's my first time in New York, but can you really say "in New York" from the confines of an airport?

I head for the nearest Starbucks, knowing I'm about to leave the land of designer coffee far behind. I want one more *venti*, lite, caramel Frappuccino for the road. With extra whip.

Two

I wake to the sound of the landing gears lowering our tiny little tires in preparation for setting our great big airplane on that narrow strip of blacktop some distance below, thinking the man-sized tires on Opa's John Deere would be far more preferable to the bicycle tires I see out my window. I'm not fond of flying. And I'm amazed I actually slept over the whole of the dark Atlantic. Three Tylenol PM didn't hurt the cause. But oh, my neck. And my mouth. It feels like an incubator for huitlacoche, which I only know about because of my dad the chef. But moldy corn by any other name is still moldy corn.

I take a swig of water and unwrap a root beer barrel candy from the little stash Opa tucked in my pocket before I left home. Opa always has root beer barrel candies in his pocket, along with guitar picks, and it doesn't matter that Johnnie and I aren't tots anymore. The candies are for us. I can see me one day, years from now, burping my own grandbaby over my shoulder, while I suck away on one of Opa's root beer barrel candies.

I brace myself for the landing, eyes shut tight, and flinch when the rubber hits the road, bounces twice, then settles into a hard brake as we roar down the landing strip. Only when the plane decelerates into a less heart-stopping speed do I breathe again.

"Thank you," I say out loud, eyes turned toward the metal arc of a ceiling overhead.

"Check the seat pocket for anything you might have forgotten," says our flight attendant, "because I *will* put it on e-Bay." He's been the most entertaining element of the flight, in the brief time I was awake, anyway.

It's 3 A.M. California time, noon in Chisinau, the capital of Moldova. Only nine hours' difference instead of ten because of Daylight Savings Time, which, honestly, I wish they'd put an end to. Set the time how absolutely ever you want, then leave it alone for crying out loud. That's how I feel about it. Of course, when I was a kid, there was hardly anything better than getting that extra hour of daylight for playing outside after dinner. But I'm over it. Now, that extra hour of sleep means a whole lot more to me. And for seven long months, from mid-March to the end of October, every time my alarm slams its hideous racket into the middle of my REM sleep cycle like a gatecrasher at a Hollywood party, I think of that one Sunday morning in the fall when I'll get my hour back. I'm not a morning person. Now, thanks to the ungodly hour, since I'm still on California time, and the three Tylenol PMs, I feel as hung-over as a Russian vodka quality control specialist.

I stand, scrunched down until I can reach the aisle, then retrieve my carry-on from the overhead bin. I can't wait to use the toothbrush I packed inside. And the mousse, to add some pizzazz to my hair. The blue plastic travel-size bottle contains two point eight ounces, which should last me all of three uses. I have a pair of the gigantic Costco bottles, shrink-wrapped, in my checked baggage, and hope they'll last until I get my first care package from home. I'm new to this mousse thing and have no idea what to expect in the way of economy.

Whoever thought of the international drawings that identify his and her restrooms in public places deserves early retirement with full pay, but I check twice to make sure my figure is wearing a skirt before I enter, since the Romanian letters don't begin to register. I have a moment of panic standing outside the stall, and am relieved to see a real toilet with a seat when I push open the door. I've heard missionary horror stories of holes in the ground, though I can't say I listened with as much empathy as I might have, and while my knees are sound I can't imagine what they'd be like after a whole year of squatting. I make sure there's toilet paper before I sit down.

When I'm through I wash my hands, without soap because the dispenser is empty, then look around for something to dry them on. Not seeing a paper towel anywhere, I shake them till most of the water is gone, then reach in my bag for my toothbrush and paste. Simple pleasures, I think, and load my toothbrush three times before it's over. I run my tongue over my teeth. What on earth did people do before Colgate? Baking soda comes to mind, since that's what Mam says they used in her grandmother's day. So then, what did they do before Arm and Hammer?

I shake the bottle of mousse and spray a wad of foam the size of a Russian snowball into my palm, rub my hands together, and ruffle it through my hair the way Tana showed me. Then I shake my hair and ruffle it some more. A little girl about five studies me intently, her head craned back on her neck as she watches my unpracticed movements, with huge translucent eyes. I smile and say, "*Salut!*" She backs up, drops her head and puts two fingers in her mouth.

"Nadia," her mother says, followed by a half dozen words that are lost on me. Nadia grabs onto her mother's leg and casts another glance or two my way, and smiles from her place of safety. Her mother says something to me in Romanian, or maybe Russian. I really don't know which, or if it's either.

"American," I say in reply, feeling as if I just failed my first international test.

"Ah," the woman says. She nods, says something to Nadia, who waves, and then they're gone.

Language school is not required for MAs—missionary associates—in our denomination. Only full-time, career missionaries are required to learn the language of the people they're assigned to minister to. And in my case there wasn't time anyway. When I filled out my application, I put myself up for grabs for anyone who needed an MA for one year, trusting God to be my Guidance Counselor. As long as my primary responsibility was to teach English to the local children, it didn't matter what continent I landed on. I found out I was going to Moldova only in time to apply for my visa.

I study myself in the water-splattered glass, feeling like a stranger even to me, then grab my bag and head off to find the rest of my luggage. I don't know if I'll see my name on a sign before or after I retrieve my checked bags, but I hope it's before, because I have way more luggage than I can handle alone.

Dang, I wish there were a Starbucks, or even a Coke machine. Anything with enough caffeine to quell this headache.

———————————

His eyes grow enormous for the briefest second, the man with the sign bearing my name, but long enough for me to know I've over packed. But come on. Fifty pounds of baggage plus one little carry-on? For a whole year? It was worth what they charged me for being overweight. In the cargo department, that is.

My arms feel as if they'll pull right out of their sockets as I lug my suitcases behind me, and try to keep my shoulder bag from sliding down my arm. It doesn't help that a wheel on the largest Pullman, the one I bought just three days ago at Wilson's Leather, has busted clean off. The strap on bag number two looks ready to burst. But it's not like you're packing for just one season, or even two. You have to have shorts for the summer and sweaters for the winter. Heavy sweaters. And long johns. We're talking Soviet winters. At least they used to be Soviet. Now they're just plain old eastern European winters. But don't let that fool you. Only the name has changed.

I know from the photos they emailed me that the man holding the sign with my name scrawled in fat black Magic Marker is Clark Mitchell. I've made a point of saying his name over and over again to myself, because I know it's just a matter of time till I slip and call him Mitchell Clark. I can't help wonder if his middle name is something like Sanford or Warren, to keep the whole surname thing going. At least Clark and Mitchell are in alphabetical order. That's been my only help. It must be tough to be saddled with two last names. And no, I haven't missed the irony that this observation comes from the offspring of krystal blue karma. I wish Johnnie were here to share in the humor.

Clark is so much taller than his photo lets on. And thin? He and I could have shared the airplane seat I just vacated without him once infringing on my half. I suddenly have this fear that Sally, his wife, is going to turn out looking like a penguin, and that I'll not be able to keep from laughing when I see her. I bite the inside of my cheek in advance and extend my hand.

"Mister—" Already I hesitate. "Mitchell?"

"You must be Miss Winters. Here, let me get that." He takes over the suitcase with the busted wheel, easing my burden considerably, and not ever letting on that I've undoubtedly broken the first rules of MA etiquette by showing up with more than one little bag in my possession. "How was your flight? You must be exhausted. It's still the middle of the night for you, isn't it?"

"Uh-huh," I say, as I try to keep pace with his stilt-like legs.

I know from reading their profile online that Mitchell, I mean Clark, turned sixty-one last May, and Sally is fifty-nine. He looks every bit his age, but I also know he and Sally have spent the better part of four decades on the mission field, on one continent or another. Their life hasn't been cushy, by any means, but I look forward to the details. I intend to keep a journal.

Clark turns to see how far behind I've lagged, and waits for me to catch up. "Sally's with the car. We don't dare leave it unsupervised."

Unsupervised? I have visions of it sneaking out the window at night, like I used to do in high school, or telling its parents it's spending the night with a friend, when that friend tells its parents it's spending the night with you, thus setting up a whole night of unsupervised freedom. Which I only did once. I hold back a laugh and remind myself it's a car.

"Crime's a problem everywhere," Clark Mitchell says.

"Ah."

As we step outside we're walloped with a blanket of heat and humidity that takes my breath away. The outside of Chisinau feels like the inside of my *dojo* after a workout of the entire brown belt class. I've taken Tae Kwon Do since I was seven, and believe me, there's nothing hotter than a canvas *gi* during a workout. Or so I thought. I'm from California, where the humidity on a really bad day might top the charts at twenty percent, but this feels like one hundred twenty percent. Am I ever glad I packed all my shorts, T-shirts and flip-flops.

"You get used to it," Clark says, and I wonder how he stands the long sleeves he's wearing.

He halts as a white van in desperate need of a wash rolls to a stop before him. He pulls open the back doors, hoists up the big bag and heaves it into the back. My face glows, and not just from the heat. I remember it took both Dad and Opa to lift that single bag, and that I'd laughed at the two of them as they wrestled it into Opa's Hummer, but now I'm really embarrassed. I try to lift the bag I've wheeled to the back of the van, but Clark takes over.

I turn around and there stands Sally. Instantly, "Long Tall Sally," that old rock and roll classic, comes to mind, for she's almost as tall as her husband, and nearly as thin. I have one immediate thought: man, I hope they have carbs in Moldova. Sally's hair, a blend of dark brown and cotton white, is pulled back in a fluffy ponytail. Short, curly tendrils line her face, and I think without the band to hold the rest of her hair together she'd look something like Opa at Woodstock.

And then she smiles, and I think she might be enchanted, because I've never seen such a smile in all my life. Her teeth are large and not quite straight, though they're white as fresh water pearls, and if you saw them alone you'd think it was a "before braces" picture in an ADA ad. But the smile is radiant, and the way it transforms her face is magic.

She pulls me into a hug. "Aria," she says, "how good it is to have you. I'm Sally, and you've met Clark, my better half by miles."

Nice as he may be, that seems unlikely. And if I thought the woman on the plane could be Mam's cousin, well, Sally *is* Mam, who is one of my best gifts from God. Not in looks, like the woman on the plane, but in heart she's Mam, I can tell it already. And in spunk she's Mam, I'm willing to bet.

"Here we go." Sally directs me to the front passenger seat of the van. "You sit up here." I start to object when she adds, "Where Clark can hear you better." She touches her ear and winks.

It's cool in the van and I perk up a little, like a parched violet after a long drink of water. I position myself so the air from the vent hits me full in the face. I push up the sleeves on my thermal Henley tee, and run my hand over my forehead. My jeans cling to my legs, and if it were just Sally and me I'd take off my shoes and get rid of the socks. I don't know what I was thinking when I dressed yesterday morning.

"Hot as the dickens, and only June." Sally leans her long body forward between the two front seats and looks at me. "You're so different from your photo."

I tug on my scrap of bangs. "It's the hair."

"The hair! Of course."

"It's gone," I add, as if she might have missed that.

"Oh, but you look positively with it. I'd love to try something like that, but with all this curl if I cut it short I'm afraid I'd look like a pinwheel." She sits back and laughs, her hands tucked together between her knees.

She's wearing a light blue cotton jumper, the kind with the dropped waistline, a sleeveless tee beneath it, and brown leather sandals. Birks, I'm sure. Her arms are lean and suntanned. Except for the fact her toenails are unpolished and she has no chest to speak of, she honestly could be Mam. It's weird actually.

"Are you hungry? I made sandwiches. It's a bit of a drive from Chisinau to our little town of Leoccesni. Or you may want to nap. It's such a long flight from the States, and who can sleep on planes? Now trains, I can sleep. But planes? Never. Clark here can sleep just about anywhere, can't you, love?" She pats her husband's arm. "Except behind the wheel," she's quick to add.

A nap would be heaven, but already I'm captured by the countryside, which is nothing close to what I imagined. I really expected the landscape to resemble the buildings in the city—dull and drab. But the view spread out before us could have come right out of a travel guide. The terrain is a great expanse of rolling hills, blanketed in the distance with fir trees of some sort. They look as if someone with a paintbrush and a pallet loaded with smoky blue and avocado, stirred it all together and dabbed it, like arrowheads, onto the backdrop of sky that's all but bleached of color. And in the foreground, acres upon acres—or hectares upon hectares—of sunflowers, their leafy stalks a glistening primary green, topped by ochre, brown-centered blooms that sway, en masse, in an unfettered wind.

"Sunflowers?"

"That was my response, too," Sally says, "when we first came here."

"You'll find it's much like your part of the world for agriculture," Clark says. "Like California, Moldova is known for its vineyards and orchards. Specifically apples and walnuts."

Walnuts? I think of Dad and Opa, and my stomach dips, which surprises me, for it's much too soon to be homesick. Besides, this is me we're talking about, not Johnnie. "I had no idea."

I know I should have made time to research the country, but—and now I see how wrong I was—I assumed I knew what eastern Europe would be like. Bland and boring. Not even a little. I find myself smiling. I can't wait to email home. Of course, I already know it's dial-up, and that service isn't the least bit dependable, but that will be part of the adventure.

Sally hands me a sandwich. "Egg salad." She unwraps another one for Clark and passes it forward. "And Coke." She passes that forward too.

I'm a Pepsi person myself, but if eastern Europe is anything like the eastern United States, it'll be Coke for the duration. And really, I can handle the sacrifice. It too will be part of the adventure.

"I didn't realize how hungry I was," I say, and take a bite. I pause after two or three chews and take inventory of what's in my mouth. Egg, bread—very good bread at that, coarse and grainy—red onion if I'm not mistaken, and—pickles? Yes, pickles. Sweet, not dill. Back home, egg salad isn't much of a salad at all. It's egg and mayo with a dash of salt and pepper, spread between two pieces of Oroweat. Sort of the Caesar salad of sandwich salads for content. I resume chewing, but slower, unaccustomed as I am to crunchy things in my egg sandwiches. I try to forget that sweet pickles are right up there with Brussels sprouts on the top of my what-not-to-eat list.

Sally chews away, and looks out the window as if the scenery is new to her, too. "It doesn't get old," she says. She's read my mind.

I take another bite and pretend it's tuna salad, in which pickles belong, and pretend the pickles are dill. "How long have you been in Moldova?" This is something I already know, but I'm certain it will be a good conversation starter.

"The country became independent in 1991, when the Soviet Union collapsed. We came—when was it Clark? Ninety-six?"

He nods, one efficient movement of his head. "June of '96. This is our fourth term. Here."

I know a term is four years on the mission field, then a year home itinerating and presumably resting up for the next term. But there's nothing restful about traveling throughout a state, or even half a state if it's California, speaking in a church on Sunday morning, then high-tailing it to another church a hundred miles away for Sunday night small groups. And that doesn't touch the Wednesday night services or miscellaneous meetings. No, I have an idea they only get rested up after they return to the mission field.

"Do you have family?" I ask.

"Two sons," Sally says, with a smile that is deeply connected to the womb. "James and Jesse."

"James and Jesse?" I turn my eyes forward and try not to laugh.

"Of course, we'd never have done Jesse and James." Sally giggles and I feel better. "We wanted to honor Bible characters, not outlaws. When the boys were small, if the two of them got out of hand in public, particularly at a church we were visiting—and believe me they did on occasion—I always made it a point to reprimand them in their birth order, and not the other way around." Sally takes a drink of her Coke. "But they did love their pistols and holsters, didn't they, love?" She rests her hand on Clark's shoulder. The fingers are long and tapered, like a musician's. Like mine. "Do you have brothers?"

I shake my head. "Only one sister. Johnnie."

"Johnnie?" Sally leans forward as if she's sure she didn't hear me right. "Is she a tomboy?"

I laugh. "Not in the least. Her name is Johanna, after Bach."

"And Aria. Okay, I get it. Music lovers. Isn't that nice? Johanna and Aria, James and Jesse. Themes everywhere. I like the symmetry of it."

We've left the sunflowers behind. Now there are wooded hills for our landscape. An occasional farmhouse sits back off the road, looking for all the world like something you'd see in Colorado or Montana. And there's that dip again, right in the pit of my stomach.

"We love it here," Sally says. "Love the people, love the land. I think you will too, Aria." She touches my shoulder. "We're so glad you're here."

———————————

I wake sometime later as the van turns onto an unpaved lane and comes to a stop outside an old building whose block façade has faded to a tired periwinkle blue. There's a sign above the door written in Romanian, I assume, that I'm pretty sure, interpreted, reads Evangel Worship Center. This, then, is Leoccesni, where I'll spend the next twelve months. A house stands across a gravel path, and by its matching color I take it to be the parsonage. It's tall and narrow, three stories high, and has a small porch with concrete steps. A planter box positioned on the top step, popping with petunias in fuchsia and lapis lazuli, adds a burst of unwashed color to the scene.

"Here we are," Sally says. "Home."

That one word rolling off her tongue has all the appeal of Mam's homemade peach cobbler just out of the oven. My mouth waters, and I too am glad I'm here.

Three

I try to reach for the biggest of my suitcases before Clark can get to it, but his long arm slips in ahead of mine. He pulls it out of the van along with my second largest suitcase and rolls them behind him as he heads for the house, or tries. But the broken wheel does not cooperate along the gravel path. He's left my carry-on for me to handle. I sling it over my shoulder before Sally can take it from me. My eyes rise to the full height of the house. I just know my room is on the top floor, maybe the little one on the left with the dormer, and I'm embarrassed all over again. I hurry to catch up, hoping Clark will let me carry one or the other to my room.

"Wait, wait!" Sally says as we pass the petunias. She plucks one the color of the three packages of Post-it notes somewhere in my bags, and puts it in my hair. Then she crosses the threshold, turns and opens her arms to me. "Welcome!"

My heavens, she's so much like Mam it's a moment before I can step forward to receive her embrace. I hope she doesn't take my hesitation for reticence. I hug her extra hard to compensate.

"Here, Clark," she says, "let me take one of those."

He passes off the smaller suitcase, and the three of us hitch-step our way up the narrow staircase.

Sally stops in front of the first door we come to on the third floor. "Here we are."

I'm right. My room is the one in the front, the one with the dormer, which contains the only window in the room. The window is small, about two feet square, but it's open and allows a light breeze to pass through. There's isn't a curtain, only a shade that pulls down for privacy. A box fan in the corner stirs the warm air. I can't wait to get into my shorts.

The bed is narrow and has an aluminum tube frame. There's a small table beside it with a reading lamp, a straight-back chair, and a three-drawer dresser. The top drawer is half the height of the two below it. I shift my eyes from one side of the room to the other, seeking, hoping, but there is no closet. Only a portable wardrobe the approximate width of the bed. It's open, and I count nine wire clothes hangers. Combine the furnishings and the three of us squeezed in, and we've eliminated all the standing room available.

Yes, I've over packed.

Clark takes inventory. "I'll bring over that chest of drawers from the storeroom in the church. It might fit there under the window."

If it does, it can't be more than two feet wide and three feet tall. My smile looks more like gas pains, I'm sure, but I say thank you, and I mean it.

"I think your smaller suitcase will slide right under the bed. And the larger one, well, maybe you can use it to store whatever you're not using at the moment. We can find someplace to keep it, I think. I'll see if I can round up more hangers.

Six maybe, because the wardrobe won't hold many more than that.

"The bathroom's on the second floor. Come, I'll show you."

It's larger than I expect, though smaller than anything I'm used to. There's a sink with no vanity, and a mirrored medicine chest hanging over it. There's a toilet, and a bathtub completely encircled with a plastic shower curtain. It's open a foot or so, and I see the showerhead is nothing to write home about. Or maybe it's just the type of detail Celie and Johnnie would love to hear. There are built-in cupboards on the wall opposite the sink. I think someone added them long after the house was built. Maybe Clark.

"This is your towel and washcloth." Sally indicates the set in faded wintergreen, hanging on a long rod over the tub. "We change them about every fourth day. We try to keep our wash to a minimum. And we hang everything outside to dry."

Everything?

I've just decided I'm leaving my thongs in the big suitcase, no matter the season. I don't think panty lines will matter as much as the image of my barely there underwear flapping in the wind for all of Moldova to see. And as for my Victoria Secrets bras, maybe Celie can pick up something plain and unassuming at JC Penney before she sends my care package. I'm going online to look the first chance I get.

Three other sets of towels hang on the rod. One set is basic white. The other two are embroidered with Sally and Clark's initials. "Women's Ministries sent us these for Christmas."

"Ah, nice." I think of my own church and the small cluster of women who work all year long on crafts for the missionaries, and I have a whole new appreciation for what they do.

Sally moves to the cupboard, opens one of the doors, and runs her hand along the empty half of a shelf. "You can put any of your, um, personal supplies here. And shampoo and soap, things like that."

"Great," I say. And I'm glad, really glad, for the haircut—though how I'll maintain it I haven't quite figured out—because it allowed me to leave my blow dryer, curling iron, claw clips and rubber bands at home. If my eye is even close to accurate, my Costco mousse will never fit on that shelf.

If I didn't know me better, I'd say I was a spoiled little rich girl from California. I fear I'm going to have to work hard to dispel the image.

"You look about ready to drop," Sally says. "Would you like a nap?"

I nod. I haven't begun to work off the three Tylenol PMs I took on the plane.

"Go on up and stretch out. I'll get you a glass of water."

"Oh, lovely. Thank you."

On the landing, I go up the stairs and Sally goes down. I can touch the papered walls, elbow to elbow, and my size eight foot only half covers the treads. I wonder how long before I tumble down on a potty run in the night, like Jill gone to fetch a pail of water.

In my room I open the suitcase that contains my summer clothes, and tug out my favorite pair of distressed denim shorts and a navy blue tee that says Abercrombie in white letters, going sideways from top to bottom down the left side of the shirt. I finish changing just as Sally knocks on my door.

"Well, that should be cooler," Sally says of my outfit. She places the glass of water on the bedside table. The ice cubes tinkle in tune, then quickly grow still. "Can I get you anything else?"

"No, this is fine. Thank you for everything." I stifle a yawn and realize just how tired I am.

"Okay then."

She leaves me and I position the fan to blow directly toward the bed. I curl up on my side, hugging the thin pillow in the crook of my arm. And sleep.

I have no idea where I am when I awake. I'm startled for a moment, but when my eyes fall on the open wardrobe with the nine hangers, I remember.

I sit up and work to get my bearings. It's still light outside, so I couldn't have slept long, though my head seems to weigh a ton, and the ache between my temples reminds me of my one and only hangover. I was fourteen and foolish, shunning my youth group and hanging out with my new high school friends. After two hours of downing Budweiser and sweet wine one night when I was supposed to be in a study group, my new *friends* dumped me at the entrance to the compound. I staggered up the road and into our house and threw up all over Celie's Italian marble. Then continued to throw up until I was sure I saw my gall bladder floating in the mess. Seeing Celie's eyes afloat with tears did more to put me back on the narrow path than the slamming headache or the puking. Because I knew how she prayed for me and Johnnie. I heard the murmur of her prayers often in the early morning, knowing she was calling out my name, among others, while I was tucked snugly in my nice warm bed.

The air is thick, but the fan has kept me somewhat comfortable. Still, I feel sluggish as honey straight from the fridge. I hang my feet over the side of the bed, stand and get my balance. I'd better get to the john. I'm careful with the stairs and am glad to see the bathroom door wide open when I reach the landing. When I finish, I go back up and retrieve my toothbrush from my travel bag. Back down I go to freshen up.

"Well, hello." Sally's in the kitchen when I get there, working on . . . lunch? Again? I think of the eggs and the pickles. Well, okay. You're not in California anymore, Ree. Sally turns to me. "Coffee or tea?"

"Better make it coffee. I don't think I got my nap out."

"Not got your—?" Sally laughs and fills up a cup. "Sweetie, you've been sleeping for, oh, about twenty hours."

"Twenty *hours*?"

"I tried to wake you for dinner, then again for breakfast. When you didn't budge, I decided you needed rest more than food. Though if you were a plate of ribs I'd have to send you back for something with meat." She laughs again.

I'm barely able to follow what she says, but take the coffee and drink as much of the hot stuff as my mouth can handle at one time. "It's, it's Sunday?"

"You missed the morning service, but we meet again at six."

"Oh, Sally, I'm sorry." And embarrassed.

"Nonsense. But I do hope you can sleep tonight so you're on schedule in the morning. The children are so eager to meet you."

"The way I feel right now, that won't be a problem."

"Clark's over at the church," Sally says. "He prays between services. I knew you'd want something to eat once you woke up. I hope you like BLTs."

"I love BLTs."

"On toast?"

I nod.

Sally lays six thick strips of bacon in a hot cast iron skillet, then points a fork in my direction as they immediately begin to sizzle. "Crisp or lethargic?"

I laugh. "Crisp."

"Me too. Otherwise, what's the point?"

The tomatoes are sliced and the lettuce leaves are rinsed. But I offer to make the toast when she's ready for it. She's sliced an apple and placed it in a bowl of cold water with a wedge of lemon that's been squeezed to keep the fruit from turning brown.

The toaster looks retro, stainless steel with a rounded top. But it's not new made to look old. It is old. You can tell by the thick rope-like cord in that vintage striped pattern, the kind you see on steam irons in antique shops. And by the fact that a bagel would never fit in the slots.

We take our sandwiches outside and sit on the top step of the porch, Sally on one side, me on the other. The temperature is right on the cusp between tolerable and hot, but there's a breeze and that helps.

I chew and swallow my first bite after Sally says grace. "At home we have a delta breeze that comes in off the bay most every night and feels like it's sent from heaven. No matter how hot it's been during the day, it's cool enough for a sweatshirt once the breeze kicks in."

Sally washes down a bit of sandwich with her Coke. "I've never been to California."

"If you ask me, it's the Promised Land." I take a bite from a wedge of apple and my taste buds come alive. "Ooh, nice and tart."

"I've heard it called lots of things, but never the Promised Land."

"Well, it might not flow with milk and honey, but we have everything in the way of agriculture. And two hours in any direction from the com— our house—you can be in the mountains, at the beach, in the redwoods, almost to the desert. We have it all. There's not another state like it."

"Clark and I grew up in Nebraska. We never saw the ocean till we came here. Not once. Now we go to the Black Sea once a year for a short vacation, or at least we try."

"The Black Sea. Oh, I can't believe I'm here." I take another bite of sandwich. "So is it? Black?"

Sally shakes her head. "Not in the least. But there are several theories of how it came to be called the Black Sea, from compass points to hydrogen sulfide."

"Hydrogen sulfide." My nose wrinkles. "Science was not my favorite subject."

"Well, don't ask me what it is, but there's a layer of the stuff about six hundred feet below the water's surface. There's no marine life at all below it."

"Wow, that's odd."

"There's no oxygen in the water from two hundred meters down. And, as any of us who at least took basic science knows, nothing can live without oxygen."

The voice comes from behind us and belongs to a man who isn't Clark. I look over my shoulder and have to stop myself from smiling. Definitely not Clark. A nice-looking guy about my age is standing in the open doorway and I wonder where he came from. I don't know why, but I put my sandwich aside and stand.

"You must be Aria," he says.

"People call me Ree." I haven't yet gotten around to telling Sally that, but now she knows too.

"Why?" There's absolutely no trace of an accent in his voice. My guess is he's from the Western US.

"Well because. No one uses a name with three syllables."

"Really." He puts out his hand. "Hamilton."

Hamilton? I count the syllables as we shake hands, and wilt a bit. I say the name in my mind, hoping, really hoping it's his last name. "Is there a first name that goes with that?"

Sally, who's also standing now, chuckles.

"That's it," he says. "Hamilton."

There's a moment of silence as I decide if I'm really going to call him Hamilton. Or worse, Ham or Milton. Then he smiles and comes close to a laugh, but not quite. "Andrews," he adds. "People call me Andy."

I want to say "phew." Instead I say, "Well there you are. Nice to meet you."

He smirks. "You may want to withhold judgment."

Sally's eyes are wide with mirth, and she nods. "He isn't kidding."

I don't know what to say to that.

"Can I talk to you for a sec?" he says to Sally. He nods toward the open door.

"Sure." Sally steps through the door to lead the way.

I'm halfway back to a sitting position when he turns back to me. "Nice to meet you. Aria."

He disappears before I can respond. But I will, sooner or later. You can count on it.

I go upstairs to dress for the evening service. I doubt jeans and a T-shirt are kosher, but Sally's already walked over to the church, so I can't ask. I select one of the half dozen dresses I brought, but I hope I find tonight I'll only need them for Sunday mornings. I hope this is like home, that Sunday night services are more laid back.

Before I pull down the shade, I lean my elbows on the blistered sill and rest my chin in my cupped palms. If you look beyond the immediate landscape, it really is a beautiful view. The mountains are a smoky blue and fade into the sky like someone skilled with a brush has done the blending. The neighborhood below is nothing like the compound, and yet that's all I think about.

Opa never meant to be a land-holding, entrepreneurial member of The Establishment. When he dropped out he did not intend to drop back in. But he did, in a big way. Ten acres became a hundred and twenty acres in only seven years. He could have owned two or three times that, but Opa said a hundred and twenty acres were manageable, and he liked the sound of it. Whenever Dad talked of expansion Opa would say, "There's something right about one hundred and twenty."

By "right" he meant biblical. On the day of Pentecost, of course, there were one hundred twenty disciples in the upper room. Then divide Opa's one hundred twenty acres by his original ten and you get the twelve tribes of Israel, the twelve Apostles, the twelve foundations and gates of the heavenly Jerusalem. And on it goes. Opa's big on numbers.

And while every landholder up and down the San Joaquin Valley was planting grapevines by the thousands, Opa opted for nuts. He laughed at every pun thrown his way, all the way to the bank, where he deposited his earnings like the King of Squirrels stocking up for a long winter.

I love an orchard, our orchards in particular. Dad and Opa are meticulous farmers, keeping away the weeds and any debris the wind blows in. And now here I am in Moldova of all places, surrounded by orchards and vineyards almost as beautiful as our own. The only difference between this and our landscape at home is that the mountains on either side of the valley are much closer here than they are there. I kind of like that. They make me feel secure, as if I'm nestled in the hands of God.

Four

The sanctuary is a rectangle maybe twenty feet wide by thirty feet long, with wooden pews like park benches on either side of a narrow center aisle. The front six on either side are already full. On a hot Sunday night. I'm certain that would not be the case at home if it meant crowding into an un-airconditioned smokehouse of a box for service. But there are windows on one side of the aisle, and they're open, though there's not much of a breeze to offer relief. There are box fans, one on the platform and one in the back of the church. They're stirring up the air, and though my dress is almost sleeveless, and pure cotton, my skin glows with perspiration. It's not the look I favor.

Sixty pairs of eyes are on me and have been since the moment I walked through the door. Two thirds of them belong to women, all of whom wear head coverings. The remaining third is an even split between children and men. All the faces smile and nod. I hear a word or two I understand: *salut, buná seara. Hello, gut evening.* I return the smiles and slide into a pew near a window, and hope the breeze picks up. I fetch an old church bulletin from my Bible to use as a fan.

Clark sits on a bench at the back of a slightly raised platform. He leans forward, elbows on knees, head resting in his hands, praying. Sally greets the congregation one by one, as fluent in her adopted tongue as she is in English. Her smile continues to captivate me. And not only me. The young girls rise to give her hugs as if she were their grandmother. Or Jesus. *Suffer the children to come unto me,* the Savior said. I think this is exactly what he meant. The young boys hold back from giving or accepting hugs, but they shake the hand Sally extends, and squirm shyly under the attention she gives.

Andy stands just to the right of the wooden pulpit situated front and center of the platform. He straps on an acoustic guitar, then strums the strings with a turquoise pick. He adjusts two of the tuning keys and strums again. My ear detects the minute difference as the strings give off a perfect tone.

I know this because of Opa. An acoustic guitar in his able hands . . . well, if there's a folk rock band in Heaven, he'll be the lead guitar player. No question. He'll be the lead singer too. I close my eyes and Opa's voice is there, inside my head, making something mighty good out of an everyday song. His voice is smooth as a cool, deep pool that's been just the least bit troubled. It's the troubling that gives it the sound I love above any other. It's earthy, and heavenly—a perfect blend of heart and soul. A sound as healing as the troubled Pool of Bethesda.

Andy plays an intro then begins to sing a hymn I recognize. The words are another matter, but even in Romanian my spirit understands and responds. I close my eyes and sway, hands lifted, and hum along with the tune. Then I stop, cock my head and listen. Because Andy's that good. In fact, he could do backup in Opa's heavenly band.

I can't wait to tell Johnnie.

"Aria, Aria. Come up here, love." Sally calls me forward. The music part of the service is over, and I'm next on the agenda.

I don't know when I've felt so self-conscious, but I think it had something to do with the first time I wore a bra to school. Our sixth grade classroom was divided into three groups: girls who wore bras, girls who didn't, and the boys, all of whom cackled like hyenas at both sets of girls for two obviously different reasons. I had just joined Group A, and there wasn't a student in Mr. Parker's class who didn't know it.

I make my way to the platform, turn, and smile at the congregation. Sally introduces me in Romanian, then bends at the waist and calls the children forth. I only know this because they rush forward en masse, but stop a foot or so short of the place where we stand.

"Good even, teacher," they say as one. A knot of emotion blocks my throat because it touches me to know they've rehearsed this. That they, or someone, anticipated my coming as much as I did.

So then, these are my students. "Good evening," I say, and I shake every one of their hands. Like children the world over, some are shy, some are not, and while I'm taken with all of their smiles, there's one in particular, a girl about eleven, who catches my eye. I'm almost sorry for how lovely she is, because it will make her life charmed, but it won't make it easy. Already a look in her eye seems to agree with my assessment.

As I return to my seat, Andy is watching me. I can't begin to read the look on his face. I slide back in the pew and pick up my makeshift fan. I feel his eyes on me and can't resist turning to look. But Andy's eyes are on Clark, who has just placed his Bible on the pulpit, and has just begun to pray.

It's an intimate prayer, which touches my heart as deeply as the notes on Opa's guitar when he plays for no one but God. I wish I knew the words, but that doesn't seem to matter. With my head bowed and my eyes cast downward, tears drop on my lap, tiny splotches as telling as a Rorschach test, because I can't tell you the last time I cried in church. But I feel such anticipation, such a sense that I actually managed to get to the right place on purpose. That redemption for me might yet be a reality. I outline one of the splotches with my fingernail, but it evaporates quickly in this heat.

John fifteen is Clark's text. I open my Bible. Every verse is in red, and nearly every one is underlined, for this is my favorite chapter in the

Bible. "Ask whatever you wish, and it will be given you," verse seven says. Whatever you wish. That catches me up every time I read it, because it's such a huge boast. I'm sure Jesus meant it, but I'm saving my wish for when I really need it, in case we only get one.

———————————

Moldova has long given up the sun to the other side of the globe by the time service is over. Black moths the size of Shunk-Winters' prize-winning walnuts, drawn through the open windows to the bare bulbs that hang throughout the church from the low ceiling, have distracted me for a good part of the sermon. If I were Catholic such inattention would earn me a dozen Hail Marys, I'm sure. But as it is, these dull but determined creatures have preached me a three-point sermon of their own.

Point one: how easily we are drawn to the white-hot allure of this world, only to be burnt up and consumed in the process. Point two: there is another Light that draws us just as surely, and burns us up just as thoroughly, but like the Burning Bush we aren't consumed. Point three: to which light am I more consistently drawn—the big L or the little l? I search my Bible's concordance for the scripture in Jeremiah that runs through my head. Finding it, I read, ". . . his word is in my heart like a fire, a fire shut up in my bones. I am weary of holding it in; indeed, I cannot."

I want to be consumed like that, I think. Then I say that again in my mind the way I know it really is. I *want to be consumed like that . . . I think.*

With such wandering thoughts you can see why I had to work exceptionally hard to earn a B minus average all through high school and college. There was no honors stole for me. That blue and gold accolade was bestowed upon Johnnie when she graduated from Linden High, and she'll no doubt be draped again when she leaves Sac State in May.

I adore my sister, and believe if there's one mistake God made where our family is concerned, it's that I'm the big sister. Because I'm so not. In maturity, Johnnie beats me as surely as if I'd started the trek to wisdom ages after she did. Which I guess is true. I spent my teenage years in front of my computer, IM-ing my friends for hours at a time, while Johnnie devoted the same hours to growing up. In kindness she's the honey, while I'm the pollen that never made it into the mix. I'm okay with that. Mam says most recipes call for both sugar and salt. I don't need anyone to tell me which one I am.

One more thing. Johnnie is as selfless as I am self-centered. You know how they say on airplanes to secure your own mask before helping others? Well, I've been in the habit of securing my own mask since I was, I don't know, a day and a half old. Which is why I'm in Moldova, to learn to quit thinking life is all about me. The thought makes my stomach flip, because I know what a hard nut I am to crack. That's a little Shunk-Winters humor we use at the compound. But there's nothing funny about courting the hammer of God. And that's exactly what I'm doing here. I only hope that when the shell falls away, the nut that emerges isn't hopelessly spoiled.

Five

"Good morning, teacher."

The children greet me in one sing-song voice. There are an even dozen, four boys and eight girls in the little classroom off the sanctuary, which doubles as a Sunday school room. I'll be teaching that as well, I'm told. The youngest student looks to be about six, while the oldest is a lovely girl of twelve. I know that for certain because I asked Sally about her last night after church, the one I guessed to be eleven. Her name is Anya Moravec, and she's one of the shy ones.

"Good morning, class," I reply, but I have no idea what to say or do next. I'm glad Sally will work with me for a day or two.

The children move to their desks, surprisingly similar to the ones I used in grammar school. The smallest of the children, whose feet can't yet reach the floor, swing their legs back and forth, each in contrasting symmetry.

"Who would like to pray for us this morning?" Sally asks, and four little hands shoot up. "Let's see. Nicolai, I think it's your turn."

Nicolai, who looks to be seven or eight, bows his head and folds his hands, all very formal. His classmates follow suit. "Dear Jesus," he begins, in a voice that endears him to me straight away, "good morning." Good morning? It's never, ever occurred to me to start a prayer this way, and self-consciously I dig one sandaled foot into the floor. Already I'm asking myself, who's the teacher here? "Thank you for our new teacher. I hope we learn a lot. Amen."

"Amen," the others say in unison.

"Thank you, Nicky." Sally turns to me. "We begin our day with devotions. Would you like to read the story?"

I take the book Sally offers. "Okay. Sure." I start to move toward the chair beside the teacher's desk, and expect Sally to take the one behind it. Then I see she's moved to a small clearing and sits like an Indian chief on the old wooden floor. The drop-waist jumper she's wearing accommodates the movement nicely, then covers her folded legs like a lap quilt. Except for the color, it's identical to the one she wore on my arrival, and I'm willing to bet she has more in other colors for every day of the week, with tags that say *Handmade by Sally*.

The children rush forward and join her on the floor, getting as close to Sally as they can, with the youngest ones in the front of the slapdash semi-circle. Sally flashes me a smile and pats the floor beside her. I tug at the hem of my walking shorts, glad for my selection this morning, for they're the longest ones I own. They'll cover most of my thighs when I sit, not Indian style like Sally, but for modesty's sake, more in the shape of a Z—like I imagine Princess Di might have sat in her kindergarten-teacher days.

I'm going to ask Sally about my dress code the minute school is out, to find out what is and isn't proper. I'm sure I've already earned a semester's worth of demerits for violations.

"Jesus and the Little Children," I begin, and all eyes are on me. I read slowly, because I don't yet know how fluent they are in English. "'One day Jesus was teaching in a certain place, maybe Nazareth or maybe Jerusalem. Many people pressed in around him, because they loved to hear the great Teacher's stories. He taught them about widows and tax collectors, lost sheep and rich young rulers. And every story he told taught them more about God.'

"'But Jesus wasn't just a Teacher. He could do what no man had ever done before him. He prayed for sick people and they were made well. He touched blind eyes, and they could see. He touched deaf ears and they could hear. He was a miracle worker!'"

The children's eyes grow big as Moldovan sunflowers, so I guess they understand well enough.

"'Well, parents in that city began to bring their babies to Jesus just so he could touch them and bless them. But Jesus' disciples—' "

"I know what disciple means," one of the boys says. "It means follower."

"That's right, Peter." Sally gives the boy a wink then nods for me to continue.

I run my finger over the text, hunting for where I left off. "'But Jesus' disciples said, "Go away! Can't you see you're bothering the Master?" Sadly, the people turned to go, but Jesus said, "No, don't leave. Bring the children here to me."'"

Without taking her eyes off mine, the smallest—and I'm sure the youngest—girl in the group moves almost unnoticed into Sally's lap and leans her head against Sally's chest. I think her name is Tanya, or maybe it's Olga. I'll get them straight before long. She puts her thumb in her mouth and looks as content as can be. But then, so does Sally, and I can't help wonder if her sons have children, and how much Sally has sacrificed in her life.

I find my place again. "'Then he gathered as many as he could into his arms, and didn't mind at all when the others clung to his legs and even stepped on his toes.'" The children in our little group giggle. "'"If you want to know what the kingdom of God is like," Jesus continued, "open your eyes"'—and this is the memory verse," I say—"'for the kingdom of heaven belongs to such as these.' Matthew 19:14."

"Shall we all say that together?" Sally says. "For the kingdom of heaven," she prompts, "belongs to such as these." They say it in two parts, two more times, then say it almost flawlessly without a break, adding the reference the final time.

There are questions and answers for a good five minutes. When Sally unfolds herself I hear her knees pop. No surprise there. The woman is all angles and bones.

We breeze through the next three hours, teaching math, grammar and science on three different levels. Then Sally teaches European history to the older children, while I take the younger ones out for recess. There's been no break at all for the kids eight and above, but they don't complain, and, surprisingly, I haven't noticed even the teeniest sign of ADD from anyone. That never happened in the US, even in my college classes. The children use the restroom as needed, then get right back to work.

We break for lunch at noon and the children head off to their respective houses. Only the youngest ones are met by their mothers and escorted home.

"Is it okay? To let them go alone, I mean?"

"Oh, sure," Sally says. "It would be different in the city, of course. But out here we all look out for one another."

She and I cross the drive to the house. The gravel crunches under my sandals and a pebble finds its way between my toes. I stop and wiggle it out, then follow Sally up the back steps that lead to the kitchen. Even before we open the screen door, I smell something delicious and I realize how hungry I am. I breathe in deeply as Sally ties an apron around her thin frame.

"The crock pot really is the eighth wonder of the world, don't you think?"

"I do today," I say. There are two on the counter top from which a blend of mouth-watering aromas emanate. "When did you find time to put all this together?"

"Oh, it's nothing," Sally says. "Would you mind setting the table? The silverware's there, and the plates and bowls up there." She nods, first in one direction then in another to show me the way. I take note that the dishes and utensils are exactly where Celie would store them. Now me, I'd put the silverware in the drawer closer to the— I look around. Okay, well, if there *were* a dishwasher, I'd put them in the drawer closest to it, and I'd put the plates and bowls in the cupboard right above it, to make unloading the dishwasher as easy as possible. I hate to empty the dishwasher, and for that matter, put away folded clothes. Johnnie and I have a pact: I load, she unloads. I fold, she puts away.

I turn on the faucet in the big, single-tub sink and reach for the bar of soap, which is a dull brown, grainy lump, which smells strong and pungent. I'm willing to bet the pH-balance concept hasn't made it this far east. I think of my own papaya and melon bars, clear enough to see through, upstairs on my shelf in the bathroom. I make a mental note to ask Celie to add extra soap to the care package she'll be sending. I can't imagine scrubbing my body with this Moldovan concoction.

Clark stomps his boots outside the screen door, then smiles his way into the kitchen. "I could eat a wild boar, tusks and all," he says. "I'm that hungry." He heads straight to the sink and that brown bar of soap.

"You'll have to settle for roasted chicken." Sally leans toward her husband to receive a kiss.

I hear another set of boots stomping outside the door, and turn to see Andy just as the screen door closes behind him. He sends a *hey* in my direction, only because our eyes have met, I sense, then falls in line at the sink behind Clark.

I've given no thought to what the men might have been up to today, other than to assume Clark would have been secreted away in his study, preparing his mid-week message. By all appearances I've assumed incorrectly. He and Andy look as if they might have been plowing fields with nothing more than a team of oxen. It's *Little House on the Prairie*, European style.

Clark takes a seat at the table and lets out a long breath. "It's hot as Hades out there." The air from the box fan quickly dries then ruffles the fringe of hair that hems the back of his head. It's exactly the color of steel wool, but the texture appears much finer.

"And only June," Sally says. "I'm afraid we're in for it."

I assess the food she begins to dish up. There's one steaming crock pot full of soup with nearly every vegetable I recognize and then some. The other crock pot is filled with a whole chicken and quartered potatoes. There's fresh bread that smells nothing short of decadent. My mouth waters at the prospect, but if this were my gig, the weather being what it is, I'd toss a salad, slice an apple and leave it at that. But I already know the noon meal is the main meal of the day in this little village, and that meal is taken seriously. I also know, no matter the season, soup is always served.

I unfold a napkin and lay it across my lap when Sally says, "Aria, would you like to pray?"

There are butterflies in my stomach all of a sudden, and I think it's because of Nicky's prayer in school this morning. I could never sound as, I don't know, acquainted with Jesus as Nicky already seems to be at his young age. But I clear my throat and decide *Good afternoon, Jesus* is not the beginning for me. "Gracious Heavenly Father," I say, then wish I hadn't, because that isn't me either, but I forge ahead. "Thank you for your bountiful provision and for the hospitality of this home." I relax, then, and say what's really on my mind. "Thank you, Lord, for letting me be here. I hope I don't let you down."

Sally pats my hand and gives me a wink, a vote of confidence if ever there was one.

We begin with soup and bread, and if I ever thought I'd had vegetable soup before, I have to think again. "The potatoes are different here," I say.

Sally chuckles. "It's rutabaga. More like a turnip than a potato. And sweeter."

"Huh. I thought you made pies out of rutabaga."

Sally and Clark give me a raised-eyebrow look, then return wordlessly to their lunch, while Andy smiles into his soup. It's the smile that tells me I've misspoken, though for the life of me—

"I bet you're handy in the kitchen."

"Andy." Sally's voice has the exact tone Celie still uses back home when I get smarmy with my sister.

Andy smiles again and I feel my cheeks grow hot, not because of his smarminess, which I already know I'll have to learn to ignore, but because I don't know where my error is, and, therefore, don't know how embarrassed to be.

"Well, it's good," I say directly to Sally, shunning Andy with every bit of body language I can muster. And believe me, if there's one thing I'm fluent in it's body language.

Clark tears off a piece of bread from the loaf and dunks it in his soup. Before I can fully identify the vegetables in my bowl, he finishes his soup and hides a belch behind his hand. "My tank was past empty."

"Love, it's always past empty," Sally says.

"It's hard work digging a well."

Andy looks at the palms of his hands, and I notice matching blisters. "That it is," he says.

"You're digging a well by hand?" No wonder they both look like they sprang from Middle-earth. "Whose well?"

"A man by the name of Janic Rotaru," Clark says.

"Was he at church yesterday?" There are too many unusual names for me to keep up with. Unusual for me, at least.

"He's not a believer," Sally says.

"But he is a neighbor," Clark adds. "His well collapsed after the rains. We had an exceptionally wet winter."

My throat tightens all at once as I think of Dad and Opa, because they would have had the same reply. Clark has risen more than a notch in my estimation. And I hate to say it, but Andy has too.

"How was school?" Andy asks. He addresses the question somewhere between Sally and me. I get the feeling I'm a non-entity where he's concerned, but a glance from Sally makes it clear the question belongs to me.

"The kids are great," I say. "And smart. I have a feeling I'm going to learn more from them than they learn from me."

The look Andy gives says he completely agrees. It makes my cheeks burn again. I resist tossing back a look of my own and decide he's not on an even keel with Clark after all. I dip my spoon in the bowl and take another bite.

Clark tears off another hunk of bread and digs into a second bowl of soup. Man, if I had a metabolism like his I could be a runway model. Or a poster child for anorexia. Not that I aspire to either, but as I push away the uneaten half of my soup, I decide life isn't fair.

Sally makes small talk while Clark finishes his first course, then she dishes up the next from the second crock pot. The chicken falls off the bone, it's so tender. And those are red potatoes, this time I'm sure of it. Sally heaps a plate and adds plenty of juice, then passes it to me to pass to Andy. I'm tempted to let it slop onto his hand, but even I realize how immature that would be. Instead I make sure my hand doesn't touch his as he takes the plate.

I take a thigh and half of one potato for myself. This bird didn't come out of a frozen bag of boneless, skinless precut pieces, I can tell you that, and oh the flavor. Not even Dad's chicken is this juicy. Wisely, I peel back the chicken's skin with my fork. I don't dare eat like the natives, adopted or otherwise, or I'll outgrow my wardrobe before the summer's gone, and I happen to know there's not an Abercrombie and Fitch east of the English Channel. I checked. But when Sally brings out a mixed berry pie I allow myself a small, small slice, but that's it for the week. I swear.

"We'll work till dark," Clark says. Just the thought of digging a well in this heat makes me want to fall in front of the fan. He kisses Sally's forehead and thanks her for the meal.

"Me too," Andy says. Then the screen door slams.

"And me," I say. "You cook as well as my Dad."

"Let's get these dishes done, then we'll sit on the porch and you can tell me all about your family."

"Let me, please," I say in regards to the dishes. "You cooked.

Really," I add when she doesn't seem convinced. "Go sit and rest. I'll be out soon."

"Oh, but I hate—"

"Please."

"Well, then, just stack them in the drainer to dry. In this heat it takes just a minute. And, Aria, thank you."

Six

Even after the sun sets, a shimmery red fireball in the west, there isn't a lot of relief from the heat. But aside from a slightly higher degree of humidity it isn't much different from a summer night back home whenever a high pressure front keeps the delta breeze from reaching us. Sally and I sit on the porch steps talking away, our sweating glasses of iced tea leaving rings on the concrete. The ice has long melted and my slice of lemon floats like a dead fish in the brew. I dunk it three times with my finger, then lick off what's left of the tartness.

The men have not returned from their work, and if my calculations are correct, they've put in a fourteen-hour day.

"Are all wells dug by hand in Moldova?" I ask.

Sally plucks a dying petunia and twirls it between her thumb and forefinger. "Out here where everyone is poor, yes. We're decades behind the modern world. But that's not always bad."

"That's how Opa feels. He's perfectly content to live a simpler life in ways that matter."

"Opa. And Mam. Not heard those names for grandparents before."

"Opa's German for grandfather, and with a name like Shunk . . ." My voice trails off and I shrug.

"And Mam?"

"Early on I called her Mamaw. I eventually dropped the "aw" part and Mam stuck. We tend to abbreviate names in our family."

"Yes." Sally sounds relaxed enough to fall asleep where she sits. "Ree. Isn't that what they call you?"

"Ree. Sis. Whatever comes to mind."

"Mmm." She's winding down fast.

"Will our schedule be the same at school tomorrow?"

"Pretty much, but we add current events on Tuesdays and we take field trips on Fridays."

Field trips. Sounds fun. I should benefit as much as the children. "I expected to go back to class after lunch today."

"School hours are eight to noon, but as you saw, it's comprehensive teaching. These children soak up knowledge like sun worshipers soak up the rays."

"Why these twelve? Are they hand picked?"

"Most definitely," Sally says. "But it's not my hand that does the picking." She looks up at an indigo sky that's beginning to sparkle like a sequined spread. "It's his hand. We opened our schoolhouse doors four years ago with Anya, Peter and Lazlo as students. We've added two or three every year. All from the congregation."

"How do they afford it?" I ask. "You indicated there's a good deal of poverty here."

"Oh, there's no tuition. The Lord provides everything we need."

"Is that why you came to Moldova? To teach the children?"

Sally shakes her head, then finishes off the last of her tea. "Tomorrow after school we'll take a field trip of our own, you and I." She rises, stretches, and looks up the dark road. "They'll be in soon. I think I'll run Clark a bath."

––––––––––––––––

I'm upstairs sending an email to Kari Zalasky, my best friend next to Johnnie, when I hear boots stomping on the porch. The clock on my laptop says 8:52. It has indeed been a long day for Clark and Andy. In no time at all the bathroom door downstairs closes. The voices that filter up remind me of adult-speak in a Charlie Brown cartoon. Sound without structure. The abstract conversation lasts twenty minutes or more, as I imagine Sally scrubbing away Moldovan dirt from her husband's back with pungent brown soap. Privacy must be difficult to come by under our living conditions. Another minute more and I actually hear the water swirling down the pipes as the tub empties.

I wait for one door to open and another to close, a sign Sally and Clark have retired for the night, then scoop up my tank top and boxers which serve as pajamas from May to October, after which it's flannel from my neck to my toes. I grab my *People Magazine's* "50 Most Beautiful People" issue, which I intentionally saved for my arrival in Moldova. I'm on Beautiful Person #44, counting down from 50, and I intend to savor the magazine like fine chocolate, making it last as long as possible. I take a peek inside the page where I've stuck a gum wrapper as a book mark. My only hope is that Ryan Gosling is on one of the pages I haven't yet gotten to. I dance down the stairs. Ooh, yes, I'm looking forward to my bath.

"Oh," I hear, and look up from a full-page glossy of #44.

Andy, with a towel thrown over his shoulder, and looking as if the well-digging team used him as a drill bit, reaches the bathroom door at the exact moment I do. He looks at my magazine, then at the boxers slung over my arm—a purple and apple-green striped pair Johnnie hid in my suitcase as a going away gift—and takes a reluctant step back. He extends an upturned hand toward the door as if to say, "Be my guest." He's almost to the stairs when I find my voice.

"No, wait. I mean, I'll wait."

He turns and shrugs. "I'll come back."

"No, really." I hold up my magazine. "I'll be a while."

He takes an inventory of what he can see of himself. "So will I."

"Please." I take a backward step in the direction of the stairs that lead up to my room. "You first."

"You sure you don't mind?"

"I'm sure." I turn and jog up the stairs, giving him no room for further debate.

With the click of a mouse my half-written email to Kari appears on my screen. I'm poised to type just as the water begins to run into the tub downstairs. Another moment and the running water changes to a shower spray, then the fat rings that hold up the yellow-daisied shower curtain screech over the rod they're connected to as the plastic shield is pulled close. I swear I can smell the pungent scent of the soap seeping up through the floorboards in my room.

I feel like a voyeur. I turn up the box fan, which I've moved to within arm's reach of the bed, and stick a CD into my laptop. Then turn up the volume one more notch. A candle would be nice in the bathroom, I decide. I'm pretty sure I have one.

Kari Zalasky begged me not to come to Moldova. In fact, she begged me not to go to Bible college, but to join her at UC San Diego instead, and boy was I tempted. I mean, shorts and sandals year round, beach volleyball. Sailors. The decision weighed heavy on my mind, and Kari nearly had me convinced as she recounted her first three years there as vividly as if I were watching UC San Diego: The Movie. Kari went to UCSD right out of high school. But I wanted to do something with my life, not just with my education. So I headed off to Santa Cruz, a beach community in northern California that's as unlike San Diego as a sandbox is the Sahara. Four years later, here I am.

But I miss Kari almost as much as I miss Johnnie. She's as cute as she is spunky. I can tell you her Slavic father and Puerto Rican mother clinched the gold when they conceived her during a brief honeymoon to Yosemite, then before they knew the rabbit had died, Kari's father left for work one day and was never heard from again. His passport and a few items of clothing went missing with him. Kari said her mama, the original Red Hot Chili Pepper, was way too much spice for the poor boy. She sought and won an annulment, and has been blissfully single ever since, but never without a good-looking fella to take her dancing on a Friday night.

Kari asked me to keep my eyes open for an albino-looking man by the name of Ivan Zalasky, who'd now be creeping up on middle age, but I imagine I'd have as much luck finding him as I did the contact lens I lost while snorkeling in Kapalua Bay two summers ago. Still, I did promise to ask everyone I met if they know anyone by the name of Zalasky.

Kari is the only one who knows almost all my secrets. Not that I have that many, but the things I've hidden from everyone else in the world are common knowledge to Kari, because she was there for most of them. Plus, when it comes to prying, she's a pro. So if she wasn't there when it happened, whatever *it* was, I open up like a clam in the stew pot with one little nudge from Kari.

But there's one thing no one knows. Not anyone. Well, except God, and even now it leaves me concerned about my standing with him. That may be the biggest reason of all I'm in Moldova, to show him that second chances aren't always wasted.

Just as I hit send, catapulting my missive to Kari into cyberspace, the water shuts off downstairs. But I open my Bible and read a sermon-on-the-mount chapter in Matthew, partly to wait for Andy to clear out of the bathroom, and partly to let the steam evaporate. On my list of things I hate is wading through someone else's steam.

I've started reading the New Testament again since awakening from my marathon nap yesterday afternoon. Was it really only yesterday? I expect to get all the way through Revelation before this year is up, plus the Psalms and Proverbs. Some might think that's not much of a goal, but like never before I want the Holy Spirit to teach me as I study the life of Christ and the New Testament church at work. I have a feeling the real revelation will be just how far off the plumb line I am, and that's okay. Mam always says awareness is a big step toward the solution.

I get through a chapter then gather my things up again, adding an apple spice candle to the mix. I drop everything off in the bathroom, then open the window a little more to eliminate the last bit of moisture in the air. The warm breeze is just the thing. Then I run downstairs to the kitchen in search of matches.

I stop short when I find Andy sitting at the kitchen table, a chicken leg in one hand and a can of cola in the other.

"I came down for some matches," I say, then point toward the upstairs bath, "for a candle."

It looks to me like he stops just short of rolling his eyes, then nods toward a drawer by the stove. That's exactly where I'd have looked if his unexpected presence hadn't stopped me, but of course there's no point in saying that.

"Hard day?" I ask. Then, as he continues to chew his chicken, I say, "Of course it was."

He swallows and takes a drink of cola. "Ever dug a well?"

I take a moment to decide if his question is genuine or just pure sarcasm.

"It's not a hard question," he says.

I bristle. "I helped dig over two hundred holes when we planted a new almond orchard on the compound a few years ago."

The truth is I was rounded up and handed a shovel along with every available laborer on the compound when the drill bit on Opa's auger broke right in two. There were trees to be planted and we couldn't wait for a new part. So we dug. Johnnie and I shoveled out the soft earth where each tree was to go, while the men came behind us and did the real work. I made Opa proud, but I'm ashamed to say that back in my room I cried real tears over the blisters that erupted on both hands.

"The compound? What, were you in juvenile detention?"

I hate it when my nostrils flare, but there's no stopping them sometimes. "No. The compound happens to be where I live. With my family."

"Sounds like a great place." Andy wipes his mouth with a paper napkin and places his dish in the sink. Then he runs soapy water and actually washes the plate.

"It's a great place." My defense sounds weak even to me.

"Lock up," he says, then the screen door slams.

I listen to the gravel crunch beneath his flip-flops as he heads over to the church. I'd have expected him to turn in as hard as he worked, but he obviously has things to do. I close the door and turn the lock on the knob as instructed. I suppose he has a key to get back in.

The matches are right where he indicated. I can't read a word on the cover, but I slip them into my pocket and jog back up the stairs. Finally, it's my turn. I slide back the shower curtain and stop just short of kicking the tub. "In our house," I mutter, "we clean the tub when we're through." I find a sponge and a can of something in one of the cupboards that looks like the Moldovan equivalent to Comet and sprinkle it over the enamel, or what's left of it. Then I kneel down and scrub away Andy's dirt.

I haven't written anything about Andy to either Kari or Johnnie, but when I get around to it I doubt I'll be able to disguise the fact I plain don't like the guy. He reminds me of a pointer Opa had when I was a kid. His name was Thaddeus, and he was one surly dog. Opa's current best friend is a pug named Wolf. When I asked Opa why he gave him such a ridiculous name, he said, "God calls things that are not as though they were. That's all I'm doin', darlin'."

"You think he wants to be a wolf?"

Opa flashed me one of his smiles that never fails to remind me just why Mam fell in love with him. "He's an unneutered male, Ree. Of course he wants to be a wolf. In the true and proper sense of the word," he added with a wink.

I can hear Opa's voice in my head. It's a beautiful voice, and places high on the chart, if there is such a thing. With your eyes closed you can hear the smile. It's always there. Even when he sings. I don't believe for a minute God's voice is anything like the resounding, thunderous, soul-shaking, boom-box of a noise most of us hear internally when we think of God. No, I think his voice is a lot like Opa's.

It's way too soon to be thinking these thoughts. I chide myself and light my candle, get my soap out of the cupboard, lay out my PJs and towel. With the tub clean, I pour in a capful of coconut bath bubbles and begin to run the water, heavy on the hot. Even in summer I like my bath a skin-shriveling temperature. And I love the scent of coconut.

I test the water, then turn the hot water handle all the way to the left and test again. I reduce the cold, test, reduce some more. Then I really do kick the tub. There's not a trace of hot water left.

Seven

Tuesday is a repeat of Monday, except for current events. Nadine reads a clipping, in Romanian, from a Chisinau newspaper. Everyone laughs at the end of the story, including Sally. Then in her heavily accented, though fairly accurate English, Nadine translates the article, which is about a goat that wandered into a library and ate up a whole shelf of how-to books before they could run him out. I can just imagine the, ahem, paper trail he left.

The exercise is designed to help the children with their English, but I appreciate hearing the story, thinking it's exactly what you'd expect to read about in the, oh, say, *Mobile Register*, if there were a copy handy.

Then Peter takes his turn. He lives close to where the well is being dug and tells us all about it. "Pastor Clark and Mister Andy look funny in the dirt," he says. I can't help but agree, though I certainly know better than to say so. "Mister Andy, he is inside the hole with Mister Janic, and he fills up the bucket with dirt. Over and over he fills up the bucket. And Pastor Clark, he pulls up the bucket and pours out the bucket and makes a dirt mountain"—Peter demonstrates by standing on tiptoe and reaching as high as he can with both hands—"together with Mister Janic's house."

"*Beside* Mister Janic's house," Sally says.

"But far away," Peter adds. "Anatol, we play in the mountain."

Sally applauds when Peter sits down. "Very nice, Peter, but when you say Mister Andy is inside the hole, you say it just like that: Mister Andy is inside the hole, instead of Mister Andy, he is inside the hole. Because that's the same as saying Mister Andy Mister Andy is inside the hole."

The children laugh, including Peter, who isn't the least bit fazed at being corrected.

"And I'm guessing that you and Anatol play *on* the mountain?"

Peter smiles and nods, and Anatol comes off his seat with excitement.

"So you would say, 'Anatol and I play on the mountain.'"

The children repeat the phrase along with Sally. But I've been transported, as if in a time machine, back more than a dozen years, to April, near the end of my fifth grade year. We were finally adding a swimming pool to the compound. It was placed like a hub, central to where all four houses would eventually stand, and made large enough to accommodate nearly everyone in Linden. The contractor promised it would be ready by Memorial Day, the magical division between spring and summer in northern California, all the way from the Grapevine to Sacramento and beyond.

I couldn't wait to dive in, but in the meantime, Kari, Matt, myself and any number of neighborhood friends had an ongoing game of King of the Mountain where the dirt was dug out and piled up beside the growing hole that would soon become the pool. It was girls against the guys, and we held our own while it was King of the Mound, but as that pile of dirt grew, our prowess shrunk, while the guys got braver and feistier by the backhoe bucketful. By day three we were getting our butts whipped—all except for jacks-playing Johnnie, who didn't have a tomboy bone in her body—and when Jacob Landers snatched the flag out of my back pocket and pushed me off the top of that dirt so hard I tumbled down the hill and into the hole, I decided a jacks tournament between Johnnie, Kari and me didn't sound all that bad. I brushed myself off, went straight to the garage and borrowed a golf ball out of Dad's bag, got a knife and went to peeling it. Because there's nothing so good for playing jacks as the little rubber ball underneath all those rubber bands beneath that dimpled white coating. That little sphere will bounce like it's king of kinetic energy, just right for "around the world" and "eggs in a basket." I won the tournament without trying, and to this day I've never told anyone about my secret weapon.

"That was a fetching story, Peter," Sally is saying when I zone back in.

I smile and shake my head, for that's exactly what Mam would say, fetching.

————————————

After lunch, and after Clark and Andy go back to work, Sally and I start out for our field trip. She hops behind the steering wheel of the van and I take my place in the passenger seat. The cracked Naugahyde is hot on my bare legs and I stuff my hands under my thighs until the seat cools off.

We leave the windows down waiting for the air conditioner to kick in, and that takes a while. Dogs, thin and parched-looking with tongues hanging out, run loose all over the neighborhood, but they're friendly, Sally says. Still, if and when I decide to go for a walk on my own, I'll make sure I have a nice stick in hand.

We drive away from the little town, but in a direction opposite the airport. There are fields of sunflowers as far as you can see on either side of the road. They sway in the breeze like sun-worshiping dancers, their strange faces uplifted, soaking in the sustaining rays.

Sally rolls up her window, as the vents are finally putting out a cool stream of air, and I follow suit. "They're heliotropic, you know.

Sunflowers."

"Helio—?"

"Tropic. At sunrise their faces are turned toward the east. Then they follow the sun throughout the day. At night, they turn back to the east, and wait." She demonstrates this with her own head, as if in time-lapse photography.

"Hmm. I thought only houseplants did that." And even that seems creepy to me. I think it, but I don't say it.

"Nope," Sally says.

I get the feeling I can learn a lot from this woman. And so I take this opportunity to ask. "What did I say wrong yesterday?"

"Wrong?"

"You know, about the rutabaga."

Sally chuckles, reaches over and pats my knee. "I think you meant rhubarb."

I close my eyes and pinch the bridge of my nose. "Rhubarb. Oh man. How dumb can I be?"

"Oh, sweetie, think nothing of it. Or of Andy. He—" She pauses, then laughs again. "I started to say he means well, but—" She changes direction again. "Andy is very focused."

I look out my side window. If this were Celie or Mam or someone I'm not trying to impress, I'd tell her what I think of Andy's *focused* remarks and attitude. Instead, I say, "Hmm," and leave it at that.

We've driven ten or twelve miles from the house. I'm in the process of converting that to kilometers—and failing—when Sally pulls off the road. A cloud of dust rises up around us. She waits for it to settle before she opens her door. When she slides out, I do too.

We wade through a field of shin-high grass that's fighting hard for its life, but this time next week I expect what little bit of green is present today will be gone. Unless a storm blows through, that is, and brings a reprieve. I'm told summer rains are much more common here than at home.

The dry stalks leave little white scratches on my suntanned legs. I'm very glad Sally suggested tennis shoes over flip-flops. This would have been much worse to walk through if I hadn't changed. I see our destination, and it's not far now.

"Here we are." Sally steps up onto a concrete foundation someone, for some reason, poured out in the middle of nowhere, then she spins a full circle with arms outstretched. "This," she says, coming to a stop, "is Hope House."

I decide not to point out that it doesn't look like a house, nor does it look hopeful. In fact, it looks forgotten.

"I know what you're thinking." Sally's face crinkles with a sly smile, and I wonder if there's something in this generation of women that gives them an extra sense, like mind reading, because Mam, too, always seems to know what I'm thinking. "It's a start," Sally says. And I get it. The hope is inside her and it spills out like water gushing forth from one of Opa's irrigation pipes back home. There's nothing like that water on a hot summer day, pure and refreshing. If hope were a color, it would look like that water. And Sally would be that exact color right here in this place.

"What is Hope House?" I step over rebar that sprouts up like field corn around the perimeter of the foundation, and join Sally, who's taken a seat on the dusty concrete. She pulls her knees up and hugs them to her chest. The skirt of her yellow denim jumper provides plenty of modestly.

Yellow denim. I love it.

Sally's eyes fill with tears, which she doesn't even try to hide. She swallows, and I know she's waiting for her voice to hurdle the swell of emotion before she answers. Birds call back and forth across the countryside, and not for the first time I wonder if they're really having a conversation or if the sound they make is only so much noise that hasn't an ounce of significance attached to it.

Sally clears her throat and turns a thoughtful eye toward the easternmost hills. A scripture spills into my thoughts like a wave washing the shore. *I lift up my eyes to the hills—where does my help come from? My help comes from the Lord, the Maker of heaven and earth.* It's from the Psalms, though I couldn't say which one. I can only quote the verse because of a song Opa sings.

"Hope House," Sally says, "is just that, Aria. Tell me, what were your greatest cares when you were twelve years old? Or thirteen."

That was half a lifetime ago, but the question is easy to answer. "Fighting zits. And split ends." I'm only being a little bit facetious.

Sally nods, then shakes her head, and it's like a division mark separating one thought from the next. "Those aren't the greatest cares of young girls in many places in our world."

I think I know where Sally is going with this, and my stomach flutters as if I've leapt off the huge rocks underneath the old Knights Ferry Bridge into the Stanislaus River, a favorite summertime exploit for my friends and me. Celie would have had a cow and Dad would have put me in my room and nailed the door shut if they knew how daring I was on those rocks. But I sense all that is nothing compared to the subject we're closing in on.

Sally confirms the worst. "Hope House will be a refuge for girls rescued from human trafficking."

"Girls?" My stomach really does take a dive. "How, how young?"

"Young, Aria. Some are very young."

I level out an anthill with the sole of my shoe, because I need to do something with the revulsion I feel. "My age?" I hope she says yes. My age and no younger.

Sally nods, but she doesn't stop there. "I was in Chisinau a year and a half ago, for a get-together of missionary wives who live in the region. One afternoon a friend asked if I'd go with her to the hospital to pray with a girl she'd visited a few days before." Sally looks off to the mountains. "She was, I think fourteen or fifteen, and had been found on the streets, very ill, a victim of the sex trade." She doesn't want to go on, I can tell, but she does. "These girls are abused in the worst ways and they feel so tarnished. They don't understand they aren't the ones who are dirty. But this girl in an effort to—how do I put it delicately?—

cleanse herself internally, used bleach. You can only imagine the damage. She inspired this place. She's the reason we're building this home."

I feel sick in the center of my gut as I look around at the beautiful valley in which I sit. The fertile ground offers up a potpourri of trees and vegetation sustained completely by nature. Silver-gray mountains rise in the distance like a wall of protection.

And out of this beauty children are snatched and sold for the vilest of reasons.

"Mostly it's young women lured from their homes with the promise of honest work overseas. Housekeeping, childcare, factory work, anything that sounds realistic for their circumstances. Then, once they leave their homes, they wind up in brothels in forced prostitution with no way out. It's a huge problem in eastern Europe, and in many parts of the world. But I can't let myself look at the big picture. I have to focus on what we can do right here." She taps the foundation with a determined finger. "For the twenty-four precious girls and young women we can love back to life at Hope House. And the next twenty-four, and the next." Her eyes puddle with tears.

The foundation looks as if it's been here a while, evidenced by smatterings of wildflowers—weeds really—that have broken through cracks in the concrete. "How long till this is finished?" I open my hands and look up as if there's already a ceiling above our heads. In my mind I calculate how long it will take for Johnnie and Matt's house to go from concrete to curtains. They have six months allotted from the day they break ground to the day they say "I do," and that should be just about right. The decorating will begin after the honeymoon, because who would want to rush that? Johnnie's only desire is that the rooms that matter the most are completed by the holidays, because that's where we all plan to congregate not this Christmas, but next, with the new Mrs. Farmer as hostess. And with Rudolph Mangini of San Francisco already selecting fabrics, I'd say we can all rest easy.

And then I remember what led me down that rabbit trail and my thoughts seem trivial.

"It won't be this year," Sally says.

"But why? It's only June."

Sally gives me a patient smile. "Even if everything were lined up and ready to go, construction projects don't move as quickly as they do in the States. But the issue, of course, is money. We do what we can as the funds dribble in."

"But if people knew how urgent the need is . . ."

"Most of our support comes from small congregations." Sally gives me the smile again and says as if it were a secret, "There aren't a lot of megachurches in Nebraska. Our supporters do what they can, and a few give beyond what they've pledged toward our support, which is why we're no longer sitting in the dirt. Still, it took a year to raise enough to pour this foundation."

A year? "But at that rate . . ." I don't even want to think of all the young women who won't be helped in the meantime. But I do think about them. I think one day must seem like an eternity for women in their situation. But a year of days that stretches on forever? Lord God Almighty. It makes my stomach hurt. "What about the Moldovan government? Won't they help?"

"The completion of Hope House is our number one desire, but no, help won't come from our host government. They say they're against trafficking, but they look the other way. And as for us, well, as I'm sure you've seen, Moldova is an Eastern Orthodox country and the Orthodox are opposed to anything that isn't. Their influence on the government keeps us under a good deal of suspicion. We're just glad to be allowed to work here."

"So then, at least when it comes to the people, Moldova is a religious country?"

Sally thinks a moment before answering. "It's more a country of religious agnostics, which I'm sure doesn't make any sense to you. But you have to remember the communist influence these people lived under for so many years." She pushes herself up. The skirt of her jumper catches the breeze and whips like a banner in the wind. "We'd better get back. I've a lesson to prepare."

"For?"

"I teach a Bible study for the women on Wednesday nights, while Andy teaches the men. As you saw on Sunday, the sexes don't mingle during service. That too is part of their Orthodox heritage. So we divide them up proper on Wednesdays, and try to do our best by them. Maybe you'd like to teach on occasion? After you're acclimated."

Immediately, my head starts to itch, which is what happens when I'm nervous or scared. But then I decide, if Andy can, I certainly can. I smile and nod, and shoo away the butterflies that have already begun to flutter inside.

That night I compile notes in a file from which I will prepare my first newsletter at the end of the month to send to all my supporters. Okay, that's mostly my parents and grandparents. But the folks at my church back home—which is miles from the nearest megachurch—have sponsored me too. I plan to tell them all about Hope House, and why it's needed. More than ever I'm glad I'm here, because I really want to be a part of this.

Eight

I've taken to showering in the morning. It's the only way I can ensure I'll have enough hot water to get the job done. But I must say I miss my baths. Of course, showering has taken on a whole new meaning in Moldova. The showerhead resembles the lid of a tin can, not aluminum mind you, that's been peppered with little nail holes, each one ringed in a handsome shade of rust. "It's safe," I tell myself every time I step under the spray. But then, *spray* has taken on a whole new meaning too, as it's entirely possible to stand under the nozzle and keep one half of my body perfectly dry. I can't begin to imagine what this will be like in the dead of an eastern European winter.

Kari commiserates with me in her emails, but my bathing habits are a never-ending source of hilarity for Johnnie, who knows what a water hog I am. She can probably tell you how many countless times I've drained the 100-gallon hot water tank at our home back on the compound in one marathon bath event after another.

It's payback, she says. This from Johnnie, the queen of compassion. Friday nights I save for baths. I don't mind waiting up till after everyone has gone to bed, counting the quarter hours it takes to restore the water to a temperature that will shrivel my toes. I can almost hear it heating up in the pipes, and then I take my candle, my *People*, my green-apple-striped PJs down the stairs and shut myself in. Those baths have come to be the vanilla cream icing on the petit fours of life.

But before Friday nights, we have Friday mornings—the most fun day of the school week because it's field trip day. The air is so charged with expectation our twelve little scholars can barely stay in their seats for story time, only after which is our destination finally revealed.

This is what I wrote in a perpetual email Kari and I have been sending back and forth like a tennis volley since I arrived. And to see just how weirdly I can mix my metaphors, this email might as well be a kite, the tail has grown so long. But I can't bring myself to snip it off, it's such a link to home.

K: My first Friday here—which was a week ago already, can you believe it?—our field trip was to Mr. Janic's house to see how the well was progressing. It's the talk of the neighborhood, and after Peter gave his current-event report on how funny Pastor Clark and Mister Andy look in the dirt, the children could hardly wait to see for themselves. They were not disappointed. The entire field trip was a huge success, especially when each child was given the task of hoisting up a bucket of dirt, with Clark's capable assistance. In spite of the seeming novelty of it all, I'm certain these children know a whole lot more about work than their American counterparts.

Just so you know, my plan was to give Mister Andy some slack after finding out how the poor guy spends his days. And nights. Because after hearing Andy trek over to the church night after night, but never hearing him come back, I just had to ask Sally about it. You know what a light sleeper I am—when I haven't drugged myself to oblivion with three Tylenol PMs—so you'd think I'd hear him come back in the house once in a while. But I never do. So I wait till Sally and I are alone in the kitchen cleaning things up after dinner. Andy and Clark are in the living room, one of them rustling a newspaper and one of them snoring loud enough to keep the folks awake all the way back home. Since I happen to have learned Andy doesn't read Romanian, it's obvious whose pipes are clanging. I decide right then he could spend all night, every night at the church if he wants, and more power to him. But I had to ask. "What's he do over there every night?" I was thinking maybe he uses the church computer to connect with home or some such thing.

So with my question hanging in the air, Sally gives me a look mingled with surprise and mirth. "Why, Aria," she says—they don't believe in nicknames here—"he sleeps."

I glance upward in response—to the empty bedroom on the same floor as mine—but Sally just laughs. "Darling," she says, "we can't have two unmarried young people of the opposite sex sleeping in such close proximity."

"Well, but you and Clark are, I mean, practically right there."

"Which changes absolutely nothing," she says, sweet as Mam but with the same kind of "caught ya" look Mam gave us when she found us trying to push your Bug off the compound that Saturday night. Remember? I still think she was born with radar.

Anyway, after Sally says this I turn just enough to see Andy standing in the doorway, one side of his mouth raised in a smirk, while snoring continues to drift in from the living room. No kidding, Kari, it felt like someone had taken a blowtorch to my cheeks.

Mister Hamilton Andrews relished in my discomfort for who knows how many infuriating seconds, then he says directly to me, "I'm heading to the coffeehouse. You can come if you want."

Now, how inclined do you think I was to go along with an

invitation like that? I felt like Opa's pathetic Wolf waiting for someone to toss me a bone.

But then, Sally tugs the dishtowel out of my hand and smiles like Celie seeing me off to the prom. "Oh, yes, Aria, you should go."

"Coffeehouse?" That's the first I've heard of it. I stuff my hands in my pockets to keep from scratching my scalp. In the end I say I have things to catch up on, which is what I'm doing now. But—oh, there's my phone. It's Johnnie.

I press send without signing off.

Kari's volley, which she smacked right back at me, contained nothing but a stupid winking smiley face, which nearly drove me to cut the tail.

I was going to finish my email with "but I've changed my mind." About giving Andy some slack. But the fact is, I've changed it back again. Anyone who gives up a perfectly good bedroom for what was surely a secondary office a third smaller than my own quarters, with a window not the least bit worth bragging about, and a cot, deserves some slack— though that'll never go into an email to Miss Smiley-Face.

Even so, my generous behavior doesn't seem to have made an impression on Hamilton Andrews. Well, fine.

This is my second Friday and since the early morning it's been raining elephant tears, as Celie says when the raindrops are big enough to sting. Don't think this summer rain has helped one bit to cool things down, because it's only served to turn our window on the world into one huge sauna.

No matter how much mousse I apply, my hair is completely listless. I'm not used to this one little bit, and suddenly I can see the value in covering up with a *basma*, or headscarf, as all the older Moldovan women steeped in orthodoxy do.

Because of the weather our field trip to Lazlo's uncle's vegetable garden is postponed till the following week. Instead, we dart through the rain, single file, like a loose-linked caterpillar, and hurry up the concrete steps to the periwinkle porch for a picnic. The children are as excited about one set of plans as the other.

Already I find them all irresistible, but if I have a favorite, and I admit I do, it's twelve-year old Anya. She reminds me nothing of myself at her age, or ever. She's shy, thoughtful, eager to please, and in her young eyes I see wisdom I've yet to attain. She's a tiny bud waiting to emerge and when at last she blossoms I hope I'm there to smell the perfume.

The children sit cross-legged in clusters, the four boys forming their own little clump. This separation has nothing to do with orthodoxy, I'm certain, and everything to do with cooties, which hop from one continent to another, I've just learned, even if they're called by a different name.

Lunch makes me smile. Peanut butter and honey sandwiches, but the bread looks homemade, and so do the cookies.

As if reading my thoughts, Sally says, "Riya Moraru, Hedy's mother, makes our bread every week. It's her offering to God." She waggles her eyebrows. "And he shares."

The little girl looks up at the sound of her name. She smiles, showing the newly-formed gap where a front tooth used to be. As adorable as it is, I have a sad feeling there's no Tooth Fairy in Moldova.

The peanut butter tastes like the stir-your-own-stuff Celie brings home from the health food store, dry but nutty. Still, for my money it's Skippy, extra crunchy, or why bother?

Sally runs her finger along the edge of her sandwich. "The honey's from local hives." She appreciatively licks the mixture off the tip of her finger.

My taste buds pop with the sweetness, and I decide I'll trade the Tooth Fairy for this any day.

But I'm not fond of the milk. There's a lot to be said for homogenized. And one percent. This stuff is thick as cream, which I happen to know was ladled off the top of the one-gallon jug only this morning. Sally will churn her own butter from it. That's not to say there's not homogenized somewhere in Moldova. It's just that we get our milk directly from the cow down the road, except in this case I'm pretty sure it's a goat.

I've opted for water since my arrival. Boiled.

Sally says to the children, "It's English-only day," for my benefit, I'm sure. So the children grin and talk in bashful whispers, casting enamored looks my way. The newness of our relationship is still upon us. I hope it never ends.

Anya, the oldest child by two years, has inched her way to my side. I scoot over to make room for her on the step and she fits her pubescent self into the gap. She seems as uncomfortable in her changing body as I was at twelve. I pat her knee and wink. The smile she returns makes me think of one of those credit card commercials on TV: Flight to Moldova: $2,000. Inconveniences: Still calculating. The light on the face of this beautiful girl beside me: Priceless.

And I do mean beautiful. Slavic women are in a class all their own. Skin as creamy and flawless as almond milk, eyes the truest and most translucent blue in the universe. And in Anya's case, hair as fair and fine as corn silk, with sparkles of gold that shimmer in the light of the summer sun, which is trying to peek through the clouds even now. Honest to goodness, she's the poster child for what happens when the perfect genes collide. Right up there with Halle Berry, Lucy Liu, and Kari Zalasky. Trust me on that one.

In her own diffident way, Anya scoots just enough so that her hip touches mine, then, satisfied, takes a bite of her sandwich. I think of Peter Pan, certain I've just found my shadow. Her downcast eyes find my filigree ring tattoo, which I've had since high school, on the second toe of my left foot. I call it the Lookout—the toe, not the ring—because it's long enough to peek over my big toe without having to stretch. Johnnie calls them our Shunk toes, because she has them too, but I like the Lookout much better. The tattoo has faded to a dull blue-green and is only partly hidden by the silver toe ring I wear over it.

Anya looks at me with wide eyes and a conspiratorial smile that makes me genuinely glad I've adorned my toe in this particular fashion.

Next, she reaches over and traces the daisy painted on the nail of my ring finger. The piece of art, which is only now beginning to chip, is compliments of Johnnie, part of a going-away manicure. She's only fairly artistic, but has the steadiest hand you ever saw. And who in their right mind wouldn't take a free manicure?

"My sister painted this," I say, displaying the nail.

Again, Anya smiles up at me, and I think I must look like a walking canvas to her. She gives me a quick looking over, but I've nothing else to surprise her with. As I take another bite of my sandwich Anya leans even closer and says, "I vish could be your sisters."

A lump the size of a luxury liner closes off my throat and I can't say a word. But I slip my arm around her and give a squeeze. I look at Sally, who's looking at me with a cryptic smile. She nods slightly then leans in my direction and stops mid-chew. I think I must have peanut butter on my face, when all of a sudden she says, "I love your freckles," as if she's just discovered them. "They're the exact color of your eyes, which are the exact color of . . . sarsaparilla."

She's sweet to say so, but I do not love my freckles. Not in the least. I have seventeen of them across my nose, like a moose trail, and she's right, they're a perfect match to the color of my eyes. I've counted them—the freckles, that is—on many occasions, hoping they would decrease as I grew from teeny bopper to woman. But no.

"I look like a Brittany spaniel," I say.

Sally laughs, but in her eyes I clearly see she agrees with me. "There's nothing like a spaniel. Who wants popcorn?"

Well, you'd think she'd told the children Santa Claus was coming for a slumber party, only I'm thinking he may be on hiatus with the Tooth Fairy and the Easter Bunny. The little ones whoop and bounce, hands wiggling above their heads. "I do!" "Me!" "Yes, please." That, of course, from Anya.

So off Sally goes.

I'll bet it's not microwave, and only then do I realize I haven't seen a microwave anywhere in the kitchen in the almost-two weeks I've been here. I stand and follow Sally into the house, because if there's a way to make popcorn without a microwave, I want to see it.

———————————

I've a sense of déjà vu when Andy, dressed in the same worn jeans and black T-shirt as the week before, appears in the kitchen doorway and says to me, "I'm going to the coffeehouse." He lets one eyebrow ask the question, *want to come?* And there's Sally, tugging the dishtowel out of my hand again.

"Maybe I should change," I say, but Sally says no, the crops and the Vans are stylish. Only they're not Vans, they're Converse. Cute little checked ones, pink and green. Her error, I'm sure, comes from having two boys who undoubtedly wore Vans—a decade or more before I was born.

Andy doesn't say anything, but he wears this look as though he's secretly amused. At me. No surprise there.

"I'll just be a minute." I slip past him and on up the stairs. I do a close-up check of my face in the bathroom mirror to make sure I'm not having a crisis moment I'm unaware of. That happened once on a youth group ski trip. I swear it wasn't snot on the rim of my nostril, but do you think the youth group guys were convinced? Not on your life. They called me things reminiscent of second-grade-playground banter. Well, sticks and stones is all I have to say.

But I won't let it happen again.

I do another inspection. Everything looks as it should, but on a whim I dispense a dollop of foam into my hand and scrunch it through my hair. My cute do is beginning to morph into something I'd never accounted for. The word *hideous* comes to mind. And *scarf*. I wonder if I can find something in a pink and green check.

Nine

The rain has stopped, leaving the atmosphere warm and heavy, but surprisingly not unpleasant. The clouds have begun to part, like curtains drawn back on a stage, revealing one incredible set. The night is dark and our only light as we walk the quiet street is the moon and the stars. Billions and billions of stars, blinking out a celestial Morse code. I've never seen so many, not even on a good night at the compound. And I thought it was as good as it got back home when it came to stars.

"It always boggles my mind," I say, and Andy waits for more without asking what. "I mean, who knows how many millions of them burned out light years ago, and yet their light is just now reaching us. Hard to fathom."

"Like an arrow, finally hitting its bulls-eye."

I cast a glance his way and see he's completely serious. "Now there's a happy thought." If he's trying to be philosophic I'd say he's missed it. By a million miles.

We pass two more houses before he replies. "I bet you see a lot of stars from your . . . compound."

I shrug even though the effort is wasted. "I suppose."

"Sounds to me like you've taken a lot for granted."

I sputter for a moment, then say, "I've been busy. Getting my degree to come here, for one thing." And there's that stupid smirk again. "You so do not get it."

"What, that your Umpa has spent a good portion of his life turning that compound you are so down on into a safe place? I get that even if you don't."

"It's Opa. And oh sure, come over here and let me smother *you*. Then we'll talk."

Andy laughs, and I'm surprised it sounds halfway normal, he's so unpracticed at it.

"If you're such a homebody, what are you doing here? And what do you call *your* grandpa?"

"Grandpa."

"Well, that doesn't surprise me one bit."

"And as for what I'm doing here, same thing you are. Escaping."

"I am not!" At that I'm inclined to turn around and go back, but we've come far enough that I'm not sure I could find my way home in the dark. "So, where's this coffeehouse you're so fond of?"

"Up a ways." That's all he says till he stops all of a sudden and tugs open a brown door with blistered paint. There's one weak light bulb a foot or so above the entrance, otherwise there's not the slightest indication an establishment of any kind is on the other side of the doorway.

I'm fully expecting a Moldovan knock-off of Starbucks, complete with whirring steam wands and *baristas*, and I'm practically salivating with the thought. Not even close. As I step inside I feel as though I've stepped back in time a good half a century. The room is small and not much brighter than the darkness through which Andy and I walked to get here. There are perhaps a dozen small tables, no two alike from what I can see so far, with more bodies than you'd imagine in folding chairs crowded around each one. On the back wall, a card table holds a commercial-sized coffee urn and a stack of Styrofoam cups. Eight ounce, if I'm not mistaken. There's a diner-style sugar dispenser that needs filling, and a jar of milk on the table.

But the atmosphere is, well, not upbeat exactly. More like it's humming. Think beatniks—which were a decade or more before krystal blue karma even made the scene—and you'll have a good feel of the gathering. Cigarette smoke rises from every table, and like intermittent tower lights, red hot tips of cigarettes glow in the dark as smokers draw on the filtered ends. I feel as if I've been zapped back to the San Joaquin Valley at the heart of tule fog season, the smoke is so thick. I resist fanning my hand in front of my face and try not to choke. Most everyone is dressed in something dark. Dark jeans, dark T-shirts, dark everything. And combat boots. There's not a *basma* in the place.

By the time my eyes adjust, we've been noticed. "Pastor Andy," a choir of voices calls out, all heavily accented. *Pos Tor Ondy* is how it comes out. He smiles and waves and I suddenly get the garb he wears. This is his mission field.

And speaking of choirs. A lone guitarist on a stool strums his instrument in the corner, no mic, no anything, barely heard over the rumble. He would not be in Opa's heavenly band. But he bends over the guitar and strums its strings as if caressing his true love. If this is church, this is his love offering.

Chairs scoot over the rough wooden floor as everyone moves to make room for us at their tables. Andy deposits me at the nearest one, then goes off to greet his compatriots, stopping as though to bless each table, the veritable godfather of Leoccesni.

I'm left to make my own introductions, so I put out my hand and say, "Ree." As if they might not get it, I point with both index fingers to my chest, then put my hand out again. One by one they shake it. Four guys and three girls. There's Sasha to my left, a tall, sturdy looking guy about Andy's age. His head is nearly buzzed, leaving the outline of a dark head of hair that comes to a sharp point in the center of his forehead as if someone had drawn it on with a Magic Marker. I immediately think of Eddie on *The Munsters*, an old black and white sitcom from the sixties. Mam and I used to watch the reruns on *Nickelodeon* when I was a kid. The absence of color in this place only adds to the image.

Next to Sasha is Svetlana, one of those Slavic beauties I was talking about. Beside her, Andrea, emphasis on the middle syllable. The name is exotic the way she says it, and I repeat it in my head several times. I even roll the "r" the way she does. Something glitters when she smiles and I see there's a tiny jewel just above the crease between her lower lip and her chin. Kari would so love that.

I try to make a mental roster of the other names, knowing I'll forget them long before I leave this place, but my mind stops at Boris. Won't go any farther. Boris? Really?

Their English is heavily accented and something short of proper, but understandable. Still, I follow Andy with my eyes, hoping he'll soon come and bless *this* little group with his presence. I can only carry the introductions out for so long.

"You are from where?" Sasha asks. All the w's in Moldova sound like v's. And the question sounds like an interrogation. It's not meant to, I think, because he leans in and waits for my reply, his eyes wide and eager.

"California," I say.

"California!" They all say it at once, and suddenly I'm a rock star. There are smiles all around and more murmurings. "California." "Vow." And that takes care of the conversation. I've been thrust into an interview and all I have to do is decipher and answer the questions they throw my way. "You are not upset by earthquake?" "You live on beach?" "You know Mel Gibson?"

Andy brings me coffee and pulls up another chair. "Sugar," he says.

I turn a frown his way, but he points to the cup. "You won't want to drink this black."

Which, if he'd had any sense of observation the past couple of weeks, he would know I never do. But as I look into my cup it's clear he's not bothered about the cream. "Thank you," I say. It's fairly obvious I have not put my heart and soul into those two little words.

Andy chats with all the guys at the table, completely in Romanian, though his is not nearly so fluid as Clark and Sally's. Boris throws his head back and laughs at something Andy says, and the others join in. I smile weakly, and get the uneasy feeling the joke is on me. No one bothers to interpret.

The group continues to chatter, drink coffee and smoke cigarettes, while the lone guitarist strums away. I actually recognize two of the songs, and I'm right, this is church.

All the girls in the place take turns casting appreciative glances in Andy's direction. Except me. It's the foreign mystique, that's all I can say, because of all the billions of cells in Hamilton Andrew's body, there is not one labeled charm. Not that it's hard to look at him, but whatever genius said beauty is only skin deep got it so right.

I've finished my coffee, and amuse myself by swirling the grounds in the little bit of espresso-colored liquid left in the bottom of the cup. I've picked one or two off the end of my tongue, like bits of tobacco, and decline the refill Andy offers. I'm thinking of the humdinger of a bow I can add to the tail of my and Kari's email kite later tonight, when Andy stands. I recite the phrase *buná seara*—good evening—in my head, ready to recite it to those at my table, and push back my chair, but then Andy turns his chair around, plants one foot on the seat, and pulls a little book out of his rear pocket.

A New Testament.

So this really is church. I scoot back in to the table.

The noise in the room subsides as if someone has turned down the volume on a radio talk show, and the cigarettes are stubbed out. No smoking in church, I take it. Andy opens the New Testament, and judging from the few pages he turns, I'm guessing we're in the Gospels. Then Andy begins to offer up a prayer in Romanian with a quiet passion that startles me. I sneak a peek and see his face is upturned, eyes looking way beyond the ceiling, hands open, as if he's giving something away.

He reads, "'A farmer went out to sow his seed.' "

Sasha, who sometime during Andy's prayer pulled his chair up beside Andy's and assumed the same stance, says something in Romanian. He's the translator, I'm guessing.

Andy continues. "'As he was scattering his seed, some fell along the path.' "

And so they continue to the end of the parable. There's the nodding of heads and some quiet exchanges between those present. Then Andy says, "This is the meaning of the parable," and the room comes to attention once again. He goes on to paraphrase the explanation Jesus gave his disciples, who were surely as dense as Riya Moraru's exceptional bread for even needing an explanation.

"The seed is this, the word of God." Andy holds up the Testament. "You are the soil that receives the seed." He pauses for Sasha to translate. "Some of you are good, fertile soil, and this"—again he holds up the Bible—"takes root in here." He taps his chest with his free hand. "It sprouts like fields of sunflowers soaking up the sun." Pleasant laughter follows his analogy and I have a word picture of this parable such as I've never had before. Sunflowers. In God's garden. All heliotropic. Imagine.

"Some of you,"—Andy's voice carries a warning—"are as hard as the dirt in Janic Rotaru's field. Not so easy to penetrate." The guys in the crowd seem to know just how hard the Moldovan soil can be, judging by their sudden animation. "But even Janic's soil yields to the pickax, with the help of heaven's rain."

Sasha frowns and repeats, "Pickax?" Only it sounds like *peacocks*? Andy pantomimes the act of digging with that same tool, displaying the motion he's no doubt made thousands of times in the past two weeks. "Ah," Sasha says. He nods, then repeats Andy's words in his native tongue. He even copies the motion to get the point across.

"With the help of heaven's rain," Andy says again. "And that's the key." He leans forward, as if speaking to each one there individually.

"We're not born with fertile soil. Good things don't just naturally sprout out of us. We all have rocks and briars and very hard places. But the rain"—he looks and points heavenward—"the rain softens the soil. This is the rain." Again he holds up the Bible. "As the rain comes down from heaven and does not return without watering the earth, so is the word of God. It accomplishes what he desires."

This is a paraphrase of a verse from somewhere in the Old Testament, one that Opa often quotes. I tap my forehead with the tips of my fingers. Jeremiah? Isaiah? It's one of those. I think.

"The Bible," someone says through the dissipating fog, "it is the seed *and* the rain? Bote these things?"

"The seed and the rain," Andy says. "And food and a sword. A consuming fire, a crushing hammer. It's exactly what we need it to be. We can handle the rain, even the crushing hammer. What we can't handle is the barren soil, where there's not even one seed to germinate."

Andy nods to the guitar player, who retrieves his instrument from its stand and begins to play another song I recognize. Andy moves to a corner in the back of the room, while all who heard his mini-sermon do a soils analysis right there on the spot. In a few minutes the afterglow fades, and more coffee is dispensed, more cigarettes lit. But one young man has made his way to Andy's corner. If God is eavesdropping, and I'm willing to bet he is, I'm also willing to bet their conversation brings a smile to his face.

I sigh and shake my head. The neat little bow on the end of my kite tail just came untied.

Ten

Whoever came up with the word *ribbit* for the sound a frog makes was a linguistic genius. There's a bullfrog, big enough for a skillet by the sound of it, right outside my window. And, yep, *ribbit* is exactly right. If he's calling for a mate, I wish she'd quit playing hard to get and let us have some peace in the neighborhood again, for crying out loud.

For crying out loud. It's a term all three generations of Shunk women use, but I don't have a clue as to what it means. I mean, *for crying out loud?* As opposed to *not crying out loud?* Wherever it came from I bet it had something to do with a bullfrog.

All this talk about seeds and soils reports has made me homesick. It's nearly one o'clock, Saturday morning, which means it's mid-afternoon on Friday back home. Because I haven't gotten a European version of my cell phone charger, I creep downstairs to use the kitchen telephone. I flip on a burner as I pass the stove and put on the kettle for a cup of tea.

Dang! I forgot my calling card, so I go back up the stairs in the dark, slip on one of the narrow treads, and come down hard on my knee. I plaster my hands over my mouth to hold in the moan, while the pain clangs through my body like a marble in a pin ball machine. I'm racking up all kinds of points here, believe you me.

You know that weak feeling you get when you bang your elbow smack dab on the crazy bone? Well, I'll have you know there's a crazy bone in the center of your kneecap and it hurts just as bad as the one in your elbow when you hit it. I hobble up the rest of the stairs and into my room, a female Quasimodo, retrieve my card, then hobble back down. I press both palms against the wall on either side of me for support since there is no banister, and nowhere to put one anyway, because the stairwell is so narrow.

The water isn't boiling yet, but it's hot enough. I click off the knob, fix a mug of plain old tea, and mentally add orange spice tea to my care package list. I realize I'll have to pare the list way back before I send it to Celie, but for now orange spice is up there with Tootsie Pops, which I'm guessing the kids will love.

I dial the phone and hold my breath till someone finally picks up on the fourth ring.

"Johnnie!" I catch myself and lower my voice. "Hey."

"Ree!" She sounds exactly like I hoped she would. Happy, happy, happy to hear my voice. "How's it going, sis?"

Great, I start to say, but "Good," comes out of my mouth. Just good. I say it again.

"Really?" There's a question within the question.

"It's good. Honest. The children are amazing. I wish you could meet them."

"I'm sure they are, but it's so funny to me to hear you say that. You've never exactly been the maternal type, you know?"

I bristle just the tiniest bit. "It's not like I plan to adopt them."

"You were never the kindergarten teacher type either," she says, and I know she's right. "But, oh, it's good to hear your voice. Mom and Mam are going to be so upset they missed you."

"They're gone? Both of them?" The disappointment turns my voice to a whine.

"Went to the city with Matt's mom." The city, of course, is San Francisco. "Something to do with centerpieces for the reception. Premature if you ask me, but they never do."

"Premature? Everything's okay, isn't it?"

"Oh, sure." There's a smile in her voice, as always. "But the wedding's still fifteen months away. Honestly, you'd think they were planning The Royal Wedding. If I could talk Matt into it we'd elope right after graduation next May. It would be so much easier."

"You're my only sister. No way are you getting married without me." I take a sip of tea in the silence that follows.

"Hey, Ree, it's, what, one-thirty in the morning there? Are you sure everything's okay?"

"Between the bullfrog outside my window and the espresso surging through my veins I just couldn't sleep. But yeah, things are fine."

I start and turn at the sound of a key in the kitchen door. It opens and in steps Andy. I do a quick check to make sure I'm adequately clothed, so glad I hadn't yet slipped into my T-shirt and boxers, thinking surely no one would see me at one-thirty in the morning. As it is I've only changed from crops to shorts because the night is still so warm. Let that be a lesson, I tell myself. And don't forget it!

"Oh," I say.

"Someone there?" Johnnie asks.

"Andy," I say.

"Yeah?" He bends to step under the phone cord that stretches from the wall to the kitchen table, then straightens up and waits for my answer.

"No, I was just—" I point to the phone.

"Ah." He disappears into the darkness of the living room.

"He's there?" Johnnie says.

"He just came in," I murmur into the phone.

"Why are you whispering?" she asks in a whisper.

A light switches on in the living room and I hear the chair pulled out from the corner desk. He's staying? I suddenly feel my space has been violated. Only it really isn't my space. Still, at one-thirty in the morning you'd think you could count on a bit of privacy. Besides—and this is what really matters—he's the one I wanted to talk about.

"Oh, hello." Sally's voice filters in from the living room, then there she is in the doorway. "Hello again," she says, this time to me. Then she puts an index finger across her lips as she realizes I'm on the phone. *Sorry*, she mouths.

"Are you there?" Johnnie asks.

"Yes," I whisper, then say it again out loud. "Yes." I feel as though I've been caught ransacking the silver, and hold up my calling card for Sally to see. I really must find a charger. Or a new phone.

Sally smiles and waves me off.

"Are you there?" Johnnie asks again.

"I'm here, but I have to go."

Nonsense, Sally mouths.

"I'll call again in a few days. Say hello to everyone."

"Take care," Johnnie says. "I love you."

"I love you too." I stand and hang up the phone. "Johnnie," I say to Sally by way of explanation, just as Andy steps around her into the kitchen on his way to the door.

That eyebrow of his shoots up and he smirks without bothering to look my way. I think he even rolls his eyes this time. Wordlessly, he steps outside and locks us in. I hear the crunch of his shoes on the gravel as he crosses back over to the church.

Then Sally laughs. "Have you introduced Andy to your family yet?"

"Not everyone."

She laughs again, fills a glass with water, then says goodnight. "Oh, and feel free to use the phone any time you want."

That's nice of her, but I'd never consider calling home or anywhere else without using my calling card. I know a little something about missions budgets. Not that I'm on one, but our instructors spent the whole last quarter of my World Missions class going over budgets, and

I'm glad I'm not, is all I can say.

I dump the rest of my tea and turn out the light. My knee smarts as I climb the stairs. Back in my room I see there's already a bruise in the middle of my kneecap. I quickly change, and realize I've missed my Friday night bath—and aren't I glad I have? That certainly puts the excitement of my new life into perspective.

The bullfrog has either found his mate or given up and gone on to bed. I turn out the light and listen to the quiet night, broken only by the waxing and waning of Clark's snores rattling the floorboards. I reach over and turn my fan up a notch.

Poor Sally. That's the thought that jumps into my mind, but when I picture her smile, I think maybe not so poor. Maybe not so poor at all.

Sunday morning service is a repeat of the week before. Andy plays his guitar, and even though the songs are in Romanian, their message seeps into my soul like winter sunshine, warming all the right spots.

The journey I'm on is like riding a carousel. Up one minute, down the next. Inflated with faith, then, *whoosh*, all the air is gone. I'm a leaky vessel, but can't see where to patch up the holes. So I fill and fill and fill, hoping one of these days it'll hold.

Like Opa. Nothing leaks out of him, except faith, hope and love, the Big Three. It oozes out of him, in his music, his counsel, even the way he trims his trees. Don't ask me to explain, there's just something holy about everything he does. He should be in the Bible, right there along with Moses, Daniel and Paul, but even I realize that if krystal blue karma had gotten lost in the wilderness with a whole tribe of kin, he'd have turned it into a sanctified love-in, and I somehow think that wasn't quite what God had in mind.

Sally makes her way to my pew as the final strains of Andy's guitar float out the open windows. She asks if I would like her to interpret the sermon, but I thank her and say no. She smiles, winks, then returns to the front row, where for the next hour she will lovingly hang on every word her husband utters from behind the pulpit. I turn to the scripture reference Clark announces, and read in English what he's reading aloud in Romanian. Then I let the Holy Spirit do his work, applying the words, not like a Band-Aid, but like wet clay that fills in the chinks. When it's fired, will it finally be whole, this vessel that is me?

Coming to church here is different in more than just the obvious ways. Heading the list is that I'm here for the right reasons. At home, church is as much a social event as a religious one. It's a time to connect with friends, to check out the new guys if there happen to be any, to rate all the girls' outfits. Oh, sure, I settle down and listen to the sermon, but halfway through I'm trying to decide where to have lunch. *Red Lobster was last week. Besides—and I tap my watch in case it's stopped—the way the pastor is going long today, there'd be a thirty-minute wait by the time we got there. So maybe . . .* And I run through the list of restaurants in town. All the while I'm taking notes on the message, expecting it to work its magic the way garlic permeates Dad's pasta sauce if it simmers long enough.

Not here. I'm simmering all right, and I can almost feel the stirring of the spoon. I want to give in to the process, the sooner for God to ladle me out, a savory sauce to be poured over someone's life.

And then I wonder, do I really have much to offer?

Eleven

The boys have something up their collective sleeve, I can tell by the gleam in their eyes. Mischief is their mission this bright Monday morning. This is my first solo flight as their teacher and I have the feeling they want to make it memorable. They giggle behind their hands and cast sideways glances at Peter, their leader by default as he's the oldest boy in the class.

We make a circle for devotions. The story I've chosen and printed out from the internet is folded in my lap. I have no pictures to show them because I have no storybook, but I think they'll like the story just the same. Really, it's a parable but I could barely explain the word *parable* to a classroom full of children whose first language is English. I won't even try here. Instead, I sit with folded legs, seven-year-old Hedy occupying my lap on this occasion, and unfold the page, wary of the giggling that continues among the boys.

I begin to read. "'There once was a jaguar named Emoo, who lived in the most beautiful part of a beautiful jungle. His lean body rippled as he walked the paths of the jungle, and all the other animals bowed as he passed.' "

I look up at my students and see that even the boys have begun to settle down. The jaguar has captured their attention as I hoped it would.

"'With hardly an effort, Emoo leapt onto the low branch of a capirona tree, then followed its thick trunk high above the jungle floor, his body perfectly vertical as he climbed ever higher.

"'The capirona, king of the jungle trees, spread wide its branches, a huge umbrella against the sun that rose high above the treetops. Not even the hot rays of the sun could penetrate the thick foliage as one capirona tree reached out to another, and another, and another, until the entire jungle rested in the shade these trees provided.

"'Emoo climbed as high as the capirona would allow, then, like a tightrope walker, he moved outward on a branch that bounced every time his padded paws came down on its smooth gray bark. Just when the branch began to bend under the weight of the great jaguar, Emoo leapt onto the outstretched branch of the next capirona. And on he traveled, high above the jungle, as sleek a creature as God ever made.'"

All the children listen intently now, their bodies leaning toward me, mouths open, eyes keen and studious.

"'Far below, the other animals of the jungle watched with awe and wonder, for only the monkeys and the birds and a snake or two could match Emoo's ability to reach the great heights. Though none was nearly so imposing.' "

I look up to see the boys turn their eyes toward Peter, then look back at me, the spell somehow broken. I find my place and continue to read, casting a guarded glance at my audience from time to time.

"'When Emoo reached the farthest capirona tree in the jungle, he descended the trunk as gracefully as he'd climbed the first.

"'Well, you'd think he'd have been the most satisfied creature of all, having viewed his environment from such lofty heights. You'd think he'd have thanked God for such a grand gift, but Emoo's mood was as low as the depths to which he'd returned.

"'The other animals did not understand Emoo's dejection, and they asked him, "What is wrong, Emoo? Have you seen something from the treetops that has filled you with sadness?" "Oh, yes," Emoo replied, "I have." And with that, all the animals were alarmed.' "

One glance reveals my audience is back.

"' "Has something dangerous invaded our jungle?" "Should we run and hide?" The animals could barely ask their questions because of the fear that had taken hold of them. But the jaguar merely laid his head in his paws and sighed. "Nothing has invaded the jungle. We're as safe as we've always been." With that, the animals ceased their quivering, as relief settled over them as thick as the shade of the capirona trees. "Then what has made you so sorrowful?" asked the tapir.

"' "Of all the animals of the jungle, none can climb higher than I," said the jaguar, "none has seen the sights I have seen. None, save one. The great harpy eagle. He alone soars the heights of the heavens, able to see from one side to the other, nothing obstructing his view. I should have been born a harpy eagle instead of a lowly jaguar." And with a deep sigh, he laid his head once again on his paws.' "

Just then, Hedy reaches up and touches my face. "Teacher Aria, I'm thirsty."

"Oh, okay." I stand her up, then unfold myself off the floor. "Let's all take a water break." I go to the water jug, and as I lift the lid I turn at the sound of giggling. The boys are at it again. I turn back to my task, dipper in hand, wondering what on earth is so entertaining.

As if in slow motion I lower the dipper just as a gold serpentine head emerges from the jug, a black, forked tongue flicking the air. With eyes unnaturally wide, I suck in a startled breath, and before I can stop myself, it comes back out in a screechy, pathetic scream. Most of the girls follow suit, but I doubt if they know why they're screaming. Then they see the snake and now they scream in earnest, including Anya, while the four little boys squeal with laughter.

In the midst of the bedlam a figure appears in the open doorway. Clark. It takes him only a handful of seconds to assess the situation, and, with legs as long as a stilt walker, only a few seconds more to reach the jug. He grabs the snake by the head and carries it out the door. Its lean, foot-long body writhes, splattering water like a runaway hose in its wake.

I shudder as furiously as old Thaddeus shaking off water from the pond after he's chased a frog, and want to say, "Thanks, Clark, we needed you." But how absurd is that?

And then another figure appears in the doorway. His white-toothed smirk reminds me of the Cheshire cat, and I wish, like his counterpart, he'd disappear into thin air. "It's just a rat snake," Andy says. "Perfectly harmless. Right boys?"

As if set free in freeze tag, the boys become animated again and laugh, though when they see the set of my jaw, the arch of my brow, and the slits of my eyes, their laughter is not so unrestrained as before. My nostrils flare with the surge of breath I cannot control. I count to twenty before I trust my voice, and even then it shakes. "Shouldn't you have your head in a hole somewhere?" I say to Andy.

And he laughs. I hear him as he crunches his way across the gravel, back toward the periwinkle house. My fists are tight at my sides, and I continue to shiver. If there's anything I hate, it's a snake. I love that there are four corners to the classroom. One for each of the boys, and I send them there. They have no trouble understanding my meaning, and bury their noses in the ninety degree angles of the walls. That's where they'll stay as long as it takes my heart rate to get back to normal. Which could be the rest of the day.

I steel myself and creep to the jug, then from a safe distance I crane my neck to peek inside. Nothing but water, I'm relieved to find. Yucky, contaminated water. I snatch up the jug, go outside and toss out its contents, then I turn it upside down and shake it until every drop is gone. It will not be refilled until I've given it a good scrubbing with a bar of Moldovan soap, but even then I doubt I'll ever drink from it again. I give each of the girls a drink from the hose, give in to one last shudder, then gather my wits and the girls for the end of the story.

Hedy's in my lap again the moment I sit down. I find my place in the story and begin to read. "'I should have been born a harpy eagle instead of a lowly jaguar,' " I repeat. The boys inch their heads in my direction, and that's okay. I'll allow them that, but they won't leave their corners till the story's finished and all the girls have had recess.

""But Emoo," said the agouti, brave for one so small—' "

"Agouti?" Ivana aks.

Fortunately, I'd looked it up. "An agouti is a rodent," I say. "A rat."

"Rat?" Katrina asks, still not understanding.

"Şobolan," Lazlo says, to which the girls respond as every little girl might, with plenty of eewws and yucks. "Should beware of snake, yes?" he gamely adds.

I clear my throat and draw my class back to the story. ""God has given you agility and great strength. You can climb higher than all the four-legged animals in the jungle. Is that not enough?" The eyes of the jaguar became slits' "—no doubt like mine a few minutes before—"'and the menacing rumble in his throat sent the other animals scurrying. Still the lowly agouti stood his ground. "Is that not enough?" he repeated. "Should you not be grateful for all God has given you?"'

"'Angered by the agouti's words, Emoo lifted a mighty paw and batted it away like a fly, then he resumed his stalking, sleekly ascending the nearest capirona tree and spanning the heights of the jungle, over and over again, always with the same doleful result.' "

The story closes with the Scripture verse from I Timothy 6:6: "'But godliness with contentment is great gain.' Which means," I say, "we should be content with what God gives us, no matter what."

"Satisfăcut," Sally says from the doorway. "Content." Then she applauds. "Wonderful story. At least the little bit I heard." With one eyebrow raised she takes note of the squirming boys in the corners of the room. "I haven't tried that one," she says. "We'll see how it works."

"You heard?"

"Oh, yes. I'm sure Clark and Andy are still laughing. They're such men."

I smile at that and my embarrassment ebbs away. "I should have known the boys were up to something, the way they kept giggling and looking at Peter." Peter turns his eyes to mine at the mention of his name. The appeal on his face almost undoes me.

"Little boys are always up to something. Big boys, too, for that matter. Ready for a real drink of water?" she asks the girls.

We follow them across the gravel and into the kitchen.

"How long are the boys under restriction?"

"Till after recess," I say. "Am I being too harsh?"

"Good heavens, no! If they had pulled that stunt on me I'd have turned every one of them over my knee."

"You can do that?"

"I certainly can. Not that I have, mind you." She smiles, and that says it all. Yes, she is Mam all over again.

It's Friday evening, and as we walk to the coffeehouse Andy asks if I'll find a corner to go to after his message in case there are any young women who would like someone to talk to. He senses my hesitation. "How are your language skills?"

Language skills? "Andy, I teach English."

"Those aren't the skills I mean. Your Romanian language skills."

I know what he means! He's the one not getting it. "I'm here to teach English." I say each word distinctly, as if he won't get it otherwise.

He looks over his shoulder, because he's three steps ahead of me. Like always. I'm out of breath just trying to keep up, because if there's anything I hate, it's someone who's always three steps ahead. "So they learn your language but you don't have to learn theirs?" He might as well add *snooty American*.

"No. I don't have to learn theirs. That's the whole point."

He stops, and suddenly *I'm* three steps ahead. "What would have happened if Christ had only spoken *Heaven* when he came to our planet?"

"Heaven? Excuse me?" What on earth is he talking about?

"You know, the language with which he speaks to the Father, the Holy Spirit, the angels? You think it's English? Or Hebrew or Greek maybe?"

I put my hands on my hips and wait. My nostrils flare as I breathe.

"No. When he came to Earth, he spoke our language. He wouldn't have gotten far otherwise. And I don't just mean in communication. He became one of us, and look what happened because of it."

"He was crucified," I say, then wince at my own sarcasm. I can't resist sarcasm, but even I know when I cross the line.

Now Andy's three steps in front again, and shaking his head.

"Well, I'm certainly not going to learn Russian by the end of your sermon," I say to his back.

"Romanian," he says.

"Whatever." And yes, actually, I did think the Trinity spoke English. The King James version.

He doesn't say another word till we reach the peeling door of the coffeehouse. "Svetlana's English is good, relatively. She'll interpret." And there I have it, my assignment.

I pass on the coffee and smile at all the unfamiliar faces, afraid to open my mouth.

"They do know conversational English," Andy whispers as he passes by. "You heard them last week."

And then Svetlana comes to my rescue, wearing black jeans and boots. Her smile shows perfect white teeth, and I doubt they're the work of an orthodontist. I rub my tongue over my own manipulated enamel, glad the whole braces thing is behind me. "Hello, Aria," she says.

Never has my name sounded so fluid as it rolls off her tongue. I only wish it could sound that way with everyone. Here at least I'll be— And then I catch myself. "Content." I whisper the word as I think of Emoo.

The man with the guitar is at his post, his head down as he embraces the instrument. What a union they have, he and his guitar. When I listen with a less critical ear, he maybe could be third string in the heavenly band. I certainly have to applaud his effort. And with time…

That's one of Opa's favorite phrases. *"With time, baby girl, these will be more than saplings,"* he said of a new orchard he'd planted when I was maybe eleven. *"They'll grow and produce sweet fruit."* Then he put his arm around my shoulders. *"With time, baby girl, you will too."*

Oh, I don't want to let him or the rest of my family down.

Andy's pulpit is just what it was last week, a chair to rest his foot on, his knee a dais for his little Testament. He speaks from Hebrews, chapter four. "'Today, if you hear his voice, do not harden your hearts.' "

That's a big if, hearing God's voice, because even I struggle to know, and I've been immersed in the world of Christianity since birth. Any lawyer could tell you what a huge loophole that little two-letter word provides, *if.*

If I had to pin it down, I'm not sure I could say I ever heard, "Thus saith the Lord." Not that I think he would actually talk to me that way. No, if his voice is anything like Opa's then maybe his words would be too. Maybe he'd call me baby girl, but then I could be fooling myself, because there's that secret. The one only God and I know about. So, yeah, on second thought he'd probably look like a glaring Uncle Sam, with his hand pointing me right back out the pearly gates.

There's a lot to be said for not hearing voices in your head.

Andy's wrapped up his sermon in the time it's taken my thoughts to find resolution. He's found his corner and looks my way while he waits for someone in his unique congregation to join him. I take the hint and migrate to a corner close to the guitar player. I want to hear him better. And there we are, in our corners. A lot like the boys in my classroom earlier in the week. Except that our noses point away from the wall.

Matches are struck and put to the end of cigarettes all over the room. The noise level has gone up a decibel or two, just another Friday night at the coffeehouse. But one lone girl dodges chairs and bodies on her way to where I stand. I know she's coming my way because her eyes are fixed on mine. But there's an apology in the way she carries herself, like she already knows what a burden she'll be. I smile when she's closer to put her at ease. I don't think it helps either one of us.

"Hello," she says, and nervously fingers her long blonde hair behind her ears again and again. Her eyes are now focused on her combat boots.

My heart pounds as I say hello. Before I can scan the room for Svetlana, she's there, one lean arm around the girl's shoulders. She says something in Romanian and the girl nods slightly in response. Then she looks up at me. Her eyes, that same ethereal blue, are rimmed with heavy black liner. She whispers something to Svetlana, who seems to encourage her with her own whispered words.

"My boyfriend— Oh." She stops. "My name Stasya." Her accent is heavy, and exactly what you'd imagine a Romanian to sound like.

"Hello, Stasya." I take her hands in mine. They're ice cold, but mine aren't much warmer. "Is there a problem with your boyfriend?"

Stasya's eyes are on Svetlana, who translates my words. Stasya turns to me and nods, then seems to change her mind. "Not problem with boyfriend. Problem of boyfriend."

Well, that's as clear as Mam's famous hamless split pea soup.

Svetlana chimes in again in her native tongue, this time using her hands for emphasis. "Just say," she concludes.

Stasya looks from Svetlana to me, then lowers her gaze. She leans close and whispers, "Boyfriend wants sex. All the time, sex. I think is wrong. Pastor Andy say."

Pastor Andy, huh? Does he have any idea how he's set me up? I'm going to kill him when this is over. And if he thinks I will ever again save the hot water for him, well, he's dead wrong.

"Is wrong?" Stasya asks.

"Yes," I say, and shrug, because honestly, where do I go from here?

This hasn't been an issue with me since . . . man, this has never been an issue with me. Matt was my last steady boyfriend and I was fourteen. Thank the good Lord we don't have a history to contend with, other than an innocuous kiss or two, now that he'll be my brother-in-law instead of my husband. I am so out of my league here. "Yes," I say again, "it is wrong, but only because God wants to protect you." I wait for Svetlana to translate, all the while thinking like crazy what I'll say next.

"I want make God happy," Stasya says. Her "h" must scratch her throat on the way out, it's so heavy.

"That's good." I fight to keep from lapsing into her accent, and wonder where on earth that's coming from.

"But boyfriend," Stasya continues, "he does not care to please God."

Tends to be a universal problem, I think. Then I think of Andy. Probably not so much with him. Or if it is, he's quite the hypocrite.

"He vants only sex," Stasya says. "And more sex."

She's like a wind-up doll, I decide. Get her going and there's no stopping her.

"So vat I do?"

For lack of a better idea I want to ask her if she's prayed the sinner's prayer, but what a copout that would be. *God*, I scream, *what do I say?*

Then, as if someone's reading a Teleprompter inside my head, the answer comes back clear as can be. *What would you tell Johnnie?*

What would I—? I'd tell her to lose the bum and don't look back. Ever. To save herself for a man who loves God more than he loves her. Which I'm certain is exactly what she's done. And then I realize I've just heard the voice of God. My knees want to buckle and I grab the back of a chair. I've heard the voice of God! I want to scream. Wait, wait, what did it sound like? Oh, man! What did it sound like? Think, *think!* It was, was, nondescript. Could that be right? Could you hear God's voice in your head, know it for what it is, and then not remember what it sounded like? Could you—

Stasya and Svetlana are looking at me with scrunched up faces.

I clear my throat. "This is just my recommendation, but, Stasya, you must put God first. If your boyfriend doesn't understand, then maybe God has another boyfriend for you. Somewhere."

Stasya's eyes fill with tears as Svetlana interprets my words.

Great.

But then she grabs my shoulders with more power than I would have imagined the tiny young woman capable of and pulls me into an embrace. "Tonk you," she says. "Tonk you so much."

And I realize all she wants is someone to validate that voice inside *her* head telling her what is and isn't right, for heaven's sake.

I let out a heavy breath as she walks away, and I pray for her resolve. A saying of Mam's comes to mind. "What man's going to buy the cow when he can get the milk for free?" I always thought it crude, but right now I'm wondering how it would translate.

I glance over at Andy's corner and see that he's watching me. He doesn't smile, doesn't give me a thumbs up, nothing. Finally, I look away. When I glance back he's turned his attention to the guy in black. Oh, wait, that could be any guy in the room, so let's just say he's turned his attention to the next guy in line.

There's no one else waiting to talk to me. I'd really love to step outside to grab a breath of smokeless air. But I'd have to step around Svetlana to get away, and she seems on the brink of asking me something. So I wait, as my heart beats out of rhythm.

Svetlana twirls a silver filigree ring on her right index finger, then takes a step that closes the gap between us. We're eye level, but only because she's in boots with four inch heels. Even so, she's all legs and arms, thin and sleek as a gazelle.

"What you say to Stasya is true?" She holds my gaze in her own sky blue eyes. "About sex with boyfriend?"

I nod and try not to look apologetic, because I know I'm rocking their world. "You've never been told you should wait?"

She looks confused. "For what?"

"Marriage."

"We're told use—" She says something in Romanian. I have no idea what. She knows that, of course, and pulls a small packet out of her pocket to serve as an interpreter.

"I see," I say, and close her hand over the condom. I steal a peek at Andy and offer up a great big *thank you!* to heaven when I see that his eyes are looking up in prayer and not in our direction. "It's more than protecting yourself against pregnancy or sexually transmitted disease. If you want to obey the Lord, you can't have sex until you're married. And only with your husband," I add, in case my meaning isn't clear enough.

Svetlana bites her lower lip as she studies me. "What about you?" she says.

"Me?" I reach up and scratch my scalp.

"Are you wait till marriage?"

"Yes. Of course."

Her eyes grow large. "Vow. Your boyfriend does not complain?"

I'm not about to say I don't have a boyfriend at the moment. Instead I say, "It vouldn't—wouldn't matter. I have to do what I know is right. God holds me accountable for my own conduct." I have no clue how much of this is getting across. "You understand?"

She steps back, and I'm glad when she returns the condom to her pocket. "Vow," she says again. She gives me a little wave and works her way through the tables to where her boyfriend Sasha is waiting.

Now that I am alone I make my way outside. The late night air is warm and heavy, but refreshing after the hot, smoky atmosphere inside the coffeehouse. What I wouldn't give for a frigid *venti* Frappuccino. Or at least a Pepsi. With endless ice. I lean against the building and wonder how long Andy has been in Moldova, how long he's been holding church inside the brown door. Regardless, I'd say he has his work cut out for him.

———————————

Andy's his typical non-conversant self as we walk back to the parsonage. It annoys me that I'd like him to at least acknowledge I stepped up to the plate tonight. Accolades aren't necessary, but recognition would be nice. I don't even care that he's several steps ahead of me, until I hear something howl in the distance. I quicken my pace to catch up.

"So what makes you think I'm running away from something?" I blurt the question and it catches even me by surprise. I don't expect an answer, a civil one that is, but the silence is way too loud.

And then he surprises me with a response. "More likely some*one*."

"Oh, really? Like who?"

His laugh sounds more like a snort. "Could it be—let me guess. Johnnie?"

"Johnnie?" I fall back again, thinking of all the great ways I could run with this. "You've been listening to my conversations?"

He stops and turns. "Kinda hard not to if you get what I mean."

I do. And it ticks me off. "One would reasonably expect a bit of privacy in one's own kitchen in the middle of the night."

"You'd do well not to expect too much here."

"That's a bit cynical."

"Give it time," he says.

He stops in front of the church then nods toward the parsonage. "I'll wait till you're inside."

"Well then, good night."

I make it all the way up the back steps and open the door before I turn back to him. "No," I call. "I'm not running from Johnnie."

"Whatever," he says, and disappears into the darkness of the church.

Twelve

I keep thinking about that bare foundation, and the wildflowers springing up through the cracks. More than that, I think about why it's there. I know about human trafficking, of course, in that vague way most people know about it. That it exists around the world is an awful testimony to the baseness of humankind, and it sickens me. But that it's enough of a problem in eastern Europe for missionaries to address? That I didn't know.

I think of the young people—I don't say girls because I don't think the problem is gender specific—who are forced into the worst kind of bondage, and it makes me sick. But I want to do more than pay it lip service. I want to help. I want to rescue and restore the victims, and protect young women, and even children like Anya, who are the targets of these vile abusers.

Like Mary, I ponder these thoughts in my heart, because I don't know how to send them home. I don't know how to adequately describe the state of that Hope House foundation, and what its solitary presence in a field of wildflowers represents. I don't know where God is going with this, with me. I came here to teach English to Moldovan children. The folks back home get and applaud that. Not that they wouldn't be sympathetic to the plight of those who are lured from their homes and dropped smack dab into the middle of the worst kind of nightmare; it's just so much darker a situation than the one they bought into.

These thoughts I pen in my journal because I have to do something with them.

I've turned the page on my virtual calendar from June to July. School is out for two months, but my students still come for Sunday school, along with other children in the church who are not students at our school. I smile at how quickly I've taken ownership. This afternoon I'll prepare my lesson, but it's Saturday morning and I need to get downstairs to help Sally with the laundry. I strip the sheets off my bed and take them with me.

"'Morning," I say as I enter the kitchen. Sally's busy at the sink. Clark and Andy are at the table finishing their breakfast. I glance at the clock, which shows it's only 7:30. Still, I feel like a slacker.

Clark looks up from his newspaper and nods. He's not a man who wastes his words, I've learned. But Andy, well, he's just Andy. I've learned that too.

Sally gives me a quick, one-armed hug. "Sleep well?"

"Yes. You?"

"Like a bear in hibernation. Coffee or tea?"

"Tea, but I'll get it." I grab a mug out of the dish drainer and fill it with hot water from the kettle, glad I don't have to wait for it to boil. I really need to put my care package list together and send it to Celie, because I'd just love something that wakes up my taste buds, unlike the black pekoe, which is all we can get here in Leoccesni. A slice of lemon helps, but we don't always have lemon on hand.

"It's going to be a scorcher today," Sally says. "Let's get our work finished early so we can hide out inside near the fans this afternoon."

Sounds like a plan, but first I want a piece of toast made from Riya Moraru's bread. Honestly, I can't get enough. It's better than cheesecake, and in my book there's not much better than that. If it's homemade.

"How's the well coming?" I ask.

Clark pushes back from his empty breakfast plate and pats his stomach with both hands. "Finished last night. Andy's one happy man, not to mention Janic Rotaru."

Well, he might have mentioned that during his long silences as we walked to and from the coffeehouse.

"You think he might eventually make it to church?" I ask. "Janic, not Andy." I feel foolish for my addendum, because obviously I meant Janic.

Clark stands and picks up the newspaper he's ready to read. "The better question is, will he eventually make it to heaven?"

A strange comment for a pastor, I think. "Doesn't one lead to the other?"

"Church is just a greenhouse," Clark says. "The fields where we're planted and plucked are out there." He winks and points a thumb in the general vicinity of *the world*.

Odd. "That's exactly what my Sunday school lesson is going to be about, the parable of the sower."

Andy gives me a quick glance and I want to say, *No, I'm not copying your sermon. It happens to be the lesson in the book I teach from. The one Sally gave me.* But I don't say that or anything else.

Andy shifts his eyes to Sally. "Thanks for breakfast," he says, then he's out the door.

"A wonderful lesson. One of my favorites." Sally wipes her hands on a dishtowel, then walks over to kiss her husband. "You did a lot of planting in helping to dig that well. You and Andy both. Janic Rotaru will be plucked one of these days, you wait and see."

He pats her hand. "I'll be across the way, preparing my sermon. After . . ." He holds up the newspaper and lets it finish his sentence.

Once we're alone, Sally flashes a smile and says to me, "We've company coming. On Tuesday."

"Company?" I can tell by her enthusiasm she doesn't mean someone local. I'm thinking maybe one of their sons or other family members, and for a brief moment I'm homesick for my own family.

"A team from Wichita, or is it Wisconsin?" She drums her fingers on her lips as she thinks. "Cheese! Yes, Wisconsin."

"A team?" I'm thinking basketball or, I don't know, soccer? "To play what, and who?"

Sally laughs. "Not that kind of team, Aria. A work team for Hope House. They're bringing funds to buy the block for the first story and a group of workers to lay it. Can you believe it?"

Not only can I not believe it, but I especially can't believe it in light of my thoughts, written in my journal this morning before I came downstairs. That I might actually be on the same page as God strikes me as amazing. "That's awesome."

"Yes. Clark is thrilled. But now I'm scrambling to find housing for the men. The women will stay here with us."

"Women?"

"Two." Sally beams, and I realize how much she looks forward to this connection from home. "About your age, I understand, along with five men of varying age and experience. I'm thinking the Dinescus can house one of the men. And the Moravecs too. If there's a young man, I'd like to put him up with Andy. He could use the company, don't you think? Especially after so long in that hole of Janic's."

Poor guy, is what I think—the visitor, not Andy. "His room's pretty small, isn't it?" Come to think of it, the room upstairs the girls will share is small too, with only a twin-sized bed.

"Oh, we have a cot or two somewhere. It's not the Hilton, but I think it's part of the experience, don't you? It gives them something to go home and talk about."

Sally is popping with energy, and I sense she doesn't know where to start.

And then a thought comes to mind. "Sally?"

She looks up from the list she's creating.

"Do you think, well, I was wondering, since there are women

working on Hope House, if I could work too? I mean, with school out and all?" I feel like a kid asking her mom about a sleepover. *Can I, Mom, huh, please can I?*

"It's hard work, Aria, laying block. Especially in this heat." As if to make a point she picks up her pad of paper and fans herself.

"I know, but—" I don't have much with which to plead my case, having zero experience at laying block, or anything else to do with construction, so I simply say, "I would really love to help."

She's quiet a moment, then she nods. "I'll speak to Clark." She might as well have said, *I'll ask your father*, and I can't help think, *there goes the sleepover.*

———————————

I've just dried the last of the breakfast dishes when a light tap sounds at the screen door. I look over to see Anya. Sally and I both welcome her in. Anya is wearing a yellow sleeveless blouse, blue shorts, and tennis shoes without socks. Her sinewy legs remind me of a colt. She's still shy around me, but treats Sally like a *bunica*, a grandmother. Sally relishes it.

"Have you had breakfast?" she asks.

Anya nods. "Mama let me come to offer help."

"How nice," Sally says, "but this is your vacation. You should at least sleep in."

"Not sleep," she says. "If I not help you, I help Mama." She says this to Sally, but glances at me.

I think back to summer vacations when I was twelve and thirteen. One of the best things was staying up late, then sleeping in until you couldn't stand one more minute of being in bed. How different things are here. How spoiled my life has been is beginning to sink in and bother me.

"Well then, we'd love your help. Aria—Miss Winters—was just about to hang out the wash. The first load's in the machine," Sally says to me.

"You should have waited." I say this because this is my job, the Saturday laundry. Now I really am a slacker.

"I put the men's clothes from last night in the wash first thing this morning, that's all. They're ready to hang on the line."

"Well, the rest I'll—we'll—do." I hand Anya the jar of clothespins and open the lid to the washing machine.

Outside it's one giant notch above warm. "Sally's right," I say to Anya, "it'll be a scorcher before long." She nods and reaches in the jar for a clothespin to be ready for me. She's so very shy.

Growing up, this is the kind of summer day I used to love on the compound, when we could swim from mid-morning to midnight. By the end of the day, we could barely keep our eyes from squinting from all the sun and chlorine. The tender skin beneath our eyes would be as red as the ruby seedless grapes Mam buys at the fruit stand down the way. The one drawback was that the sun also made my freckles pop. Still does, actually. I look up at the blazing fireball and wish I'd dabbed on some SPF 45. Johnnie says she wouldn't mind having my freckles, thinks they're cute in fact, but believe me, come her wedding day she'll be one happy girl when she doesn't have to Photoshop the moose tracks out of her pictures.

Our pool back home is Olympic size and is the hub of our four parcels, assuming hubs can be rectangular. As an eleven-year-old, early that summer, I invited all the kids in the area to use our pool, and I only charged them a dollar each for the privilege. But Celie got wind of my entrepreneurial efforts and said I had to give all the money back. When I said that would not only be impossible, but mortifying to boot, she confiscated the money and only gave it back the next Sunday morning, instructing me to put it all in the offering plate at church. It happened to go into a missionary offering that morning, so who knows, that may have been the seed God used to call me to Moldova.

Assuming I have been called. I'm still sorting that out.

I take a clothespin from Anya and pin one side of a pair of blue plaid boxers to the line, then I pin the other side. I feel weird handling either

Clark or Andy's underwear. And later, when I hang Sally's plain white, high-waist briefs and AA bra to the line, I'll make sure there's a bed sheet up to hide them from the neighborhood. I mean, there aren't even any fences. Which is the second reason my own little dainties will be drying over the rail of my bed in the wind of my box fan when they come out of the washing machine in a load or two. The first reason, of course, is Andy.

Anya and I giggle together as I pin up another pair of boxers. These are red with vertical gray stripes. Elastic shows through the worn spots around the waistline. Finally we get to blue jeans and overalls, items a bit less entertaining.

"Do you like to swim?" I ask.

"We play in water, but there's not—what you call . . . ?" She says something in Romanian, then, "Pool. Pool?"

I love her accent. All the v's in place of the w's, and when she says pool, it's in two syllables, pooh-elle. "Yes, pool. So you don't know how to swim?"

She shakes her head, and I sense she feels she's gone down a notch in my estimation.

"I'm not so good myself," I say. "I don't know what it is about me, but I get in the water and it's all I can do to keep from sinking." That's not really true. I'm a good swimmer and can do a dozen laps in our pool—short side to short side—without a break. "You'd think I had a lead kidney or something."

"Lead kidney? Vat is dis?" She looks so serious.

I laugh and say, "It's nothing. I'm kidding."

With the shirts hung, we go back inside. The next load of laundry is in the spin cycle. "How about some iced tea while we wait?"

"Yes, please," Anya says.

Sally's unsweetened sun tea is nothing like Mam's who makes Southern-style sweet tea, so sweet one glass will give you a sugar high. So one glass at any one time is always enough for me. There's an art to making sweet tea, one I haven't mastered. But this much I know: you don't simply boil your tea then add sugar to the jar. No sir. You add the sugar to the tea as it's cooking so it's absorbed into the tea, becoming one with the drink instead of sinking to the bottom of the glass, which is exactly what happens to me now. I stir it briskly again, hand the glass to Anya, and pour one for myself. I leave out the sugar this time. No sense worrying over the calories if they're not going to give me a bang for my buck.

I hear Sally upstairs singing away as she works. In Romanian. Her voice strains to reach the high notes, but there's passion in the sound even if there isn't artistry. I love that Opa has both. Andy has both as well, though I hate to admit it. If he could just be as engaging in dialogue as he is in song. But talking with him is like hand-to-hand combat. And if we're keeping score, he's ahead. Dang. And yet, when it comes to the guys at the coffeehouse he verges on the edge of civility.

I realize I've allowed my mind to wander when I look to see Anya's eyes focused on me.

"What will you do all summer now that school's out?"

I've caught her mid-drink and she hurries to swallow. Everything about this adorable girl is a desire to please. "Help Mama with chores. Help with brother." She says *brother* without the roll of the eyes I'd get in America.

"He doesn't come to our school?"

"In fall. He is just now"—she counts in her head, I think much the way I do in Spanish to get to the right number—"five." She holds up a hand, all five fingers at attention. "His name is Victor."

"I have one sister. She's younger too, but only by two years." Less actually, but this is close enough for Anya. "She's my best friend. Well, she and Kari Zalasky. By the way, do you know of anyone in Leoccesni whose last name is Zalasky?"

"Zalasky? No. No Zalasky."

"Ah. Well." It was a long shot. Of course, I'll ask an adult or two, but again, what are the odds? "Do you have a best friend?"

She turns her lovely eyes on me, and shrugs. There's a longing in the action, a request.

"Let's be friends," I say, and her smile causes me to smile. My eyes sting with the surprise of tears, which I quickly blink away. "For the summer you may call me Ree. But when school starts, we must go back to Miss Winters." I wink and lift my glass to her. She knows just what to do, and clinks my glass with her own.

"Ree?" she asks.

"It's a nickname. Short for Aria. Do you use nicknames here?"

She thinks a moment. "Mama calls Victor *Viki*."

I pull my eyebrows back down and decide not to tell her that Vicki is a girl's name where I come from. "Well then, there you are."

"I call him little brother." Of course, it comes out leetle brudder.

"Well, that would be a nickname too, of sorts."

She nods, as if she gets the concept.

"What do you want to do with your life, Anya? Any idea?"

"Oh, yes." She doesn't hesitate. Her face becomes as serious as ever I've seen it. "I want be missionary."

"Missionary." I'm absolutely certain this has nothing to do with a student wanting to be like her teacher—in this case, a missionary teacher. Inwardly, I point to myself. No, I get the sense this comes from a deep place in her heart, where it's germinated for some time. "Where do you want to go?"

"Go?" She shakes her head. "Not go. I want be missionary in Moldova. To tell my people God loves them."

"Wow. That's an excellent goal."

She says, "When Mama become Christian, my grandparents don't talk to her no more. I know just little about them." She holds her thumb and finger almost together. "Victor? They not see."

"Never?"

"Never."

"But why?"

"They go to church, but Orthodox. Not same as our church. Grandparents not like."

"Ah. That's sad."

"I want them know Jesus loves them. I want be missionary."

"Your father comes to church?" I ask.

"Yes. Always he come."

I'm still unused to families sitting on different sides of the aisle. I'll have to ask Sally to point him out. "I'm glad. My father does too."

"And mother?"

I nod. "Mother, sister, grandparents. My whole family goes to church together."

"They know Jesus loves them?"

Of course, I start to say, then I think of Clark's comment earlier. *Church is just a greenhouse. The fields where we're planted and plucked are out there.* Anya would know this since he's her pastor. And I know he's right. Church is not a one-way elevator to Heaven. But I think I'm just now getting it. My stomach takes a tumble as I think about Bible school. It's not an elevator either. Neither is membership in the Shunk-Winters household, for that matter. I'm somewhat distracted as I answer, "Yes. They know Jesus loves them."

But do I?

Thirteen

My hair has become a problem. No amount of mousse gives it the lift I loved when I first had it cut. Today it's pulled back with a headband, lying flat as the earth before Columbus. But it's out of my way as I work. Three loads of laundry are hanging out to dry. All that's left are my clothes and bed sheets. I've taken much for granted in my charmed life. I see that oh so clearly in this environment, and for the dozenth time since arriving I vow to change that. Here and at home. I don't want to be a rich American do-gooder, bestowing favors on the plebes just because I can. I want my heart to show, like Sally's, like Anya's.

"Are you this much help at home?" I ask Anya. She's worked tirelessly since arriving this morning, not just with the laundry, but she's dusted every surface in the house she can find to dust.

She smiles and shrugs, but Sally hugs her and says, "If not more."

We all look like char women, covered in grime and sweat, and when it comes time for my shower I won't complain about the tin can showerhead, nor the water, even if it's nothing but cold. Right now I'd welcome it. I would, in fact, love to walk right out the door, twist on the faucet that juts out of the side of the house, and stick my head underneath the flow. And if that faucet weren't in view of Clark and Andy—mostly Andy—just across the gravel, that's what I'd do. Instead, I pull off my headband, smooth back my hair, then put the band on again.

"I thought going short would solve the hair problem," I say. "What a mistake."

"Oh, but it looks so with it," Sally says. She's collapsed at the table, enjoying the blast from the oscillating fan whenever it hits her. I know just how she feels.

"It did for a while, but I didn't think this through."

Tana was so right. Dang, and dang again.

"There's a young woman in town who trims Clark whenever he gets shaggy. Perhaps we could—"

I know my eyes go as round as the white walls on Dad's '62 Thunderbird Coupe.

"Or maybe I could try my hand at a light trim . . ." Sally leaves off with a smile and a shrug.

"I have buzz shears," Andy says, appearing out of nowhere. He disappears just as quickly, like a comet that's shot through the kitchen—minus the dazzling tail, or anything else that dazzles, and there goes the mood.

"Whatever you do, don't take him seriously," Sally says. "He's such a prankster."

There are words I could use to describe Hamilton Andrews. Prankster doesn't make the list.

The washing machine stops its spin cycle. I push myself up from the table and unload the sheets into the laundry basket. I add my blouses and shorts to the basket, but my personals are going upstairs. "I'll be down in a minute," I say, then see Anya watching me. "Want to come?"

She's on her feet in a flash and follows me up the narrow stairway. "This is your room?" she asks when we get there. I nod. She seems to approve. I hang my bras and panties and sleepwear over the rail of my bed and click on the fan. They'll be dry in no time in this heat. Anya watches me, then giggles behind an open hand.

She's found the photo on my dresser of Johnnie and me. She picks it up and holds it like a treasure. "This is you?"

"With hair."

"Is beautiful. Why you"—she makes clipping motions with her fingers—"make short?"

I realize she didn't understand much of the conversation downstairs. "I thought it would be easier to care for." I say this slowly, watching for understanding.

"Ah," she says. "This is sister?"

"Yes, that's Johnnie. She's beautiful, yes?"

"Oh, yes. Very beautiful."

I half turn toward the open door when I hear a faint thud in the hallway, but all is quiet again.

"You both are beautiful."

"Thank you, Anya." I give her a one-armed hug. "I guess we better hang out those sheets. And then I'd like to take you for a treat.

"Treat?"

"For all the help."

"Oh, no, that is not—"

"Yes, it is. And you'll love it." I hope. The café a few blocks away should have what I'm craving.

———————————

The waitress gives me a confused look when Anya translates our order, but then Anya is just as confused. "Root. Beer. Float." I say it again, slowly, as if that'll make a difference. There's still no comprehension from either Anya or the waitress. "You have ice cream?" I ask. Anya translates.

"*Da.*"

"And root beer?"

"Root beer?" They both look perplexed, and I'm afraid my surprise isn't going to be what I hoped it would be. "Soda pop?"

"Soda pop. *Da, da.*"

"Root beer soda pop?"

Here come the frowns and we're back to square one.

"Root beer soda pop." The waitress mimics my words, then holds up a finger. "*Unul minute.*"

"One minute," Anya says, though I've gotten it.

True to her word, the waitress returns with a man I'm assuming is the owner of the café, or at least the manager. She says something to him in Romanian, but I clearly hear *root beer* in the mix.

"Root beer soda pop," I repeat, with high expectations.

But he shakes his head. "*Nu, nu* root beer." Then his face brightens. "Beer. Beer? Budweiser? *Da?*"

"Budweiser? No, no," I say emphatically. "Not Budweiser." Oh man, just the idea gives my stomach a tumble. Hmm. "Pepsi?" I ask, hoping, though even I know a Pepsi float is a distant second to a root beer float. Still, desperate times and all that.

The man shakes his head again. "*Nu, nu.* Ah, Coca-Cola?" The rest of what he says is lost on me.

I deflate like the rubber raft Kari and I once tried to navigate down the Stanislaus River, but hey, when in Rome . . . "Coca-Cola. *Da.*" I hold up two fingers. "*Doi.* And ice cream. Vanilla. *Doi.*" I'm afraid a fountain glass is too much to hope for.

One little scoop of ice cream comes in each of our dishes, and I didn't think to ask them to hold the ice in the Coca-Colas. But unlike at home, there aren't many cubes to deal with. The waitress smiles, and I know she's pleased with her accomplishment. But there's one more thing. "Two empty glasses," I say to Anya. She doesn't understand why I want two empty glasses, but she translates it just the same. The waitress eyes me narrowly, as if wondering what sort of experiment I'm about to conduct on her table, but she complies.

And then, finally, we have everything I need for our Coca-Cola floats. I spoon the ice cream into the glasses, ignoring the strange looks this gets me. Then I spoon the ice out of our Coke glasses and put the cubes in the empty bowls. Now comes the tricky part. Pouring quickly to keep from dribbling all over the tablecloth, I douse the ice cream with the soda. Of course it begins to fizz as if the concoction will soon erupt. Anya pushes back in her chair, but when she sees I'm not alarmed she leans in for a closer look, and laughs when the fizz hits her nose. All the patrons are watching us now, laughing and pointing. When the fizz subsides, we're left with one little ball of ice cream each bobbing in our drinks. But I pick up my spoon and dig in. Anya follows my lead. The smile she flashes after that first bite is worth what we went through to achieve it, but man, what I wouldn't give for one single bottle of Dad's Old Fashioned Root Beer right now.

"Good, *da*?"

"*Da*!"

We part ways at the corner that leads to her house at half past one. She's due home to work at her own chores. It's been a productive day, and fun this last half hour. The only thing left, besides bringing in that last load of laundry, is my Sunday school lesson. Saturday is the only day we have dinner at what I consider the traditional time, and I should have it done by then.

I'm folding clothes right off the line, thankful for a bit of breeze that cools the sweat on my face. I'm trying to keep the sheet I'm folding off the bare ground, and just barely succeeding. My thoughts are on portions of my conversation with Anya, portions that reveal the depth of the heart and soul of my little student. I've been much too lackadaisical about my faith, methinks. In fact, there's not a doubt in my mind. The question is, what do I plan to do about it?

"You might have said Johnnie's your sister."

I'm so startled at Andy's voice coming out of nowhere that I lose my stance, and there goes the sheet. Dang. But that explains the thud I heard earlier. "So you *were* listening the other night."

He tugs his boxers off the line, the blue plaid ones, then his jeans. "Like I said, how could I help it?"

"Excuse me for stating the obvious, but it was the middle of the night. I thought I was having a private conversation."

"We've been over all that. You just might have said." With his laundered clothes slung over his arm he heads back to the church.

Now my temper kicks in. I drop the clothespins I'm holding into the jar, then run to catch up to him. "What's the big deal?" When he stops short, my momentum takes me three steps past him. Really, interacting with him makes me feel like a Slinky.

"Who said it's a big deal?"

"Well, obviously it is to you."

"It's just weird, having a sister named Johnnie." There's loads of accusation in the way he says it.

"It's not weird. It's short for Johanna."

"Johanna. Oh, that's right. You don't do three syllables."

"Apparently, Andy, neither do you."

He glares for a full half minute. "Thanks," he says, raising the arm with the laundered clothes. But if that's a real thank you, I'll take a nice long swig out of the classroom water jug.

"And why haven't you asked me to the coffeehouse the last two weeks?" I call to his back.

He stops and turns. "You're not very popular there."

Not pop—? "What's that supposed to mean?"

"The guys would like to draw and quarter you."

"Because?"

He raises an eyebrow.

And then I get it. "Well, is that my fault? You're the one who sent me to the corner."

"Yes, I did," he says.

"And I didn't say anything wrong to those girls."

"No, you didn't. You said nothing different than I've been saying to the guys. But now the girls know and that changes things. In a good way." His voice has lost some of its condescension and I'm not sure where to go from here. "But you asked and that's why." When he turns back to the church his blue plaid boxers fall off his arm. He scoops them up with a bare toe without missing a beat, then disappears through the open doorway.

I want to laugh, but I'm just too angry.

It's a long email I write to Kari before I've settled down enough to prepare my Sunday school lesson. The one about all that good seed.

Dang. Dang. *Dang*.

We're just about to sit down to dinner when a knock sounds at the front door. "Shall I get it?" I ask.

"Oh, would you?" Sally's got her hands full with something just out of the oven. I don't know what it is yet, but it smells delicious.

When I get to the door Clark has beat me to it. Anya's mother stands on the other side of the screen. She holds the hand of a boy I'm assuming is Victor. Every motion of her body apologizes for her being here, and it's obvious where her daughter gets her shyness. "We come for Anya," she says, and I'm surprised at the strength of her English.

"Oh, certainly," Clark says. "I'll round her up for you." He turns and nearly plows me down. "Oh, oh. Sorry. Didn't know you were there." When he sees my face he stops short, then turns back to the screen door.

"Anya? She went home this afternoon," I say. "I walked her to the corner." The feeling I get whenever lightening strikes nearby starts at my scalp and the current trips down my body all the way to my toes.

Her mother isn't sure what to do with this information. "This afternoon?" she says.

"About one-thirty. Are you saying she didn't come home?"

Clark translates my question, concerned as I am that Anya's mother gets it right.

"*Nu.* Anya not come home."

Sally is with us now, wiping her hands on a dishtowel draped over her shoulder. She pushes open the screen door. "Georgeta, please come in."

Georgeta and Victor step into the room. With one hand behind her back she catches the screen and keeps it from slapping against the jamb. With the other hand she pulls Victor tightly against her skirt.

"Now, what's this?" Sally says. "You're looking for Anya?"

Georgeta nods, her eyes wide with worry. "*Da.*"

Sally turns to me. "Aria?"

"I left her about one-thirty," I say again to Georgeta. "At the corner near your house. At least Anya said it was near your house." I begin to feel like I'm trapped in a parent's nightmare, the one where they forget where they put the baby. "Does she have a friend nearby where she might have stopped?"

For four hours? That's the unspoken question that hangs in the air.

Sally interprets even as Georgeta shakes her head. "*Nu.* No friend. From here she come home to work." She says something to Sally in Romanian, a repeat of what she's just said in English, I sense. Sally nods.

"Did Anya say she was going right home?" Clark asks.

My shrug is empty and helpless. "I assumed so."

He gives Sally a quick nod. "I'll get Andy. We'll check the neighborhood."

"Please, Georgeta, come sit."

Georgeta pulls Victor closer and inches back toward the screen. "I look too."

That's exactly what I'd do in her place. In fact, it's what I plan to do myself. "I'll help."

I trade my flip-flops for tennis shoes, then trot the few blocks to the corner where I left Anya four hours before. Clark and Andy are right behind me. "Here," I say, stopping at the spot. I rest my hands on my knees and pull in a few deep breaths. My heart is pounding, and not just from the sprint. There's a dread that leaves me cold in the hot July sun. "Right here."

"I'll start over there." Andy lopes across the street and knocks on the front door of the corner house. Clark has done the same thing to the house on our side of the street. I'm useless myself, restricted as I am to English, so I wait and join Clark as he goes to the next house. And the next.

We've reached the end of the street, two houses beyond the house where Anya lives. No one has seen the girl. My prayers are desperate and unceasing. I fight back tears, because if I fall apart I'll feel so silly when at last we find she's indeed spent the afternoon with a friend. Not like her to be so irresponsible, I know, but she's only twelve after all.

"I'll look at Sonja's," Sally says. Sonja, at ten, is the next oldest girl in our school.

"I'll come," I say, because I don't know what else to do. *How are your language skills coming*? Andy's words play over and over in my head, and I see how foolishly unequipped I am at the moment, and the moment is what matters like never before.

In thirty minutes' time we've checked the homes of all the kids in our school. Several church members, including Anya's father, have joined in the search.

Two hours later we gather at the Moravec home. There are more people than space in the little house, and several of our group mill around in the front yard, waiting for further instructions. Georgeta frequently uses the end of her *basma* to wipe her eyes as the women do their best to encourage her. Poor Victor seems not to understand what all the trouble is about. Anya has been missing now for six hours. We're reluctant to use that term, *missing*, because it has darker connotations than simply being late for dinner. But we're not fooling anyone, including ourselves. Anya is indeed missing. Following Clark's advice, Mr. Moravec calls the local *politia*.

Georgeta Moravec slumps in a chair, flanked by women from our church. Her hands are balled at her eyes and she weeps without sound, but now and again a pitiful wail escapes, like a whistle barely blown. The women take turns kneeling beside Georgeta's chair, pulling her head to their breasts, kneading her hands, wiping her face with fingers that do not end in acrylic nails, that have never had a manicure or hot wax treatment to tender up the skin, that anyone in my circle of friends would hide with shame. But they're hands bursting with love. Hands like Jesus' hands.

I'd never noticed before, but I see now that just beneath the surface of Georgeta's unadorned features resides the beauty so conspicuous in the face of her daughter. Georgeta's lips, though not so soft and pink as Anya's, are as full and as beautifully shaped. Her eyes, void now understandably of the sparkle contained in Anya's the last time I saw her, are the pattern for her daughter's. Where I'd seen only plainness and sobriety before, I look deeper now and find the beauty I've overlooked, a beauty I've overlooked in all the women here. How arrogant I feel, how vain.

Each woman cries with Georgeta, their tears mingling as if in a bloodless blood-sisters ceremony. Like the one Kari and I performed years ago under a walnut tree at the back of the compound, using Mam's little embroidery scissors—the sharpest thing we could—

With a glance at Georgeta I reclaim my thoughts, ashamed of the silly rabbit trail they've taken me on at such a time. *God, oh God, I'm sorry*.

Just then the—I'm not sure what to call him, sheriff, constable, or what—arrives, and after a brief explanation from Clark and Mr. Moravec, I'm questioned for thirty minutes or more, the process extended by the fact that everything has to be translated. I tell them about the Coca Cola float, and exactly where I last saw Anya. I try to remember our parting words and gasp back a sob as I see Anya in my mind, smiling and waving as she turns toward home. She's wearing a yellow top and blue shorts, I say. Tennis shoes, no socks. But that won't help us find her. There's one who sees, though, and he's the one I want to talk to right now. When finally we're through, I step outside and find a solitary place on the side of the house.

"'An ever present help in time of trouble'," I recite. "That's what you said. An ever present help. And this is the time of trouble. Father, please." My heart swells and tears too long delayed fall onto my knees as I crouch on the grassless earth. I beg. I bargain, with all that I have, all that I am. I cash in my chip from John fifteen, because when would I ever need it more? "Do whatever you want with me," I say, because how will I live with this? This is my fault. "Just bring her home. Safe, Lord. Please."

A hand is on my shoulder. I turn and look into eyes filled with compassion, then bow my head and brace as another wave of emotion hits. Sally rests her hand on my back and waits as my tears fall on the dusty ground and leave little pools that are slowly sucked up by the earth. Finally I wipe my eyes on the sleeves of my blouse and wish for something with which to blow my nose. As if on cue, Sally reaches into the pocket of her jumper and hands me a tissue.

"'The Lord is full of compassion and mercy'," she quotes. Her eyes are closed and her face reflects how deeply she believes this. "Those are not just words, Aria, they're truth. God is not a despot we have to bargain one life for another with. That trade was already made, long ago."

I know this in my head, but my heart doesn't get it. It never has. "It's my fault," I say. And God knows it.

"What? No." Sally shakes her head. "No."

"I should have taken her all the way home. I never should have left her."

"No, Aria, if it's anyone's fault, it's mine. I told you it's safe here, when in truth there isn't an inch of this world that's safe. Not really. Not for innocence."

Another wave of panic hits and the tears just won't stop. "We have to find her. God, please, we have to find her."

"I'm staying here with Georgeta, but Clark, Andy, some of the others, are going back to the church to pray. You should go."

"I don't know." My knees protest as I stand. "If she comes home . . . I mean, if they . . . I'd like to . . . oh, Sally, I feel so helpless." The tissue is barely of use at this point.

"I'll let you know the moment anything changes."

Just then Clark comes around the corner. He motions with his head for Sally to join him. I don't like the look on his face.

"What? What have you heard?"

He looks away, then says, "Three other girls are missing. All about Anya's age."

Fourteen

The prayer vigil lasts all night. Somewhere around one A.M., I slip away and call home. Celie answers and knows right away something is wrong. "Ree? Baby, what is it?"

I break at the sound of her voice, unable to speak. I know my silence prolongs her distress, but I can't get a word out, can't catch a breath. Celie talks to someone there with her, then Dad's firm voice comes across the line. "Aria. What's wrong?"

I gasp, and finally my lungs fill with air. "Anya," I say. "Someone's taken her."

They know about Anya from my emails and phone calls. They don't yet know about her missionary heart. I've only just learned that myself.

"What do you mean, taken?" Dad says, then Celie's there too.

"Ree? What's this?"

"Anya's been stolen. And three others." I don't need to say more, because I've also told them about Hope House.

"Dear God," Celie says.

"We're praying here and I want you to pray."

"Of course. We will. All of us."

"The church too."

"I'll take care of it," Celie says. And then her words become a prayer. The words are so simple, come so easily, as if God's right there in the room with her, like best friends hanging out. Well, I know for a fact they are. But how on earth does that happen? How?

There's no bargaining as Celie prays, just pure supplication with honest expectation. The fear that pounds me from head to toe isn't quite so intense when I hang up.

Downstairs, I find Andy in the kitchen making coffee. I know from the stop I made in the bathroom how awful I look. My eyes are fire red, and the skin underneath is swollen and raw. My nose is nearly as red as my eyes and won't stop dripping, and my upper lip looks like I took one for the team. But I don't care. Any embarrassment I might have felt seeps away at the softness in Andy's face. Without its intensity it's a different face.

"I called home to ask—" My voice breaks, and I wait, but here I go again. I don't know that I've ever cried so many tears.

Andy nods his understanding, then opens cupboard doors looking for something. "Styrofoam cups?" he finally asks. "I'm out of my element."

"Here," I say, and get a stack out of the far cupboard. I grab a paper napkin and dab my eyes. "I'll get the milk and sugar if you want to get the coffee." I see he's filled two thermoses besides the full carafe.

He nods, clamps one thermos under each arm, then picks up the pot full of coffee. He takes a step toward the kitchen door, then stops and turns to me. "She walked to and from school by herself every day. It could have happened then as easily as now."

I know what he's saying and it touches me. Even so, I start to argue, start to say it didn't happen on her way to or from school. It happened because of my carelessness. But the look on his face stops me. So what I say instead is, "Thank you." The words come out as broken as I feel. I'm dripping from eyes and nose. "I'll catch up."

I hear the crunch of his shoes on the gravel, but this time it doesn't have the same grating effect as the feedback we sometimes hear at church back home when the worship band is getting ready to play. I dab again and fear I'll never stop crying.

_____

The rising sun spreads its rays on the horizon like the open arms of God long before I see the yellow ball. We've prayed through the night, Clark, Andy, myself, and a handful of men from the church. The women are home keeping watch over their own daughters and sons. The fine veneer of safety they've existed in for who knows how long has been grossly shattered in the past eighteen hours. From here on out the children of Leoccesni will be kept on a mighty short tether.

I've never spent a whole night in prayer before now, never knew I could. It taught me a lot about prayer. For one thing, there are as many styles of prayer as there are people. There couldn't have been a better object lesson for me to finally realize that prayer is simply talking to God. I've heard that all my life, but I'd always think: there's talking, and then there's talking. I mean, who wouldn't rather listen to a great communicator over a novice? Not God, I used to think.

For another thing, there's no right posture, no right approach. There were some in our group who knelt at a pew and stayed that way throughout the long night. Others paced as they prayed, the way I imagine expectant fathers used to do before birthing rooms were open to the entire family and any number of friends. Andy mostly prayed with his guitar. If anything could have soothed our ravaged souls, it was his playing. But it wasn't for our benefit he played. It was his personal outpouring of prayer and supplication to God. We just got to listen in.

For myself, I sat on the altar, offering whatever pitiful part of me God might want. My prayer consisted of _please, God_, and hardly anything else. It's all I could think to say. Please keep them safe, please bring them back, please let this not be real. Please, God, oh please. If there's such a thing in heaven as receiving prayers in their order of ascent, like, say, calls to a support center, I hope mine get there last of our little group, for in my opinion, mine have the least to offer.

As long as the night was for us, it rips my soul to shreds to think what the hours have been for Anya and the other abducted girls. Our fear can be nothing compared to theirs. Not even Georgeta's. In comparison, we're spectators of the nightmare, while they're living it in 3-D.

I can hardly pull myself away from my little upstairs window. From here I can see nearly to the end of our road in the direction of Anya's house. I keep hoping for a messenger who'll come with the news we all want to hear. There are still remote places in the world where runners carry important news from village to village. All we need is one. But I can't hold out another minute, I'm so tired. I push aside my finished Sunday school lesson that will not be taught this day, and drop onto my bed. With the whirr of the box fan filling my ears, I fall gratefully into sleep.

The sound of the phone ringing downstairs coaxes me awake. A glance at the clock shows I've slept for several hours. I force myself to a sitting position and run my hand through my hair. It's wet from perspiration, and there's a pillow crease in my cheek so deep I can feel it when I run my finger over it. Feeling as I did my first Sunday here, so groggy I stagger like a drunkard, I make my way downstairs. Twice my foot slips on the narrow treads. I could easily maim or kill myself before I reach the landing, but I press on. There might be news. Clark stands at the phone in the kitchen, Sally at his side. There's no sign of Andy.

"Aria." Sally holds out an arm to me and I move in for her to curl it around me. We wait for Clark to say something revealing, but he only listens. Then, with a "*Da*, yes," he hangs up.

"That was the *politia*," he says. "A brother of one of the girls who's missing saw a van near his house late yesterday morning. It was just there a short while, so he didn't think anything of it."

"What kind of van?" Sally asks.

"Not like ours. A worker van. Plain. No lettering."

"The kind without windows?" I ask. Just right for hiding stolen girls in?

Clark nods.

The panic rises with a feeling that makes me fear I'll throw up. "What do we do? How do we find it?"

"They'll want to get across the nearest border. Who knows where they'll go from there?"

"But how do we find it?" I say again.

"They'll do the equivalent of an APB," Clark says. "Hopefully, someone in law enforcement will see the vehicle."

"What if it already crossed the border?"

"It most probably has," Sally says. "And with how many other girls?" Her voice sounds as weary as my own.

"It will be up to the authorities wherever it is to find it. But you do realize," Clark says, "the odds are not in our favor."

"And yet, with God . . ." Sally doesn't have to finish the thought for us to get her meaning.

Fifteen

It's Tuesday morning and Anya is still missing. Her mother and father are immersed in their grief, but they've not been left alone in their crisis. Women from the church have provided meals for the family, helped with Victor, prayed with the family, and cried with them too. Sally and I have taken our turn as well, but today the team comes from Wisconsin, and we have them to focus on for the next seven days. I will be allowed to work on Hope House, and I'm grateful. Not that I relish the thought of hard labor in the hot Moldovan sun. But more than anyone else on the work crew—save Clark and Andy, perhaps—every ounce of energy I expend will come straight from the heart.

It's a two-hour drive to the airport. Before Saturday, this might have been an excursion to relish. I could have tagged along with Clark and Sally for some shopping and sightseeing before meeting the team at the airport, but today it will be nothing more than a drive there and back. This is not a time for pleasure.

Accordingly, I'll stay behind and not take up space in the van. With nine passengers and luggage for seven, that space is valuable, though

I'll bet none of them has more than one small bag and a carry-on.

"Aria, please, go in my place," Sally coaxes. "See the country. You slept much of the way here the day you arrived. Besides, I've plenty to do," she adds, as if that will win her argument. But Clark and I have talked this over. Sally has hardly stopped or slept since Saturday. The four hours of travel will provide a much needed rest for her, maybe even a good long nap on the way to the airport.

"You should greet the team," I say, "not me."

"But I've dinner to prepare."

"Which I can do most ably." I don't believe that for a minute, not in comparison to Sally's cooking, but I'll never let on.

Sally doesn't say what she's thinking, that she wants to make a good first impression on our guests from Wisconsin. The original plan was to disperse the men among five families in the church, four if one of the guys could room with Andy. But now, so many of the families are helping the Moravecs, that Clark and Sally don't want to burden them further. So we'll host the whole team for the entire week. We've set up a barracks of sorts in the church for the men, with cots and fans. The two women, as planned, will share a room upstairs on my floor. Our poor little shower doesn't know what it's in for. Neither does the team, for that matter.

But back to dinner. "I can fry chicken," I say. Because I've watched Celie, whose fried chicken is even better than Dad's, and really, how hard can it be? "And boil red beans with onions and bacon as good as any you've ever eaten. I can steam vegetables. And make sweet tea." I add that last part as if it's the thing that'll seal the deal.

"Oh. Well," Sally says. "The chicken is thawed. I was going to roast it, but fried sounds wonderful. You're sure?"

"Absolutely."

"We may have some beans in the pantry, but if not—"

"I'll take care of it. Really."

And still she frets. "It's a lot to do."

Clark takes her hand and gives a tug. "Sally, come on now. We have to go. The plane arrives at ten-thirty and it's already after eight."

"Don't worry," I say, as I see them to the door. "I'll have everything ready when you get back."

There are purple circles under Sally's eyes, and I know this is the right thing to do. But I can't help think, as Opa would say, I've grabbed the stick from the big dogs. Well, all I can do now is run with it.

So. What would Celie do? That's my catchphrase as I watch the van turn the corner at the end of the road. I decide to worry about that later. For now, I'll wash up our cereal bowls. That done, I do all the other little things Sally would do. If I were home I'd cut some daylilies out of the garden. But I'm not home, and fresh flowers are hard to come by in our neighborhood.

When I've done all I can do to make the house ready for our guests I sit down with a glass of weak sun tea and call home. It's Celie I want to talk to, and Celie who answers.

"Have they found that precious girl?" That's the first thing she asks.

How I wish I could say yes. "There's not been a word from anyone. Please, please keep praying."

"We haven't stopped, Aria. You know we won't."

There's not much news from home, but everyone's fine, and that's news enough. I get down to the reason for the call. "There's a team coming from Wisconsin today to work on Hope House. The Mitchells have gone to the airport and I've volunteered to cook dinner."

"Dinner. Well."

Oh, the volumes that are spoken between those two little words. I'd break out laughing if life weren't so terribly serious just now. "I can do this, Celie, but you have to tell me how."

"Electric skillet or cast iron?" she asks.

I've washed enough pots and pans here to know the answer to that. "There are two electric skillets and lots of cast iron."

"Cast iron's the best, but electric skillet's the easiest for a newbie. I'd say go for the easiest this time around."

"My thoughts, too." I reach for Sally's notepad and pencil. "Okay, shoot."

I write down her instructions, word for word, for the chicken, the beans, and even the tea. It doesn't sound so hard, but I have sense enough to know that if I think I can come even close to Celie's fried chicken on my first try—or fiftieth, for that matter—it's only me I'm fooling.

"And the thing about fried chicken," she adds as a footnote, "is that it's good hot or cold. Do your best to time it, but if you have to go one way or the other, have it ready sooner rather than later."

"Got it." I look over the notepad before signing off, and hope I can read what I've scratched on the pad.

"Ree? I'm really proud of you."

"Thanks, but don't get ahead of yourself."

And now I'm ready to start. Sally's right, there are two pounds of red beans in the pantry. I find a colander and rinse them, then pour them into a large pot and cover them with water. I add salt for now. I'll add the other seasonings later. I put the lid on the pot, then leave them to soak for an hour. This isn't so hard. My confidence soars.

"The chicken's in the fridge." That's the last thing Sally said on her way to the van, besides "thank you." I tug open the door.

"Uh oh." The chicken's in the fridge all right. Three of them, just like Sally said. But they don't look anything like the chickens they have back home. They're . . . connected. "So now what?"

"You'll have to cut them," Celie says when I call back.

Right then I lose my swagger. "Cut them?"

"In pieces. You know, legs, thighs, wings. Pieces, Ree."

I inspect the birds that are now in the sink. "Yes, but how?"

She's quiet a moment. "Is there anyone there who can help?"

"Only me."

"Okay." I can practically see her roll up her sleeves. "You're going to start with the leg and thigh sections. Oh, but first, there's a cavity, baby." She eases up on that bit of information in a voice as soft as if she's trying to re-cage a canary.

"Cavity?"

"Just reach in and pull out whatever you find."

"Whatever I find? Like what?" Suddenly, all I can think of is the snake in the water jug.

"We'll get to that. For now, just pull it out and set it aside. Here at home it's in a little sack. I don't know about there." She waits a moment. "Did you find it?"

I did, and nearly scald my hand trying to rinse it off. "There wasn't a sack."

"Ah, yes. Sorry, Ree." It's hard to believe her when she doesn't even try to hide the laugh. "The chickens probably didn't come from Raleys."

"I thought this stuff"—I look at the commingled blob in the sink—"only came with turkeys."

"No, they pretty much come with all manner of fowl."

"And people eat them?"

"Not all people, but I bet they do there. Back to the thighs. You're going to cut them away from the body of the bird. Do you have a sharp knife?"

"I'll soon find out," I mumble.

"You need a sharp knife."

I feel like a med student taking an on-line course in surgery. *On-line. Hey, maybe . . .* "Celie, I'll call you back. Don't you dare go anywhere."

Sure enough, I find a site that shows me how to cut a chicken, and showing is exactly what I want. Now, I don't feel as if I'm, ha, stabbing in the dark. If I do this right I should end up with eight pieces per chicken. Twenty-four pieces total for the dinner table. That should be about right, because who doesn't love leftover fried chicken?

Okay. I'm poised to do this. I insert the tip of the knife at the point where I should sever the thigh from the body. That thought alone is enough to make me gag, but add to it the goose-pimply skin that slides around like the loose skin on a puppy, and I soon realize there's no way I can do this. I'm used to freeze-dried, boneless, skinless chicken breasts, someone else has cooked, and they're nothing like the birds laid out before me. I lay the knife on the counter and wonder how the team will feel about red beans and egg salad sandwiches. With pickles.

I'm desperate. I know that because I'm crunching my way across the gravel to the church. I open the door. "Hello?"

"Back here," Andy calls. "Oh, hey," he says when I poke my head around the corner that leads to his room. He sets his guitar aside and slides a pencil behind his ear.

"Am I bothering you?" *I can come back*, I start to say, but catch myself. That's not even remotely possible. I need help and I need it now.

"Nah. What's up?"

"I have a really huge favor to ask."

His left eyebrow shoots up, and he leans back on one elbow. "Yeah?"

And I wouldn't be here at all if I weren't such a coward. "I volunteered to cook dinner today and—"

The eyebrow takes another hike and I lose my concentration. "And?" he prompts.

"Have you ever dissected a chicken?"

"A chicken. Don't they usually do that to frogs?"

I ignore his stab at humor. "I have to cut up three chickens and I don't know where to begin. Well, I know *where* to begin, right where the thigh connects to the body. I just don't know how."

He studies me for a minute, then all of a sudden he laughs. "You're joking, right?"

"It's that or egg salad."

The look that crosses Andy's face says he's had the egg salad. He's on his feet in an instant, and we're crunching back across the gravel to the parsonage.

"There," I say, and point to the chickens in the sink as if they were a body I thought he should know about. "The website shows that, first, you cut off the leg and the thigh, about here—" I show him the place I think he should begin, then stop. "What?"

"You saw this on a website?"

"It's faster than looking for Sally's cookbooks, which may still be in Nebraska for all I know. The internet's just *there*." He gives a nod and I relax the tiniest bit. "You do that on both sides. Then you cut the legs from the thighs." It all sounds so obscene as I say it.

Andy blows out a breath. "You need a hole dug, I'm your man. But this . . ." He shakes his head and turns to leave.

"Wait! Andy, please. I can't do this alone."

He hesitates, but I'm not convinced he'll stay. "Isn't there some way to cook them whole?"

"Not in a skillet, and I promised fried chicken. I could print out a diagram." I know just how desperate that sounds. "Can't you please try?"

He picks up the knife as if he's never seen one before, places the blade where I show him, and begins to saw back and forth. Disgustingly, the pimply skin moves with the motion of the blade. The look Andy gives me says he too is used to the boneless, skinless variety. He tries again, putting more muscle into his sawing. The knife blade immediately locks up, stuck in the bone.

"I think we missed the joint," I say. I can almost hear Andy's thoughts as his eyebrow goes up again. *We*? "Maybe if you—"

He holds up a hand to silence me, then frees the knife. He finds the joint and tries again. It looks like we are about to sever our first thigh from the carcass, and while that is a small victory in light of what's left to do, it's a victory nonetheless. I want to cheer. But no, the knife suddenly becomes lodged again. Evidently there are bones everywhere.

Andy tugs the knife out of whatever has gripped it and lays it on the counter. "I have an idea. I'll be back." Without the slightest indication of what his idea is, he jogs out of the kitchen.

Whatever it is, I'm all for it.

While I wait, I put the beans on the stove and light the fire under the pot. Then I put water on to boil for the sweet tea. Mam would add loose leaf tea if she were here, but all I have is teabags. I drop six in and wait for the water to boil. All the while I'm watching the clock, wondering *where is he*? I've removed the teabags from the pot and am stirring in the sugar when Andy finally returns. Janic Rotaru is with him.

I say hello, but this has certainly caught me off guard. We have work to do!

Andy says something to Janic in Romanian, then hands him the knife. Mr. Rotaru gives one firm nod then sets to work. Before my sugar is fully dissolved in the tea, one whole chicken has been cut into pieces—nine pieces at that, counting the back—and pushed aside. Janic goes to work on the second. I'm so enthralled at his handiwork I forget about my own. A hissing, sputtering noise draws my attention to the stove, where my beans are boiling over the rim of the pot. The lid dances on top as if possessed. I lift it, letting the steam escape, replace it at an angle the way I've seen Dad do, then lower the flame a bit. When I turn back to the men, Andy gives me a thumbs up and the closest thing to a smile I've seen in days. Or ever. Janic works until the third bird is severed into perfect pieces.

"Please, Andy, invite him to join us for dinner." It's the best way I can think of to thank him.

"*Nu, nu*," Janic says. The explanation is short and in Romanian, but I thank him again and again as he leaves.

"Whatever made you think to ask him for help?"

Andy shrugs. "I could have asked just about anyone in town. He happened to be the one who came to mind."

"I like how you think." I start to high five him, catch myself, then slip Sally's apron over my head and tie it in back. I give Andy a look of dismissal, thinking surely he's ready to get back to what he was doing before I interrupted him, ready to get away from me. But he pulls a chair out from the table and straddles it.

My scalp begins to itch. I prefer not to have an audience until I've perfected a thing, and I'm light years from perfection. "Thanks for rescuing me," I say, and wait. But he rests his chin on his hands. He's not going anywhere.

"All right, then," I mutter, and set to work.

I plug in both electric skillets and search the pantry for cooking oil. There's nothing that looks remotely like a bottle of Wesson. Not even olive oil. What I find is a large can of lard.

Celie, who's been expecting my call and applauds my good fortune at having Janic Rotaru on hand, assures me that lard is the absolute best thing in the world to fry chicken in.

"Then why don't you use it?" I ask.

"Because it's a heart attack in a can, sweet girl. I love you all too much for that."

Well, then. I say a prayer I don't kill anyone with my meal as I spoon several globs into the skillets, then think that Sally and Clark, at least, could use more meat on their bones, so I may be doing them a favor. By the time I've seasoned the chicken, the lard is hot and ready to go.

"I need a lunch bag," I say to Andy, as if he could actually help me find one.

"Lunch bag?"

"You know, the little brown bag that— Oh, here."

I've found exactly what I need in a drawer. I pour in two cups of flour and drop in a large, seasoned breast. I close the top, give the bag a good shake, then reach inside and pull out the perfectly flour-coated fowl. I place it just so in the skillet, and snap back my hand when the lard pops. "Whoa." I rub the three little blisters that instantly erupt and look in the utensil drawer for a pair of tongs.

I repeat the process of flouring the chicken and adding it to the skillet until there are five pieces sizzling in the pan. I turn and give Andy a smug little smile, thinking *this is a breeze*, and drop the next piece of chicken into the bag. "Nothing to it," I say, exactly as the bottom of the bag breaks open and a chicken leg splats on the floor. A snow flurry of flour coats my legs and feet and everything else around me.

"Five second rule," Andy says. He reaches over to pick up the leg, and doesn't even try to hide his amusement.

"Funny." I take the leg and drop it in the sink. I'll rinse and re-season it after I clean up my mess.

Andy heads for the screen door. "Later."

I swear he just waited around for something like this to happen.

_____

I know you have to keep the beans covered with water as they cook, but I forget to check until the smell alerts me. They're only slightly scorched. I add more water and a bit more salt. Now they taste only slightly scorched, and salty. I know about an old trick of Dad's, so I peel and quarter a potato and add it to the pot. That will at least absorb the extra salt. There's nothing I can do about the scorching, unless I throw them out and start over. One glance at the clock tells me there's not time for that.

"Lord? Please?" Nothing else is necessary. He knows what I mean.

I've turned the chicken until all the pieces are golden brown and crispy. I'm completely impressed with myself. Now the vegetables.

I feel like a master juggler as I stir the beans, turn the chicken, and slice squashes, onions, mushrooms, and bell peppers. Things are nicely up in the air, to stick with my juggling theme, until my nose detects another problem. I lift the lid on the beans and see plenty of juice in the pot. Dang, it's the chicken. One skillet is cooking hotter than the other, don't ask me how that happens, so one side of the chicken in that pan is a bit beyond golden grown. Quite a bit beyond.

I glance at the clock again. If the flight was on time and nothing hindered their progress, Clark and Sally should be here soon with our guests. I recall that Celie said better to have the chicken done too soon than too late, so I prepare a platter with paper napkins, since there are no paper towels to drain the extra lard, and pile all the chicken on it. It's a lovely golden brown mountain, if you don't consider the extra-done parts, which I've hidden on the bottom. The beans are simmering nicely, minus the potato, which did its job, and the vegetables are ready to steam the minute everyone gets here. The tea is chilling in the fridge, and I feel like I've conquered the world.

I think it's especially nice Sally did the baking the day before, so I don't have to worry about dessert.

Andy's back to check on my progress. I detect a hint of disappointment that I've managed so well without him.

"I was just coming to get you. Can you help me extend the table?"

Andy pulls one end as I pull the other, and we fit in the extra leaf. I retrieve the tablecloth Sally uses on Sundays, and whip it over the table. It settles over the old wood like snow over the Alps.

Back in the kitchen Andy's inspecting my three little globs in the sink. "What about these?"

I wrinkle my nose. "What about them?"

"Sally cooks them too."

"Really?" I was afraid of that. I use the end of the knife to separate the mass. Something purplish-brown quivers and I think *nope, can't do it*. "Really?" I say again.

"At least do the gizzards. Clark likes those."

I look at Andy as if he's asked me to read hieroglyphics without the Rosetta Stone. "And which piece might that be?"

He uses his finger to check through what is most certainly the heart, liver, kidneys—do they cook kidneys?—and whatever else is in the sink to try and locate the gizzards. Finally, he pushes something roundish to the side. "I think that's it."

"Yeah?" I wouldn't know a gizzard from a gall bladder.

"I think. There should be three. Right?"

"You're asking me?" I study the poor birds' innards with mounting reluctance. "Maybe we better not chance it."

Andy shrugs. "Whatever."

I don't like the tone he's taken. "Clark really likes these?"

"He always eats them."

"Well, then." I find two other pieces that look like this one and discard the remaining organs.

Andy has the hands of a musician, which is probably one of the reasons he plays so well. A thought suddenly hits me. "Were you writing a song back there?" I nod toward the church. "When I interrupted you?"

The question seems to surprise him. "I'm working on something."

"Really? Worship or secular?"

He lifts one shoulder. "Not sure yet."

"Ah," I say, but I'm really thinking, how can you not know? "Have you written other songs?"

"A few."

Honestly, talking with Andy is like pulling taffy. Let up just a bit and you're snapped back to where you started. "Have I heard any of them?"

He shakes his head. "Nah."

"I'd like to."

"Does your Opa write songs?" He says Opa's name like he's indulging a dim-witted child.

"Yes," I say firmly. "And he plays like no one you ever heard."

"I've heard some good guitar players."

"Did they make you cry?"

He gives me a roll of the eyes. "No."

"Then you haven't heard the best." I turn back to the gizzards. At least I think they're gizzards. "Who in the world was the first person to try these?"

"I always wonder," Andy says. I can't tell, but I think he's making fun of me again.

At least they appear to be the least slimy of the organs. I drop all three of them into the flour, give them a good shake, reheat the skillet, then pull them out of the bag with tongs like a doctor gripping snipped adenoids. These gizzards, if that's indeed what they are, don't look the least bit appetizing, but I'm doing this for Clark. They're half cooked when I realize I forgot the seasoning. I shake some salt, pepper and garlic powder over them and hope it sticks.

I've just set the table when I hear the crunch of tires on gravel. They're here. Suddenly I feel as nervous as a girl on her first date. I don't know whether to go out and greet them or fill the glasses with ice. Oh, yeah, the veggies. I turn the fire under the pot and repeat three times, "Do not forget, do Not forget, DO NOT FORGET," because there's only a small amount of water in the pot for steam.

I stand behind the cover of the screen door and take my first look at our team. The guys are exactly what you'd expect: construction type guys in their thirties, forties, and one looks to be somewhere between Dad and Opa's age, the leader I suspect. But the girls. Well. Andy's just come through the church door, and judging by the look on his face they're not what he expected either. He actually smiles and I can practically see his pulse pounding in his neck from here.

Sally sees me at the door and calls to me. "Aria. Darling, come meet our guests."

I step out into the hot sunshine and stop five feet short of the group. I nod and smile as the introductions are made: James, Matt, Phil, Tom and Pete. Counting Andy, half the disciples have come to Moldova.

"And this is Joni and Isabel."

Along with the saints.

Sally smiles with motherly pride. But that's Sally.

"Can I help?" I ask, but I was right. They each—including Barbie and Barbie—grab one small duffle bag apiece.

"This way," Sally says to the girls, while Andy leads the guys into the church to drop off their belongings. I catch him as he turns and steals a glance at Joni and Isabel. The sensation that courses through me is anything but sanctified.

The moment I enter the kitchen I remember the vegetables. Dang! There's not a drop of water left in the pot. The bottom layer is stuck to the pan, but the rest might be salvageable.

Right.

"Oh, it smells delicious in here."

Yep, that's Sally for you.

Sixteen

As Clark leads us in prayer over the food, I feel like a kindergartner showing Teacher my crayon drawing. I was way out of my league to try this. A third of the chicken has a burn strip down one side, the beans retained their scorched taste in spite of my humble prayer, and what's left of the vegetables has turned to mush. The sweet tea is a hit with all but Barbie and Barbie. They, of course, have opted for unsweetened water.

But Clark blesses the meal anyway, and smiles over the three gizzards—which indeed they are—that find their way onto his plate, as everyone else has passed on them. Sally oohs and aahs over each dish, though the only really good thing about the meal is Riya Moraru's bread. Our guests dive in with a fervor, the male contingents, that is, and I'm sure it's only because they've been on an airplane for hours with one small prepackaged meal to get them through. B & B, on the other hand, use knife and fork to cut away the crispy brown skin to get to the white meat beneath. The juice of the red beans has run into everyone's vegetables, and that's when I remember Celie always sets bowls on the table when she serves those beans. Speaking of diving, I'd be happy to jump headfirst into Janic Rotaru's well at this point.

"Aria," Sally says, "you've outdone yourself. This is wonderful."

As if she has anything to compare it to. I burn with embarrassment at what I feel is a compliment undeserved, though I know she doesn't mean it as such.

"Aria?" the blonde Barbie says. She's poised with a chunk of chicken breast on the tines of her fork. "What a beautiful name." Her smile is a real invitation to friendship.

I stammer out a thank you. Dang, dang, dang! Once again I've judged according to appearance, like a high school girl hating the cheerleaders because they're beautiful. I strongly begin to feel Joni and Isabel are not at all what I deemed them to be in the five full minutes I've known them.

"Isn't it though?" Sally's taken a dark-striped thigh and seems to be enjoying it immensely.

I swallow back a surge of emotion at the graciousness of my tablemates, and take my first bite of food. It's not bad, I decide. Not great either. Not like Celie's fried chicken. I can't wait for the team to get a taste of Sally's cooking—minus the egg salad—because it's so much better than mine. I don't want them to think this is as good as it gets. I catch Andy studying me, though I can't begin to read his expression. The moment my eyes meet his, he turns back to his food and dunks a slice of bread into his beans.

"Where are you all from?" I ask, then wish I'd asked something else, because I remember now Sally already told me. Wisconsin.

"Wisconsin," one of the guys says. Tom, I think.

"Eau Claire," Isabel adds.

"Tom is Isabel's father," Sally says, and instantly the makeup of the team makes sense. "And Joni is Isabel's best friend."

There's something oddly familiar about Joni, now that I get a good look at her. It's like I've seen her before—though I know that's impossible—but it's one of those out-of-context situations, you know, where she could be the receptionist at the dentist's office you've visited all your life. But if you see her outside the dentist's office, well, you just can't put it together. That's how I feel, looking at her.

"Since first grade," Joni says. I can just see them, two little beauties with ponytails and no front teeth, pinky swearing to be best friends forever. Like Kari and me. "And now we've both just finished our second year of college."

"We've been so looking forward to coming. Dad's promised me a trip since I was sixteen."

"None of the places we've been were safe enough for you girls." Tom sends Isabel a wink.

My heart does a somersault as I think of Anya. Leoccesni isn't nearly as safe as it was before Saturday. "You guys have worked together before?"

Tom nods and swallows a bite of bread. "Many times."

All the guys begin calling off places they've been. "Colombia."

"Zimbabwe.

"Indonesia."

"Turkey."

"But when our church heard about Hope House, I knew this was the place." Isabel's long cascade of hair ripples like a silk scarf in the breeze of the fan. Reflexively, I whip my head back to push my hair over my shoulder like I used to do, only it's not there. If anyone happened to see, they'd surely think I have a nervous tic. I better watch that. And speaking of watching, Andy can barely pull his eyes away from Isabel. I don't know why that bothers me the way it does.

"It's the perfect project," Joni says. She reaches out to touch Sally's hand. "Thank you so much for letting us come."

The gesture brings that feeling of familiarity again. "Have you ever been to California?" I ask, just as Sally says, "Oh, my dear, thank you for coming."

We laugh, the way people do when they tumble over one another with their words, but when Joni says, no, she's never been to California,

I'm left with a question mark in my head. Why do I feel I know her?

"How long have you been here and where are you from?" Isabel asks. I start to reply, then quickly press a hand to my lips when I see the question is directed at Andy.

"Eight months," he says. "I'm from Sacramento."

Sacramento? I do a double take to discover we're practically neighbors.

Sally's face beams with pride. "Andy's here on a two-year assignment. We can't tell you how invaluable he's been to us already. Right, love?"

"Never saw anyone dig a hole like Andy," Clark says, then goes back to his gizzards.

Sally's laugh is not as carefree as it was three days ago. "Andy's job description would fill a full sheet of paper. Legal size. You'll see."

"Laid much block?" Tom asks, for that's what we'll be doing, starting tomorrow.

"Built a small kitchen for a church in Honduras, and a classroom for an orphanage in Jamaica."

I do another double take. This is more than I've learned about Andy in all the weeks I've been here. That could partly be my fault for not asking the right questions, but he might have offered a thing or two on a Friday night instead of walking three steps ahead to the coffeehouse without a word of conversation.

"Aria's our school teacher. But now it's summer break, so she's my right-hand man."

I catch Andy looking at me again with that enigmatic look. I reach once more for the hair that's no longer there, feeling stripped of my identity, as if not one person here knows the real me. Right hand man. Yep, that's a good description.

———————

Our meal is finished, the table cleared, and the guys have gone across to the church to discuss tomorrow's work. Joni and Isabel are intent on helping with the cleanup, but Sally is adamant. "You girls have had a long trip and you're exhausted. You need some real sleep before the work begins. Go." She takes the dishtowel from Joni and nods toward the door that leads to the stairs. "I wish we had better accommodations for you."

"They're perfect," Joni says. "Really."

She's a peacemaker, I decide as I watch her and Isabel disappear through the doorway. Like Johnnie.

"Sweet girls," Sally says. She turns on the hot water and reaches for the dish soap.

"No you don't." I take the bottle out of her hand. "This is my mess to clean up." And a true mess it is.

"I can't leave you to do this by yourself, Aria."

"Yes, you can. I know you're dying to see Mrs. Moravec." Not for news because if there were any we'd have already heard. But to comfort her. "You go."

Sally hesitates, but I see in her eyes I'm right. "Are you sure?"

"Absolutely. Please."

The moment I'm alone the tears I've kept back all day stream down my face. I don't even try to stop them as they drip down my chin and onto my T-shirt. I haven't dared let myself think too much of Anya with so much to do today. Though she's ever on the surface of my mind and in my constant prayers, it's the chasing of the thoughts that gets me into trouble, like Alice down the rabbit hole in Wonderland. Only this is more like hell. When I let myself imagine what those girls are going through and how terrified they must be I want to scream for my inability to do something to help them. And so I cry, because it's all I can do.

My prayers have become angry and militant since our all-night vigil. Not that I'm angry with God, but I'm outraged at a world where this kind of horror occurs. What kind of monster snatches little girls from their homes and their families? What kind of monster uses them in such vile ways?

What kind of God allows it to happen?

I'm caught off guard by the thought. *It's not mine*, I say in my head. *I don't know where it came from*, but I feel as if I should do penance. I know this wasn't God's doing, nor was it his will.

Still.

I push back the thought and begin to recite the Lord's Prayer.

I feel like I've put in a full day when I climb the stairs, but it's only three in the afternoon. It's not just the heat that contributes to my exhaustion. It's that none of us has really slept since all this happened. We're lucky to grab a few hours here, a few hours there, but always the sleep is fitful. I never get past semi-consciousness into genuine sleep, and alone at night in the dark the tears flow freely.

Not a sound comes from behind the closed door next to my room. I'm pretty sure the girls are down for the count. I bid them a good night's rest as I close my own door, switch on the fan, then drop onto the bed. I want nothing more than to sink into a really deep sleep for an hour or two, though I don't expect that will happen, but first I reach for my laptop.

K: What is it about hair that matters so much to guys? You there?

I don't have to wait long for a reply.

I'M HERE. WHAT'S THIS ABOUT HAIR? AND WHAT GUY?!?

You should have stopped me.

RIGHT. LIKE I KNEW. SO WHAT'S THIS REALLY ABOUT?

Miss Wisconsin and her first runner up just arrived.

I look at the words I've typed. They're not at all fair to Isabel and Joni, who are sweet girls on a hard mission. I hit the backspace till the sentence is erased, and start over.

Our team arrived today and two lovely girls are part of it. And I do mean lovely.

AND THIS MATTERS BECAUSE . . . ?

It doesn't matter. At all. It's just that everything's so awful around here right now. I guess my thoughts are out of whack.

JOHNNIE TOLD ME ABOUT YOUR STUDENT, REE. YOU KNOW I HAVEN'T STOPPED PRAYING.

My eyes can hardly stand another bout of tears, but they come just the same. Though I try, I can't stop speculating what's happening with Anya and the others this very minute. My heart would have already imploded if I were her mother. I'm certain of that. I don't know where she gets her strength. And then I think, yes, I do. Of course I do.

Why are you online so early? Shouldn't you be getting ready for work?

WHO WAS IT THAT SAID, "AM I MY SISTER'S KEEPER?" OH, WAIT, THAT WAS BROTHER, WASN'T IT?

And the speaker had just committed murder, so your point is. . . ?

TESTY, TESTY.

Sorry, K. I need to sleep off this headache. Note: If you have a choice between cast iron and electric, don't even think about it. Cast iron.

Because as far as I know, Celie never had a burn stripe down one single piece of her chicken. Ever.

The delay between my Send and Kari's response is much longer this time and I can just about see the question mark her face has become. Finally an envelope icon appears on my Application Bar.

WE'LL GET BACK TO THIS JUST AS SOON AS I GET TO WORK. THE WHOLE HAIR THING TOO. LOVE YOU. K.

Seventeen

It's dark when I emerge from what Dad always refers to as the sleep of death. "Like Juliet in the tomb," he'd say. "There aren't any star-crossed lovers lurking around, are there?" I'd laugh as a girl at the melodramatic look on his face, and the way he'd waggle his eyebrows, and I'd say, no, not one. But for now I just try to hold my head on. The headache is not only not gone, it's ratcheted up a couple of notches. Heavy sleep during a nap always does this to me. But at least I slept. The red numbers on the alarm clock on my nightstand read 3:49. Twelve hours? No wonder I feel like Cyclops.

I tiptoe out of my bedroom and carefully make my way downstairs to the bathroom. My bladder is screaming for relief. The door creaks with a vengeance as I push it to. Why do we never remember to do something about it until the middle of the night? Do they even have WD-40 in Moldova? I clamp my eyes shut and flip on the light switch, then ease open my lids as slowly as I can. Still, the light sends a shaft of pain deep into my brain. I moan, and stagger to the toilet.

Who knew I could hold so much liquid?

The toilet could use a muffler, because to me it sounds as loud as a jumbo jet when I flush, but a minute later when it's quiet again, the sawing sound of Clark snoring assures me he at least slept through the racket. And if Sally can sleep through Clark, then maybe she's slept through the flushing too.

I go to the sink to wash my hands and splash water on my face. "Wow," I say to the mirror when I get a good look at myself. I press down on tufts of hair that shoot from my head like lemon grass, but they spring back as soon as I move my hand away. Wish I'd thought to bring my khaki brown "We're Nuts!" cap, because I sure could use it in the morning. I brush my teeth, brush them again, then stagger back up the stairs.

Here's my dilemma. I have to be up in an hour to get ready to go work with the team on Hope House. If I go back to sleep I'll have to go through waking up all over again, and who wants to do that? But have my eyelids ever been this heavy? I tell myself twelve hours of sleep ought to count for something, so I switch on the lamp by my bed and reach for my laptop. But before it even boots up I turn it off again. My Bible is on the dresser where I left it after Wednesday night Bible study almost a week ago. How irreparably things have changed in that week.

I don't read my Bible like I should, I know that. I'm not at all like Celie or Mam, whose Bibles are roadmaps of their journeys in the faith when you look at the underlined passages and the notes squeezed into the margins, Celie's with purple ink, Mam's with red. More than once I've spent an afternoon with Mam's NKJV, just reading the notes, which are like little doors that open to reveal the meaning of a passage—like an advent calendar without the chocolate. Not only that, but they reveal the heart of Mam as well. Every one of them says, *This is what matters most to me*.

Today is July tenth, so I turn to the tenth Psalm and begin to read: "Why, O Lord, do you stand far off? Why do you hide yourself in times of trouble?"

My stomach rises and falls as my thoughts bear witness to the lament of the Psalmist. *Why, God? Why?* I can't read any further than that first verse, stuck as I am on that question. Because God does seem far away. Hidden. When we need him not to be. His promise to be an ever-present help in time of trouble seems not to hold true. And yet I know God is wholly Truth. If there's a discrepancy here, it's on my part, but why can't I find an answer? How do I reconcile what I believe with what has happened?

I'm the first one downstairs after Sally, who's already made the coffee and is frying bacon for our breakfast. My hair is plastered with water and pulled back with my green plaid headband. That should keep it down.

"'Morning," I say, not nearly as chipper as I would be two hours from now, which is when I usually show up in the kitchen. Clark has crafted a schedule that will have us back home by the hottest part of the afternoon, working six to two, with a half hour for lunch stuck in the middle. "Can I help?"

Sally seems not to mind the early hour. She's her usual cheerful self. "I have breakfast under control if you'd like to start on lunch."

"Sure." I move toward the fridge.

"Let's put in the rest of your delicious chicken. Then I've made hard-boiled eggs, and there's a loaf of Riya's bread and a bag of apples. Oh, and put in lots of napkins."

"Perfect." I set to work.

Joni and Isabel enter the kitchen at the exact time the screen door opens and the men file in, with Andy in the rear.

"Sleep well?" Sally asks everyone.

I know she's sorry she doesn't have real beds for all the team, but judging by the replies, no one seems to mind. Tomorrow that could be a whole 'nother matter, as Opa would say, after laying brick for eight hours today. But I suspect the men have tolerated much worse conditions.

Sally's whipping eggs in a bowl, as scrambled will be quicker than fried. I start making toast of Riya's bread.

"Here, let me," Isabel says. I don't know how she looks and sounds so perky. I was first runner up to the queen of the living dead after my marathon sleep when I first arrived. But both girls look as though they spent the night at a health spa.

"Who got the cot?" Sally asks.

Joni raises a hand. "I lost the coin toss, but I have a feeling I'll be glad tonight when I get the bed."

"Oh, I'm sure of it." Sally, who usually takes a positive tack on things, casts a sympathetic glance at Isabel.

"We've loaded the van," Andy says to Clark, who is pouring mugs of coffee for those who want it. Clark nods his appreciation.

"Cream's in the fridge," Sally says.

And it's real cream. I'm just not sure it comes from a cow. "Aria, would you mind, love?"

I get it and the sugar—no such thing as Sweet'n'Low in the parsonage—and put it on the table where it will be easy to get to. Isabel has taken my place at the toaster.

Both girls are in jeans and light blue T-shirts that say Hope House on the front, and on the back: No one whose hope is in Christ will ever be put to shame ~ Psalm 25:3.

I wonder if they've brought enough of the shirts to wear one each day they work.

When everything's ready we sit down to eat. I'm not one for such a heavy breakfast, but I eat as heartily as the rest, knowing I'll be starved by the time lunch rolls around. We talk at the table as though we're old friends. I'm excited to be part of the team.

"I hate to leave you with the cleanup," I say to Sally when breakfast is over. Everyone else is out by the van.

"After the mess I left you with yesterday? Don't be sorry, love. Go, and work hard." She might as well have added "for Anya," because that's what she means.

"I will." I hug her and hurry out the door.

Andy seems surprised to see me, or maybe disappointed. "You're coming?"

"Yep." I slide onto the second row of seats along with the other girls. A look that skitters across Andy's face makes me think I've taken the place he wanted for himself, but if I move now it will just be obvious. He climbs in behind me, and the van rocks with the weight of his body as he drops onto the seat.

The windows are down and the morning air is relatively cool as we drive down the highway toward Hope House. The coolness won't last, but it feels good right now. In fact, my bare arms and legs have goose bumps, but I'm not about to complain. I have a feeling I'll yearn to have the goose bumps back before long.

The fields of sunflowers shimmer in the breeze. The stalks have grown two feet since I saw them on my first trip to Hope House. And the heads—all listing to the east—are enormous. Their chocolate brown centers framed by silky golden petals soak up the rays like sunbathers at the beach.

I feel a tap on my shoulder and turn as far as my seatbelt will allow. It's Matt, who's seated right behind me. He talks loud enough to be heard over the yawl of the wind as it rushes in and around us.

"I don't think I heard how long you've been here," he says.

Not counting the girls, Matt appears to be the youngest on the team. Even so, he looks older than Andy.

I count on my fingers then say, "Seven weeks, almost. I'm here for a year."

"Ah." He nods. "First missions trip?"

"Very first. I graduated from Bible college in May, then came straight here. I teach school."

"Yeah, I remember hearing that. Where ya from?"

"Northern California." I give him the specifics and am not at all surprised he hasn't heard of Linden. No one ever has.

"But it's nice, I bet."

I give a noncommittal nod. "I suppose." I hope he doesn't take this wrong, but, "I get carsick. I better . . ." I say, pointing toward the front.

"Oh, sure."

So I turn around, but it actually would have been nice to sit next to him in order to talk. I'll do my best to arrange it on the way home. That at least should make Andy happy. And Isabel too, I'd say. She's seated on the driver's side, and has shifted her position so her back rests against the side of the van instead of the back of the seat. She keeps stealing glances at Andy, who happens to be one row back on the opposite side of the van, which makes it easy for her. Her long ponytail whips about like a windsock, with loose wisps going every which way. The overall look is charming, but I think she knows that. I sincerely mean it in a good way. I guess.

By the time we've spilled out of the van the guys have unloaded the tools Andy brought. We girls are milling about, waiting for instructions. I notice Joni and Isabel have work gloves in their back pockets, and light work boots on their feet. Dang. I didn't bring work boots from home—don't have work boots period—but I wish I'd thought about the gloves. Clark calls us all together at the middle of the foundation. As I step up onto the slab I notice more wildflowers have broken through the cracks. There's a lesson, I realize, right here under my tennis shoes, about adversity and perseverance, seeming to say that if we persevere in hope and prayer, Anya and the other girls will come home. Then another voice inside my head says, *but if God really is God, couldn't he just pluck them out of this nightmare like one of these wildflowers and bring them home? And if he could, why doesn't he?*

I'm startled by the thought. *Lord, I'm sorry. I don't know where that came from.* That's twice in a short time I've offered such an apology. I feel the need again to do penance. And I will. I'll work hard, really hard.

And I won't complain, gloves or not.

". . . with our endeavors, Lord." Clark is praying. "We thank you for those who have come to help, and ask thy protection on everyone who labors in your field. In thy name we pray." And we all say amen.

But what about Anya, the girl with the missionary heart? Who's protecting her?

I feel as if there's a devil on my shoulder, like in the cartoons, whispering into my ear. But this is no cartoon, no laughing matter. I pray for myself that God will stop this voice from getting through. Then, subconsciously, I brush my shoulder with my hands, but when I think about it I do it again, and yet again.

"Tom, you're the man of the hour. We defer to you." Clark passes his authority over to the team leader, the man who knows what we're here to do.

Tom steps to the middle of our group. "Okay. The truck carrying the block should be here any time." He turns to Clark for confirmation, and Clark nods. "We'll unload the block, chain-gang style, if you know what I mean. That'll take most of today. It'll be the worst part, so come tomorrow it's all downhill." Everyone chuckles. "We'll put you gals in the middle. I think that'll be the easiest spot for you."

I want to protest, because I don't want easy, I want penance. But, of course, I don't say that.

"I hope to finish the bottom floor in the time we have here."

"Wow," I say. "The whole floor?"

"It'll go like clockwork once we get started."

"Wow," I say again, this time under my breath, to myself.

Joni and Isabel smell like a tropical fruit salad. In the van, I thought it was their shampoo, but now I figure out it's their sun block. Dang. Didn't think of that either. But I come to my own defense. I came to teach school, they came to lay block.

The truck arrives, throwing up a thick cloud of dust as its humongous tires amble over the rough, dry ground. I cough, clamp my eyes closed, and wave a hand in front of my face to clear the air, then move out of the dust, along with Joni and Isabel. Tom and Phil help direct the driver to a spot close to the foundation, so close that not one link of the chain gang will stand on the dirt ground. We'll either be in the trailer or on the concrete, thus shortening the gap from the block to its destination.

"Sure beats Colombia," Matt says to Pete with a laugh.

"Had to haul the block in wheelbarrows to the site," Pete explains. "A good thirty yards or more."

Matt slaps Pete on the back. "How many loads did you dump?"

"One or two fewer than you, bud."

The guys laugh, and as I watch their interaction I think what a bonding experience it must be to travel the world together to work on behalf of others. I suddenly wish Kari were here, or Johnnie. Wish they knew what a sweet girl Anya was. *Is*. Is. So they'd really get why I'm out here on this slab in the middle of a Moldovan prairie, with my sleeves rolled up, metaphorically speaking. And then it comes to me that a face makes all the difference, a face makes it personal. It's what drives me today. I look around and wonder what drives my fellow laborers.

Tom watches as the driver jumps out of the truck, walks around to the back, and slides up the door to the cargo hold. It's filled with huge sacks of concrete and sand-colored blocks. Hundreds and hundreds of them. Tom removes one, inspects it, then nods. He says something to Clark, but I don't hear what it is. And then the work begins.

Eighteen

James climbs into the back of the truck, slips on his leather gloves, as do the other members of our team, and we all line up. Andy closest to James, then Matt, Pete, me, Isabel, Joni, Phil, Clark, and Tom at the head of the line. I watch as the first block is passed from James to Andy to Matt to Pete, and then it gets to me. I brace for it because I've seen how the muscles expand in the guys' upper arms as they handle the block, but I'm completely unprepared for its weight. To me, it doesn't look any heavier than my Webster's New World College Dictionary, but it bends me forward, almost in half, and I stop just short of hitting the ground with it. I heave it up, and with a grunt pass it on to Isabel. It has to weigh as much as a large sack of potatoes. I look back at the cargo hold and wonder just how many tons we're dealing with.

I'm more prepared for the next block, and before long we've got a rhythm going. I think it's Phil who starts the singing that establishes our pace. I know the song, but I don't join in. I think it only smart to save my breath. But I like what it adds to the atmosphere. This really does feel like a chain gang. In a good way.

Johnnie's gift manicure has long worn off and my fingernails are waging a desperate war, and losing, along with the skin on my hands, which feels like Peggotty's "pocket nutmeg-scraper of a finger" in *David Copperfield*, a masterpiece of fiction I've savored more than once. But like my hair, my nails will grow back. And speaking of hair, I've gathered it into a stub of a ponytail, which sticks out the back of my head like the nub of a broom worn down to nothing. What doesn't reach the rubber band is held back with the green plaid headband. It's not even close to matching the jean shorts and navy T-shirt that are my newly designated work clothes. It's my favorite Abercrombie and Fitch T-shirt, and I know this will ruin it, but the mall will still be there when I get home ten months from now, right?

I know what a sight I am compared to Joni and Isabel. Their long tresses have been smoothed out from the wind and hang down their backs in real ponytails. "I had hair like that once," I want to tell them. "I gave it up for the Lord." But how lame would that be?

Something brushes my arm and I turn. "Here." Andy hands me his worn leather gloves.

I shake my head. "No, I can't—"

"Take them."

"But—"

"Take them." Andy sets them firmly in my sandpaper hands and goes back to his place in the chain, three links behind me. Isabel watches and smiles, then wipes her face with the sleeve of her shirt in the lull this glove issue has created.

Tom, at the head of the link, takes off his cap and looks to see what the holdup is. "Let's take a water break," he calls. Make use of the interruption, is what I think he means.

I hadn't noticed the well toward the back of the property before now, but as I think about it, the digging of the well would be priority. The water is cool and tastes better than anything I could think of at the moment. I take my fill, then go and lean against the shady side of the truck. The driver is in the cab, head leaned back at a crazy angle with a newspaper spread across his face.

Tough duty.

We girls get the longer break, having gotten our water first, because after the last guy gets his drink, we all go back to work. It's all downhill from here. That becomes my mantra, and I say it over and over in my head as I take a block and pass it on. It's all downhill from here.

We stop for lunch at 11:00. I don't know when I've eaten anything that tastes as good as that cold chicken, which wasn't all that appetizing the day before. I'd even eat a gizzard, I'm that hungry. But of course, that's easy to say since I can't be put to the test. Judging by the lack of conversation as we sit and eat, I think my coworkers would too. The apples—though I prefer them cold, right out of the fridge—are tart and juicy, and Riya Moraru's brown bread is like manna from heaven. By the time I get around to peeling a hard-boiled egg, conversation begins to overpower the sounds of nature around us: the soft hiss of the dry grass as it dances in the breeze, the shrill call of the birds overhead, the constant, rhythmic clacking of grasshoppers that blend in perfectly with the ochre grass.

"Sorry about the salt," I say, as I take my first bite of egg. I didn't think to bring any along. If you ask me, eggs without salt have a high-pitched taste. Like unsalted popcorn.

"Better for the cholesterol," Phil says.

As if he needs to worry about cholesterol. He could be the July cover for *Shape* magazine, but then I remember that Matt Farmer's dad, when we were in high school, had a physique like Phil's and high cholesterol too. Looks, as they say, can fool you.

Great lunch," Matt says, and everyone agrees.

It's all relative, I want to say. Instead, I say, "Thanks."

"You ladies are doing fine." Tom winks at his daughter.

"You expected less?" She reminds me of me with my dad.

Tom's not a bad looking guy, but I have a feeling Isabel gets her beauty from her mother. She's dark-haired, brown-eyed, olive-skinned and lithe, while Tom is blond and built like a bull. Like Opa, only younger.

"We saved the easy trip for you," James says, with a young man's bluster, though the tone is good natured.

"Easy?" Joni says.

My thoughts exactly. My back is screaming its displeasure, though I'd never say so. From my shoulders to my fingertips, my arms have begun to tremble with the strain of the work. They feel ten inches longer, too. But it's all downhill from here.

All downhill.

"Try hauling blocks like these up five floors with a bucket and a rope."

"What? No way," Isabel says.

"No kidding." James holds up a hand, on-my-honor style. "In Colombia, wasn't it?"

Matt and Phil both say, "Guatemala."

"Guatemala. Right."

"Why?" I ask.

"No other way to get the block up there unless you carried them up the stairs. We weren't about to do that."

"Wow." I find myself using that expression over and over today. "How long have you guys been working together?"

"How long, Tom?" James asks.

"This is the"—he stops a minute to count—"seventh trip for you, Pete and me."

My fourth," Matt says.

Phil tosses an apple core to the birds. "Mine too."

While the guys continue to talk about past missions trips, Joni reaches over and touches my arm. I still can't shake the feeling she's somehow familiar to me. "The young girl who disappeared, she was your student?"

"Is my student, yes. Her name's Anya."

"Another beautiful name."

"She's a beautiful girl in every way." My eyes sting as if they're about to tear up again, but I manage to hold back the flood. My heart feels like a dead weight in my chest every time I think of what she and the others must be going through.

"Is it for sure she's a victim of trafficking, and not a runaway or something?"

I shake my head. "Three other girls went missing the same day." I don't say that if I'd been as careful as I should have been Anya would be home where she belongs. But I know it. And furthermore, God knows it. "Besides, Anya wouldn't run away. Kids here aren't like what we're used to in the States." I think suddenly of the coffeehouse crowd and amend my answer. "For the most part."

"It's a sad world," Isabel says.

Sad? It's way more than sad. It's egregious, atrocious, heinous. There aren't enough o-u-s words in my vocabulary to express how I feel. I hate whoever took Anya. I know all about the scripture that says hate is equal to murder. But I feel I could do that too to this beast. Yes. Let me introduce myself. I'm Aria, the murdering missionary. Bet I could have my ministerial degree revoked for that. Yes, indeed. I see my heart as something black and toxic. How then must God see it?

"Let's pray for them." Without a wasted moment Isabel reaches for my hand and Joni's hand, and murmurs a prayer. I bow my head, but at her tender and earnest words I open my eyes and watch as she communes with the Lord in a way I would never have thought to. But then, knowing what a mess I am, I can't see he'd be eager to hear from me. There's nothing formal about Isabel's approach. It's intimate, poetic, and I can't help wonder what it would have been like to hear David, the poet king, offer up a psalm of praise.

A sweet savor, that's what. And truly, that's what I want my prayers to be, but I wouldn't know how to begin.

I whisper amen after Joni and Isabel. "You said when you heard about Hope House you knew this was the project you wanted to work on. Why?"

"I can't think of a worse fate than what these young women are forced into. I'd want someone to help me."

"Like God?" I never meant to say that, and certainly not with such cynicism, but there it is. Out of the overflow of the heart the mouth speaks. How many times have I heard Mam chastise me with those words when my mouth got the better of me? Well, I don't need Mam to tell me I've done it again. "I'm sorry. I didn't mean that."

Joni and Isabel exchange a look, but it carries more compassion than condemnation. "You must wonder where God is in all of this," Joni says. I wait for an answer, something that will explain his ill-timed absence, but a shine in Joni's eyes is all I get. "We won't stop praying till they're home, Aria. I promise you."

Well, okay, but I was hoping for more.

Okay, here's the thing. Having men and women on the same work team out in the middle of nowhere poses one major problem. All my water consumption has caught up with me and there's not a port-a-potty in sight. "Where do you suppose we, um, you know . . . ?"

Isabel catches my meaning at once. She holds up a finger as if to say, "Hold on one sec." She jogs to the van and returns with a blanket under one arm, a roll of toilet paper in one hand, a small shovel in the other. Then she nods toward a fallen tree in the distance, black with age and decay. Joni and I follow.

"This is the best we can do," Isabel says.

I look around, not getting her meaning at all. "What's the best we can do?"

She takes one corner of the blanket and Joni takes the other, holding it up like a shield. Then Isabel tosses me the paper.

"You're kidding." I look back toward the guys, who are beginning to stir from our lunch break. "I'm not gonna—" I point to the blanket and shake my head. "No way."

"Well, then, would you take this corner?" Isabel asks.

I know my eyes betray my surprise. "You're really gonna—?"

"We're three hours from a real toilet." She takes the paper and steps her way through the foot-high grass to the back of the fallen tree. "Would you—?" She motions for us to raise the blanket. Two minutes later she emerges, looking as relieved as I'd like to be.

That's all the encouragement Joni needs. "Here." She hands her corner of the blanket to Isabel, then retreats behind the blanket.

"Bury your t.p.," Isabel instructs.

Ah. Hence the shovel.

In the two minutes it takes for Joni to reappear I have come to a conclusion. Three hours from a toilet is three hours too many. With reluctance I hand off my corner of the blanket to Joni and make my way through the tall grass, especially since not one of the guys is paying a bit of attention to what we're doing out here. The whole time I'm crouched I'm watching for things that crawl. A hawk—Opa could tell you exactly what type—circles overhead and lets me know there are things in this grass he wants for lunch, like mice and bugs and snakes, an outdoor smorgasbord for the bird world. Thankfully, nothing encroaches on my territory. Still, I hasten to do my business and get back to the slab where I have a clear view of my feet.

We no sooner return to the van when Phil and Matt snatch the blanket and accessories from Isabel. "Good thinking," Matt says, and off they go, followed by all the guys on the team.

As I tug on Andy's gloves I tell myself again, it's all downhill from here.

————————————

First thing I do when we return from our day's work is ask Sally if there's any news, but I know by the look on her face, even before I ask, that Anya is still hopelessly lost. The rock in my chest crumbles a bit and I begin to despair of a happy ending here.

The girls and I decided on the ride home that today we'll take showers according to the alphabetical order of our given names, so I go first, though I do protest and insist we reverse the order tomorrow, and the day after that, Isabel will go first. Then we'll start the order all over again. I climb the stairs to the third floor, fetch my clean clothes and head for the bathroom. I'm looking forward to this. I have never worked so hard in my life. While I'm proud to say I managed to keep up with my fellow laborers, I'm ashamed to say I had every reason to doubt that I'd make it.

I stand under the cool shower, not just to conserve the warm water, but because it feels so blessedly good after a long day of hard labor under a hot sun. And though I ate a hearty breakfast and a substantial lunch, I'm famished. Sally has something good prepared, I know by the smells that greeted us when we stepped through the back door, but I'm so tired I could head right up to bed and sleep straight through to tomorrow.

I wouldn't say I've gotten my second wind, but the shower has revived me enough to get me through till bedtime, though there's little doubt that will be much earlier than usual.

"You look like a new woman," Sally says, when I get downstairs.

She's beginning to set the table, but I take the plates out of her hand. "Let me."

"You've done enough for one day," she protests, but I insist and she hands the plates over. "Are you sure you want to keep this up all week?"

"Tom assures us it's all downhill from here." I'm actually thinking *slope* as opposed to *hill*, but whatever we do tomorrow will have to be easier than unloading a truckload of blocks. We must have handled a ton or more of the gritty, ten-pound rectangles.

Sally lifts the lid off a crock pot and stirs what's inside. I nearly swoon with delight at the aroma. "Hungry?" she asks.

"Oh," is all I can manage.

"We'll eat once everyone's cleaned up."

I multiply nine more showers by five minutes minimum. Forty-five minutes at least. The thought leaves me faint, but I stifle another groan, this one of protest.

As if reading my thoughts, Sally says, "Shouldn't be long. Last evening Andy rigged a camp shower for the men between the clotheslines, with sheets all around for privacy. I gather it's working just fine."

"A camp shower?"

"With two stalls. Andy's so inventive. Such a blessing to us. As are you, Aria."

My lips turn up but there's nothing behind the smile. I don't feel like a blessing. I feel like a curse, and I've no doubt the Moravecs would agree.

"Of course, there's no hot water," Sally says, "but in this heat I doubt the men are complaining. Not that they would."

I pull open the silverware drawer and count out the forks and knives, most of which don't match. "There'd be no hot water after the third or fourth shower anyway, if they were in the house."

"That's true, and I bet the sprays outside are better besides."

I hadn't thought of that. Maybe tomorrow we could label one of those stalls *Girls*.

It's Wednesday night, which means church. We gather in the sanctuary after dinner, but things don't look like they did on Sunday. The platform is littered with seven cots, neatly made up, but still out of place. The podium has been moved as close to the front of the platform as it can be without toppling off. And instead of his usual stool, Andy sits on the altar bench fingering his guitar. I'm sorry for how raw his fingers must be and wonder how he can even play. But the acoustic notes that fill the church sound as good as ever.

The moment I sit down, the full day's workload hits me and I fear I'll fade in the middle of Sally's teaching. Joni and Isabel enter the building moments before the meeting begins and slide into the wooden pew beside me. Both of them have changed from the shorts they wore at dinner into modest dresses that cover their knees, and they both wear a bandana on their hair. Obviously, they did their homework before packing.

Something this teacher didn't do.

I give the girls a sickly smile and tug on my crops just as Clark opens the service.

"We're going to do things differently tonight. We'll all stay together in the sanctuary and pray."

He doesn't need to say what for.

With those few words Clark makes his way to a corner of the platform, behind a cot, and kneels. There's a low rustling sound as others in the small congregation find their own places to pray. As before, not everyone kneels. Some pace the one and only aisle between the two rows of pews, and some the path in front of the platform. Andy stays seated on the altar, the minor chords coming from his guitar a prayer all their own. Slowly a rumbling begins to rise, soft at first, then louder and more urgent, as the prayers of the faithful rise to heaven like so much incense.

I don't count myself among the faithful, for if I could form a prayer I doubt it would reach the wooden beams that span the length of the ceiling from which the bare light bulbs hang. Instead, I watch Anya's mother and father, for once together in the house of God, Georgeta's large, veined hand in her husband's, their heads touching as they bow. Her tears fall silently and run off their entwined fingers, or maybe they're his tears as well.

And another piece of my heart crumbles away.

Johnnie and K: I miss the delta breeze. Really miss it. The way it tiptoes up in the early evening, stirring up Celie's bamboo chimes on the patio, and shimmering the uncountable leaves on the mélange of trees on the compound. Watching that breeze grow from a whisper to a bluster that dissipates the heat of the day, like the breath of God making things fresh again. But God seems far away from here. You there?

THOSE BAMBOO CHIMES ALWAYS REMIND ME OF THAT CRAZY LITTLE SONG YOUR MAM TAUGHT US WHEN WE WERE IN BROWNIES. YOU KNOW, THAT AMERICAN INDIAN SONG WE'D SING WHILE WE TAPPED OUR STICKS TOGETHER? MOK SOMETHING SOMETHING, KOTAYO SOMETHING SOMETHING. MAN, NOW I'M GOING TO HAVE THAT TUNE IN MY HEAD ALL DAY.

Wow, haven't thought of that in years. I hum the tune myself, and slowly the words come back to me. I have no idea what they mean or if I'm even remembering them correctly. *Yeah, yeah, here it is: mokoway kotayo a kooytama, mokoway kotayo a kooytama. Of course, I'm spelling it phonetically. Have no idea if I'm even close.*

OKAY, I'M IMPRESSED. I GOOGLED IT. GOT NOTHING. HOW'S OUR BRICK MASON TODAY?

Block layer. And I'm whipped. I'm feeling this, I don't know, spiritual imbalance in my head. It's freaky. Pray for me?

The next message is from Johnnie.

Ree? You okay???

Those three little words make me as homesick as I've ever been and would bring me to tears if I had any left. But I used them all up at the prayer meeting. I soaked the thighs of my crops, and still, when my tears were gone there was a weeping in my soul so intense I began to believe a broken heart is more literal than figurative. I've never felt such sorrow, such aloneness. Oh, God, where is my faith?

Hey, Johnnie. I'm good. Really. Just tired. We moved a ton of blocks today. Literally. Maybe two. But you should see my biceps. ☺

WHAT ABOUT YOUR FORCEPS?

Funny. Ha.

Forceps??

You never heard?

Heard what??

Thanks, K!

Seventh grade health. Mr. Moore has this diagram of a human body—you know, one of those sexless outlines—and we're filling in the names of the muscles. Mr. Moore points to the upper arm and someone calls out "biceps." Then he points to the forearm and without a moment's hesitation—or thought—Ree calls out "forceps." The whole class lost it. You never heard that one?

In spite of myself I'm laughing.

Good one. Ree. Thanks, Kari. Somehow that story never made it home.

That's Ree, the modest one.

I miss you, sis.

I sign off, turn out the light and close my eyes. I'm so tired I feel almost weightless, like I'm not quite here, but it's a good tired, born of good work. The whir of the fan drowns out all other sounds and soothes me as I drift away. My fading thoughts are of the chain gang, of Isabel, of Joni. Of Joni. My drifting away gets hung up here and I find myself coming back. I just want to sleep. But . . . dang! What is it about Joni?

And then it hits me. I'm fully awake now. My stomach lurches then starts a slow churning. Joni could be the twin of Patti Mitchell, a girl I knew in high school. The girl I—

I didn't mean for it to turn out the way it did. It was just an April Fool's Day prank. Who knew she'd take it so hard? Who knew she'd—? I tell this to myself for the thousandth time, but I'm no more convinced now, eight years later, than I was then. I knew what was at stake. I knew how low it was. I knew. And in Joni, I get the hammering sense God's reminding me just why I need a second chance.

Nineteen

You know those cartoons where a character's eyes are like pinwheels because he's either exhausted or hypnotized? That's how I feel out on the slab at Hope House. It's day two, and I'm a zombie. After my revelation that Joni could be Patti's clone, there was no chance of sleep. I picked up my Bible and spent the next couple of hours reading—and rereading—scriptures about forgiveness. How it's a gift. Not earned. I have to keep telling myself that.

I can hardly stand to look Joni in the eye, as if by virtue of her resemblance to Patti she intuitively knows what a jerk I was. But that's in the past. I keep telling myself that too.

Still, it doesn't feel in the past. It feels as ugly now as it did when I was sixteen and stupid.

"You look wiped out," Isabel says. "Didn't sleep well?"

"Didn't sleep, period."

"I know how concerned you must be for Anya." Joni rests her hand on my arm, just as I saw her do with Isabel last night at dinner. Just the way Patti would have done it. "But our prayers won't be wasted. You'll see. And our work here today will be another form of prayer." She turns her attention to Tom, who is laying out the day's assignments.

"We'll start with the west wall," he says. "That way we're not working right into the sun. We'll go up so high"—he holds his hand at his knee—"then move on to the next wall, clockwise. Phil, James and I will lay the block, tie the rebar, etcetera. Pete and Matt will mix the mortar and concrete in buckets and bring them to us. We need the rest of you to keep us supplied with block. It'll go fast once we get started, and by Monday afternoon we'll have four walls. You'll love how that feels."

So we're carrying block again, just not as far. I was right, our "downhill" is just a slope. "Concrete and mortar? Aren't they the same?"

"Not exactly. Mortar has cement in it, but they're two different substances. The concrete will fill the hollow space inside the blocks; the mortar will fill the gaps between them."

"Ah." I nod, but it's no clearer to me now than it was before the explanation. I'll just have to wait and see. I pull on the leather gloves I borrowed last night from Sally, ready to go to work, and hold my hands up for Andy to see. He's looking this way, but I'll bet it's only because Isabel is beside me. At that he reaches for his own gloves, which are hanging out the back pocket of his jeans, and tugs them on.

Andy looks good in jeans. Really good.

But that and every other thought leaves my mind as I dive into the task at hand.

"I'll take Dad," Isabel says, "if you and Joni take James and Phil."

I don't get her meaning. Maybe it's because I'm brain dead from lack of sleep, I don't know. "Take them where?"

Isabel's smile reveals that one front tooth overlaps the other one just a bit. It doesn't take away from her looks at all. "Take wasn't the right word. I just mean I'll supply blocks to my dad. If you want to supply them to, say, Phil, Joni can supply them to James."

"Oh. Oh, I see." Dolt. "What about Andy and Clark?"

"They can work in between. That way we're not bumping into each other all day."

The morning sun reflects off the concrete slab, zapping my eyes with its brilliance, and I squint. "You've done this before?"

Isabel shakes her head. "I've just heard Dad talk about how they do things."

And so we set to work. The blocks are heavier than they were the day before, if that's possible. Clark and Andy carry two apiece with each lap from the wall of block we created yesterday, to the wall the men are building today, while I barely manage one. The other girls carry one at a time as well. I find great satisfaction in that.

And so it goes.

Tom is right. By the end of another long day the four walls stand four feet above the foundation, the mortar surrounding every block drying in the sun. I take heart from our progress as I'm sure Clark and Andy do, but when this team leaves there will be four walls standing, that's all. And who knows when the next team will come with laborers and money for supplies to continue the work?

———————————

Friday night Andy invites some of the team—Joni and Isabel included, or maybe especially—to go to the coffeehouse. Because there's no way around it, I'm included in the invitation. Matt smiles in my direction, then at my hesitation he encourages me to come along.

"It's Friday night. Time to let your hair down."

Oh. He has no idea how that wounds.

"I don't know. It's been a long few days." My chin is practically dragging the ground, but more to the point I have visions of tar and feathers or whatever it is young men in Moldova do to people who encourage their women to withhold sex until marriage. Especially when that's a whole new concept, if you get my drift. But I'm hoping Matt, and maybe Andy, will protect me should any of the natives become restless. I return a weak smile. "Okay."

"Great," Matt says. I get the feeling he means it.

At thirty, Matt is the youngest guy on the Wisconsin team. And speaking of Matt, his last name is Belcher. Yes, Belcher. So here we are again. The problem, of course is not *this* Matt's last name or even Matt Farmer's last name. It's prefacing them with Aria. Any guy with a last name that doubles as a noun just won't work, especially a noun like belcher. Not that I'm thinking wedding bells. It's just, well, things like that matter. In fact, my cousin Birdie legally changed her first name to Fiona right after her wedding because it went so much better with her new last name of Fry. Extreme maybe—unless you consider that she too sprang from the lineage of krystal blue karma, being the daughter of my mother's brother, Donovan Mellow-Yellow Karma Shunk—but she said no way could she write Birdie I. Fry on everything she signed from here to forever. I can't fault her. If I had to write Aria Belcher on everything I signed for the rest of my life, I'd be perfectly happy to keep Winters for better or worse, and probably will regardless.

I'm nervous as we approach the peeling brown door. I'm wearing a ball cap I borrowed from Joni, but I don't think it's much of a disguise. Especially since I'm with Andy. Well, not *with* him, but with him. If anyone's *with* him it's Isabel. And I needn't have worried. Every set of eyes that belongs to a face with whiskers is fastened on our female guests. No one even knows I'm here.

Except Matt.

So much for being a rock star.

We find a table near the back of the room that will accommodate the seven of us.

"Coffee?" Andy nods in the direction of the table with the urn, the little Styrofoam cups and sugar dispenser, still in need of filling. There's no milk tonight as far as I can tell.

"Sure," Isabel says.

"Joni?" Mark follows Andy the moment she says yes, and Phil follows Pete.

"Aria?" Matt raises an eyebrow in my direction.

Looks like the guys are playing host. "Thanks, but no. I really want to sleep tonight."

"Okay, I'll just—" He throws a thumb in the direction of the urn.

"Please, help yourself."

"Wow," Joni says, when we're alone. "This is so . . ."

"Not what you expected?"

She looks over the room. "Retro."

"No kidding," Isabel says. "When Andy said coffeehouse ministry, I envisioned a cross between Starbucks and Saddleback Church."

"I thought the same thing the first time I came. You kinda get used to it."

The guitar player is tuning up just as the guys return with the coffee. Matt lifts his cup in my direction. "Sure you don't want any?"

I glance at the cup he sets on the table as he takes a seat beside me. The little bit of light in the room reflects off the dark, oily liquid. "I'm good, thanks."

Joni and Isabel provide the only real color in the room. The T-shirts they wear are daisy yellow and cherry red, over white crops, both of them. Personally, I dug out a black tee, which I don't usually wear, but tonight I want only to blend.

Right away our table is surrounded by smiling faces, girls and guys alike. The flirting from both sexes is instant and shameless.

"Hallo," a deep voice says.

I recognize it at once as Sasha's. I slide down a bit and lower the bill of my cap. His eyes flit back and forth between Joni and Isabel, a toothy smile stuck on his face. I know they're attractive girls, but come on. If it's about beauty, all these Slavic guys have to do is take a look around. There's plenty of it everywhere. Must be the foreign mystique, I decide. And speaking of beauty, I don't see Svetlana.

Andy introduces our guests to the pressing crowd, while I do my best to look invisible. Sasha pulls a chair away from a neighboring table and joins our circle. Dang. He stretches out his long arms and the masses retreat back to their own places.

"You from United States?" he asks the girls. When they say yes, he adds, "California?"

"Wisconsin," Isabel says.

"Visconsin. Ver dat?"

"Northeastern US."

Sasha thinks a moment. "You know Mel Gibson?"

Joni and Isabel laugh. "No."

"Ah." Sasha doesn't look terribly disappointed. "Vat you do here?"

"We're building a house," Pete says.

"A refuge," Joni adds.

"Building?" Sasha wags his finger back and forth between the girls. "You build?"

"We do," Isabel says. "Aria too." She smiles in my direction as I sink lower in my chair.

Sasha turns his eyes to me, reaches across Matt and lifts off my cap.

"Hi," I say, trying to ignore the way the muscles in his jaw flex.

He forces my cap onto his own big head, bill facing backwards, then points his finger my way. "You trouble."

My tablemates respond in a variety of ways, while I pray no one asks him to explain. It looks like Matt is about to come to my defense when Andy says something to Sasha in Romanian. Sasha gives me another sideways glance, hands me my cap, then gives a reluctant nod. "*Da*," he says, and Andy seems satisfied. I'll have to ask about this later. Judging by the looks on the faces of my compatriots, they'll sure be asking me.

The guitar player is lost in his music. Besides him, I may be the only one in the room listening to him play. His style is growing on me, sort of early Bob Dylan—a favorite of Mam's, so it's a sound I know well. In my head I'm able to anticipate the next note almost every time, though it could be that I've heard him play this song before.

Andy swallows the last of his coffee, stands, and pulls his pulpit-chair to him. Behind me I hear the scraping of chair legs on the concrete floor as people turn to face him. I can't hear it, but I know cigarettes are being stubbed out. Andy nods to our worship leader and he begins to play a song I know in English, but of course everyone but those at our table are singing in Romanian. Joni closes her eyes and hums along. She really is a beautiful girl.

I wait for that stirring in my spirit I usually feel during this part of a service, even one as casual as this. It doesn't come. I'm wiped out, I tell myself, spent in so many ways. But I know it's more than that. Something's going on inside. Something not good. I don't feel the things I should feel, and do feel the things I shouldn't. Things like fear, despair, and worst of all, anger. I try to talk myself out of it, pretend I don't know what I'm talking about. But who am I kidding?

I'd like to think God hasn't noticed, but I know better. *I'm sorry*. It's all I know to say, but I don't think it means much.

Andy opens his Bible as the guitar player slides down off his stool and the last note fades away. Though I see Andy just across the table, my thoughts are still on the music, on the note that's no longer with us, but not really gone. I wonder where sound goes to, out there in the universe, and if there's anyone to hear it as it passes by. I wonder if it travels forever, catching up with other notes, forming melodies we can't even imagine, with a dimension unknown to us as yet. I wonder what music sounds like in heaven. Wonder if I'll ever know.

"'. . . who planted a vineyard.' " Andy stops reading, motions for Sasha to come and stand beside him, then waits for him to translate. Sasha seems reluctant tonight, and I think it's because of whatever it was Andy said to him. Still, he responds and translates as Andy tells the parable of the tenants. "'This man rented a vineyard to some farmers, then went off on a journey. When it came time for the harvest, the landowner sent his own workers to gather the grapes. But the farmers beat up the workers, even killing one. The landowner sent more workers, but the farmers beat them up as well.' "

Andy pauses and looks around the room, and I wonder where in the world he's going with this. "God is like that man who owns the vineyard," he says, and Sasha translates. "He sends workers into that vineyard." He makes a motion with his hand that encompasses everyone in the room. "Those workers bring the message that God loves them and has a plan for their lives. And that message contains do's and don'ts."

Sasha stops. "Do's and don'ts. Vat dat?"

There are a few chuckles from our table. "Things you can do and things you can't do," Andy says.

"So you mean can do's and can't do's."

Andy shrugs. "Okay, that'll work. The can do's we're usually okay with. But the can't do's, sometimes they tick us off."

And now I get where he's going.

"But the can't do's are can't do's for a reason." Andy's taking this slow, making sure Sasha gets it. "God knows his children well. He knows what will bring them harm, and so, like a good father, he says you can't do this, or you can't do that. Because he wants to protect us."

A low murmur arises as Andy's audience begins to get his meaning.

"Some of you haven't liked the message, so you want to stone the messenger."

I feel a hundred eyes on me. All of a sudden it's really warm in here, and I wish I were closer to the fan in the corner. In fact, I wish I were at the parsonage tucked away in my own little bed. I reach up under the bill of my cap and wipe my forehead.

Johnnie and I used to play a game when we were little girls and took bubble baths together. We called it "tickle." With my bare back to Johnnie she'd say she was going to tickle it, but I never knew when. I'd wait with nervous anticipation, giggling long before she ever made contact. But as I waited, feeling her finger near but not yet touching, involuntarily my back would arc away from her hand. And that's how I feel at this moment, my back wanting to arc away from the touch of all these eyes on me.

"'After all this,'" Andy continues the story, "'the landowner sent his son to receive the harvest. But the farmers killed him too.'" Andy closes his Testament and slips it back in his pocket. "If you're not willing to receive the worker who is telling you the truth, how will you receive the Son, who is the truth?"

Sasha squirms as he stands there, looking everywhere but at me. Joni leans across Mark and whispers, "What's this all about?"

"S-E-X," I whisper back. "And I'm the messenger."

Her eyes grow wide with understanding. "Ouch."

"I gather they're not happy that your message falls under the can't do category?" Phil says.

"Exactly."

"And yet they've come back. That says something about the openness of their hearts."

Andy closes in prayer, then makes his way to a corner. I sit absolutely still and don't give Andy the slightest chance of catching my eye. No more corners for me. I'm surprised to see Sasha move in Andy's direction, and I think maybe Phil is right, maybe Sasha is open to the complete gospel, but no, he goes only as far as the coffee table. He pours a cup, screws the lid off the sugar and shakes out what little is in it into his coffee, goes back to a table and lights a cigarette. He smiles at his comrades and jumps into the conversation. Sasha is tall and muscular, a natural leader, the life of the party. Tonight, minus Svetlana, he's the recipient of uninhibited flirting, and enjoys it enough that I could slap him on her behalf.

Matt is about to ask me something when I feel a tap on my shoulder. I turn to see a young Slavic woman standing behind me. I've seen her here before, but I don't know her name. She seems nervous, as though she doesn't want to interrupt, and yet she knows she is.

"*Buená seara*," I say.

"Gut efening," she replies. The greeting is extended to our entire table. Then she leans closer and says, "Could ve talk?"

I smile and nod, but inside I'm groaning. Not again. Please? I scoot out my chair, stand, and motion for my new friend to lead the way. Across the room Andy's eyes meet mine for just a moment, then he turns back to the young man he's been talking with. But a look crosses his face that—though I can't say why—makes me glad I'm here.

Twenty

"They've found the van." Those are the words out of Sally's mouth when we return from working at Hope House on Monday. "And the driver."

"What? Where?" The words I utter are so rough they sound as if they were delivered over a pumice stone.

"I just got word." Sally turns to Clark. "I think you should go to the police station with Mr. Moravec.

"I'll go too," Andy says.

"What about Anya? The girls?" I ask.

Sally's eyes are downcast as she shakes her head. The spark of hope I felt at the news dies as suddenly as it was ignited. Clark washes his hands at the kitchen sink, then he's out the door with Andy at his side. The meal Sally prepared is put on hold.

"Do you know anything else?"

"Only that they found a van matching the description the boy gave them and that they've taken the driver in for questioning." That last word sounds ominous coming out of her mouth, and then I think, *no Miranda rights here.*

"What boy?" Isabel asks.

Sally wraps her thin arms around her middle. "The brother of one of the abducted girls. We're hopeful the driver will at least tell us where he took them."

Please, God. Please. It's my feeble prayer, started up again.

Joni and Isabel offer me the shower even though it's not my day to go first.

"Thanks, really, but I'll wait." I don't want to be out of earshot should we get any more news. I hear their soft conversation fade as they climb the stairs. The men take their leave as well, and head for the camp showers.

We've had a long day of work trying to finish the four bottom walls of Hope House, as the team returns home tomorrow. We worked as hard today as we did the first day unloading our tons of block, but when we left this afternoon, two hours later than usual, four walls were standing. We shared a great sense of accomplishment when that last block was put in place, whooping and high-fiving each other, but as we stripped away the scaffolding and drove back to Leoccesni and the parsonage I couldn't help wish they were staying long enough to lay the block for all three floors, and complete the finish work too. Somehow I'm going to do whatever I can to bring another work crew here so it's not another year between this stage of progress and the next.

"Sally?"

It's all I say before she pulls me into her bony embrace. Though I don't hear or feel it, I know that the beat of our hearts mingle as surely as the tears of the church women and Georgeta Moravec mingled the night Anya disappeared, and as surely as mine and Kari's blood mingled to seal our girlish pact. We're forever sisters now, Sally and I, forever bound with the kind of bond that's forged only with shared joy and shared tragedy.

Sally tugs tissues out of the box and hands me a couple. She wipes her face and I wipe mine. "You should have gone yesterday to the monastery," she says. "You worked as hard as the rest. You earned the reward."

I shake my head. "It just wasn't the time for me."

"We'll be sure to go sometime while you're here. You'll enjoy it."

"It" is the Cave Monastery north of Chisinau, built into the mountain overlooking the Raut River by monks in the 13th century. It's a place I want to go while I'm here, but when Clark announced after church yesterday that the team would still like to visit Old Orhei that afternoon as planned, I had no problem declining. After a quick lunch they all squeezed into the van. I thought it odd that Andy would go until I saw him sitting next to Isabel in the middle seat as they drove away.

I spent the afternoon stewing on my bed under the wind of the box fan, telling myself—out loud even—that I was upset they could take a pleasure trip when our community of friends was in such turmoil. But I kept seeing Andy's arm stretched along the top of the seat, encompassing Isabel's position beside him. The vision made my stomach roil, and I couldn't quite account for that.

It's an hour and a half before Clark and Andy return. The girls and I help Sally serve the supper she's kept on hold, and though I'm eager for news, my stomach rumbles shamelessly and I admit I'm as hungry as the rest of the group assembled around the table. But the moment Tom's prayer dies on his lips, we clamor for information.

"Did they really find the van?" Sally asks.

"And the driver?" We're passing food every which way. My serving bowl collides with Joni's, spilling mixed vegetable juice onto the tablecloth. "Sorry," I say.

Clark takes a pork chop that's not as moist as it would have been two hours ago and arranges it on his plate just so. The thing I've noticed about Clark in the two months I've been here is that he's meticulous about most everything. His meat goes on his plate in the twelve o'clock position, his starch, if there is one, is placed at three o'clock, and his vegetables, no matter if there's one or three, are positioned at nine o'clock. Six o'clock is left open for miscellaneous items. His bread goes on a saucer at the top left of his plate, and his drink sits at the top right. He eats in a circle, starting at twelve o'clock high, and finishes each round with a sip of iced tea, which is what Sally serves with our meals. At the moment, his obsession bothers me more than it has the whole time I've been here. I want to pull the answer to our questions from him, but he waits to speak again until his plate is completely served.

"Yes, on both counts," he finally says as he cuts a bite off his pork chop. "The van was spotted crossing into Moldova from Romania early this morning. It was stopped and the driver detained and questioned. He was returned to Leoccesni a couple of hours later for more questioning."

"His interrogation's been on the rough side," Andy says, "in both locations."

I'm not the least bit sorry. "You saw him?"

"Andrej Moravec and we saw him only briefly."

"He's not a local," Clark says. "There's a little satisfaction in that, I guess. But he's not the trafficker either. All he does is deliver the girls."

"All?" I regret that I sound so disrespectful, but come on, delivering the girls is enough! And whether or not he personally dumps them into a brothel, he's still trafficking.

Sally pats my hand without taking her eyes off her husband. "To whom? Where?"

"Always to the same person, but the girls' destinations vary."

"So this, this driver doesn't know where they are?"

Clark gives me a sober look. "Not definitively."

"What are the options?" Joni asks. "Are they at least here in Moldova?"

Clark shakes his head. "They never stay in Moldova."

Not in Moldova? I know God's hand is big, but right now I feel our girls have slipped beyond his grasp.

Like me, Andy hasn't touched his food. "There are any number of places they're taken. But"—he holds up a hand to stop my interruption—

"there's a strong indication this time the destination was Macedonia."

"Skopje," Clark adds.

"So how do we find them?"

"Once they get the name of the trafficker—"

"And they will get it," Andy interjects.

"—they'll follow the lead."

"And so we pray." Sally pats my hand again. "Aria, eat. Please. We all need our strength."

———————

K: Remember the fight we had in 6th grade, the really bad one over Jason Milner?

BECAUSE HE ASKED ME OUT AND NOT YOU?

Asked you out? Ha! Knowing how the two of us competed for his attention, he played us as deftly as his Nintendo Game Boy—actually eeny, meeny, miny moed back and forth between us to make up his mind. I'd hardly call that asking you out.

YES, BUT I WON AND YOU HATED ME FOR IT.

Only until he eeny meeny miny moed his way into asking Carly What's-her-name into going steady a week later. And then, as I recall, I was only too happy to give you my shoulder to cry on.

YOU WERE HAPPY BECAUSE HE DUMPED ME. SO WHAT'S YOUR POINT?

I was thinking about that silly blood sisters ceremony we performed in the walnut orchard after we made up. I rub my thumb over my index finger and can almost feel the prick of Mam's scissors as they punctured the skin. *Remember?*

I BET NO ONE DOES THAT ANY MORE, WHAT WITH ALL THOSE BODY FLUID WARNINGS AND HAZMAT HYSTERIA. BESIDES, SWAPPING BLOOD? IT IS KINDA CREEPY.

In my mind I see the mingling of tears between Georgeta and her friends, feel the tenderness of that night, and remind myself more of Johnnie than me at the moment. *We didn't swap, we shared.*

REALLY, REE, WHAT'S THIS ALL ABOUT?

I feel lost. I think it but I don't write it. *The team left this morning and I have nothing to do except the mundane. I can't stand just waiting. I'm as restless as Emoo. I need to do something.*

EMOO??

Never mind. It's just a story I told my class. But the point is, it's all I can do to stay here, going through the motions day after day as if nothing's amiss. I don't mean that Anya isn't first on everyone's mind. But how do you just continue?

YOU STAY IN AN ATTITUDE OF PRAYER, REE. PRAY WITHOUT CEASING, LIKE PAUL SAID, AS YOU GO THROUGH THE MOTIONS. THAT'S NOT DOING NOTHING.

No one gets it, not even Kari. But I say thank you, and sign off. Then out of desperation more than faith I close my eyes and bow my head. The words I offer up are respectful, but who am I kidding? Inside I'm railing. *Because you could have stopped this.* That's the thought that bounces around in my soul. *You could have stopped this.*

Twenty-One

It's been two days since the team left. My thoughts are no easier than they were Monday night. When I should be sleeping I pound the darkness with questions instead, but I always come back to the same conclusion: God could have prevented this—and didn't. This Thursday night my thoughts are no different. But a God who can fail isn't the only thought that troubles my mind. Andy's there as well, and much too often. As I lay on my bed in the dark, offering prayers that are more apology than petition, the notes of a song being played drift in through my little window. I turn my head just enough to listen better, and slow my breathing for the same purpose. Then I reach over and click off the fan. As the whirr of the blades slow then stop, the notes become clearer. The tone is pure and compelling, and there's no question they flow forth from Andy's guitar. How a sound so tender comes from fingers made rough by the labor of the week before is still a mystery. But tender it is.

I rise in the darkness, my T-shirt and boxers clinging to my body where the air of the fan didn't reach, and move to the window. I get as close as I can, my bare toes stubbed against the dresser. The screen smells of Moldovan dirt as it clings to the mesh, blown there by who knows how many seasons of wind.

I can't see him, but I'm sure Andy sits on the steps of the church, across the gravel, playing his guitar. I slip on a pair of shorts and creep down the stairs. The house is quiet, though the sound of Clark's hard, steady breathing as I hit the second floor makes me glad I sleep upstairs away from the snoring. With just the tiniest squeak, I open the front door, ease open the screen, and step out onto the periwinkle porch.

Sally's petunias are in full bloom and their fragrance is sweet as I sit on the step beside the flowerbox. The night air is warm, of course, with more moisture than I like or am used to, but it feels almost like the air of a sauna. All I need is a towel wrapped over my head like a honeybee hive to feel right at home, because I am quite the sauna queen. An occasional breeze that would never make it in through my dollhouse window upstairs keeps me comfortable, and even plays with my hair, which is in such embarrassing need of attention. A waning moon hangs in the sky and sheds its meager light on the porch where I sit. Though Andy is perhaps only thirty yards away, directly off to my right, I'm sure he doesn't see me, and that's just how I want it.

He's singing now, though softly, a song I don't recognize. I remember the pencil behind his ear the day I enlisted his help with the chicken, and wonder if this is the song he was writing. A few of the words of the chorus drift by on the breeze, about the everlasting faithfulness of God. But it's Andy's voice and the melody, not the message, that kindle my tears. They slip down my face unhindered, an outpouring of my grief.

The message, in fact, kindles another emotion entirely. All my life I've been taught about the faithfulness of God. I've believed in it, sang about it, depended on it in the crises of my life—though I'm aware now of how pathetic my crises have been compared to those who know what real crisis is. People like Georgeta Moravec. Anya. I never would have articulated it this way before, but now I see I had this Superman image of a God who was able to leap tall buildings in a single bound.

But not protect a little girl.

Hence the apology of my prayers.

I've never felt so forlorn.

Out of the darkness a moth the size of Maine, or maybe it's a bat, dive bombs my head. I let out a squeal and blow my cover. Dang and dang again. The music stops. I see Andy lean forward and look toward the porch where I sit. There's nothing to do but give myself up. I stand, descend the steps, send a wave his direction, and wipe my nose on the sleeve of my T-shirt.

I cross the gravel on bare feet and yelp when I get a sticker in my big toe. I don't get any sympathy from Andy. I limp the rest of the way and invite myself to have a seat beside him. The concrete step still holds the warmth of the day.

"Hey," I say.

"Hey." He sounds suspicious, and who can blame him?

"I was just"—I shrug—"listening." Might as well come clean.

He leans back and looks away, his arm draped over the guitar.

"It's nice, what you were playing." I hope the moonlight is subdued enough that he can't tell I've been crying, but I really needn't worry since he'd have to actually look at me to see. And he doesn't. "Did you write it?"

He lays the guitar across his lap. It's a Gibson acoustic a lot like Opa's. My grandfather wouldn't own anything but a Gibson. "It's not finished yet."

"I like what I heard. I love minor chords."

He does look at me then. "You play?"

"Nah. Well, a few chords. Picked up a little watching Opa."

I expect him to say something snide about Opa. Instead he says, "You have the hands for it."

"Yeah, right, me and my Go-Go-Gadget fingers." Long and skinny, like twigs attached to my knuckles.

"That's not what I meant. You have nice hands."

Nice hands? I never expected to hear a compliment from Andy. The truth is, all my life I've been told I have the hands of a musician. But do you think I was even the least bit interested in anything that required that kind of discipline? Not on your life.

Now Johnnie, whose hands are from the Winters gene pool and are anything but the hands of a musician, plays the piano almost as beautifully as Opa plays the guitar. Because Johnnie, the quintessence of discipline, devoted herself to practice for years. She made up for her lack of natural resources with hard work. More than once I wondered if God didn't give my sister the wrong hands, if somehow he inadvertently switched that part of her anatomy with mine. And that was before I began to question God's ability to make a mistake.

That concept is relatively new to me.

A gust of wind rattles the thirsty bush growing near the steps where we sit, and dries the perspiration that coats my arms. I shiver though I'm not at all cold. "Who taught you to play?"

"My brother Stuart."

There's a downturn in Andy's voice that sends the vibe that not all things are kosher with brother Stuart. "I assume he's older?"

"Younger. By a year."

"What's he do, besides play guitar?"

Andy runs his finger down the length of the low E string, then positions his guitar and adjusts a nut or two. Just when I think he's decided to ignore my question, he says, "Not much of anything." He plays a chord, A minor, I think, then turns another nut and strums again. "Stu's on a path that's different from the path he once was on."

So I was right. "That doesn't have to be a bad thing," I say, even though I didn't miss the letdown in Andy's voice. "I mean, sometimes the detours have a way of leading us where we were meant to be all along."

"Sometimes," he says, but I can tell he's not buying it.

As I sit there I realize I've just delivered a mini pep talk I have no intention of embracing myself, even though I can almost visualize the veering path that woos me. I'm beginning to understand how good it can feel to break away. To spring like a jack-in-the-box and not hurry to stuff your anger and doubt and discontent back inside before someone notices. I feel myself on the verge. One more little crank of the handle—that's all it'll take.

Andy shifts on the step until he's facing me. "Can I ask you a question?"

I shift a bit in response, not at all sure I want him to. "Okay."

"What did Andrea want to talk to you about the other night?"

"Andrea?"

"At the coffeehouse."

"Oh. Right." I remember the name now from my first time at the Friday night service, though I couldn't have put it with the face of the girl who asked to talk with me a few days ago. I'm not sure I want to answer his question.

"If it's personal I don't want you to break a confidence. It's just that I care about these people and she seemed really troubled."

I try to decide if what Andrea told me is privileged, then I realize that for all intents and purposes Andy is her pastor so I guess it's okay to share. "She wanted to know if being pregnant is a sin. They all seem hung up on the whole concept of sin just now."

Andy's lips turn up in what can only be labeled a miniscule smile. "I'm doing my best to drive the 'whole concept' home. What did you tell her?"

"I asked her if she's pregnant."

"And?"

"She thinks so. In fact, she's sure. I take it she's not married?"

Andy shakes his head. "She and Ivan are a thing, but who knows how committed they are."

"I'd say she's committed. And scared."

"She's barely eighteen."

Something darts across the road, pulling our attention with it. A cat, I think, but there are critters here I'm not familiar with, so I can't be sure.

"So, is it? A sin?" Andy lifts an eyebrow and waits to hear what I said to Andrea."

"I told her the alternative—and she is thinking alternative—is a greater sin. I invited her to come talk to Sally. She has so much wisdom. But I don't know, Andrea didn't seem inclined to take me up on it. Has anyone from the coffeehouse ever come to church here?"

"Not so far. And don't sell yourself short. I think your response was a good one."

A good one? "Thank you."

Andy plays the chord again.

"Can I hear your song?"

He looks at me for a second then says, "Remember, it's not finished."

But what is finished is beautiful. It stirs me, and as hard as I try I can't keep the tears from spilling down my face. As if that's not enough, I'm beyond mortified when I begin to squeak like a balloon seeping air, but I just can't contain the emotion.

Andy's voice dies off and he stops playing. "That bad, huh?" I know his words are meant to quell my embarrassment.

But there's nothing playful about the depth of my anguish. "Do you think we'll find them?"

"Aria." Andy seems to look for just what he wants to say. "They're lost to us, but they're not lost to God. I can't remember which Psalm it is, but David wrote something to the effect, 'If I ascend up into heaven, you are there; if I make my bed in hell, you are there.' There's nowhere we can go where God doesn't see us."

I know this isn't the intended result, but I'm incensed by Andy's words. "So right this minute God might be watching four little girls as they're hurt and violated and crying for their mothers? Ignoring our prayers that he rescue them? Is that what you're saying? Because if you are, I have to tell you I can't pretend to love a God like that. And I sure don't want to work for him."

"That's not what—Ree, wait—"

The rest of his words are lost to me as I limp back across the gravel. I take the narrow stairs to my room two at a time and am breathless when I close my bedroom door behind me. I turn the fan on high, not just to blow away the sweat, but if Andy were inclined to play again, which seems highly unlikely, I don't want to hear another note. I sit in the dark and let the artificial air swirl around me until I'm no longer shaking. I offer up one more prayer for Anya—and firmly believe it's my last, on any subject, ever—then close with my resignation. The way I've worded it leaves no chance that I'll ever be rehired in God's organization. Against Mam's good advice, I've thoroughly burned a bridge.

I switch on the lamp by my bed and fire up my laptop. In less than ten minutes I've booked a flight home, then I switch off the light again and place a call to Kari's cell phone.

Twenty-Two

I didn't sleep my last night in Moldova, evident by the deep circles under my eyes. I know Andy meant to encourage me, but like advice gone bad, so was his choice of scripture. It backfired. Completely. And now I have to break my news to Sally and Clark. That's the worst part, disappointing them—even worse than disappointing God, because, as it turns out, he has disappointed me, big time.

But Sally and Clark are a different matter. They've taken me into their home, treated me kindly, with love even, at least Sally has, so I face this as enthusiastically as I would a second period in one month.

I descend the stairs to the kitchen just as the coffee stops percolating. The aroma fills the kitchen and wakes my salivary glands.

"Aria. Good morning." Sally reaches into the cupboard for another cup. "You're up early." She fills the heavy white mug and hands it to me. "Milk's there on the table."

"Thanks." I slide onto my chair and barely acknowledge Clark and Andy, to whom Sally serves matching mugs of coffee.

"There's toast there," she says. "I'll make a few more slices."

"Not for me." I'm sure I sound as glum as I look.

It's not lost on Sally. She joins us at the table. "Did you have a bad night?"

"A long night." I glance at Andy, who catches my eye then looks down into the dark liquid in his cup. "I don't know an easy way to say this so I'll just say it."

"Oh, sweetie." Sally touches my arm. "What is it?"

"I'm going home." I can't look at anyone when I make my announcement. "Tonight."

"Tonight?" Sally's voice is a whisper of surprise and sadness. "But why?"

In the space between her question and my answer Andy's jaw flexes, then he says, "Excuse me." He leaves his coffee and exits through the screen door, which bounces three times against the paint-blistered jamb. His familiar crunch on the gravel induces my first spark of emotion.

"Aria?" Sally's hand is warm on my arm.

I sniff and shrug. How do I tell a couple like Clark and Sally that I quit, that I no longer believe in what I'm doing, or rather for whom I'm doing it? They've been faithful workers in God's kingdom for years. They've sacrificed comfort and basic necessities, not to mention time away from their own sons to minister to the temporal and eternal needs of others a half world away from where I'm sure they'd rather be. And I sit here saying I quit?

Yes.

There is no alternative. Not for me. Even if I wanted to change my mind I couldn't. Not after the way I ranted at God last night. Oh, I know Celie would tell me he's big enough to take it and then some. The problem is he's evidently not big enough to prevent the catastrophe in the first place or run interference once it's occurred. He's not the omniscient, merciful one I believed him to be. So why waste one more breath trying to convince others he is?

"Are you sure this is what you want to do?"

I look at Sally's face, tender in all its sharp plainness. She exudes compassion. Just a short time ago I would have attributed it to the work of the Spirit flowing through and out of her, but now I think it's just Sally's nature and nothing more. "I can't stay." That's the simple truth.

There's a pleading in Sally's eyes that pierces me as she looks at Clark. "Love?"

Clark glances at the screen door then back at me. "Has something happened we should know about?"

Instantly, I catch his meaning. "No! Absolutely not." I shake my head for emphasis. "I'm sorry," I say to both of them, "for letting you down. For the inconvenience." Twice to the airport in three days.

Clark rises. "Well then, I'll bring up your trunks."

I can tell that isn't what Sally wants to hear. She seems to be looking for something persuasive to say, but I know she won't find it. I've made up my mind.

Bring up my trunks. Like a faulty CD, Clark's words play over and over in my head as I wait for him in my room. They're not trunks, they're suitcases. Oversized, yes, but still not trunks. The thing is, they might as well be since that's Clark's impression of them, of me, of the dumb girl wannabe missionary who doesn't even know how to pack for her first and only term overseas. Of the dumb girl wannabe missionary who cuts her hair in a style that can't possibly be maintained, leaving her to look like a dumb *boy* wannabe missionary in need of a haircut almost before the tires of the airplane that brought her here lift off again, with shorts too short, flip-flops, and not a pair of work gloves or a headscarf in all that stuff.

I obviously missed something in Bible school.

"Thank you," I say, when Clark deposits the accursed luggage in the middle of my room. The big one takes up half my bed when I plop it down on the spread. More than half of what I brought is still inside, untouched in the nine weeks since my arrival. Nine weeks? Only? Yeah, but look at the damage I managed to accomplish in that short amount of time.

I start shoving things in the enormous bag with none of the care I took when I packed them back at the compound. The big suitcase bulges when I zip it shut. It's all I can do to lift it off the bed. Its broken wheel makes me groan even more than the weight, for I know what a miserable experience it will make of my trip home. The mid-sized bag will have to hold the rest of my things. I utter a sardonic laugh when I think of all the space I've created by using up several of the papaya and melon bars of soap—the others I'll leave in the bathroom cupboard for Sally—not to mention the king-sized bottle of mousse I won't be taking home. What little is left can go in the trash.

I leave a brief note of thanks and apology in an envelope on the bed. Inside I've added all the Moldovan *leus* I have left. They will buy a few groceries and cover the cost of fuel for the trip to and from the airport, which I know Clark and Sally won't allow me to pay for outright. It's the least I can do.

I tote the smaller of my suitcases downstairs, along with my carry-on bag, and deposit them by the front door. Then I head back upstairs for the big one. I check the dresser drawers and wardrobe once more, though I know I haven't left anything and wouldn't have room if I did, then clunk my way down, both hands gripping the handle of the behemoth leading the way.

Sally turns the corner as I reach the last step. She has a tissue at her nose and I'd guess she's shed a few tears. "Aria, sweetheart, you should have said something. We'd have helped." I can't help catch the double meaning of her words.

Clark steps around her and relieves me of both suitcases and wheels them out to the waiting van. All its doors are open, letting the built-up sauna-like heat escape before we climb in.

I deposit my carry-on in the back, alongside my other luggage, glance at the church and ask them to give me a moment. Then I crunch my way across the gravel one last time.

It's hot inside the church with the windows shut and no fans running, but this is Friday and services aren't scheduled on Fridays.

Except at the coffeehouse. Clark will open things up and get the fans going early Sunday morning to cool things down before the congregation gathers.

My floppy bangs are wet with perspiration with me just standing in the sanctuary saying my goodbyes. Andy's been living in a back room since I arrived, with a window smaller than the one in my borrowed room upstairs, sleeping on a cot, and as far as I know he hasn't complained about the cramped quarters or the heat. Sure, he has a fan, but that box of a room has to be miserably hot, even at night. I've no doubt he'll be glad to have a bedroom in the house once again.

My heart races as I turn the corner that leads to his room. I'm sure he thinks my time here has been a waste, and worse, for everyone concerned, and he's absolutely right. Anything I've accomplished could only be logged on the what-not-to-do side of the page in your everyday missions how-to manual. Still, I want to say goodbye.

I knock on Andy's door and wait, then knock again. No answer. My hand hovers over the knob. I really shouldn't do this, I know, but I turn it and inch the door open. I hate to leave on a bad note, hate to think that his flexing jaw is the last thing I see of him.

"Andy? Are you here?" I stick my head in and see that he's not in the room. I already know he's not in the church or the house. So I guess I can keep my goodbye. My throat constricts, but that's all the emotion I allow myself. This is no less than what I deserve.

Sally reads my disappointment and squeezes my hand as I pass by her on my way to the van. This time I insist she sits up front. I strap myself into the seat behind hers and start to slide the door shut. But Sally puts her hand on the edge and leans inside. "It's not too late to change your mind." She entreats with her eyes and touches my knee. "Aria, this wasn't your fault."

It takes everything in me to keep my resolve, but here's the thing: "If I hadn't come here, Anya would still be safe." And my trust in the God of the universe would still be intact.

"You can't know—"

"She wouldn't have been on that corner at that moment. I left her there. And that's the truth."

My words make her sad, and I'm sorry for that. But I can't stay and pretend I'm here to do the Lord's work. Not now, with me on the opposing side of the God-is-good debate. I may be many unsavory things, but hypocrite isn't one of them.

I turn my eyes to the periwinkle church as we pull out of the drive and watch it till we round the corner. An interested audience might think me nostalgic in my moment of departure. But since the only audience is me, I won't bother to deny that all I really want is to see Andy walk out the door and beckon us to stop. To say goodbye, nothing more. But it's not to be.

There are no egg salad and pickle sandwiches on this trip, no getting-acquainted conversation. Just silence if you don't count the steady blast of the air conditioner and the drone of the tires on the road. There are things I'd like to say. I want to thank Sally and Clark for opening their lives to me and letting me work in their vineyard, so to speak. I want them to know I've come to like this little patch of the quilt that is the world, and that I care about the people here. But none of it matters now, so I'll save my final thank you for the airport and leave it at that.

I watch the acres and acres of sunflowers that line the highway out my window. Of course, the land unit here is the hectare and not the acre. One is larger than the other, but I couldn't tell you which—yet another indication of what a poor study I've been. The sun is halfway between high noon and sundown, a perfect three o'clock in the sky. Amazingly, all those beautiful brown and ochre, seeded heads have turned to follow its solar path, their faces lifted toward the light, absorbing all the life and energy they can before day's end. I never get over how human and yet other-worldly that seems. And no, the spiritual application is not lost on me. I just have no intention of turning my face to the Light, only to get burnt.

It's harder than I expect to say goodbye. Sally wraps me in an embrace, and though she feels fragile under my touch, with all those bones everywhere, there's nothing fragile about her. She's an M&M, this one, strong on the outside, gooey on the inside. I will miss her.

Her prayer for me is tender yet imploring. Her voice breaks more than once as she sends her petitions—all for me—to heaven. Under other circumstances, her prayer would move me to tears, but standing here I don't feel much. I want to for Sally's sake if not my own, but it just isn't there. And I can't fake it.

I'm humming "It's Too Late" by Carole King as I locate my seat on the plane. Booking at the last minute never bodes well for optimum seating, and today is no exception. I'm all the way in the back of the plane, in a middle seat, between two large men. Think sumo, only Caucasian. I squeeze my carry-on into the overhead bin, then apologize as I point out my seat to the man on the aisle. He groans as he hefts himself to his feet, not the least bit happy about it if looks mean anything, and steps past me. I thank him and strap myself to the gray tweed seat, then adjust the air to blow right on me. Someone needs a shower and it isn't me, that's all I can say.

Between the elbow on my left and the elbow on my right, this is going to be one long flight. I'm thinking this is only the first backlash, out of many to come I'm sure, of being out of God's favor. But there's an open aisle seat six rows up on this side of the middle aisle I have my eye on. I furtively unstrap my belt, and am as attentive as my students were when I told them the story of Emoo. Finally, an attendant speaks into the microphone and says what I've been waiting to hear.

"The doors to the cabin have been closed," she says. "If you're going to change seats, now is the time."

I'm on my feet in a flash, bumping my head on the underside of the overhead bin, but everything's slow motion from there. My outside aisle mate gives me an are-you-kidding? look, then drops his hands onto the armrests to hoist himself up. But dang! A guy in tropical board shorts and flip-flops beats me to the draw. I almost cry as I sit back down and click my seatbelt closed.

But then, another attendant stops at our aisle. "Miss," he says, "would you come with me? And bring your carry-on."

Would I come with him? Any bring my carry-on? What could I possibly have done in these few short minutes to draw the attention of the flight crew?

As I walk the aisle behind him toward the front of the plane, uncomfortably conspicuous, I try to think what this might be about. There's nothing in my suitcase I didn't come with, nothing to catch a scanner's attention, is there? Well, only the trinkets I bought in the airport gift shop, and those should be okay. I planned to bring home the perfect souvenirs for my family and Kari at the end of my term, finding just the right things in just the right places, but that was before my whirlwind decision to leave the country. As it is, I grabbed two baseball caps for Dad and Opa, one blue and one black that say Moldova, with the first O a golden sunflower. Then I bought a sunflower light catcher for Celie, a sunflower salt and pepper shaker set for Mam, a sunflower key chain for Johnnie, and these dangling sterling silver sunflower earrings for Kari. Okay, I bought two pairs of those, only because a random woman customer in the gift shop said, "Oh, yes, those were made for you."

Otherwise I know of no contraband I might be carrying. But still. I force my breathing to slow down. Then the attendant stops, and with a sweep of his hand directs me to an aisle seat. In an exit row. In business class! The tiny woman in the window seat beside me is already whiffle-snoring. She has a sleep mask over her eyes and ear pods in her ears.

"I'll stow your carry-on," the attendant says. His smile is conspiratorial.

Honestly, I could kiss his feet. Don't ask me why an exit seat is still empty at this stage of the game. I just know it's not empty any more. Yes! There is a—

I abruptly stop my thought, because I know where I'm going with this, and I can't go there anymore.

You'd think after one complete sleepless night I'd be out for the count. But I'm not. Not even with the assistance of two Tylenol PMs I bought in the gift shop for five dollars US. Five dollars. For two caplets. And here I sit, the endless drone of the 777's engines anything but a lullaby in my ears. I'm as restless as Opa waiting for Mam's apple and raisin kuchen to come out of the oven. Every time, you'd think he was eating it for the first time, and after all these years. And who can blame him? No one makes kuchen like Mam. Dad doesn't even try. The odd thing to me is how an old hippie like Mam, Italian at that, ever learned to bake anything but brownies. But to hear her tell it, her mother-in-law's kuchen was far superior to her own. Well, if that's true, all I can say is great-grandma Shunk's kuchen was too good for mere mortals.

I've read the *People* magazine I bought at the airport from Contents to Chatter, and I don't have a book. That was a huge oversight, getting out of the gift shop without one. It occurs to me with a sinking in the pit of my stomach that my "50 Most Beautiful" is still on the shelf in the parsonage bathroom cupboard, with the gum wrapper bookmark stuck in Beautiful Person #27. Ryan Gosling was still a no-show, but I had every confidence he'd be in the top ten. Now I'll never know. I close my eyes and try to self-hypnotize. You are getting sleepy, very, very sleepy. Not even.

And then a small blond head appears above the seatback in front of me. It belongs to a girl, maybe three years old. But I can only see her from the nose up, so that's just a guess.

"Sweetie," a woman I assume is her mother, says, "come back and lie down." The woman sounds as tired as I feel. "Baby, come on."

But Baby has other ideas. She doesn't want to lie down. I'm guessing she wants to stand and stare at me, because she warms up for a nice little fit when Mommy pulls her away. The woman shushes her, then placates her when the shushing doesn't work. She's already getting angry looks from the passengers sitting around us.

So Blondie pops back up, her eyes round and brown as she stares at me. "Hello," I say. But she continues to interrogate me with those Tootsie Pop eyes. If I could see her mouth I might know how to proceed. I'd know if there was the trace of a smile or the quiver of her chin. Then, two little hands appear on the seatback. Her tiny fingernails are painted sky blue. They match the bands that hold two little ponytails on either side of her head. She's adorable from what I can see, and could be the model for one of those Kim Anderson cards, like where the little boy offers the little girl a rose, or where the boy and girl are looking back as they walk off into a mist, holding hands.

If only life were that serene.

"Who painted your fingernails?" I don't even know if she understands.

But then, Baby grips the seatback with one hand and splays the fingers of the other as she examines the polish. "Mommy."

I barely hear her reply with her mouth hidden behind the seat, but it's a start. "And did Mommy fix your ponytails?"

Baby nods.

"They're lovely."

She disappears behind the seat and I think, *it was nice while it lasted*. But then she appears again, struggling to lift a baby doll half as big as she is by the hair. She holds it up for my inspection, though I can hardly see more of the doll than I can see of the girl.

"This must be your favorite doll."

She looks at the doll, whose hair has seen better days and whose eyes are stuck open in a glassy stare. She nods. "Baby Abbie."

"Abbie. That's a nice name. And what's yours?"

She raises herself, on tiptoe I suppose, and almost gets her shin to the top of the seatback. "Meggie."

"Well, hello, Meggie. I'm Aria." I don't know why I don't say Ree.

"Are you going on a visit, or are you going home?"

She looks down at her mother, then back at me. "Home. To see Daddy."

"I bet he'll be glad to see you."

She nods.

"I'm going home too."

Meggie's mother sits up and we chat for a few minutes. They live in a town in Iowa, and have been to visit Meggie's grandparents in Romania, where—the woman hasn't told me her name—but where she lived till she was five. She moved to America with her aunt and uncle, which explains the absence of a strong accent, though there's a trace now that I know where she's from. Finally she says, "Baby, we really need to sleep so we'll be ready to see Daddy."

We say goodnight, and Meggie seems finally ready to lay her head down and rest.

Tired as I am my mind still won't shut down. I wonder what type of parents would send their little girl off to live in another country with her aunt and uncle. Then I think of Romanian history over the past twenty or so years. *Selfless parents* is the answer that comes to me. Instead of growing up in a country riddled with unrest and poverty, Meggie's mother grew up in America, where the possibilities for a good life are endless. So instead of growing up in a country where beautiful little girls, like she certainly must have been, are stolen and supplied like toys to deviant monsters, she was given a better life. I don't know that to be a fact. I merely hope that her parents' sacrifice was worth it.

I know America has its share of perversion. Still, I feel safe within its borders and I'm glad to be going home.

Unfortunately, this string of thought leads me right back to Anya. My five dollar Tylenol PM purchase was a waste. I acknowledge defeat and ring my call button. The same attendant who led me to my current seat responds.

"Could I get a cup of coffee—the real thing? And is there any chance a passenger left behind a book on a previous flight?" Not likely, I know, but it can't hurt to ask.

"Time clock off?"

I smile and nod.

"I'll see what I can find."

In three minutes he returns with the coffee, in a larger-than-normal Styrofoam cup, along with two individually wrapped chocolate chip cookies the size of a compact disc. Then he hands me a book, and I know by his smile it's a treasure. Sure enough. It's a hardback of James Patterson's latest. Someone was ticked, I'll bet, when he or she found it missing when they got where they were going. But their loss is my gain. Not that Patterson would be my first choice in a novelist, but I'm the proverbial beggar here. "You rock." Again, I could kiss his feet.

He smiles. "Call if you want more," he says of the coffee.

I vow to write a letter of praise about this young man—Justin his name badge says. Handwritten and mailed through the USPS, no less.

I crack open the book and turn to chapter one.

Twenty-Three

Unlike so many towns that sprang up along the old Highway 99, Linden isn't a quick pit-stop of an exit off the highway, with a mini-mart, a McDonald's, and a good old-fashioned truck stop. It isn't off the highway at all. It's several miles east of 99, and you have to be going there on purpose or you'd never find it in all that farmland. For those partial to cities, Linden would seem like nothing more than a patch of dirt too far from everywhere. Our version of "high rise" is the acres and acres of old English walnut trees that spread their umbrella of branches thirty feet up or more. This time of year, the nuts are encased in velvety olive-green hulls the size of eggs. The fruit inside will continue to grow until late August, when the harvest begins.

Same with almonds, only their hulls are gray-green and smaller. Pistachios are smaller yet. Both pistachio and almond trees are much smaller than walnut trees, but unlike walnut trees, which are self-pollinating, having male and female flowers on the same tree, almond and pistachio—and any number of fruit trees—have male and female trees. The male tree is the pollinator and the female the producer, naturally, and pollination depends not on bees, but entirely on the wind. There should be, on average, one male to every ten female trees, which when translated to human terms is not much off the mark if you ask most any guy, and just plain disgusting if you ask me.

For trivia nuts—pun intended—pistachios were a favorite of the Queen of Sheba, and they're Mam's favorite too. But in my opinion almonds win hands down. Fresh, roasted, seasoned, I love them all. Except candied. *Candied* and *almonds* don't belong in the same sentence, let alone all wrapped up into one treat.

I've always thought of our nut trees in terms of papa bear, mama bear and baby bear trees—walnut, almond and pistachio, respectively. Odd I know, but there it is.

It's beyond me why a pair of hippies would settle in Linden, when to my knowledge there's never been a commune within seventy-five miles in any direction. But settle they did. And I'm forced to admit I'm as rooted to that patch of dirt as the nut trees Opa planted long before I was born. I'm glad to be going home, and that amazes me.

I exit the plane, so tired I practically stumble as I search out the carousel that will deliver my bags to me. It's fifteen minutes before the first piece of luggage from our plane appears on the conveyer belt, and a few more minutes before I finally see the broken wheel of my bag emerge from the dark hole that belches out the luggage. The smaller bag isn't far behind. I wrestle both pieces off the track while still trying to manage my carry-on. When I turn back toward the terminal, there's Kari, holding a cardboard sign that reads, "Are you NUTS?!"

That makes me laugh. "I am." I let go of my bags and throw my arms around her. "Thanks, K."

"Are you kidding? I never pass up an opportunity to come into the city. Wait till you see the jeans I bought."

She has the perfect figure if you ask me. We're the same size from the waist down, if you don't count the four inches of height I have on her. But up top, well, let's just say there's lots more of Kari to love. She's not vain about it, nor is she self-conscious. "God given," she's said more than once, "so, girl, why should I be shy?" Don't get me wrong, she's modest enough, but she does turn heads.

I console myself by reminding me there'll be less to sag one of these days. Those jokes about slinging them over your shoulder to get them out of the way when you're old won't apply to me.

Still.

"Hungry?"

"Starved."

Kari grabs the handle of the bag with the broken wheel and stops me from even opening my mouth when I try to object. "You pick."

She won't believe what I'm about to say. "Fuddruckers."

I'm right. She looks at me with both eyebrows lost beneath her sassy curls. "Are you sure about that?"

"I want a good old American cheeseburger."

"All right, then. You got it."

"And a milkshake."

"Let's go." She winks and picks up her speed as much as that crazy wheel and her four-inch stilettos will let her.

The lights of the city are behind us as we cross the San Mateo Bridge on our way to Dublin. The night sky above the outline of the inland mountains engulfs us in a twinkling midnight blue embrace. The water some thirty feet below us is black and fathomless.

"You didn't tell anyone you were picking me up, did you?"

Kari has one hand draped over the steering wheel. "You said not to. Do they still not know you're coming home?"

"I thought I'd go for the surprise factor."

Kari turns my way for a moment. I don't need the artificial light from oncoming headlamps to know exactly the expression that's on her face, or what it says. "Surprise factor? That's so not fair, Ree."

"If I'd called to say I'm coming home they'd have had hours to worry. This way they won't."

"Have hours?"

"Worry. They won't need to because there I'll be. I mean, they can see I'm fine."

"Uh huh. Except you're not."

I've been up nearly forty-eight hours, dozing a few minutes here and there, so I'm not on my game. And where Kari's concerned that's a huge disadvantage. "Let's talk later. After some food and about a week's worth of sleep."

The minute we walk into the burger joint, with every bit of breathing space filled with the odor of frying meat and onions, my stomach gives me this not-on-your-life vibe. I'm smart enough to listen. "Um, you know, I think I'll just have a chocolate shake." I direct Kari to the ice cream fountain. "With vanilla ice cream," I say to the girl behind the counter. "To go." Kari, who's only too happy to pass up the burger, or anything with meat for that matter, orders a designer shake with one scoop of Butterfinger and one of peanut butter and chocolate, then adds two squirts of caramel sauce. Within ten minutes we're back on the road.

———————————

I'm jostled awake as Kari turns onto the mile-long gravel road that leads to the compound. A third of my shake is melted in the cup in the center console cup holder. I don't even remember putting it there.

"I forgot you talk in your sleep." Kari says it with a laugh in her voice.

I, on the other hand, don't see the humor. "What did I say?"

"That's the thing, Ree, you mumble." She snaps her fingers as if to say, *Drats!*

Well that's a relief, especially considering I woke with Andy on my mind. "Slow down," I say, even though Kari's barely creeping along. I could throw up I'm so nervous. "Maybe I should stay with you tonight." The digital clock on the dash reads 11:11.

Kari brakes. "Whatever you want. I can turn around."

I seriously consider the offer, disgusted that I'm such a coward. "I don't know what I'm doing here, Kari."

"We go home when we don't know what else to do. That's what you're doing here."

She's right about that.

I blow out a breath and nod forward. "Let's go."

I don't know if the houses that anchor two of the four corners of the compound look larger or smaller than I remember as we approach. But they do look different from what I've been used to the past two months. I ask Kari to turn off her headlights and coast into the driveway of our house. And here we sit.

The moon resembles the sickle on the old Soviet flag, only bleached of its color. It offers little illumination. A faint glow from the front windows of our house is the only other light, other than the stars, for Mam and Opa's house is just a black silhouette in the night. That little glow tells me Celie is still up and in the sitting room on the opposite side of the house.

Dad turns in almost the moment their upstairs bedroom loses all its natural light. But then he's up before there's even a hint of color in the eastern horizon. Same with Opa. Natural for farmers, I guess. But the women on the compound get their second wind about that time. I'm certain there's a strong correlation there. The sitting room, which is really just a small family room minus the fireplace where we women love to gather and chat, has always been Celie's favorite. Even more than the kitchen, which is the room Mam prefers no matter whose house she's in. The sitting room was built at the southeastern-most corner of the house and couldn't get any farther from the master bedroom upstairs at the northwestern-most corner. Dad's not a light sleeper, but still, that was good foresight on Celie's part in the design of the house. We've never had to shush ourselves for fear of waking anyone when the entertainment got out of hand.

For the most part it serves as a reading room for Celie. And she does love to read. She has a wine-colored velour Queen Anne wing chair molded and worn to her form, with a matching footstool for Snickers, her Lhasa apso, who is now entitled to his own AARP card, and therefore coddled more than ever. There's a floor lamp over the left shoulder of the chair, whose shade is tilted forward just slightly to shed the perfect light for Celie's eyes, which are beginning to lose their sharpness. She doesn't know that we know she hides a pair of drugstore magnifiers down the side of the seat cushion. She only wears them when no one else is around. She doesn't know we know that too. But her hearing is as sharp as it ever was, maybe sharper, so there's little chance she'll get caught with them on.

We think it's cute.

Celie has never loved a dog the way she loves Snickers, or spoiled one so shamelessly. No other dog has been allowed free run of our house, and certainly never slept on her and Dad's bed. But every night, Snick curls up at Celie's feet, and he gets plain nasty if you try to move him before he's good and ready to be moved.

When he was a pup, his fine, curling fur was a blend of chocolate and caramel, hence the name. Now it's a smoky gray. His pronounced under bite gives him the look of a bulldog, and though small, he was fearless back in the day. At the moment he's my biggest problem, because in all my life there's never been a better watchdog on the compound. I know Opa will argue the point from here till forever, but Opa's wrong. Plain and simple.

I can predict how this will go down. Celie's reading in her Queen Anne chair with Snickers curled up on the footstool. The moment Kari and I step onto the porch, Snick will lift his head and flex his long ears— the better to hear you with, my dear—then a low growl will form in his throat.

Celie will be alerted the moment he lifts his head from the footrest, and being a lot braver than me, will go on her own to investigate. I'm amazed he isn't already yapping from the other side of the front door, which even Mam and Opa can hear all the way to their house if all the windows are open and the wind is just right.

"What?" Kari asks as I hesitate.

"Snickers." I say it in the softest of whispers and put a finger to my lips.

Kari pulls her cell phone from her pocket, since mine hasn't been charged in several hours. "Maybe you should call."

But unexpected phone calls late at night are no less jarring than an unexpected knock at the door. Of course, I could just pull my key out and let myself in. But that would startle Celie even more, and what if the alarm's set?

Kari's giving me a look that says, Well, what now? when suddenly the porch light comes on. We both jump and clutch our hearts, then Celie opens the front door. Before I can say hello or anything, Snickers is sniffing my shoes and licking my shins. Celie watches with a thought-you-could-fool-me? smile. If Kari's not thinking the same thing I am—that Shunk women are most definitely equipped with radar—then I don't know my best friend. I just wonder when mine's finally going to kick in.

"Hi," I say, and Celie opens her arms to me. Her hair smells of citrus fruit from the shampoo she's used for a long while now. Tana, our hairdresser, says to mix it up for the best effect, but Celie isn't into change.

She holds me at arm's length and studies my eyes. It's a psychological shakedown, equivalent to smelling my breath for alcohol the way she did that one time in high school I came home drunk, only instead of booze, tonight she's looking for brokenness. "Hi." There's not the hint of a question in her voice about why I might be standing here at this moment, and it occurs to me Sally may have phoned my parents. I swear there are some things I will not do when I'm a mother.

"You girls come in. I'll put on water for tea."

Kari pulls my suitcase onto the porch. "Not for me, thanks. I need to get going." She gives me a sideways glance and it's plain I'm on my own for this one.

Thanks, I want to say. A lot. Instead I hug her. "I'll call you tomorrow."

"Or the day after. Get some sleep, huh?"

Celie and I stand shoulder to shoulder and watch as Kari disappears down the lane, then Celie leads me into the house. "Let's get that tea started."

All I really want is to climb the stairs and drop into my own bed, but I owe my mother more than that. "Sounds good."

In no time we're seated at the kitchen table, which she's selected for a closer, more intimate arrangement. "How did you know we were here?"

"Snickers told me."

I raise an eyebrow. "I didn't hear him bark."

Celie smiles her all-knowing smile, the one that did more to keep me on the straight and narrow than any amount of preaching from Pastor Cash. Yeah, that's his real name. "Of course you didn't. When it's Johnnie coming in, or lurking out here on the porch, Snick raises his tail and shakes it like a pompom." Fitting for Johnnie, my pep club sister. "When it's you, he lifts his head and sniffs the air three times. Like this." She looks like a rabbit as she demonstrates.

"Yeah? You never told us that before."

"Ha, and give away my secrets? They came in handy when you girls were in school."

"Mom"—she looks as surprised as I am when I call her that—"Johnnie and I both were straight as Carly Underhill's bangs"—and it doesn't get much straighter than that. "Well, almost."

"It's the almost that mattered. And whatever made you think of Carly Underhill? You were in—"

"Second grade together. And I have no idea."

"Say a prayer for her tonight."

The look on her face tells me she means it. "Okay."

I love the simple, classic look of Celie. On the sliding scale of natural hair color, hers falls right in the middle of Johnnie's and mine. It's the color of almonds right out of the shell. Tana does an adequate job of keeping it looking as natural as possible, and adds the perfect highlights. I love how Celie's bangs swoop down right to her eyelashes and twitch when she blinks, and how they're not so thick that they hide her eyebrows, which are one of Celie's most expressive features. She speaks volumes with those eyebrows. And her eyes, well, they say, "I can read every thought you ever thought about thinking, and don't you think I can't."

I'm thinking that may be a skill that develops along with the zygote. Not for one minute would I put that past God now that I'm getting to know the real him.

Celie knows how to make hot tea, and this cup I'm working on tastes better than anything I've had in the past twenty-four hours, including the milkshake. "So tell me the truth, did Sally call?"

Celie twirls the string on her teabag, which she never removes from her cup until all the tea is gone. Not me. I dunk it a few times, then out it comes. She doesn't answer one way or the other. Instead she says, "You want to talk about it?"

It's not her words that bring the lump to my throat, but the tone of her voice, which comforts like warm socks on a cold day. I shake my head, and that's about all I can manage.

"There'll be time." She sips her tea as if that's true. As if she has all the time in the world. Snickers is curled at her feet in a furry spiral so it's hard to tell where he begins and ends. His breathing is steady and even, a perfect representation of the environment in which his world revolves.

Conversely, a representation of my world just now would look like Pablo Picasso had gotten hold of it.

On my third yawn Celie rises and carries our cups to the sink. "We better turn in."

I don't hesitate for even one moment. "I'll lug my suitcases up in the morning. For now I'll just grab my carry-on." It has my toothbrush and . . . well, anything else is unessential right now. "Goodnight, Mom."

"'Night, baby." I've almost reached the stairs when she says, "By the way, I put clean sheets on your bed this morning. And opened your window."

Well then. I completely disregard the chill that ripples its way down my arms.

Twenty-Four

It's dark when I awake and for a moment I wonder where I am and what day, or more accurately, what night it is. But my wondering is short lived, for I know exactly where I am the instant I hear the incessant squawk of the owlets that hatched, in my absence, in Opa's owl boxes. And I do mean incessant. From dusk till dawn they never hush their screaking.

The owlets may sound like a girl band, but believe me, they don't *sound* like a girl band, if you get my drift. From late May through August they never stop. And I always know when it's dinnertime, because the screaking becomes frantic as the baby owls open wide their gullets and cry for the lion's share of whatever mouse or snake Mom and Dad have brought home to regurgitate for supper.

Yuck.

The owl boxes—there are two—are located in the orchards that surround our four home sites. They're each the size of a large rural mailbox, are painted stark white, and are perched on fifteen foot poles, one on the west side of the compound and one on the east.

Unfortunately, that particular box faces my bedroom window, which is typically open all night long from April till October. Never mind that the box is a good hundred yards from the house. Noise carries in the country. But as Mam is quick to point out, we don't have to worry about snakes or mice.

I tug my cell phone away from its charger, flip it open and check the date. I'm relieved to know I haven't slept through even one night, let alone two. Now I try to assess what woke me out of what should have been a well-earned sleep. My bladder is content for the moment, I'm neither too warm nor too cool—though I do miss the steady hum of the box fan I used in Moldova. In fact, I might buy one like it to drown out the racket of the owls, which, now that I think of it, may have been what woke me. "Note to self . . ." I say out loud and hope I'll remember to get to Lowes before another night falls.

My stomach growls and I realize I'm so hungry I hurt. That must be what really woke me. I wonder if Celie has any of those raisin-cinnamon bagels downstairs, but I'm so tired. I lay in the screaking darkness hoping, *hoping* sleep will win out, but my grumbling stomach gets the upper hand, and I go in search of food.

The house is asleep, as it should be at this hour. I open the bread drawer and search its contents by the light thrown off from the tiny bulb burning beneath the stovetop micro-hood. Celie leaves it on as a nightlight. I'm out of luck with the bagels, but reach for a package of English muffins.

"Aria?"

I jump as if super charged and let out a squeal as the drawer slams on all four fingers of my right hand. "Ah! Oh!" I shake my hand furiously as the pain radiates all the way to my toes, then hold it up to inspect. There are deep creases across the fingers between the knuckles and nails. But no blood. Yet.

"Ree?" Dad says. "You all right, babe? What are you doing here?"

I shake my hand again and give into another groan or two. "Dad, it's four o'clock in the morning. What are you doing up?"

"I'm always up at four. You sure you're okay?"

I never said I was okay. Not once. I examine my fingers again. "Yeah." This is the first of any number of lies I'm prepared to tell about the state I'm in.

Dad's in a T-shirt and boxers, and for the life of me I can't tell you why, but I think of Andy. We hug, then I move to the table while he reaches for the coffee pot and turns on the tap. "When did you get home?" He looks back at me with a scowl. "Did we know you were coming?"

"Last night. And no. Kari picked me up."

The aroma of Blue Mountain Jamaican coffee reaches me as Dad zips open the baggie Celie put it in last night after she ground the beans for him. She does that faithfully every night before she turns in. She may not know it, but I'm taking notes in case Mr. No-Noun-For-A-Last-Name ever finds me out here on the back side of the moon.

Dad presses the coffee maker's "on" button, places his mug under the flow, then turns and leans his tall form against the tiled counter. For the most part he's kept himself in good shape, from hard work and nothing but. "We could have done that." When it's full, he removes his mug and slips the pot in place. No doubt about it, he begins his day with one potent cup of joe.

"I know." I can tell he's waiting for more, but I leave it at that. I don't tell him I was afraid to call, afraid someone would talk me out of bailing on the Mitchells, of letting everyone down. Afraid they'd be as disappointed in me as I am.

"Is this about that girl?"

"Anya. Yes."

He holds up the pot of brewed coffee to offer me a cup. I shake my head. If I drink a cup of his famously strong coffee now I'll never get back to sleep, which is what I intend to do once I've eaten my English muffin. Which reminds me I forgot to start the toaster, but I don't move to do it.

"It's a bad world out there, Ree. All we can do is try our best to make it better."

"And how exactly do we do that?"

Dad takes several sips of his coffee as he's formulating his answer. "Most of us will never be in a position to impact the world at large with our actions, good or bad. We won't govern countries or serve on the Supreme Court."

"You're forgetting Johnnie." Our political science major.

He smiles. "That's true. Anyway, we both know I'm not the theological expert here. But we do whatever we can to right whatever wrongs come our way, and we don't back down from bullies."

That's something my dad has said all my life, and he's lived it. Not with fists but with guts, and most bullies don't know what to do with guts.

"You're saying I shouldn't have come home?"

"No." When I throw him a question with my eyes, he clarifies. "Not saying that at all."

But I think that's exactly what he's saying. How else do you make it better? Certainly not by hiding out here at the compound. "I'm too tired to think." The English muffin will have to wait.

Dad hugs me again, and this time he smells like coffee. "It's good to see you." He gives an extra squeeze for emphasis. "Really good."

I round the corner on my way to the stairs and meet Johnnie head on. Literally. "What the—Ree? Ree!" Her voice goes up three octaves between the question mark and the exclamation point. "What are you— when did you—? You're home!" She throws her arms around me and laughter fills the alcove.

But the laughter is all Johnnie's. Though I'm as happy to see her as she is to see me, I can barely manage a smile. Right now I'm as mixed up as the nuts we send out in our Christmas baskets every year. I've backed down, big time, and I know it. And here's the thing: I don't care. But if that's true, why do I want to hide?

Johnnie suddenly pulls away. She frowns as her eyes probe mine, just the way Celie's did. "You okay?"

"Sure." I'm quick to answer, but I know she doesn't believe me. "Tired actually. I was just"—I nod toward the stairs—"going up."

Johnnie's every bit as intuitive as Mam or Celie, but it takes little intuition to read through me. "Let's get some coffee." She leaves me no wiggle room as she nudges me back toward the kitchen.

The French doors which lead to the patio and pool deck are open. Dad's in his favorite outdoor chair, drinking his coffee and waiting for sunrise. He's all about sunrises. The cool, fresh, morning air swirls around Johnnie and me where we sit at the kitchen table. She's served us both a mug of Blue Mountain, but I've yet to take a sip. I'm still hoping to go back to sleep. I run my finger around the rim of my cup and wait for Johnnie's questions.

"This is such a surprise."

I shrug. "My phone wasn't charged." Even I know how lame that sounds. And what's that all about anyway? I mean, good grief, who's the older sister here? "The truth is, it was a last minute decision. There wasn't time to call anyone."

"How did you get home from the airport?"

Okay, she has me there. "Except Kari."

"You know I'd have come."

"Yes, I do. And thank you." I reach over and touch her hand, then go back to circling the rim of my cup.

"Did something happen? Besides Anya," she's quick to add.

"No. Not to me. I just—" What? Missed my vocation. Spent a good deal of time and money pursuing a course I was never meant to follow. Don't have a clue about what to do with my life. Other than that . . . I surrender and take a long drink of coffee. I forgot what a great barista my dad the chef is.

Johnnie tilts her head just like Celie and has that same intuitive look. "I missed you. I'm glad you're home."

And speaking of Celie, here she is, and it's barely five A.M. "Well, I see the surprise is out." She stands between us where we sit and rests her right hand on Johnnie's shoulder and her left hand on mine. She gives me a squeeze. "I didn't expect to see you up so early."

"You either." If Dad's all about sunrises, Celie's all about sunsets.

"I heard you girls down here, well, Johnnie anyway"—she winks at my sister—"and wanted in on the fun." She heads to the stove to turn on the burner where her teakettle sits. With the flame adjusted just so, she takes her barefooted self outside to say good morning to Dad. She drops onto his lap and puts her arms around his neck. That's where I turn away.

There are no perfect marriages, I know, but if I come close to finding a mate as well-suited to me as Dad is to Celie, I'll be a happy woman. Matthew Farmer may have been my one honest chance, but knowing how right he is for Johnnie, I firmly believe he was meant to be my brother-in-law and not my husband.

And if I don't find a mate, suited or otherwise?

That thought slips away as the kettle lets out a shrill cry. "I'll get it." The steam from the boiling water dampens my face as I fill Celie's waiting mug, but the rest I'll leave up to her. She knows which tea she wants and just how she likes it.

"Thanks," she says at my side.

I don't sit down, just reach for my coffee. "Might as well let everyone know I'm home." I mean, of course, Mam and Opa. It's only five, but Opa will be on his second cup of coffee by now. And Mam, well, she'd be ticked if we didn't wake her up.

"I wish I could join you," Johnnie says. She rises and refills her cup. "Wish I could stay home today, but this is only the second week of classes. Too soon to cut."

As if she'd ever miss a class.

"Then I have to work at the capital for a couple of hours, but I'll be home for dinner"—she glances at Celie—"if we can make that a little later than usual? You'll be here, won't you?"

"As far as I know," I say.

She kisses my cheek, blows a kiss to Celie, and scoots off for her shower. Besides starting her senior year at Sac State, Johnnie works as an intern for our district congresswoman. She hopes one day to fill her seat. Do I think she'll make it? I'm already practicing my curtsey.

Dad heads up to shave as Celie and I skirt the pool on our way to Mam's. Though the sun has yet to show its face, it's close to seventy degrees outside, not the least bit uncommon for mid-August in the valley. I'll be swimming laps before the day is out. But I'll wait until it's good and hot, so it's all the more refreshing. Like after a long, long nap.

I hear the strains of Opa's Gibson, hear the tiny squeals as his fingers move up and down on the steel strings as he plays his prayers. A pang pulls at my stomach as I think of Andy. Right away I shake off the thought. I love the squeals, always have. It's a sound unique to itself, like the skip of an LP. What else makes such a sound?

I tap two times on the glass door, slide open the screen and step into the breakfast nook just off the kitchen.

"Baby girl." Opa puts aside his guitar and stands. His dimples are deep as he smiles, his eyes give off their singular twinkle. I could never decipher the knowing look that resides in his eyes, not if I lived a thousand years, but it's as comforting as the timbre of his music is haunting. He wraps me in a hug, and I smell the cleanness of him.

"I missed you." My words are for his ears only. He tightens his embrace. "Will you go get Mam?"

He chuckles, smoothes his white goatee and heads for the stairs, while Celie and I sit down at the table. Mam is still much the free spirit and that equates to no nightclothes. She likes her skin to breathe, she says. Unhindered. Which is why I'll leave the waking to Opa.

"As good as it is to see you," Celie says, "I'd like to see you looking more refreshed. I hope you'll get some sleep after you see Mom."

I don't even try to compute the number of hours I've been awake, if you don't count the four short hours I was in my own bed. "That all depends on how much coffee I drink." Already I regret the caffeine I've ingested.

I hear Mam before I see her. "What's this all about, Blue? What aren't you telling me?" I hear the worry in her voice, and who can blame her when she's dragged from her bed even before the sun clears the top of the pistachio trees. Then she turns the corner, sees me and squeals. "Aria! What on earth?"

Opa's laugh pours forth, rich as liquid silk, and washes over us. If I didn't know him I would still know he's a singer, just from the quality of that laugh. It's been a favorite sound of mine all my life. "Well?" he says to Mam. "Worth getting up for?"

"I'll deal with you later," she says, then wraps her arms around me. "But yes, worth getting up for."

I see the look that passes between Mam and Celie and know that whatever intuition Celie had about me coming home was shared with her mother. Probably without words. They've always had that ability, always been on the same wavelength.

"We've been praying," Mam says.

I swallow hard to hold back the tears.

Twenty-Five

Johnnie and Matt's wedding is one year from today, which is forty-eight weeks from the day I was due to arrive home from Moldova. I'd have had four weeks to get ready for my role as maid of honor, to be fitted for my dress, find my shoes, do something with my hair. Instead, counting the four weeks I've been home, I have fifty-six weeks to do all this.

I don't guess it'll sneak up on me.

After a few days trying to sort things out I've spent the last three weeks looking for a job. Of course all the teaching positions were gobbled up way back in the spring, but in the moments I choose to be honest with myself, I admit I don't have the courage to work with children again. Not for a while anyway. There are too many ways to get hurt.

So. What does a displaced missionary with a grudge do with a degree that, in the real world, doesn't amount to a bushel of nuts? I could work in the plumbing department of a home improvement store half the size of Moldova, selling toilets at half the salary I earned in my position as office manager of the family business. Plus commission. Can't forget that. And from what I hear, toilets practically sell themselves.

Or I could go to work as the bookkeeper for a nursery in Linden that specializes in fruit trees. If there's one thing I should know, it's fruit trees. Nut trees anyway. But here's the thing: I hate numbers. Still, I'm now officially desperate. You can only float in a pool so many hours a day, for so long.

"How would you feel about coming back to work for us?" Dad asks over a Friday night dinner. "We sure could use you."

Honestly? I'd as soon have my nose caught in a nutcracker. The look on my face probably says as much, for Dad adds, "Just to get us through the harvest."

My replacement at Shunk-Winters Nut Company hasn't worked out. I might find some satisfaction in that if I were safely stashed a half world away, out of reach of this request. As it is, I swallow twice to dislodge the meatloaf stuck in my throat. "I, ah, hadn't really thought about it."

Which is such a lie. It's all I've thought about for days, wondering just how to turn down the solicitation when it came. And I knew it was coming. The gazes of Dad, Celie, Johnnie and Matt, who are seated around the dining room table, have converged on my face, all awaiting my reply.

Can anyone spell conspiracy?

Why I chose the heart of an economic downturn to lose my better judgment is a lapse of monumental proportions. But did I? Lose my better judgment? I think what I lost is something else altogether, something I don't particularly want to parse at present. Still, here I am right back where I didn't ever want to be again. Going nuts.

I sigh, give a sickly smile, and it's settled. I've rejoined the ranks of the gainfully employed.

Dang.

Matt, a frequent guest at our dinner table, comes alongside me and wraps one arm around my shoulders in what I call a chum hug. "That was the right choice."

As if I had one. "Yeah." The word is a long exhale, like the escaping of the dregs of stale air in a used up party balloon. It's all I have the heart for.

"There's something special about family businesses, don't you think?"

Matt is positively guileless, but really, I could slap him right now. I excuse myself and sigh my way to the bathroom, where I pull out my cell phone and call Kari.

"You won't believe what I just did."

"When do you start?"

The tone in her voice rankles. "I really hate it when I'm the last one to know what's going on in my life."

"Ree, you don't have a life."

Touché.

"But that's all about to change."

I read Kari as effortlessly as she reads me, and the way her voice has changed to the texture of warm taffy tells me the exact direction she's headed. "No. You are not fixing me up."

She laughs. "Trust me, Ree, this time you won't be sorry."

I count on my fingers. "That's the third time you've said that, and let's see, Wyatt the bull rider couldn't complete a sentence without the use of phrases like worm spit"—as in 'that cowboy's ride didn't amount to a bucket of worm spit in a horse trough,' comparing his own fabulous ride, which made it to the ten-count every time, without him ever losing his Stetson. So he says. "Then there was Chuck the UPS guy. Nice to look at, but he's the exclamation point on the end of the looks-aren't-everything argument. And Ducky—well, that one speaks for itself." Kari's laughing by this time. "You, my friend, are three for three. I'd rather de-husk an orchard of walnuts single-handedly Saturday night. Have I made my point?"

We both know I haven't.

"Ree, you have to trust me. Walter's different."

"Walter. That in itself is reason enough to say no."

"He works in my office and doesn't have any telling nicknames. He's tall, intelligent, loves handball."

"Oh, well then."

She ignores my sarcasm. "He's a college grad, and as far as I know he has never ridden a bull."

I hate myself for doing it, but I'm caving, because the idea of one more Saturday night on the compound makes me feel like such a loser. "So why don't you go out with him?" The pause that follows is way too long. "Kari? Hello?" I check to make sure I haven't lost her. I haven't. "Kari." The tone of my voice demands an answer and she knows it.

"I did. Once. We just didn't hit it off," she says before I can hang up. "He's heard all about you and can't wait to meet you."

I feel a headache coming on. "Just please tell me he doesn't live with his mother."

"I swear."

It's dinner at a catfish place on the San Joaquin River. Safe, loud, not a candle anywhere, the perfect surrounding for a casual, get-acquainted dinner. Kari was right, Walter is tall. I thought she meant tall in comparison to her own five-foot-three inch frame, but no. She meant tall as in "Hello, I could be on the NBA circuit but I turned down the billion dollar offers for a job with brains." And he does seem intelligent. In fact, I've been left behind in the conversation three or four times, hung up on the meaning of an obscure word he's used—like hubris or opprobrium, though I should know what they mean—and had to pick the conversation back up like a dropped call.

I hate that in between the questions he tosses my way he bites at the tuft of hair that's sprouted like field grass just below his bottom lip.

A soul patch, they call it. I get left behind in the conversation yet again when I envision a whisker getting caught between his highly polished teeth. From what I can tell this is his only quirk, but it's effectively killed my appetite. A gas pain of a smile is frozen on my face throughout the evening, but all the while I'm thinking, "You're history, Walter my boy."

Kari's date is a guy named Hugh, and if one thing is certain it's that Hugh can no more keep up with Kari than Ivan Zalasky could keep up with the original red hot chili pepper. That may be what attracts Kari to Hugh for the moment, but it's obvious there's not a relationship in their future—not that Hugh has picked up on that vibe as of yet.

"We thought we'd top off the evening with a sunset river cruise," Kari says after dinner.

Why do I get the feeling I've become the butt of every conspiracy joke ever written? "I'd love to, but I have a bushel of nuts to husk," I want to say. In fact, I'm about to spit out a fitting excuse to decline when, as if on cue, Hugh and Walter each produce a pair of pre-purchased tickets. The gas pains are for real now.

It's like I've completely lost control of my life.

Kari and Hugh, and Walter and I take the last seats available in the cabin of the riverboat, completing a foursome of couples surrounding a low cocktail table. And sitting directly across from me—no, please no, it cannot be—is Patti Mitchell. This is conspiracy of the celestial variety at its finest. Patti is wearing a slinky black dress that enhances a figure she never had in high school, and around her neck is tied a shimmery saffron scarf.

Just right for hiding the scars from the rope.

Her eyes grow enormous in the moment of recognition. The start of a how-ya-doin' smile vanishes, replaced by a look of confusion, then pure panic as her gaze darts between Kari and me. The plank has been hoisted, or whatever it is they do with riverboat planks, and the dock is fading in the distance, so there's no possibility of escape, for Patti or for me. While I can't speak for her, don't think I don't consider jumping overboard.

The next few seconds pass in high-definition slo-mo as Patti pushes up off her chair. Her knee catches the edge of the table that's fastened to the deck between us, jarring it enough to slosh our beverages, turning the glass tabletop into a miniature sea, in which spare cocktail napkins float like life rafts. Patti emits an equally slow motion groan and bends to cradle her knee, while simultaneously searching out the nearest cabin exit.

We become the evening's entertainment for a brief eternity. I suddenly understand the concept of wishing for the ground to open up and swallow you whole. Patti's escort is shocked by the actions of his date/wife?—there wasn't time to look for wedding rings—and is a beat behind everyone else. Finally, with the most perplexed of frowns, he hurries after Patti, who, I assume, has gone to the point on the boat furthest away from us. From me. Who knows, she may well have jumped overboard by now.

Kari and I can do little but stare at one another, while our dates barrage us with a stream of whispered questions. I mean what are the odds I would first see Patti Mitchell's double on the other side of the globe, and then see her on the other side of a table? I do not believe in coincidence, so what's up? *Are you trying to rub my failures in my face? Is that what this is about?* I actually look to the ceiling and aim my unspoken questions like arrows.

All I can say is there better be a restroom on this barge.

"Excuse me." I step past Walter and go in search of one, with Kari in my wake.

It's a box of a room at the stern of the boat, barely large enough for one person, let alone two. But Kari and I squeeze in. My eyes are locked on hers and hers on mine.

"Patti Mitchell?" Kari's as stunned as I am. "I mean, I thought— Didn't she move away? A long time ago?"

"Evidently she's back."

"Wow," Kari says. "The scarf was kind of weird."

"It beats a turtleneck in summer."

"You think she always hides it? You know, her neck?"

"Wouldn't you?"

"Yeah." It's just a breath of a word.

"How long is this stupid cruise? Which I didn't want to come on in the first place."

Kari slides up on her answer. "Two hours, give or take."

"Great. Just great. We can't exactly hide out in here for the duration."

"Ree, come on. It's not like it was our fault." She pulls back at the look that flashes across my face. "Not completely."

But it was. More than Kari will ever know.

"Maybe we should go find her, just clear the air."

"Kari, she tried to hang herself because of us." Because of me. "That's a lot of air to clear."

"But it was years ago."

Eight to be exact. Eighty, eight hundred, eight thousand would not be long enough. There could never be enough years to erase that kind of memory. Not ever.

"It was a misunderstanding. Now might be the time to explain."

I shake my head. This is the one secret Kari knows nothing about. I want off this boat. I want to be safely cloistered back at the compound. What a switch, what a pathetic, unbelievable switch from how I felt three short months ago.

"You're right. We can't hang out here for the next two hours. No telling what the guys are thinking."

And speaking of guys. "Kari, I have to say this one thing, and this time I mean it."

"I know, I know. No more blind dates. But really, Ree, I bet you can't name three things you don't like about Walter."

My eyebrow hitches. "Three? That's all? And what's with you and Hugh? He's worse than Wolf thinking he can keep up with the big dogs. And in this instance, that's you."

Kari crosses her arms and tilts her head. "What's gotten into you?"

She holds up her hands. "Okay, running into Patti was unfortunate, but you've been way past edgy since you got home. And I know you're terribly upset about Anya. I get that. But, Ree, I don't recognize you anymore. No one does."

"And you'd know that because . . . ?"

"Celie called me. Everyone's worried about you. You've been sullen and withdrawn. You won't go to church."

"So. That's what this is really about, isn't it? Aria's riding the slippery slope." I use my most sarcastic tone. "Well, you can quit worrying. I don't plan to go to hell anytime soon."

A knock on the door interrupts Kari's comeback. "Swell." She rolls her eyes as only Kari can, and gives me an after-you sweep of her arm. When we open the door a young woman way overdressed for the occasion gives us an arched look as we sidle past her. Her perfume hangs in the air, thick as L.A. smog.

"Go get the guys," I say to Kari. "We'll just hang out back here." Where it's safe and deserted.

She looks around at what appears to be a stock room off which the restroom is located. "Just us and the fumes?"

"Go."

"Look, I'll check things out, then give you the all-clear if—"

"Go."

Her bare shoulders slump. "Ree, honestly, this is embarrassing. And childish."

If there were any way off this boat I'd show her how childish I can be. But I'm stuck. "Fine. You go on back and I'll catch up with you after."

"After what?"

"After this ride from the dark side is over."

I haven't seen Patti Mitchell in eight years, and seeing her now reminds me of what a self-centered, cheerleader of a twit I was at sixteen. I was more secure than I should have been, not having or needing a boyfriend, and had my face on more pages of the yearbook that spring than anyone in the junior class. From that point of reference I didn't realize how insecure other girls could be, how much their identity depended on the right guy taking notice, or the right group having your number on speed dial.

Patti Mitchell fell into this category, which I discovered almost fatally late. And now here is God reminding me of just how deep my failures go, because only God could have orchestrated this little reunion. I lost Anya and nearly killed Patti. I'm chalking up quite the résumé.

Kari leads the guys to where I stand. She looks anything but happy. Walter hands me my drink, which I down in no time.

"May I . . . ?" He nods to my glass.

I chug a mouthful of ice chips and hand him the glass.

"That's 7-Up with a twist, right?"

I slide the ice into my cheek. "I'll have what you're having."

He smiles and looks more hopeful than he has at any time during the evening. "Be right back." He and Hugh high-tail it back to the bar, leaving Kari and me in our hideaway.

"What do you think you're doing?"

"What do you mean?" My mouth is numb from the ice and I sound as if I've had a shot of Novocain.

"You know exactly what I mean."

She's right, I do, but I feign ignorance.

"You don't drink."

"It's just wine."

"Which is as intoxicating as any other form of alcohol." She puts a hand on her hip. "Say it with me. Right now. Come on."

"No. Not here."

"Yes here."

"Kari, I'm over twenty-one."

She plants her other hand on her other hip. "Say it."

I roll my eyes and deliver. "'I will not put a thief into my mouth to steal my brains.' There. Are you happy?"

Up until a moment ago it was my favorite line from *True Grit*, which Kim Darby recites to a drunken Rooster Cogburn—though Hailee Steinfeld did a fine job in the remake—but when it comes to Jeff Bridges, I'm sorry but how do you compete with John Wayne? That's what Opa would ask every time he had Johnnie and me, and Kari when she could be there, over for movie night. How could you compete with John Wayne?

"You've always meant that," Kari says. "Even when I was putting my brains up for grabs all over the place. So what gives?"

Walter and Hugh return, bearing sparkling glasses of wine. I take mine without a glance at Kari, who devoutly refuses the one Hugh offers her. His smile fades and his cheeks turn firebrick red. "I just thought you might . . . you know, since . . ."

"No. Thank you."

We stand there for a minute, the four of us, looking anywhere but at one another. There's no place to sit or even lean against. So we stand and rock with the motion of the boat. I drink my wine in three quick gulps, which does strange things to my taste buds. I suck my tongue, even smack a time or two, trying to get beyond the fermented taste that lingers all the way down my throat. If this is supposed to be sweet, I'd say it's missed the mark. But then maybe this wine is dry.

"That woman back there. Someone you know? Someone you went to school with?"

I reach for the extra glass of wine in Hugh's hand. "And church," I say, though up till the moment I opened my mouth I had no intention of saying anything at all. I take another long drink.

"Church. Ah." Walter's smile is weak.

"Once."

"Once?"

"She came to our youth group exactly"—I hold up a finger I can't quite focus on—"once." I finish the last of the wine, and when my eyes light hungrily on Walter's glass, he guzzles what's left and excuses himself to make another run to the bar.

Kari makes little mmm-hmms and uh-huhs at Hugh, who's doing his best to make small talk, but all the while she's sending me telepathic signals I refuse to acknowledge. In fact, I snicker a bit, then snicker at the word snicker. Because of Snickers. When Walter returns I take the glass of wine he offers. It's fuller than the one he keeps for himself. I raise my glass. "Cheers."

"So, you work with Kari?" Hugh asks.

I shake my head, which feels as if it has a shadow that follows just a split second behind. "I'm in nuts."

"Nuts?"

"Up to my eyeballs."

"Pistachios," Kari says through clenched teeth. "And almonds."

"Ah." The guys are in unison again.

"She just"—I draw in a slow breath—"wanted a friend."

"Kari?" Hugh has a baffled look on his face.

"Patti." I point with a loose hand in what I guess to be the direction she bolted in. "Keep up with me here."

Kari, who is never silent, is silent. And I know what she's doing. She's giving me all the rope I need to—

I cough as a mouthful of wine goes down the wrong way at the unfortunate analogy that fills my head. "Whew." I fan the neck of my blouse. The wine is warm and so is the room. The rocking of the boat, which up till a moment ago I might have described as gentle, I now think of as roiling.

"You know, I think maybe—" I point to the outer deck.

"Hey, sure." Walter jumps at my suggestion. I get the feeling he's ready to be anywhere but the stuffy place in which we stand.

I move toward the door. It seems as if the boards of the deck rise up to meet my every step, which makes me feel as though I'm walking in flippers. I hurry out onto the back deck and take two gulps of air, hoping for something crisp and clean to settle my stomach. Instead, I get a lung full of diesel fumes which go right to my head. Without an ounce of dignity I lean over the rail and feed my dinner back to the fish. Ah yes, the circle of life.

Dang.

———————

"It was the fumes, and the heat, and the"—I move my hand in a rocking motion—"boat."

Kari glances my way, then looks back to the road. "Say it with me."

I lean back against the headrest and close my eyes and sour mouth in protest. When Kari doesn't press, I say what I can't get out of my head. "She just wanted friends."

"We were a snooty little clique, weren't we? And we called ourselves Christians." Kari merges onto the cross-town freeway that takes us to Highway 26, the two-lane road that leads to Linden. "But you have to admit it's extreme to want to hang yourself because a guy likes someone else. And it was obviously right, because the guy in question is going to marry your sister."

"We can't all be rocks," I quip. I don't feel one bit like a rock. In fact, never have I felt less like a rock than I do right now. I've always been the first to recognize weakness in others, the last to forgive it. Opinionated and, well, let's just say it, arrogant. If I were a tree, to mix my metaphors, I'd be the first to snap in a windstorm, as there's not the least sign of give in my trunk.

Johnnie, now she's a willow, soft and supple. But rooted. Deeply rooted. As I stare my shortcomings full in the face I see there's much to be said for a little give and take. It's that fact that won't leave me alone. Patti's face, not from tonight, but from that night eight years ago. I still see the look in her eyes when she knew she'd been played. So cruelly played. By me.

I think I might be sick again, but it has nothing to do with the wine.

Twenty-Six

I don't believe in long engagements. Me, who's never had a reason to be particular about such subjects. But here's the thing: why wait? In the old days, the groom had to build a cabin, stock the smokehouse with game, and pluck enough geese for a feather bed. Long engagements were unavoidable. But the minute he had it all together he was toting his bride over the threshold.

These are the thoughts that fill my head as I work on autopilot in my Shunk-Winters Nut Company office, though it's not an office in the real sense of the word. It's a job shack that rests on a cement slab in between the walnuts and almonds. The windows are coated with fine Linden dust that will stay there till the first autumn rains, giving everything beyond the glass a sepia tone. The old-world look makes me feel ancient.

The cooler that juts out of the wall could use a muffler, but without it, the shack would be stifling. I pull the tab on a Pepsi, and with the can halfway to my lips I suddenly think of Anya and our Coca Cola float. My stomach does this rise and fall thing, and I do what I've done for weeks whenever she comes to mind. I push her as far away from my thoughts as I can, because to think about what that young girl is living through is more than I can deal with. Selfish, I know. Very selfish.

I blot the moisture from my eyes and turn back to my computer. The orders are plentiful, and I suppose I should be grateful. After all, it's the orders that keep us afloat. More than afloat. They keep us downright comfortable. But here's the thing: I HATE BOOKKEEPING! I've scrawled it all over my notepad, my desk pad, my phone pad, just to remind myself HOW MUCH! Yes, I like coming to work in shorts and a tank top, and going for a swim over my lunch hour if I want. But I thought I'd escaped this. Not just the job but the narrow world that compresses me until I feel like a bonsai in the land of real trees.

And I can't help think how insignificant the work feels on this side of Moldova.

"Hey."

I look up to see Johnnie in the doorway.

"Thought you might like some lunch." She sets a small ice chest on the desk and opens the lid. "Dad made chicken salad."

My mouth waters, and I realize it's well past noon and I'm hungry. Dad's chicken salad stuffed inside pita bread is a lunch to get excited about. Johnnie takes out a sandwich for each of us, while I fetch another soda out of the little refrigerator.

"This is a treat," I say. I have the sandwich halfway to my mouth when Johnnie offers up a prayer. I wait without closing my eyes, then bite into my lunch.

"Are you going to work all day?"

It's Saturday, but during harvest I work ten hours a day, six days a week. Dad, Opa and the harvesters put in even more hours, working from sunup to sundown, but never on Sunday. That's been Opa's creed from day one. Give God what he asks. At the minimum. "I have to finish processing these orders." I lift a stack of papers without enthusiasm.

My sister cocks her head and gives me a sad smile. "I'm sorry, Ree. I know you're not thrilled to be back in that chair."

Don't get me started, I want to say. Instead I shrug and take a bite of my sandwich. Johnnie does the same, and as I watch my sister eat her lunch I decide she could do lip commercials, where that's the only feature the camera focuses on. I mean, she's beautiful all over, really beautiful, but her lips are perfect. They're not quite Celie's, not quite Dad's, but a combination that simply worked, with perfectly straight teeth that, unlike mine, never saw braces. My own smile if I don't really concentrate is a half up, half down affair, not nearly as appealing. I take a drink of soda to wash down a bite of sandwich. "At least I don't have to worry about rush hour."

"True. I hate the commute to Sacramento."

"But you love your classes, love your job."

"I do."

"So, what's it like to be a congressional aide? Everything you thought?" I'm glad to have the conversation turn toward her, and I give her a platform to run with.

"Oh, Ree, it's so beyond." She laughs. "You should read some of the emails we get, from both ends of the political spectrum and everything between. The accolades, the complaints. I never knew what a diverse society we really are."

"It's good training," I say. "Just don't make me call you sir when you're in office."

She's thoughtful a moment. "What are you going to do after this harvest is over? To use your degree, to fulfill your calling."

Even though it's Johnnie and I love her, I bristle. I look away and chew the inside of my lip. "I don't believe in callings." I say it as kindly as I can because I don't want to hurt her. But I don't believe, not any more. A lot of folks would have been better off if I'd just stayed here in the orchard. Oh, I'm smart enough to still believe in God, but that doesn't mean I have anything to say to him. And I'm avoiding every place he's likely to strike up a conversation with me. Johnnie covers my hand with her own. I know her eyes are glistening so I don't look at her as I slip my hand away. "Don't worry." I say to her what I said to Kari.

"I'm not going to hell anytime soon."

"Don't joke."

Believe me, I'm not.

"I know Dad wants you here, but that's just because he can't find the right person to replace you. Trish"—Johnnie shudders—"was a disaster. But with you here to find and train the right person, Dad has to let you go. You should teach. Or something."

I know what the "or something" is, but I let it slide. "I don't know, Johnnie. It's not so bad. I mean, I can do the job in my sleep."

"Which is exactly what makes it so awful."

"Well," I say dismissively, "we have to get through these nuts before I can think of going anywhere else."

She gathers up the remains of our lunch, but stops on her way to the door. "If you're interested, a few of us are getting together later for pizza and a few hands of Rook."

She says it with a nonchalance that fits her about as well as Mam's brassiere.

"A few meaning who?" Johnnie's demeanor has my radar on high alert.

"Oh, just Matt and me, Deanne, Justin, Mindy, Corey, Jenn, Christopher, Kari. You know, the gang."

Uh huh. Practically the entire college and career group from church. "I think I'll pass, but thanks."

Johnnie hesitates, wants to press further, but just gives me another sad smile and steps out of the shack.

I'd give my Kindle for a good night's sleep. I fall into bed too tired even to read the latest book I've downloaded onto the device, though my day's activities can't account for my level of exhaustion. Then I lie there with my mind whirring like a pinwheel. Anya, of course, is one point of the wheel, but Patti Mitchell is another point. I close my eyes and see that saffron scarf around her neck, knowing what it hides. I've given up caffeine and the nightly news. I try music, then no music. Tylenol PM. Nothing helps. I can't sleep, can't get things off my mind.

I climb wearily out of bed a few minutes past two, then glance out my window to make sure my grandparents aren't skinny dipping in the moonlight. All's clear, so I slide my feet into flip-flops and descend the stairs.

It's cool on the patio, a sure sign fall is all cued up and ready to go. I stretch out on a chaise and listen as a breath of wind stirs the leaves of the camphor tree. A billion stars overhead emit their white-hot light in a dazzling display that demands not to be taken for granted. I begin to relax. Even my mind slows down. Every now and then the pool sweep spits a stream of water my way. Otherwise it's pleasant out here.

"Well, hey."

Opa's voice draws me abruptly from a dreamy stupor. Dang. I was almost there. "Hey, yourself." I doubt I've disguised the disappointment in my voice. "What are you doing out here so late?" I look past him to make sure Mam isn't on her way out to take that dip.

"Wolf," he says.

Sure enough, the pug has made a beeline to the camphor tree.

"And you?"

I sit up and make room for him at the end of the chaise. "Couldn't sleep."

He gives me that look, with his dimples just engaged, smiling but not, and I swear he and Mam, and Celie too, have my number dialed in, because they seem to know my every thought, reading me as easily as neon at night. A scripture comes to mind about that very thing and God, but I give it the boot before it has a chance to settle in.

"Things on your mind?"

I shrug, an aimless thing I do a lot these days, and then I blurt out the question that drives the whirring pinwheel. "Why didn't God prevent this?"

The look on Opa's face never changes as he fingers the close-cropped beard that used to be blond. Somewhere along the way it took on an argent hue. "Have you asked him?"

"Opa, be real." I decide I could have worded that better, because if there's one thing Opa is, it's real. But I see in his eyes he understands. They're the most compassionate eyes I know, not entirely because Opa's been my hero for as long as I can remember, but that helps. "God can't be everything you say he is, and let this kind of suffering happen. I'd rather believe he doesn't exist than believe he's that indifferent."

"Indifferent," he says in that velvety voice. "Ah." He turns his gaze to the rustling camphor leaves—or someplace beyond. "Do you remember the day you were lost?"

As if I could forget. My first day of kindergarten I was put on the wrong bus after school, just one of those weird and unfortunate mistakes that happens. When I got off the bus, I was at the wrong stop and there wasn't anyone there to meet me. Celie, who was waiting at the stop I should have been left off at, was near hysterics when she discovered I was missing. I was near hysterics too as I watched the bus pull back onto the country road, leaving nothing behind but a puff of black smoke. Crying, I sat down beside a rural mailbox, not knowing what in the world to do. A mother of one of the other children saw me and came to help. I knew our number, so she wrote it down, went inside and called our house, but of course Celie wasn't there to answer. Thankfully, I also knew Mam and Opa's number. Opa was the one who came for me. Never had a familiar face meant so much. I've never thought of Opa since without wanting to wrap my arms around him and hold on tight. My nod is suspicious as I wonder where he's going with this. "I remember." Could I sound more noncommittal?

"I'll only speak for myself when I say I couldn't have been more frantic, couldn't get to you fast enough."

I knew that was true by the way he grabbed me into his arms and nearly squeezed the breath out of me, all the while whispering *baby girl, baby girl,* and me nuzzling my wet and snotty face into his neck.

"Then why?" I say at last.

"That has to be the oldest question ever, why." He looks away and murmurs an obscure proverb I've heard him quote all my life. "We grow too soon old and too late smart." Only he turns on the accent when he says *smart*, sounding like a good German, *schmart*. "I remember the days when I had an answer for everything. Now the only answer I have is not much of an answer at all. Bad things happen not just to good people, but to every person, everywhere. Yet nothing is wasted in God's economy. He'll use Anya in ways he can't use you or me, if she wants to be used. From what you tell me I believe she does.

"We don't even know if she's alive, Opa."

"No. We don't."

"And she's only twelve. But all that aside, if God kept this from happening to anyone in the first place, she wouldn't have anyone to minister to, and that would be so much better."

"You mean in a perfect world?" The lift of his brow matches the lift of his voice.

"Something like that."

"Like the one he created in the first place?" Opa smiles at my frustration. "Baby girl, we'd only just mess it up again. He rescued us once, once is enough."

"I don't feel rescued."

"I know you don't. What matters is you will."

"Not soon enough. Not soon enough for Anya. Not for a thousand, a million, like her."

"Do you know what a forlorn hope is, Ree?" It's rare for him to call me by name, so I pay attention to what follows. "In the days of musket warfare, when battle was up close and personal, forlorn hope was a military term for the first wave of soldiers attacking a stronghold. Chances were good there wouldn't be many first-string survivors. The goal was to make a breach in the enemy's defenses so those who came behind could finish the job the first soldiers had started. Those who are willing to be out there on the front lines for the work of the Lord will pay a price too."

"But a twelve-year-old girl?"

"Who loves the Lord and wants to devote her life to telling others about his love and compassion." He sighs. "It doesn't get much uglier than this, Ree, nothing much worse than seeing the innocent suffer. It makes me ashamed to be part of the human race. But pushing back the darkness doesn't come cheap."

"But why? If God is God, why doesn't he protect us better? Why doesn't he"—I struggle for what I want to say but it just doesn't come—"protect us? If he's up there watching, he could snap his fingers and make all the ugliness go away."

Opa smiles, looks away and nods. "He could. He could also have made us without a free will. He could have left us floundering without giving a thought to redeeming us. He could have done a lot of things. And before it's said and done, he will. But for now, those who pierce the darkness with their own God-given light will feel the sting."

"So let's just throw our best and brightest to the wolves?"

The smirk on Opa's face is unmistakable, even in the moonlight. "One thing I know, God nor his ways are in need of our defense."

I shake my head and look away. Arguing theology with Opa is risky business.

"Don't you know that when Anya reaches out to others who have been through what she's been through, she'll reach them in ways you never could? That when she says there's healing for those who are broken the way she's been broken, she'll have a platform she could never have gained any other way? Empathy goes so much farther than sympathy."

"I just have to say I think it's really unfair of God to put us through that."

"I tend to agree." He agrees? I'm about to high-five him, but then he adds, "Jesus could agree with you too, Ree, but I don't think he will."

It would take more mental energy than I possess to think of a comeback, so I sit in silence.

"We say we don't want to be God's puppet, then we fault him when he doesn't pull the strings. The blade of unfairness cuts both ways, wouldn't you say?" He clucks his tongue, and when Wolf trots over to where he sits, Opa scoops him up. "Look up," he says to me, "at all those stars. I'm pretty sure you'll see the outline of a pretty big hand holding them in place." He winks at me. "'Night, darlin'."

It's not two minutes when I hear the strains of Opa's guitar through the open upstairs window. And there he is, praying again.

Twenty-Seven

Sally has emailed twice in the past few weeks, though not with the news I long to hear. She's upbeat as ever, the most trusting soul I know, in spite of the obvious. The concern she bears for me comes through in every word, but between the lines my twisted mind reads what a loser I am. I haven't deleted her messages, nor have I responded.

The trees are bare of leaves and fruit, which makes it easy to see the radiant nightlights shimmering overhead when I'm out at night, but I can't make out the hand of God in spite of what Opa says. I suppose it would help if I were looking. Every nut on the compound has been harvested and packaged—unless you count me—and the orchards disked and scraped. Shunk-Winters orchards are the cleanest in the valley, a fact of which even I am proud.

"I'm glad you'll be home for Christmas." Celie looks up from the list she's writing, her grand plans for the holiday. Her Christmas cards are half-addressed and it's not yet Thanksgiving, but Celie's an elf if ever there was one.

"Who's coming this year?"

"Besides the usual, Uncle Donovan and his new"—Celie drums the eraser end of her pencil—"friend. Birdie, Jas and the twins."

The twins. "Are they staying"—I suck in a breath, and hope—"with Mam and Opa?"

Celie laughs. "Would it matter?"

The twins, Tiff and Tuck, are five-year-old dynamos in sneakers. We call them TNT with our tongue nowhere near our cheek. The title is a thousand percent applicable. Birdie and Jasper subscribe to the never-raise-your-voice-or-paddle-the-backside-of-your-offspring   mentality when it comes to raising children. And boy does it show. Tiffany, older than Tucker by a minute and a half, leads them in all manner of mischief. She learned how to pick the childproof latches on Mam's cupboards before she was two, and when they were toddlers, all the doors leading outside had to be latched up high, out of climbing reach.

Plugging the toilet is one of their favorite pastimes. The worst—in more ways than one—was when they plugged our upstairs john with Mam's prized Nuts the Squirrel Beanie Babies collectible stuffed toy. How they managed to get their hands on it and smuggle it out of Mam's house and into ours only Tiff and Tuck know, and they aren't telling. We try to TNT-proof our houses before they come, but how do you lock up a toilet? Snickers goes into hiding the moment he hears their car crackle up the driveway and doesn't reappear until they're gone. Smart dog. If I could find his hiding place, I'd join him.

"Oh, and please," Celie says, "when they arrive, remind me that Birdie is now Fiona. What is it with our family and names?"

She's asking me? "What about Thanksgiving? Are we doing anything special?"

"Of course."

I knew it was a dumb question the moment I asked.

"We thought we could all go up to the cabin at Tahoe. Well, almost all. Johnnie will spend the day with Matt's family this year." Celie gives me a tight-lipped smile that looks identical to Mam's. "That's not nearly so hard to take now you're home. Oh, I know I have to get used to sharing my children, but when I thought both of your places at our table would be empty"—she waves a hand and sniffs—"I had to come up with an alternative."

"Tahoe sounds great."

"Would you like to invite anyone? Kari, or . . . anyone?"

I know what she's asking, and no, she won't be sharing me with anyone, anytime soon. I'm not even dating, which is just fine. But at night when I'm lying in bed not sleeping, I hear the strains of Andy's guitar, see the outline of muscles through a dirty T-shirt, see him reach for the little Bible in his back pocket. That's where it's easy to turn off the vision. Still, the words from his coffeehouse sermon bounce around in my head. *The seed is this, the word of God . . . You are the soil that receives the seed . . . Some of you are good, fertile soil, sprouting like sunflowers soaking up the rays . . . Some of you are as hard as the dirt in Janic Rotaru's field.*

Don't I know it.

"Do you remember Patti Mitchell?" The question comes of its own volition, and I wish I'd only thought it.

Celie's pencil stops mid-stroke. "Patti Mitchell? You'd like to invite her?" Judging by the look on her face, Celie is more than puzzled.

"No! No, I . . . Do you remember?"

"Well, of course, sweetie. I didn't know you were still in touch with her."

"I'm not. Well, I saw her recently. On that date." I say the word as though it were a caustic blob on my tongue.

"Ah." Celie's smile is sympathetic. "I didn't know Patti was back."

"Where did she go . . . after? None of us knew."

Celie bites at her thumbnail as she tries to recall. "Her mother took her to live with an aunt, I think, somewhere out of state. It was just the two of them, right, Patti and her mom? No dad, no siblings?"

I nod to confirm.

"She was a lonely girl. A sad girl. I hope her life is better now. Well, you saw her. Is she? Better?"

"We didn't speak. Or anything."

"Oh. If you see her again, tell her hello for me."

If I see her again? My fists are tight balls at my side. I'd rather dive blindfolded and tied up like a turkey into Janic Rotaru's well to keep from seeing her again. It's all I can do to keep my eyes from looking up as I shoot my question heavenward. *Do you hear me?*

"Leave me alone!" I'm in the back orchard where only the squirrels and God can hear the words that explode from me. "I don't want to see Patti Mitchell, don't want to think about Andy and his stupid sunflower sermon, don't want to look for your hand out there among the stars. I want to be left alone."

A holdout nut in its shriveled husk falls at my feet with a thud. "I mean it," I say, and kick it into the darkness. Everywhere, the silhouettes of naked branches reach out above me, and I shudder as I think of a sixteen-year-old Patti Mitchell hanging from the rafters of her garage. "I did not mean for that to happen and you know it!" Weary, I sink like a catcher behind home plate, because the ground is too wet to sit on. "It was a joke. A stupid April Fool's Day joke, that's all. And April Fool's Day, what's with that anyway? Whoever came up with something so dumb?"

Except for the droning of bugs and things that come out after dark, it's quiet. Not that I'm looking for an answer. But if I were, one isn't anywhere to be found. There are no leaves to rustle, there's no stirring breeze. Nothing but frogs and crickets and an occasional bat darting by. I know bats have this uncanny radar that keeps them from running into things, but I'm freaked out just the same.

It occurs to me that since I'm out here I might ask God what this Patti Mitchell thing is all about, because running into her surely wasn't coincidence, but that would mean I'd have to use a more respectful tone than the one I've adopted of late. I can't bring myself to do it. Besides, my summations haven't changed since the night I saw her. He wants me to know how much I've blown it. And that unlike people whose mistakes mean they might miss a promotion at work or a sale on pork chops, mine have been life-and-death failures.

I was hoping to prove I could do better, and now I feel as though I'm living with an error message that's going to shut down my hard drive at any moment.

"Ree?"

The sound of Dad's voice calling from the distance startles me, disconnected from his body as it is out here in the dark.

"Dad?" I can't tell for sure where he's coming from, but I'd guess he's made a straight path from the house like I did. Sure enough, he appears out of the shadows exactly where I expect. "How did you know I was here?"

"Followed your footsteps. You're the only one of us who wears flip-flops in the dead of winter."

It's the first of November, hardly the dead of winter. "This is California," I remind him. Land of perpetual sun . . . except when the perpetual fog settles in.

Dad kicks the mud off one of his Wolverine work boots. "Right. I forgot."

"Did Celie send you out here to find me?"

He gives me a studied look. "Why would she do that?"

"I don't know. Dinner time?"

"We ate an hour ago. Guess we should have rung the dinner bell, huh?"

"We don't have a dinner bell."

"Well, there you are." He tugs on the bill of his red Crawdad Festival cap. "There's a guy here to see you."

A guy? "What guy?" I have visions of Walter. And fish. So it probably isn't him. Then who?

"Says his name is Andy."

Andy? My stomach lurches, then lands somewhere around my

ankles. It can't be. He's in— "He said Andy? Are you sure?"

"You can ask him yourself, unless you plan to stay out here all night."

I zip and unzip the faded gray sweatshirt I tugged off the coat rack on my way out here. I'm not sure whose it is—Dad's or Opa's—but it's clearly not mine. The navy blue T-shirt I'm wearing underneath isn't much better, and the back hems of my jeans are muddy from where they scraped the ground. My hair, which is in that worst of all stages, hangs limp at my jaw line and the roots are badly in need of a touch-up.

With a huge sigh I stand and follow Dad back through the orchard, my insides churning like a concrete mixer. "This is so not funny," I mutter through gritted teeth. Just then a shooting star cuts a swath across the sky that looks to my eyes exactly like a smirk. It's Andy all right. No question.

Dang and double dang.

———————————

On that long walk back to the house I'm figuring out how I can slip into the downstairs bathroom to see what I can do with myself before I face Andy, but as I step out of my muddy flip-flops at the sliding glass door that leads into the kitchen, there he is with Celie, chatting as if they're old chums. I bet he didn't speak half as many words to me in all the weeks I was in Moldova.

So why is he here?

"Andy, hi."

He stands and nods at me. "Aria."

Celie smiles, I think because he's so formal with me, and formal is not something we're used to in our clan.

"This is my dad, Michael Winters."

"We met." They say it in unison, then there's that awkward tension that settles into moments like this one.

Celie rises from her kitchen stool. "Mike, would you, I need to . . ."

She nods toward to stairs. "We'll be back."

This is as unexpected and awkward as running into Patti Mitchell. If I never mentioned that I hate having my cage rattled, I'll just mention it now. *God,* I want to scream, *what are you doing?*

"Want a Coke?" I say. Of course I mean Pepsi.

"Sure."

I direct him to a chair at the table, while I fill a couple of glasses with ice. I place a cold can of soda before each of us, then take the chair across from him. "This is a surprise." Inwardly I wince at the cliché.

"I told you my family lives in Sacramento?"

No, actually you told Isabel. I just happened to be within earshot. But I nod.

"So I was in the area. Sort of."

"Sort of?" The compound is not in the area of anything. You don't stumble across it or arrive by accident. If you're here, it's because you meant to get here. A current of delight runs through me. If this were a scene from a movie, this is where the chimes would give off a tell-tale tinkle.

"My brother is dying."

And this is where the curtain would fall. I swallow an ice cube, then cough it up. "Andy, I'm . . . Wow, I'm sorry."

"He OD'd on his latest drug of choice. He's been in a coma for several days. Most every organ is shutting down."

I think back to our conversation in Moldova, and of the concern for his brother I'd heard in his voice that night. "Have you been able to talk to him?"

"I talk. Only God knows if he hears."

"They say—"

"I'm not sure it was accidental."

In typical Andy fashion he gets right to the crux. I sit back and scramble to think of something to say that will help. "I know what some people say, but there's only one unforgivable sin." This from me, the prodigal theologian. As they leave my mouth, the words taste as false as any I've ever spoken.

"But then there's that whole repentance thing, that divine cause and effect."

If there's one thing I know it's cause and effect. What I don't know is how to answer Andy.

"But this isn't why I came. I thought you'd want to—"

"Hey, Ree. Oh, sorry, didn't know you had company." Johnnie and Matt stand in the kitchen doorway, a devilish look forming in my sister's eyes. "I wondered whose Honda that was."

Andy stands again. "Hope I'm not blocking anything."

"Not at all." Johnnie moves toward the table with her hand extended. "I'm—"

"Johnnie," I say. "And this is Matt."

"How's it going?" Matt shakes Andy's hand after Johnnie lets it go. The look she turns on me says, *what else haven't you told me?*

"This is Hamilton Andrews."

It takes only a moment for the name, and shock, to register. "Andy?" And just that quickly Johnnie recovers. "Ree didn't say you were back in the States."

"She—"

"I—"

"—didn't know," we say together.

Johnnie smiles that famous smile of hers and tightens her hold on Matt's arm. "I love surprises."

I clear the matter up right away, before she digs herself into an embarrassing hole. "Andy's brother is in the hospital."

"Oh, no, Andy, I'm sorry to hear that. I hope it's not too serious."

"Sorry to hear that," Matt adds.

Johnnie gives a little tug on Matt's arm. "We'll let you two talk."

"No, no, you stay." Their dinner is waiting on the stove, and as late as it is they must be starved. I ignore the rumblings of my own stomach. "We were just going out. Side," I quickly add. "Outside."

"Don't be silly. It's freezing out there."

"Not very." I scoot out my chair and stand. "This is California."

"Nice to meet you both," Andy says.

"I hope we'll see you again," Johnnie says. "We'll pray for your brother."

"Appreciate that. A lot."

There's a halo of fog around every landscape light, and our breath is visible on the night air. I force myself not to shiver inside my frumpy sweatshirt as we amble beside the pool.

"So. Johnnie really is your sister's name."

"You didn't believe me?"

He gives me a sidelong glance. "Would you?"

"Yes."

"Okay, maybe you aren't the best example. Typically, people don't have sisters named Johnnie."

I feel a thrill as I can't help wonder why this matters to him.

Andy looks around. "When you said *compound*, I had this vision of chain link fence and razor wire. To leave here you'd have to be called. Or nuts." He actually smiles. "I couldn't resist."

I ignore the pun and focus on the smile. It's the first honest smile I've seen on his face since I found him in our kitchen. "Yeah, well, the walls close in around you pretty quickly. All you want to do is escape."

"Yet here you are back in its confines." He looks away, then right back into my eyes. "You're a chick in the nest preening your wings, but you've no intention of flying."

Well, that's a mood breaker. "What's that supposed to mean?"

He looks as if he can't believe I don't get it. But I don't. "It's not hard, Aria. Just figure it out."

"Fine, Hamilton, I will."

"I hope so." My smirk falls at the surprising sincerity of his voice. "But no matter what you call me, I know who I am and what I'm meant to do. You're still pretty lost."

I have a dozen comebacks but I swallow them all. Because, dang, he's right.

"So, were you?"

"Was I what?"

"Called?"

He's two steps beyond me before he realizes I'm no longer beside him. I try to ignore the question, but then he turns to me and it's apparent he expects an answer. I catch myself zipping and unzipping the sweatshirt, then shake my head. "No. I was not called. Most definitely not called."

"Why don't you think so?"

"Well, let's see." I don't even pretend to stifle the edge in my voice. "It might have something to do with the fact that a young girl was stolen and subjected to God knows what kind of vile perversion because I. Wasn't. Careful. And speaking of God, he wasn't too careful either. And yes, I should have made sure Anya made it all the way home, but if God is so almighty omniscient, why didn't he just make the van go somewhere else that day? Or flatten its tires? Or blow it up? If I was God, I would have."

I'm no longer cold, but I am shaking.

"And speaking of omniscient, God knew that whole stupid thing with Patti Mitchell was a joke. A bad joke, granted, but a joke just the same. Still, my little joke was nothing compared to God's. He gives us these promises, then breaks every one. 'Won't give us more than we can bear'? Tell that to Anya. 'Ask whatever you will and it shall be done'? I'm not just asking, I'm begging, I'm pleading, I'm groveling. I've cried a million tears, and for what?"

I'd say the jack-in-the-box finally sprang, and it doesn't feel so good after all.

Andy takes a step in my direction. If he's startled by my outburst, he doesn't let on. "Who's Patti Mitchell?"

"What?"

"Patti Mitchell, who is she?"

Oh, Lord. Did I really say Patti Mitchell? Out loud? I consider following my flip-flop tracks back out to the orchard and hiding till

Andy's gone, but I don't know how to escape the hole I've dug for myself. "She's just"—I press the heels of my hands against my eyes—"someone I knew."

A yap and a howl draws Andy's attention away from me. I'm so grateful for the distraction I vow never again to tease Wolf about his name.

"Thought I heard someone out here." Opa skirts the pool and extends his hand to Andy. "Blue," he says, introducing himself.

There you go. Just one more Shunk-Winters name for Andy to laugh about.

"This is Andy. This is Opa." My introductions are without heart.

"I've heard a lot about you," Andy says.

I know exactly what Opa is thinking by that cryptic smile that all my life has defined him: *Haven't heard a thing about you. How come?*

"Heard you're the best there is on acoustic guitar."

"Andy plays too. Really well. We met in Moldova."

"Ah, Moldova."

Wolf continues to rumble a throaty growl at our feet, then lets loose with another yap.

"Wolf." Opa snaps his fingers, and the dog trots off toward the camphor tree. "Are you home to stay?"

"No, sir, I—"

"His brother's ill." I say the words with enough emphasis that Opa gets the seriousness of the situation.

"I see. Sorry to hear that. What's his name?"

"Stuart."

"Stuart." And just like that, Opa lifts his face to heaven and begins to pray out loud. I listen to Opa and watch Andy's lips move in silent accord. I don't even say amen when Opa closes his prayer.

"Well, I'll let you two get back to your conversation." Opa may not be all knowing, but he knows me, knows I'm as taut as a ten-pound line that's snagged a twelve-pound trout. "Baby girl." His words soothe like a hug. He winks at me and whistles for Wolf.

"Thanks for the prayer," Andy says. "Nice to meet you." Then he gives me this look I interpret to mean, *how did someone like you come from such normal people?*

"Come around when you get a chance and we'll make some music."

Boy, what a prayer session that would be. One I'd just as soon miss.

"I'd like that."

We watch Opa close the sliding glass door as he leads Wolf inside. Immediately, I jump on the conversation to keep it from turning back to Patti Mitchell. "What did you think I'd want?"

"Excuse me?"

"You were saying"—I shoot a thumb in the direction of the kitchen—"you thought I'd want . . . ?" I wait for him to fill in the blank.

"Can we sit for a minute?"

A glider is the closest thing to us, but I don't think that's what he has in mind. I lead him to a patio table on the other side of the pool. The seats are damp from the November fog that settles over the valley at night. Even so, we sit.

"They found Anya."

Twenty-Eight

Found Anya?

It takes a moment for the words to register. "They found her? Is she— Oh, God, is she—?"

"Safe. She's home."

I try to hold back the tears but it's no use. They come all at once and there's no stopping them. Andy is as ill-at-ease as I am embarrassed, but he sits quietly and waits for the wave to pass. If anyone from either my house or Mam and Opa's is looking out a window, they have to wonder what exactly is going on out here. I use my palms to dry my face, but I've nothing on which to wipe my nose except the sleeve of my—or maybe Dad's—sweatshirt. It's the icing on the cake of my humiliation. "How is she? How did they find her?"

"I haven't seen her. I was already here in California. Sally called this morning."

Sally. I'm ashamed I haven't replied to her. "This morning?"

"Since I was so close I thought you might like to hear in person."

I nod as the tears pool in my eyes again. This is the kindest Andy has ever been to me. "Do you have any idea how she was found? And what about the others?"

"There's an underground organization called U-Turn, I think that's what Sally said. They find and rescue as many as they can like Anya, and put their lives on the line to do it."

"But how? How do they find them?"

"They pose as . . . interested parties, looking for someone young. I don't know the details, just that they smuggle them out and get them home. All four girls from Leoccesni were rescued."

"All four." The relief leaves me weak. "Was anyone arrested?"

"I don't think they hung around long enough to get the authorities involved."

"But—"

"They do what they can, and that means getting the girls safely out of there. That's priority."

"Right," I say. "Of course."

"I can't help but think they do what they can to blow the whistle. I just don't know the details."

"Maybe I'll contact Sally."

Andy drums his fingers on the table, and I sense he's dancing around something else he wants to say. I look anywhere but at him, because whatever it is I don't want to go there. But that doesn't stop him. "Aria, I know this whole thing has really messed with your head. And your heart. I get that, I do. When you first came to Moldova you answered a question Sally asked you at dinner one day about what brought you there. You said you wanted to be God's hands and feet in the real world."

I remember the conversation well and blush to think how ideological I sounded. "Trite, wasn't it?"

"Maybe, maybe not. But it was your example, so here's my question. If our hands are God's hands, and our feet are his feet, what makes you think our tears aren't his tears? What makes you think he doesn't grieve for this world in ways we can't begin to imagine, or that he doesn't express it through our broken hearts? And yet he doesn't give up on us. Think about it. Would you go to the cross for the guys who stole Anya? For all the guys who victimized her?"

"You don't want to know what I'd do to those guys, Andy, if I had the chance."

"A very human response. But aren't you glad God isn't human?"

"Why should I be glad?"

"I don't know what happened between you and this Patti Mitchell person, but you don't sound too proud of it."

That takes my breath away. I start to tell him what an insensitive jerk he is, but I don't say anything. Because he's right. And because I hear the same sense of failure in his voice. "You asked me once what I was running from."

"Not quite. I said, like me, you were escaping. But okay, I guess it's nearly the same thing."

I look around and blow out a sigh. "Either way, you were right. Only I thought it was this place, not—" I shrug. "What about you?"

"What do we try the hardest to get away from? The truth. Looks like I've come full circle too."

That leaves a great big question hanging between us, but I don't expect any more of an answer than that. My hands ache with the cold. "Why don't I make some coffee?"

"Not for me, thanks. I need to get going." He stands, pulls his cell phone from his jeans pocket and checks the time. "I'm picking Isabel up at the airport."

His words come like a slap. "Isabel?"

"We've been talking," he says. "Since I'm here for a few days it seemed like a good time to connect."

"Connect. Right." I hope I sound more upbeat to him than I do to myself. "Tell her hello."

There's a look in his eyes I can't decipher. "I will."

I walk him around to the front of the house to where his car is parked. "Thanks for coming all this way to tell me about Anya. I appreciate it."

He nods, slides behind the steering wheel, and starts the ignition. I wait for him to get the car turned around, facing the long dark drive that will take him to the highway. To Isabel. But then he stops and rolls down his window. "I was the one who first turned Stu onto drugs."

I don't need to see Andy's eyes to pick up on the pain, but before I can think of a response he's gone, wheels crunching on gravel.

———————

"Where's Andy?" Johnnie asks, when I come inside alone. She and Celie are chatting in the kitchen, while Dad and Matt are watching football.

"Had to leave."

"I'm sorry about his brother. I didn't want to say, but it must be serious for him to come back to the States."

"Yeah."

"Ree?" Celie pats the stool next to hers. "Come sit. What's wrong?"

It's easy to see I've been crying. "They found Anya."

Celie and Johnnie exchange a glance and steel themselves for bad news. "And?"

"She's home." I do not say she's okay, because she most probably is far from okay, but I tell them everything I know.

"Thank God. But we need to pray now as much as ever."

"Those poor, sweet girls," Johnnie says.

"I'm going to call Sally." It takes a minute to compute the time difference. It's tomorrow morning in Moldova. Sally will be up by now, assuming she even went to bed, but no matter the time, I have to talk to her.

It takes three tries to get the international call to go through, but finally an odd-sounding ring comes over the line, then I hear Sally's voice. "Hello?"

"Sally? It's Aria."

"Aria, darling. Andy must have reached you."

"He was just here."

"In person? Isn't that just like him?"

"Sally, how is she?"

There's a catch in Sally's voice as she says, "Better than you'd think. She's a brave girl, Aria. She asked about you, practically the first thing."

"Me?" I'd think she'd never want to see my face or hear my name again.

"Well, of course. Oh, hold on just a moment, darling." I hear her say, "Clark, love, it's Aria. Yes. And Andy was there! Oh yes, let me ask." Then she's talking to me again. "Aria, how is Andy's brother?"

"I don't think he's doing well."

"No, it sounded very serious when Andy got the call. I'm just glad he made it in time."

"He doesn't think his brother can hear anything he says."

"Oh, but God hears, and he can convey to Stuart every word Andy speaks. Or thinks, for that matter."

Sally sounds so matter-of-fact I can almost believe it. In fact, my thoughts come as close to a prayer as I've uttered in weeks. *God, if that's true, he has to know how sorry Andy is.*

And if that's true, tell Anya the same thing for me. And Patti. Tell her too.

"Now the question, Aria, is how are you?"

I can't fool Sally any more than I can fool Celie or Mam, so there's no point in lying. Why then do I lie?

"Fine? Is that what you said? Because, sweetheart, forgive me, but you don't sound fine."

"I'm good, Sally. Really."

There's a span of silence, and I can't help wonder what Sally's up to. When finally she speaks, her voice is rife with compassion. "Aria, darling, none of this was your fault. No one blames you, least of all Anya. She was so disappointed last night when she couldn't see you. Would you like me to tell her anything for you?"

My throat is tight, a barricade for any words that would pass. Of course, Sally can't see my nod, so I force my voice to work, but the words come out in falsetto, a dead giveaway that I'm crying. "Tell her I'm sorry. And give her my love."

"Of course I will, but Aria—"

"I have to go Sally. Take care."

I do my best to cry in silence, but that's never been easy for me. I tend to blubber and bawl, but the last thing I want is to draw attention to myself. Johnnie's probably out of range, but Celie has this sixth sense, like when she put clean sheets on my bed the day I came home. If anyone will get the vibe that I'm up here falling apart, it will be Celie.

God, why? It's all I can think of, all I can say. If this awful thing had to happen, why to someone as innocent as Anya? Why break a heart that was already yours? I mean mine, I get that. I get that I'm so far off the mark that some breaking would do me good—not that I'm volunteering. But you have this, this *sunflower* in tune with the whole spiritual heliotropic vibe and what do you do? You crush it in your hand—

And what happens?

"What?" My head pops up and I look around the dark room. I swipe at the tears and look again. The door's still shut and I'm alone.

Swell. The last thing I want is a sermon from God. But it's too late. The words in my head won't be silenced. *What happens? What happens? What—"*

"All right!" I know where he's going with this. "The seeds fall to the ground and new flowers spring up. But that was talking about you. Your death! Your resurrection!"

I flip on the light and search the room for my Bible. I finally find it under a pile of *People* magazines. The concordance in the back directs me to the scripture this whole seed thing is about. I read the words in red from the twelfth chapter of John, thinking, *see? See? I'm right. It's about you!* But then I read on and my argument is lost in verse twenty-six. "Whoever serves me must follow me . . ."

If arguing theology with Opa is risky, then arguing it with God is just plain futile. I know that, but still I try. "You really expect a twelve year old to follow you to the grave and back?"

And then I hear Anya. *I want be missionary . . . to tell my people God loves them."*

"So why can't she simply say it? What on earth is a trip to hell going to accomplish that, say, one of Andy's Bible studies won't?"

I wait for an answer, but all I hear is a sound at my door. It's not a knock exactly. It's more like a sound made by a brush on a snare drum, as if someone rubbed against the door on their way past. I hold my breath hoping they just continue on, but then it comes again. "Ree?"

It's Celie. Dang.

"May I come in?"

She knows I'm in here, so I can't very well climb out the window as if I were ten. Nor can I do a thing about the puffiness under my eyes, so I just make sure they're dry. "Yeah." My voice is not very welcoming.

She opens the door and takes a step into the room. "Hey." Then she sees the Bible lying open on my bed. "Oh, honey, if I'm interrupting . . ."

"No!" I slam it closed. I'd rather she come in and talk than think I was actually reading the book.

"You sure?"

Actually, no. I'm not sure about a single thing in my life. But I nod.

"That's such good news about Anya and the other girls." She takes a seat at the end of my bed. "Were you able to reach Sally?"

"We just got off the phone." I don't say a thing about the conversation I've had with God in the meantime. "She said Anya's doing better than you'd—I'd—think."

"She's surrounded by people who love her." Celie lays her hand on my arm. "And so are you, Ree."

My throat constricts again. I can hardly swallow, let alone talk, so I nod, determined to hold in the stuffing that's oozing out of my broken seams.

Celie eases her hand back onto her lap. "Andy was nothing like I envisioned. He seems like such a nice guy."

I could almost laugh at that, as the idea that he was something other than nice came directly from me. But then I'd like to ask, would the real Hamilton Andrews please stand up?

"You said his brother's ill?"

"Dying, it seems. He overdosed."

"Dear Lord, that has to be tough."

She doesn't know the half of it. But this isn't the only story she isn't fully privy to. In my mind I see the look of shock on Patti's face when she recognized me that night on the riverboat, can almost feel the silk of her saffron scarf . . . and the cord of a scar that lines her neck. I hold my breath as the crush of emotion fills my chest, squeeze my eyes as tight as I can, but the tears seep onto my face. I fold myself in two and give in to the wave.

Celie rubs my butchered hair, trying to soothe. "Aria, sweetheart, it'll be okay."

"No. No. No. No." We both know this isn't just about Stuart, but Celie doesn't know it isn't just about Anya either. Nor does she know how close I came to taking someone's life eight years ago. That's how God sees it, right? If hate equates to murder, then what I did does too. "It's my fault."

"I know you feel that way, but Anya took the same route almost every day. How could you possibly know something so bad could happen?"

"No," I say again. "Not Anya."

Celie's silent for several seconds. "Then who? Sweetheart?"

I don't want to tell her, don't want to see the proof in her eyes of how much I let her down. It's one thing to know the truth about yourself, quite another for someone else to know it. And if I tell Celie, she'll be the only one besides me and God to know the whole truth. Not even Patti knows I was the one.

"Mom?"

"It's okay, honey, say what's on your mind."

I twist the frayed threads at the hem of my jeans, as I sit cross-legged on my bed, making little dreadlocks out of them. "I gave her the note." I know it's a pathetic face I lift to her.

"Well that's— I'm sure it was— What note, and to whom?"

"To Patti Mitchell."

"Patti Mitchell, oh. That was a thoughtful thing to do."

"Not *a* note, Mom, *the* note. Actually there were two." I've never called her Mom so many times in such a short period of time, and I can tell it has her worried. "I sent her the note inviting her to the formal dinner the youth group sponsored, and I signed Matt's name to it." There's no question, the plain truth is as ugly on the table as it is in my head.

"You signed— But why? The whole idea was to go as a group, not as dates."

"I know that, but Patti didn't know it."

"Why sign Matt's name? Weren't he and Johnnie beginning to—" I see the moment the truth begins to register. She drops her head into her hands. "Oh, Ree."

I'm instantly in defense mode. I hate it, but I can't help myself. "It was April first and I just thought . . . She liked Matt and it seemed like a harmless joke."

"But it wasn't harmless."

I hang my head. "No."

"What happened, exactly?"

Man, how I hate the details, which are as clear today as they were then. "Patti had just started coming to the youth group at church, but we all knew her from school. You know how she was, shy, self-conscious. But none of us knew how down she was on herself, because she was cute, you know?"

"Aria, self-esteem rarely has anything to do with what we look like on the outside. You know that."

I swear, right now I feel seven years old, as well I should.

"So, Patti had just started coming to church . . ." Celie prompts.

"A couple of weeks before the dinner. Like I said, we knew her from school and it was obvious she had a crush on Matt. So I sent her an invitation, and signed Matt's name. I thought it would help build—" *her self confidence*. That's what's on the verge of coming out of my mouth, but I taste the lie and swallow it. I never gave a thought to her self-confidence, never considered how this might hurt her. "Never mind." I go back to my story. "The day of the event Johnnie, Matt, Kari and I are on our way to the dinner and I say we need to go by Patti's to pick her up. No one thought anything of it. So when we got to her house I sent Matt to the door to get her."

"And she thinks she's Matt's date."

I nod.

"And then what?"

"You can tell she's surprised Johnnie's up front with Matt and doesn't move to the back. So Patti gets in the backseat with Kari and me, and she's quiet all the way to the church. Matt and Johnnie walk in together, sit together. Anyone with eyes can see they're a couple."

Celie is shaking her head.

"About halfway through dinner Patti says she doesn't feel well, that she's going to call her mom to get her. I know she thinks Matt's the one behind it all. Matt, who'd never hurt anyone. I felt really bad by then, but I didn't want to say anything in front of everyone. I thought that would make it worse."

"For whom?"

I don't have a comeback for that.

"Was Kari in on this?"

"No. It was all me."

"You said there were two notes."

They say confession is good for the soul, but I'd like to take the con side of that debate just now. "I put a second note in her purse. But when I saw how badly things were going I wanted to get it back. I really did. I couldn't find a way."

"What did it say, Ree?"

Just two words, but it's all I can do to say them now. "April Fools."

Celie looks as sick at heart as I feel. "What are you going to do about it?"

"What can I do about it? I have no idea how to find her. It was a fluke—a really sick fluke—that we ran into each other at all."

"A fluke? You really believe that? I suggest you ask the Lord to help you find her again. I have a strong feeling he will."

I decide this isn't the time to remind her the Lord and I are barely on speaking terms. And as for asking for help to come face to face again with Patti Mitchell, no thanks. And I'm sure she doesn't want to see me any more than I want to see her.

Twenty-Nine

It's a snowless Thanksgiving at Lake Tahoe. It's rained like crazy and is cold enough to snow, but a threat is as far as it gets. It happens that way sometimes. November doesn't always cooperate with our recreational plans. Still, we aren't used to being here with nothing to do with our snow gear.

I know Celie well enough to know she's discreet, and that my humiliating secret is safe with her. Still, I read things into my family's faces and into their comments that keep me on edge during the holiday. It probably has more to do with cabin fever than anything, but I struggle to look anyone in the eye.

On Saturday, when the gang decides to take a drive around the lake, I feign an upset stomach, saying I can't handle the curves. On those grounds, no one objects to me staying behind. Or so I think.

"Feeling better?"

I'm so startled to hear a voice as I hit the bottom step on my way to the kitchen that I actually yelp, then cover my chest with both hands to keep my heart in place. In fact, this is so unexpected that for a split second I fear I'm walking into another unsolicited conversation with God.

"Mam! You scared me to death."

She chuckles. "You're still breathing as far as I can see. Come, sit."

This isn't so much an invitation as it is a summons. I grab a can of Pepsi out of the fridge and join her at the table, taking note of the delicious, autumnal smells coming from the kitchen.

"Want a muffin to go with that? I made pumpkin-cranberry and poppy seed."

"This is good for now." It wasn't a complete lie when I said my stomach was unsettled.

"Baby girl, what's going on with you?"

I start to say not much, but who am I trying to kid? Mam knows me as well as the recipes she hasn't had to double-check for years. "Did Celie talk to you?"

"About?"

Mam isn't one to play games, so, no, Celie didn't out me about my Patti Mitchell confession. "I feel like I'm sinking, Mam. I've made so many mistakes."

The hint of a smile that crosses her face is not one of amusement but of conspiracy. "Sweetie, I know just how you feel, except I've had a lot more years than you to mess up."

"You've never messed up like I have."

She lowers her glasses just enough to look over the top of the frames. "You sure about that?"

"There are things you don't know."

"Hmm, that's what I was just about to say to you." She goes to the oven and pulls out another pan of muffins. "Cinnamon streusel," she says.

She's killing me.

When she returns she sets a napkin and a pumpkin muffin in front of me, then sits and folds her hands in front of her. "How hard it is to fall into the water of God's grace and let him hold us afloat. We want to dogpaddle all over the place, and everyone knows you can't get anywhere dogpaddling. Sure, you're in the water, but not much else."

"Grace only goes so far."

"What fool said that?"

"Me." I pinch off a bite of muffin.

"Baby girl, if you measured the grace of God against every drop of water in all the oceans on the face of the earth, they wouldn't amount to a nutshell full of salt water in the sea of God's grace. Sounds like a bad country song, but there it is. We could never use it up. And while we're on the subject of water, our experiences in life are all linked like underground springs. Sometimes they get blocked. When we clear up one blocked spring it usually leads to another blocked spring. The point is to unblock the spring."

"How?"

She looks over the top of her glasses again. "You probably never heard that Scripture is like a Roto-Rooter?"

I laugh, and think about Andy's coffeehouse message on the Word of God. This is one he missed.

"It's true. It snakes its way through all those springs and opens them right up. And when that fresh water begins to flow, there's nothing like it."

I take another bite of muffin. My stomach isn't churning quite so much as it was. "I love your earthy wisdom, Mam."

"Earthy, that's me. But I don't feel nearly so wise as I do opinionated."

"But your opinion is wise, so there you go." I give her the most genuine smile I've managed in days.

"Finish your breakfast," she says, "and help me slice the rest of the turkey for sandwiches."

A gibbous moon sheds its light through the loft window of the Lake Tahoe cabin where Johnnie and I lie in our sleeping bags, whispering the night away. We've done this since we were kids, and while there are lots of great reasons to come to the cabin, this is one of my favorites. It's our version of a nightcap. A promise from Matt to his parents to have Christmas dinner with them opened the door for him and Johnnie to be here with us for Thanksgiving. I'm glad for the trade, though I won't feel the same come Christmas Day.

"Mom says she thinks Andy's a nice guy. He's certainly nice to look at. You failed to mention that whenever you'd talk about him in your emails from Moldova."

I'm not sure what to say to that. "Your fiancé is downstairs asleep as we speak."

"I'm not looking to trade him in, and he knows it. But still."

Not trade him in, you mean like I did?

I don't know what made me think of that. Matt and I have been friends so long it's hard to remember a time when there might have been more. And if it took us hooking up, even briefly, for him and Johnnie to find each other, then it was the right thing. Because they're the right thing.

"Will you be seeing him again?"

"If you mean seeing like *seeing*, then no, we're definitely not seeing each other."

Johnnie sits up on one elbow. In the soft light I see her smile. "He came a long way *not* to see you."

"He drove from Sacramento to tell me about Anya."

"When he could have called."

"Then he drove back to Sacramento to pick up Isabel from the airport."

The smile disappears. "Isabel?"

"From the Wisconsin team."

"I know, but what's she doing here?"

"Seeing Andy. As in *seeing* Andy."

"Oh, shoot. I'm sorry, Ree."

"Sorry? Why?"

"Well, because . . . Because."

"Johnnie, there's nothing between Andy and me. He and I never meshed. It was oil and vinegar right from the start."

Johnnie chuckles. "Oil and vinegar, huh? Sounds like the right recipe to me."

"Oil and water, that's what I said."

"Uh huh."

"It's what I meant, anyway."

"You know what they say about those Freudian slips."

I give her a stern glare she probably can't see since my face is the one in shadow. "This coming from you, the political science major."

She continues to chuckle. "Psych I. We both took it."

She's right, but she's wrong. We both took Psychology, but there's nothing between Andy and me. Unless you count Isabel. "He has an edge, a really sharp edge, at least when it comes to me. Trust me, there's no attraction."

"You said he plays like Opa."

I don't remember saying that. Not to Johnnie.

"So if he has that kind of music inside him, that edge may be about something else altogether."

I don't like where she's going with this. Besides, she's so wrong. "I'm going to sleep." I turn away from her and move deeper into my sleeping bag. But even after Johnnie's breathing tells me she's drifted off, I lie awake long into the night.

I help pack our things for the trip home and all I can think of is the three hours of sleep I'll get on the drive back to the compound. But as I climb into the far rear of the family van where I can stretch out with my pillow, in my mind I'm suddenly in Clark's van in Moldova on my way to Hope House with the team from Wisconsin. And Andy. The mountains give way to valleys, the ponderosa pines become sunflowers, and I'm reminded of what a mess I've made of things.

I don't only mean Anya. Or even Patti. There's something out of kilter with me. With each mile marker we pass I delve deeper into the decisions I've made over the past five years. I evaluate my journey, examine my motives. It isn't just the curves of Highway 50 that have my stomach churning as I take a closer look at myself, at the picture I presented to Sally and Clark. And Andy.

I punch my pillow and try to understand why it matters so much. About Andy. I've prayed for him and for Stuart. Obviously, I know about guilt. I know how insidious it is, how it starts out a speck, then consumes so much of you that you become the speck. That's how I see me now. A speck of . . . what? I don't even know. Only that I'm so very inconsequential to the big picture. Which is . . . ? I punch my pillow again, and catch Johnnie watching me over her shoulder. The smile I flash is as fake as the rest of me.

How and why did I end up at Bible college? When I tossed up my mortarboard the day I graduated from Linden High I felt no compunction to run off and save the world. So what led me to Moldova seven years later? I could play some mental ping-pong here, but when you play games with yourself, who wins?

Like a scratched CD, my mind has been stuck on Andy's question for days. Was I called? And what does that even mean? Is that something you can decide for yourself, or is our destiny really out of our hands? Honestly, I don't think so. Don't think there's one path set in stone for the individual journey we're on. Oh sure, I believe Jesus absolutely when he says narrow is the road to heaven, but then I believe Jesus when he says anything. But on that narrow road I'm not sure there's just one rut with my name on it. If I take one juncture as opposed to another—had gone to San Diego for college, say, instead of Santa Cruz, or worked one job rather than another—does that mean I lose my way completely? Or if I just keep going will I eventually catch up to my one specific route, assuming there is such a thing? I don't have a problem with Jesus taking the reins of my life, at least I didn't when we were on friendlier terms. I just happen to think he holds the reins loosely enough to give us some leeway on the road to our destination.

So back to my question. What does it mean to be called?

"Ree? Hello back there."

I sit up and see that Johnnie's waiting for me to climb out of the van. We're home? Already?

Thirty

It's two weeks till Christmas and the road to my destination seems little more than a treadmill. I'm moving, but I'm not getting anywhere. Preening, not flying. I hate the image of myself Andy inserted into my brain, especially considering how accurate it is.

I would love to talk to Anya, but only if I knew for sure how she'd respond to me. And that her sweet voice wouldn't have vanished, that whatever sorrowful or angry tone that took its place wouldn't be filled with accusation. So I only pretend I'll call. Tomorrow. Or the day after.

I put my computer to sleep, turn out the lights to the job shack, and hope Dad was serious when he said we'd have homemade minestrone for dinner. I worked straight through lunch in order to finish the last of the gift baskets on order, so I'm beyond hungry.

My cell phone rings on my way to the house. "Hey," I say to Kari.

"Hey, yourself. You through working for the day?"

"Just turned out the lights."

"Perfect. Let's meet at Luigi's for pizza. Thirty minutes."

As I step into the house, the incredible aroma of Dad's minestrone makes my mouth water. "I don't know, Kari. I think I'll stay in tonight. It was a long day."

"Ree, you turned twenty-five a week ago. Long days at work mean nothing at our age. We barely need sleep, but we do need to socialize. And right now you're dangerously undernourished in that department. So, thirty minutes?"

I want nothing more than to savor a bowl of soup, then soak in a hot tub topped with citrus bubbles, and read the latest issue of *People*. But Kari's right. I'm turning into a hermit. I can have the soup for lunch tomorrow, and it's better the second day anyway, so I say okay. Don't ask me why.

"Thirty minutes," Kari says. "Oh, and wear that butter yellow sweater of yours."

"Why?"

"Because it's cold."

My eyes turn longingly to the tub as I take a curling iron to my hair. If I'd had any idea how quickly I'd bomb out in Moldova, I'd have put my hair in a French braid for the duration instead of cutting it, and I wouldn't now be dealing with that in-between stage I haven't seen since first grade. I give up and slip on a headband. I pull on the sweater, zip up my favorite jeans and dab a bit of blush on my cheeks. That's it in the way of makeup. I don't have much enthusiasm for such things now that I'm cloistered away on the compound again. But it's only Kari, and Luigi's is dark.

The fog hovers above the highway the whole way to town. It will surely be a different story on the way back as it settles in for the night. I should have looked outside before I committed.

There are more cars in the parking lot at Luigi's than I expect for a Tuesday night. I tug open the heavy door, then give my eyes a moment to adjust to the dark interior of the pizza joint. Kari isn't in any of the small booths that line the wall. I can't believe I beat her here. But then I hear, "Ree! Ree! Over here." And there she is at the biggest table in the place, with at least ten other people. I know everyone of them. From the college and career group at church.

I'm going to kill her.

She ignores the murderous look I give her as she makes room for me on the bench beside her. "Nice sweater," she says in that fake chipper way she has. "Is it new?" This whole thing smells like a setup, and when she says, "You remember Christopher, don't you?" I know that's exactly what it is.

Christopher snatches up a brown plastic glass half-filled with chipped ice, "Let me get you a soda. Coke or root beer?"

My stomach hits my toes. I haven't wanted root beer since the day Anya disappeared. "Coke." I barely get my answer out past the tightness in my throat.

"Here you go. It's nice to see you again," he says, and others in the group echo the sentiment. "I bet you're glad to be home for Christmas."

I could tell him I'd miss this and every future Christmas at home to be able to undo what happened to Anya, but I just tear the wrapper from my straw and nod.

There's something much too nice about Christopher. Too tame. Nothing he says ignites a spark, and sitting here I realize how much I like having a spark ignited, like having my words parsed and put to the test. Like every conversation I ever had with Andy.

His brother lived three days after Andy's visit to the compound. Stuart never regained consciousness. This I learned in an email from Sally two days after the funeral. It was clear Andy didn't want me there.

It occurs to me I've become a virtual stalker of Hamilton Andrews, but I'd bet the whole of next year's nut crop he hasn't given a single thought to me since the night he drove off the compound, out of my life. I wonder how long Isabel stayed, if she's even gone back to Wisconsin, wonder what transpired between them. Sally would know, but if I won't call about Anya I certainly won't call about Andy.

"We ordered already, but nothing with mushrooms," Kari says to me. "Ree hates mushrooms." She says this to the group, but if she thinks pizza without mushrooms gets her off the hook she doesn't know how wrong she is. I give her a look that says as much. "I just wanted to get you out of your cave," she whispers, but her eyes dart to Christopher and I know getting me out of my cave wasn't her only goal.

"Do not talk to me," I whisper back.

From here the plan is to go cheer on Stockton Thunder as they beat the Utah Grizzlies. That's the idea anyway. While I happen to be up for a good rumble, I'm not into ice hockey. I'm about to say so when Christopher says, "We have a ticket for you, and we're right on the ice."

I'd be happy to reimburse him the cost of the ticket and just go home, but I'm caught in the crossfire of ten sets of eyes. If I want to get the message across to Christopher I'm just not interested—and I do—it will be in private.

"Great," I say, but I'm sure no one in the group believes me.

I'm not at all surprised to find my seat is right next to Christopher's. Kari is four seats down, between Valerie Highfill and Keith Somebody. That's fine with me. I'm not ready to let Kari off the hook. I don't know why she suddenly feels the need to fix me up with any guy who happens to be single, though I plan to find out. Whatever the reason, I think she's feeling the need for herself as well. Keith is new to the group and has been held captive by Kari all evening. He doesn't seem inclined to complain.

It's downright frigid when you sit at ice level. The action of the game is so close I find myself flinching with every whack of the stick. Gets you right into the action, and I guess that's the idea. Hockey is one fast-paced sport. And rugged? There's more elbowing, head-butting and high-sticking tonight than I've ever seen, but then this is only my second game. Still, by my count there have been seven fights. Brawls actually, which paints a more accurate picture of the degree of roughness.

And if you think football fans are R-O-W-D-Y, you haven't seen hockey fans in action. They're brutal. And whatever you do, do not leave your seat during play or you might get tackled by the person whose line of vision you block as you exit your row—that on top of the R-rated verbal assaults shot like arrows from every direction. You can easily spot a newbie by how red his or her ears become.

Every few minutes Christopher leans my way and hollers a question into my ear over the ceaseless roar of the crowd. This is hardly the environment in which to get acquainted, especially with someone, namely me, who will not cooperate. But I have to give him kudos for trying.

"I didn't know you were back from Romania," he yells with the first period underway.

"Moldova."

"What's that?"

"Mol—" I shake my head. "Nothing."

I could swear he's watching the clock, because exactly two minutes later he tries again. "Haven't seen you at church."

I keep my eyes on the action. "No."

Then two minutes again. "You working or anything?"

"Yeah."

The Thunder score a hammering goal and the fans go nuts. Christopher puts his next question on hold to yell for his team. When the noise drops a decibel or two he moves in again. "Thought you were going to be gone a while longer."

He's determined, I'll say that for him. I glance his way then turn back to the ice. "That was before I wrecked a young girl's life and made a mess of my own. I wasted time and money on Bible school, and was as suited for ministry in Moldova as I would be to play goalie out there on the ice. In light of that I'd say I stayed long enough."

"Goalie?" A smile lights up his face. "Wow. How long you been playing?"

I shake my head and start to tell him what a stupid assumption he's made, but the look on his face says, for whatever reason, he genuinely cares. I'm caught up short with how flip I've been. I blow out a breath, disgusted with myself, and lean his way. "I was supposed to stay a year."

"Ah. Homesick?"

I swallow. "Yeah."

This conversation has told me one of two things. Either Kari has been the friend I'd expect her to be, and kept my miserable secret safe, or she's blabbed it to everyone in the college and career group and Christopher is one good actor, because he really seems not to know about the Aria saga.

I lean forward and look down the row of seats just as Kari leans forward in hers. She smiles and waves, and I know I have no reason to doubt her loyalty. But dang it, Kari, enough with the matchmaking.

By the second period the ice has melted a tiny bit, not in the rink, but in my behavior. My answers to Christopher's questions, though they continue to be shouted, are slightly more civil, but only because I recognize what a jerk I'm being.

"So what do you think?" Kari culls me from the herd as we leave the arena and make our way to the parking garage.

"About?"

She rolls her eyes. "Christopher."

I give her a one-shoulder shrug in reply. I mean, the evening wasn't as bad as I thought it would be, even though the group—minus me—was bummed when the Grizzlies scored the winning goal on a power play in the last four seconds of the game. It was when Christopher asked for my number that things got dicey. I mean, here's the thing: he's a nice guy but that's the problem. I don't want to make him think I'm interested when I'm not. I came despicably close to entering my number into his cell phone with one deliberately wrong digit, but I figured he'd ask Kari for the right number when he realized the mistake. So there was nothing to do but tell the truth. Sort of. I said I was seeing someone. The part of the lie that was true was that I'd like to be seeing someone. Who happens to live on a whole 'nother continent.

Dang. Whoever said the truth hurts knew what she was talking about.

I slip in the front door and am surprised to see the light on in Celie's sitting room. It's late, even for her. But when I poke my head around the corner, it's not Celie at all. It's Johnnie, waiting up for me.

"Hey," I say.

"Make a cup of tea and come sit down."

"Okay." I say it with a question in my voice. "Everything all right?"

"Sure."

I return in three minutes with a steaming cup of tea, just perfect after the ice cream that chilled me to the bone and beyond. I can't explain why I feel I've been called into the principal's office as I take the chair on the other side of the lamp table. "What's up?"

"Nothing. Just wondered how you're doing." She shifts in her chair to see me better.

"Me? Great."

She gives me a sad look, like she doesn't believe me for one minute.

"Really."

"Did you have fun tonight?"

I raise my eyebrows at her and blink, because the way she asks the question tells me the evening was indeed a setup and she was part of the conspiracy. "We lost," I say.

"Ah. Too bad."

Yep, she was part of it all right. "Why is everyone trying to fix me up all of a sudden?"

"No one's trying to fix you up, Ree, just get you out. We're concerned about you."

"Kari's trying to fix me up. And no one has to be worried. I'm trying to sort things out, that's all." I can see by the look on Johnnie's face we just arrived at the point of this chat. "But I'm fine. No plans to walk into the deep end."

"We don't think that. Well," she adds in reply to the look I give her. "Not really."

I give a little chuckle and sip my tea. I've made my point.

She fidgets a minute, working up to what she wants to say next.

"You know, if the Bible taught us life would be trouble free for Christians, that we'd never have hard things to deal with, I could see why you'd be upset with God. I'd be upset too, pounding at his door asking, 'what's up with this?' But Jesus himself said in this world we'd have trouble."

"'But take heart! I have overcome the world.' John sixteen thirty-three." My Sunday school Bible drill training shines through. "You sound like Opa." I hold up my hand. "Don't worry, that's not a bad thing."

"Ree, you know I don't want to minimize any of this. My heart breaks every time I think of Anya." True to her word, her eyes begin to shine. "And you. I know how you feel, but what happened was not your fault. But it wasn't God's fault either."

Okay, now she's losing me. "Then whose?"

She studies the carpet a moment. "If I go out and hurt someone, on purpose, really hurt them, is that God's fault?"

"No, but if you're going to hurt someone he claims is his child, I'd expect him to protect that person like any good parent. Unless he's looking somewhere else at the time, in which case he's not the God we were taught he is. So then, what's the point of trusting him?"

"You're underplaying the effect of sin on this world, Ree, in which case Jesus paid a much higher price than he needed to."

Now I'm studying the carpet. "I just don't get the plan, Johnnie. Don't feel very safe in the everlasting arms, you know?"

"Have you read Hebrews lately?"

"About all those folks cheering us on? I know—"

"No. The chapter before that. The one that talks about the faithful—"

"Right. Abraham, Moses, Joseph. All the giants of the faith." It's all I can do to keep from rolling my eyes.

"I'm talking about the others, later in the chapter, who aren't named and who weren't rescued from their circumstances. Awful circumstances." She reaches for Celie's Bible on the table, turns the pages and begins to read. "Others were tortured . . . some faced flogging . . . They were stoned, they were sawed in two'—"

"Okay. That's enough. I get it."

"Do you?" The question would sting if not for the compassion I read on her face. "In spite of everything they pressed on, because they knew what—and who—waited at the finish line. Some races are harder than others, Ree, but God knows his runners, knows exactly what kind of race they were made for. He knows what will come from Anya's experience, how it will help others get to the end of their race. If God sent you to Moldova for no other reason than to support Anya and cheer her on, I'd think now's the time she needs you most."

Thirty-One

This is the longest night of my life. For what it's worth I can say I wrestled with God, and lost. Or won, depending on your point of view. I'm going back to Moldova, but for now that's a secret between God and me. I'm not saying anything to anyone until I know that Sally and Clark will take me back. If they do I'll take that as a sign from heaven, because I wouldn't take me back if I were them.

Dad and Celie are surprised when I come downstairs ready for church Sunday morning, but to their credit they don't say a word about it. Johnnie's already left with Matt so they can stop on their way at the local Starbucks knock-off for a white mocha. But she'll be surprised too when she sees me. Or maybe not.

I've attended this church all my life, but as we pull into the driveway I'm so nervous I could puke. Instead of the college and career class, I've made up my mind to attend the sanctuary Sunday school class with Dad and Celie, as if I were five years old again, though Kari will be ticked when she figures out I'm here, but that I wasn't there. Well, she'll get over it. I'm all about easing back in.

That's my plan, but my bad string of luck continues, because there she is, walking through the sanctuary with a stack of Styrofoam cups on her way to the church library where the C&C class meets.

"Ree? Oh my—!" Half the stack of featherweight cups falls away as she runs up the middle aisle of the church. If my point was to not draw attention to myself, and it was, Kari has waylaid my plans. She grabs and hugs me as though she hadn't seen me just two nights ago.

I turn as red as the candle that decorates the piano. It's wrapped in a fat plaid bow, and is only there because it's almost Christmas. There are more candles and holly boughs throughout the sanctuary, which looks as if Celie's been at work here. She has a touch, I'm sorry to say, was not passed on to me.

"You rat. Why didn't you tell me you were coming?" She loops her arm through mine and pulls me with her toward the library. "Christopher will be so glad to see you."

It would be easier to email Sally than to call, but easy isn't right and I know it. My heart picks up speed as the phone begins to ring in my ear. It's Monday morning in Moldova, early but not too early for either Sally or Clark. Of course, I hope with everything in me that Sally answers the phone, but the voice that says hello is much too deep to be hers. Dang. There's a split second when I consider hanging up and trying again later, but like I said, easy isn't right.

"Clark, hello. It's Aria. Winters." As if he knows more than one.

"Yes, Aria, how are you?" His tone isn't rude, exactly, but it is cool. "I suppose you'd like to speak to Sally?"

"Thank you, yes." Yep, I should have emailed.

"Aria? Is that you, love?" As always, Sally is on the opposite end of the spectrum from Clark in the emotions department. "How are you?"

"Good. I'm good. How are you? And everyone?"

"As blessed as ever."

"And Anya?"

"Oh, well now. She hasn't surprised a soul. She's exactly as you'd expect."

I ponder that for a moment. I mean, is she exactly what I'd expect considering what she's been through, or exactly what I'd expect considering the girl I knew? "Please, Sally, would you give her my love?"

"I certainly will."

"How's everyone else?" I mean Andy, of course.

"Everyone's fine. Plugging away, as they say."

I have to ask. "Is Andy back?"

"Yes. He returned soon after the funeral."

"I was very sorry to hear about Stuart."

"Oh I know, love. We all were."

For not knowing the man, I feel sick at heart. "I'm really sorry, Sally. Will you tell Andy?"

"I will."

I can picture her at the gray and white Formica table, a cup of tea in front of her, the phone cord stretched across the kitchen. "It's snowing here, did you know? Oh, but you didn't call to listen to a weather report."

That's my cue, but I've no idea how to start. "Sally, I . . ." What? Let you and everyone else down, most of all Anya? Failed the first big test of my life? "I want to come back."

"Well, of course you do, love."

My breath catches and I wait for the but. It doesn't come, not even a hint. "Sally, what should I do?"

"You should come back."

"I should?"

"The sooner the better. We've been waiting for this, you know."

We? I doubt Clark is as eager for my return as Sally. "I really blew it. I know that."

"And you think we'd hold that against you? We, with our own feet of clay? We've done our share of blowing it, Aria. And we're in fine company, too. In fact, the only human being who didn't blow it, not ever, was Christ."

I know she's right about that. Still.

"A scripture in Proverbs says, 'For though a righteous man falls seven times, he rises again.' That says right up front that the best of us will fall. Not that the best of us is very good." Sally laughs. "But the point is, we get up again. That's what makes the difference. The question is, love, do you want to make a difference?"

"I do," I say, but without the idealism with which I arrived the first time.

"I'm so glad."

It's decided then. I'll return after the holidays. Now I just need to decide how and when to tell my family.

———————

We're not through wrestling, God and me. I spend another sleepless night trying to make my point. "I don't know how to find her." Of course I mean Patti Mitchell. "Wouldn't know where to begin."

I can almost hear God laugh and say, "Leave that to me."

That's what I'm afraid of. Terrified, in fact.

I give in, turn on the lamp beside my bed, and boot up my laptop. Whoever invented this Google thing didn't have a Patti Mitchell in his life, that's for sure, someone he hoped no amount of searching would turn up. Ever. I type Patricia Mitchell, California, in the search box, and hit Enter. My search is broad by design. If I can show God how futile this is, maybe he'll give me a pass. But no. I croak when I see the listing for Patricia Mitchell in Linden, California, pop up on the screen. Why on earth would she come back here?

But then, why would I? The reason is obvious, nowhere else to go.

It's three-forty in the morning, so of course I'm not going to call, but I've written down Patti's number, as haltingly as if I'm dipping the pen in my own blood, I might add, and now I'd like nothing more than to go to sleep. It's not too much to ask, I say, but apparently it is, because I see the sun come up, or at least the darkness fade to an unfocused, sunless gray. The fog is not leaving any time soon. That's December in the San Joaquin Valley for you.

The smell of yeast and cinnamon draws me downstairs to the kitchen like a cartoon character wafting on the stream of fragrance.

"'Morning." I fight off a yawn, but only succeed for a moment.

"It is, isn't it?" Celie smiles, then frowns when she gets a look at me. "Rough night?"

A grunt gets my point across.

"Coffee or tea?" she asks.

"Whichever has more caffeine."

"Since I just dumped the remains of your father's brew and am making a pot of coffee for the civilized, it's a toss-up."

"Well then, which will be ready the soonest?"

She pulls the pot out of the maker, and slips a mug beneath the flow. "This." She adds a sprinkling of creamer, and passes it to me.

I take a sip and then another. "What smells so good?" I look around the kitchen without seeing the source of the aroma that got me out of bed.

"Cinnamon rolls. They'll be out of the oven in"—Celie looks over at the timer—"three minutes."

Dad enters the kitchen, his hair still wet from the shower. He hasn't changed his aftershave in years. Like a mewling kitten I could find him in the dark, and I find that comforting. "What's in three minutes?" He kisses Celie right on the lips, unhindered by me, the spectator. And it's way more than a peck. But I love that about my parents. Mam and Opa too. *Who knows when this kiss might be your last? Don't let it get away.* That's their philosophy. One I hope to perpetuate. Some day.

"Cinnamon rolls, but they're from the freezer so don't get too excited. Who has time to bake anything extra this close to Christmas?"

"I can do frozen."

"Me too." Dang.

Dad sits on the stool beside me and ruffles my hair like he would a toddler. "Rough night?"

I should have ignored the cinnamon and stayed upstairs. "Didn't sleep much."

Celie opens the oven door and the warm, delicious scent fills the kitchen. She reaches in and pulls out the tray. "Things on your mind?"

"On whose mind?" Mam and Opa step through the slider. "Oh, yay, we're just in time." Mam fills two more mugs with Celie's civilized coffee, which hasn't yet worked its magic with me. Dad's would have been harder to swallow, but some things are worth the pain.

"Ree didn't sleep last night."

"Oh, how come?" Johnnie enters the kitchen, dressed for work.

Well, hail, the gang's all here. Johnnie fills a travel mug with coffee then turns and awaits my reply.

"Things on her mind," Mam says.

"You want to talk about it?"

No, I don't want to talk about it. Not now, anyway. I want to wait till after Christmas, so I don't ruin their holidays, so at least I can get used to the idea I'm going back to Moldova to clean up my mess. I'm not ready to deal with their doubts, or worries, or whatever they throw at me. But there they are, watching and waiting.

I play with my fork as a cinnamon roll cools on a plate in front of me. I'd like to hit rewind and take this back to where it was just Celie and me and the wonderful scent. Where I could bite into the hot pastry, savor the buttery sugar and cinnamon, chew the nuts—even if they didn't come from our trees. But like a bug on a stickpin, all eyes are on me.

"I talked to Sally last night. I think I should go back."

Johnnie's mouth opens in surprise, then she pumps her arm. "Yes!"

Yes?

Mam's face gleams as she smiles at me, while Opa wraps an arm around her shoulder and sends me a wink.

A wink?

"The timing's good," Dad says. "You got us through the season like I asked. I appreciate it."

"You do?"

"It's where you're supposed to be," Celie says, "for now anyway. When will you go?"

"And be back?" Johnnie asks.

"After New Years. And before the wedding."

"Well then." Mam lifts her mug in a toast. "Here's to getting back on track."

———————

Well, not every car of this train is chugging along. There's still the matter of Patti. I've showered, made my bed, and started a packing list, and decided what to say to Kari when I call. But Patti first. With a phone in my hand I plop cross-legged onto my bed and dial the number.

It's after eight on Monday morning. Patti will surely be at work. Maybe I can just leave a message on the—

"Hello?"

Oh, Lord, it's her.

"Hello?"

I nearly hang up, but then I'd just have to go through this again. "Patti?" The length of the pause says I've found the right person and she knows exactly who has called her. I tell her anyway. "This is Aria Winters."

I'm pretty sure I hear her breath catch. "What can I do for you?" She's all business, not a trace of the desperate girl I knew in high school who wanted to belong.

"I want to apologize, tell you how sorry I am. For what I did." What I did, finally said.

"What you—?" The pause tells me she gets it. "If you want to confess, find a priest."

"Patti, it's not like that. This isn't about me, it's about telling you how sorry I am. For hurting you, for . . ." I see the saffron scarf, but can't bring myself to say what's left.

"It was always about you, Aria. You and your little group of friends. I just picked the wrong group to try to fit in with."

"It wasn't the group, Patti, it was me. They didn't even know." She's quiet for a moment. "They never knew."

"That should get you absolution."

I know even before I hear the dial tone Patti has ended the call. My face burns with the shame of my unabsolvable behavior. I slip to my knees for the first time in far too long and do the only thing left for me to do.

Thirty-Two

My departure day comes before I'm ready. I'm packed, but not so eager this time to leave my family, nor so eager to face those on the other side of the sea. Most of all Anya. Kari is the only one not excited for me—for selfish reasons, she doesn't hesitate to admit—but that'll add more spice to her emails. Besides, she'll come around, and this time I'll only be gone seven months instead of what would have been a year. This time. But there may be others. If I get it together.

Dad and Celie are here to see me off. I said my farewells to the others last night. Celie has promised not to cry, at least until she's on the way back home.

"You know we'll pray," she says. "Continuously."

"I know."

Dad rests his arms on my shoulders, his favorite lecturing pose. For once I don't mind. "We're all fully aware it's not an adventure anymore, what you're doing. Yeah, you'll be teaching again, but this time it goes beyond that. You know we believe in you." He looks away, bites the inside of his lip, then turns back and kisses the top of my head. I reach my arms around him and rest my head against his chest. The heart that beats in there is one of the best God ever made. All I want is to find a man like him. Some day.

I board my plane at five-forty A.M. It's January tenth. Whatever enthusiasm I carried the last time I made this trip is nowhere to be found. I strap myself into a window seat and turn so that my back is to whoever might join me in this row. Like my previous seatmates, I plan to keep to myself.

When the doors are closed, the seat between me and a woman my grandmother's age remains empty. Exactly what I hoped for. Well almost. I actually hoped for an empty row, but this will do. I slip my Bible out of my carry-on, for I plan to read myself into the heavens, and after that, compose a letter to Patti. I open to the Psalms and begin to read the tenth. And there it is again. "Why, O Lord, do you stand far off? Why do you hide yourself in times of trouble?"

I remember the last time I read these words, remember the strain in my heart, and the pain that came with every breath. I'd closed the cover then, but now I read on, though tears blur the words. "In his arrogance the wicked man hunts down the weak, who are caught in the schemes he devises."

And what awful schemes they are. Just ask Anya.

"He lies in wait near the villages; from ambush he murders the innocent, watching in secret for his victims."

This is surely Anya's story.

"He lies in wait like a lion in cover; he lies in wait to catch the helpless, he catches the helpless and drags them off in his net. His victims are crushed, they collapse; they fall under his strength."

There are no Kleenex in my bag, but I find a cloth headband to at least blot my eyes. But with nothing on which to blow my nose, I sniff. And sniff.

A hand touches my arm and I turn to see the woman beside me

with a package of tissues. "Here, take these." Nurturing women seem to encircle my life. "First time away from home?"

I shake my head and thank her.

"The Psalms often make me cry," she says.

My resolve to keep to myself is slipping. I turn in my seat so that my back isn't to her.

"Beatrice Porter," she says, and laughs. "How would you like to be saddled with that all your life?"

"Aria Winters," I reply, certain I'm one-upping her. But she says twice what a lovely name.

By the time we've reached the Rockies, some thirty thousand feet below our 777, I've told Beatrice much of my story and used the whole package of tissues.

"And of course you want to know, as did that young shepherd king, why God hides himself in times of trouble."

"Or seems to." Saying that is a huge step for me.

"Ah, but there's the key. Have you read to the end of the Psalm?"

I smooth the page. "Not yet."

"Please do."

"Out loud?"

"Oh, that would be perfect."

So I read. "'Lift up your hand, O God. Do not forget the helpless. . . . But you, O God, do see trouble and grief . . . you are the helper of the fatherless. . . . You hear, O Lord, the desire of the afflicted; you encourage them, and you listen to their cry, defending the fatherless and the oppressed . . .' "

"We all so badly want instant everything, including that God would avenge the afflicted, like this sweet child you talk about." Beatrice touches my arm again. "He will, Aria. One day he will dry every tear and set all things right."

"In the fullness of time." The phrase comes out of nowhere, though I know it's from scripture.

"Exactly. God gets the last word."

I know she's right. For now, I guess, that has to suffice.

I'm going back, among obvious other reasons, to finish Hope House. Not physically perhaps, but thanks to my church and my family I have the funds pledged to complete the work. Even to me it seems like I'm hoping to buy a pass from those I let down, though what I really want is a refuge for the rescued. I try to remember that as the wheels touch down on the runway and my nerves come alive.

It's a gloomy day beyond the thick airplane window when I land in Chisinau, as cold in January as it was hot in June. I'm shaking inside as I pass through the jetway into the terminal, but not from the cold. It's nothing but nerves that have me quaking in my sheepskin Uggs.

I follow the stream of travelers toward the baggage claim, but stop to use the restroom before taking the escalator down to the main floor. I could almost laugh to recall the first time I was here, and the "*Salut!*" I threw out to the mother and child. I check my reflection in the mirror and straighten my hair. Then down I go.

Clark waits at the foot of the escalator, no sign with my name this time, no smile. But that's Clark. It doesn't have to mean he hates that I'm here.

"Aria." He nods.

"Hey, Clark."

We don't say much as we wait for the carousel to deliver my luggage. When I pull the first suitcase off the moving belt I don't look at Clark, because except for the broken wheel it's the same size bag I brought the first time. I don't look at him when I go for the second bag either, even though it's smaller. A little.

"Is that it?"

I pull out the handles and nod.

"Okay." He takes charge of the large bag and I follow him out of the airport.

"Aria!" I hear Sally before I see her. "Over here, love!"

I follow the sound of her voice, see the wave of her hand, and relax a bit. When she laughs at my luggage my face grows hot, but I feel as if we've shared a wonderful joke.

Sally stays where she is, a broad smile on her face, while Clark and I load the suitcases into the van. When I come back around to the passenger side and tug open the door, I'm left speechless, for up pops Anya. She squeals my name then I squeal hers, and we're hugging and laughing and crying. Sally claps as she looks on. Clark climbs behind the wheel. In the rearview mirror I see his eyes and I relax a bit more.

I'm glad to be here.

Our conversation is light, like old friends catching up. Sally says the children won't stop talking about Emoo, and want to hear the story again first thing. Clark says, "Emoo?" and we laugh again. I don't deserve this second chance, but I know enough to whisper a thank you to God. Anya is tucked beneath my arm. I won't lose her again.

———————————

The gravel lies beneath a thin layer of snow, but everything else looks the same. Except the petunias, of course. They won't be back till spring. The periwinkle is as faded as ever, but still it's a lovely sight. I glance up at the window that was my room, and feel a twinge. I don't want to displace Andy again.

Clark stops at the foot of the stairs with my large suitcase in tow. "Do you want this up there?" I think he holds his breath as he waits for my answer.

"Could we find a corner down here for now?"

His face registers surprise at my odd request, but I'll explain soon enough. In the meantime, Anya and I take my smaller bag and carry-on upstairs, where my old room is waiting for me.

"Take your time," Sally whispers, and I know she means for Anya and me to spend some time alone together.

I close the door and sit at one end of the bed, while Anya sits at the other. She looks up at me, with more trust in her eyes than I'm worthy of. "I am so happy you are back," she says. "I miss you too much."

"So much," I say, and reach for her hand. I'm determined to do this without tears, to be as strong as she is. "Anya, there are no words to tell you how sorry I am. How wrong I was for leaving you. For letting this happen. I'd do anything, give anything to undo it."

She drops her head and I see the color rise in her pale cheeks. She studies our hands, connected between us. I see a tear drop onto her lap and then another. Her breathing is uneven, but she doesn't make a sound as the tears continue to fall. I give just a little tug and she curls herself into my arms.

With an effort to be as silent as she, I release my own sorrow for the nightmare she's lived through. But here's the thing: she did live through it. And if love covers a multitude of sins, maybe it heals a load of injustice too. If so, I will do my part and more.

She wipes her face with hands that still belong to a child, and lifts her eyes, but only to my chin. I begin to regret the scab I've opened up. "In that place I cried too much."

"So much," I whisper. It could not have been too much.

"And I prayed"—she pauses—"so much. And then we were found."

"If I could have taken this on myself, I would have."

She nods as if she knows that. "Like Jesus."

Like—? "No, no, not— I'm not at all like Jesus."

She places a hand on her chest. "He is in your heart. He gives you love like his love. That is why."

I close my eyes and shake my head. "His love meant he would

trade places with the worst of us. I don't have love like that."

"The worst? But that is all of us, Aria."

"Yes, that's all of us. Until"—I pat my own chest—"like you said, he comes into our hearts. But even then, we don't all measure up to that kind of love."

"Measure up? Vat is that?"

"That's loving like he loves. You, Anya, you measure up." She doesn't understand, but she doesn't have to.

After dinner, which Andy conspicuously misses, Clark drives Anya home while Sally starts a pot of coffee, for I've asked if the three of us can talk. I use our few minutes alone to bring up the living arrangements.

"I'm grateful for your hospitality, Sally, but this time I don't want Andy to have to bunk down in the church. I really don't mind taking the room over there."

"Nonsense." She says it with a lilt in her voice. "Andy will be staying with Janic Rotaru for now."

"Janic Rotaru?"

"Isn't that just like God? Give him an inch, he'll take a mile. And Janic," Sally says with a wink, "gave him an inch. All thanks to Anya's return. It softened his heart just enough."

"For . . . ?"

"The opening God looked for. And now he has his very own live-in missionary. Janic, not God."

"Right."

"Welcome back, love." Sally says this to Clark as he stomps his boots on the back porch, then she pours the coffee.

I pick at a loose thread on my sweater and wonder where to begin. "I want to thank both of you," I say with a glance at Clark, "for letting me come back, though I wouldn't have blamed you for saying no. I didn't fare so well the first time around."

"Neither did John Mark, but look how that worked out."

"Still, you could have been angry. I'd have understood."

"Aria, you can't be right with Jesus and wrong with people. It's the Lord's job to sort it all out." Sally touches my hand. "And what a beautiful job he's done. We're pleased to have you back, aren't we, Clark?"

Clark clears his throat, his eyes on the floor. When the silence becomes painfully awkward, he looks across the table and holds my gaze. "That's a big suitcase you brought. Planning to stay, are you?" I'm about to choke out some ridiculous reply when he begins to chuckle. "Because a fellow could get hurt hauling it in and out of that van."

My eyes blur as I say, "I'm planning to stay. And about the suitcase, I packed almost everything I own."

"Then you're planning to stay a very long time?"

"Clark!" Sally scolds him, but only in jest, as he begins to chuckle again.

"I'm here till July, that much I know. But the clothes, they're for the women who come to Hope House, whoever can use them."

Now it's Sally's eyes that brim. "Yes, a beautiful job," she repeats.

"And I hope you have plenty of teams lined up, because we're going to finish Hope House before I go home."

Thirty-Three

I wake Friday morning to a cold but sunny day. I don't know when I've slept so well. The kitchen's empty when I go downstairs, but there's coffee in the pot. I help myself to a cup and am about to go back to my room to send an email home when the back door opens. My heart rate accelerates when I see Andy step in.

"Hey," I say.

"Hey."

I hold up my mug. "Coffee?"

"Nah, I'm . . ." He aims a thumb in the direction from which he came.

"Ah."

"Thought I'd see if you want to go tonight."

"Go?"

"The coffeehouse. It's Friday."

"Friday. Sure. That'd be— Sure." Man, could I sound like more of a ninny?

"I'll stop by about six-thirty."

"Great."

The screen door slams before I realize I didn't say a word about Stuart. What an insensitive lout he must think I am. Tonight, first thing, I'll tell him how sorry I am.

The hours pass slowly, though I don't know why they should. I've no cause to be even a little bit hopeful, considering Isabel. And everything else. I take the day to unpack, an easy job since most of what I brought will remain in the *trunk*. I hang up two dresses that actually come to my knees, and the few blouses I brought. That utilizes all the hangers, so I leave my sweaters folded in the smaller suitcase, along with my jeans, zip up the bag, and slide it under the bed. Then I locate my story of Emoo, because come Monday, I'm Teacher again.

I pick at my dinner, unable to keep my eyes off the clock, and tell myself for the dozenth time to settle down. When Andy arrives I all but leap out of my seat.

"Have a nice evening," Sally says, as though this is more than it is.

The cloudless sky is as black as ebony, which makes the host of stars shine even brighter, but it's cold enough to hurt whatever is exposed. I raise the collar on the coat I use for Tahoe and shove my hands deep into the pockets. Dang. No gloves. Again.

We make small talk about my flight and the weather, then when it quiets down again I say what I should have said this morning. "I'm really sorry about Stuart. I wish I'd known."

Andy's nod is stiff. "It was a small service. Graveside only."

I've not lost anyone close to me, though we came frightfully close with Anya, so I'm not sure what to say. How much is too much, how little too little? "Were you able to talk with him?"

"I talked, but he was in no condition to hear."

"Sally thinks he heard on a subconscious level. With his spirit. And isn't that what matters?" I feel like the great pretender as I sermonize.

"It is." He says this with conviction.

We walk another block in silence. "Andy? What you said back at the compound, just before you drove away . . . ?" I wait for him to catch up to my meaning. When he nods again I continue. "You didn't know, didn't want it to turn out like this. Maybe God will tell him."

Andy halts for just a second, then picks up the pace again. He swallows hard and blinks. "Yeah. If he sees him."

And that's the thing. He'll carry this load until he knows.

The coffeehouse is as dark and smoky as ever, but all of the tables are centered with vases of dried sunflowers. A nice addition, but they don't do a lot for the atmosphere. Nor do the candles on the bandstand in tall candelabras. Still, someone's made an effort.

I recognize a few of the faces. Svetlana the beauty, Sasha the antagonist. And there's Stasya, waving. Andrea, the girl who sought my counsel, stands beside her boyfriend. Ivan? They're holding hands, talking to Andy. Andrea's cable-knit sweater does nothing to hide the bump of her belly. Seven months pregnant, if my calculations are right.

The smile on Andrea's face touches my heart, and when Ivan nods at Andy and wraps an arm around Andrea's shoulder, I'm less inclined to judge him.

The guitarist sits half on his stool on the bandstand and plays, tuned out to all the chaos around him. He's improved since I've been away. Sort of. At least his heart is in it, as ever. When Andy steps up beside him he lets the chord he's strummed fade away, and waits for further instruction. Andy raises then lowers his hands, and the congregation takes a seat. All but Andrea and Ivan, that is. They move to the bandstand and face Andy, hands entwined, a wreath of sunflowers in Andrea's hair.

I draw in a breath and smile. This is a wedding. I don't understand a word Andy says, other than the names of the bride and groom, but I can't keep the moisture out of my eyes.

A wedding. Well.

"You might have told me." This I say on the return walk home.

"And ruin the surprise?" He stops. "You were surprised, right?"

"Oh, yeah. Completely."

And speaking of love, I have to ask. I have to. "How's Isabel?"

Andy, who for the first time maybe ever, isn't three steps ahead of me, turns my way. It's not quite a smile that engages his eyes and lifts one side of his mouth. And I wish, *wish*, I'd kept the question to myself. I think for a minute he's not going to answer, and that's fine. Really. But then he says, "It didn't work out."

Didn't work out? I compose myself then say, "I'm sorry." I am. No. No, I'm not, Lord help me. Not even a little.

"She seemed okay with it."

She?

"Nice girl, but . . ." He leaves off with that.

But? *But?*

We're at the house before I know it and there's nothing to do but go to the door. I'd give a bar of my soap to have left a glove behind, or something to go back for, to keep this conversation going. But I'm the girl with no vision, so there you are. "Want to come in?"

"It's late," he says.

And like a dolt, I agree.

He waits for me to unlock the door, says goodnight, then turns and crunches across the gravel, the resounding story of my life. But then the crunching stops. I turn as he turns. "Hey," he says, "I'm glad you're back."

———————

I lost my faith at twenty-four. What matters is that I got it back. And like a bone that's been fractured and mended, it's stronger than ever, though not without its scars. But it's the scars that tell the story of grace, a story I never tire of telling. My face is to the Son, as it should be, as steadfastly as the sunflowers that sway in the Moldovan breeze. And that's where it will stay.

About the Author

Sharon K. Souza, author of *Lying on Sunday*, *Every Good & Perfect Gift*, and *A Heavenly Christmas in Hometown*, has a passion for writing Heart-of-the-Matter Fiction . . . with a good dose of humor. She and her husband, Rick, live in Northern California. They have three grown children—one who now resides in Heaven—and seven grandchildren. Rick travels the world building churches, Bible schools, orphanages and Teen Challenge centers, and helping to strategically build the Kingdom of God in various countries and regions. Sharon travels with him on occasion, but while Rick lives the adventure, Sharon is more than happy to create her own through fiction.

Visit Sharon's website at www.sharonksouza.com.

You can also visit Sharon at the blog she co-writes with fellow authors Bonnie Grove, Patti Hill, Kathleen Popa, Latayne C. Scott, and Debbie Fuller Thomas:www.NovelMatters.blogspot.com.

Or visit her on Facebook at Sharon K. Souza, Author.

Also from Sharon K. Souza

Lying on Sunday

ISBN-13: 978-1-60006-176-9

ISBN-10: 1-60006-176-1

After learning her husband died of a heart attack—in another woman's bed—Abbie is faced with a choice: She can give in to despair, or create a new life. Abbie does both. As she searches for healing, she fights to protect her daughters from her husband's infidelity. Then a shocking revelation threatens to undo everything she's accomplished. Will the power of the truth really set Abbie free, or is forgiveness out of reach?

Every Good & Perfect Gift

ISBN-13: 978-60006-175-2

ISBN-10: 1-60006-175-3

After thirty years of close friendship, there are no secrets between Gabby and DeeDee. Except one. Thirty-eight-year-old DeeDee decides she wants a baby. And while the friends believe they have faced their greatest challenge, an unexpected turn of events alters their lives forever.

A Heavenly Christmas in Hometown

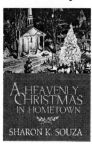

Eustace and Spencer are not your ordinary investigators. They have been given the difficult assignment a long way from home just weeks before the holidays. Hometown's annual Christmas pageant is put on hold when cantankerous Andrew Parsons insists on enforcing the new ordinance enacting separation of church and state. Not only that, he's fighting to regain the property his late wife left her nephew. It seems Andrew has his own plans for that property, and it doesn't include a new church. Will Eustace and Spencer save the pageant, the property, and make it *A Heavenly Christmas in Hometown*?

A Heavenly Christmas in Hometown – the Play

A Heavenly Christmas in Hometown by Sharon K. Souza is now a full-length play, perfect for churches, Christian high schools and colleges.

The play takes 90 minutes to perform, and can use up to 30 cast members.

For ordering information, contact Sharon at www.sharonksouza.com
Or write her at P.O. Box 1656, Woodbridge, CA 95258

CPSIA information can be obtained at www.ICGtesting.com
Printed in the USA
LVOW110923161012

303058LV00002B/142/P